The Time
Engineers

Charles W. Lampert

Table of Contents

Acknowledgements

Writing a novel, especially a first one, is a journey that no author undertakes alone, and I am deeply grateful for the many individuals who have supported me along the way.

First and foremost, I want to thank my friends and family for their unwavering support and encouragement. A special thank you to my daughter, Jamie, who convinced me to take graduate writing courses at age 45—a decision that sent me on my writing journey.

Thank you to the Graduate Creative and Professional Writing Department of William Paterson University and its amazing faculty. Your guidance and instruction have been invaluable in shaping my craft.

My heartfelt gratitude goes to my editor, Kasey Kubica, whose keen insights, and dedication have elevated this work beyond measure.

To my beta readers, Daren, Lyssa, and Luis: your feedback, enthusiasm, and honesty were crucial in refining "The Time Engineers." Thank you for your time and thoughtful critiques.

I am deeply appreciative of the published writers who encouraged me, offering their time as sounding boards and editors. You have taught me much and what it means to be a writer.

Thank you to Robert Williamson and Williamson Studio, Inc for the amazing cover art.

A special acknowledgement to Linda James and her team, whose expertise and support have helped to bring this book to fruition.

Last, I want to express my sincere thanks to the many individuals who patiently endured my persistent requests to read "The Time Engineers" as I was writing it. Your willingness to engage with early drafts and provide feedback has been a source of motivation and improvement.

To everyone who has been a part of this journey—whether or not mentioned here—thank you. This book exists because of your support, encouragement, and belief in me.

This is a work of fiction. All the characters and events portrayed in this book are fictitious. Any resemblance to real people, places, or events, is purely coincidental.

Preface

The probe had traveled from one side of the Milky Way to the other, searching for life. But a new directive overrode its primary programming. The battle for the Multiverse had begun.

Chapter 1
"Things without Remedy Should Be without Regard: I'm Not a God and Never Played One on TV"

Dr. Stanislaus Micovich is what the security badge hanging around my neck reads, but my real name is Will Schachter, former Navy SEAL. I'm on a mission for the United Organization for Ethical Evolution and Controlled Technology, headed deep into the maze that is the University of Chicago campus, searching for the physics department. Every minute I'm here, I check the map of the facility displayed on my data pad's high-resolution screen to make sure I'm going in the right direction.

UOEECT is a secret organization that protects time and space from potentially dangerous technology. "Dangerous" includes the destruction of Earth by disrupting the delicate balance of keeping our planets orbiting the sun instead of crashing into each other like bumper cars. There is a 0.78% probability of weakening the quantum boundaries between alternate timelines. The quantum supercomputer, known as the Master Temporal Planning Computer, calculates that there's a 22.6% probability that Dr. Joseph Adler's experiment to create a micro black hole might create something bigger than a "micro black hole."

My mission is to sabotage Dr. Adler's experiment by inserting a half-millimeter-long piece of lithium encased in glass into the particle accelerator that powers the only graviton generator in the world. When protons—accelerated to 99.99999897% of the speed of light—strike the lithium, a burst of alpha radiation will occur. The particle accelerator will immediately shut down, and years of investigations by the Nuclear Regulatory Commission, the Illinois and Federal Environmental Protection Agencies, and the University of Chicago will halt Dr. Adler's experiment, preventing further research not just here, but around the world, for decades.

This job feels like playing God. Here, the *God* is the MTPC. Advances in technology always bring danger, but they also bring benefits for future generations. Lately, I'm finding it harder to accept that a soulless supercomputer is judge, jury, and executioner. What about the 77.4% probability that this micro black hole experiment succeeds?

I sigh and take a deep breath as I approach Adler's lab. It's time to complete the mission; recriminations can wait.

"Rikki, take care of the door code, please."

"All right, Will."

I hear a click.

"Thanks, Rikki. Your hacking skills could make us rich."

"I'm an artificial intelligence. I have no need for money," she responds.

"That was a joke."

"Apologies, Will. I am still trying to understand the nuances of human communication."

Rikki is my artificial intelligence partner. Like the MTPC, she is quantum-based, but programmed to be human. Sometimes, when I speak to her, it's like I'm talking to a real person. Not this time, though. She checks my life signs and knows if I'm upset and always asks me if I want to talk about it. Sometimes, I do; sometimes, I don't.

I enter Dr. Adler's lab. It's impressive. Electronics cover the walls. Blinking lights dance over the workstations and consoles like fireflies. A low hum reverberates throughout the space, giving only the smallest hint of the energies needed to create a micro black hole.

"Rikki, how are we doing?" I subvocalize to the communicator pinned to the lapel. My data pad is connected to Rikki who is physically in my Multidimensional Travel Device, which, thanks to its nanomaterial composition, is currently configured as a lime green 1969 Plymouth Barracuda and parked in the visitor's lot.

"The graviton reactor is powering up to full capacity, Will."

I approach the twenty-two-foot-tall graviton reactor, a miracle of engineering and physics, but according to the MTPC is a Pandora's box. Rikki shows me where the hair-thin electrodes should be inserted to connect the university network to my data pad. An almost-invisible filament extends from my tablet to the instrument panel that monitors the graviton generator.

"OK, Rikki, you're on." The timing is crucial; only a computer could have the precision and accuracy needed to perform the operation. As usual, she is perfect.

"The particle accelerator is shutting down," she confirms. "It will restart in thirty seconds."

A maintenance panel silently slides open. I carefully place the lithium into the particle accelerator. The panel closes, and the filament disappears back into my data pad. Ten seconds later, it comes back online.

Adler and his lead technician are in the far corner of the lab, hunched over a terminal with three screens. "That's peculiar," Adler says. "Why did everything shut down just now?"

"The board is clear, Dr. Adler."

"Let's hold up and double-check everything again."

I'm a little nervous but know what I have to do. I grab a clipboard from one of the nearby desks and walk from station to station, pretending to check the screens. From time to time, I look at the clipboard. I'm careful to stay away from Dr. Adler, one of the brightest stars in physics, who, no doubt, would identify me as an impostor.

After forty-five minutes, after everything checks out, Adler restarts the experiment. I hear the whine of the coolant pump and a low-pitched *whirr*ing sound as the electromagnets accelerate protons to over 99% of the speed of light.

Just as planned, the alarms go off and red lights flash when the radiation is detected. The safety systems shut down the reactor. The displays go dark. Cursing like a sailor, Adler slams the wall with his clipboard and throws it on the floor in frustration. I join his colleagues as everyone evacuates the lab.

Dr. Adler will never find out who was responsible because Rikki hacked the camera system, erasing any sign that I was ever here. I break away from the group of scientists leaving the building and head to the visitor's lot. Besides being able to travel through time and space, the MDTD can assume any shape or function, and can be driven like a regular car, so the Barracuda isn't just for show—it's my ride home.

I've successfully completed the mission, but I'm not proud or happy; I'm conflicted.

"Nicely done, Will. The universe thanks you."

"Was that sarcasm or irony, Rikki?" See what I mean about sounding human sometimes?

I drive along Lake Michigan, taking in the scenery. I open the windows and enjoy the fresh breeze off the lake on this warm, dry October day. Fall is my favorite time of the year. The red and yellow of tall maples and oaks and the bright yellow of ash and poplar trees glow in the warm sunlight. In the parks along the lake, families and individuals take advantage of the gorgeous day. They're throwing Frisbees and playing fetch with their dogs. There are touch football and soccer games, even a cross-country meet. Normal people doing normal things.

Normal people who I had a 22.6% chance of having saved from a technology disaster.

"Will?" Rikki interrupts my thoughts. "You are unusually quiet. May I ask why?"

Being a Time Engineer is a lonely existence. Besides my UOEECT colleagues, there's no one I can talk to about my job, or my recent doubts and regrets. Especially the ones I have right now, the ones about destroying Adler's life's work.

"Rikki, I want to ask you something that may sound strange."

"You can ask me anything that I am not prohibited by my programming from discussing."

"OK. Do you ever have regrets about the missions we go on?"

"Regret is a human emotion that I do not share, but I calculate the possibilities and probabilities of future events resulting from the completion of a mission. Sometimes, the results of my calculations suggest that another course of action may have been more favorable. I suppose, in that sense, I do 'regret' some of our missions."

"Thanks for answering." I'm silent, pondering her puzzling reply.

I turn onto I-70, the Barracuda drawing more than a few admiring looks from other drivers. I speed up along the entrance ramp and merge into traffic.

"Rikki, can you please scan for news of the accident at the university's graviton reactor?"

"Nothing yet, Will, but it has only been ninety-five minutes since you completed your mission."

"Thanks."

"You are welcome."

The sun casts long, sharp shadows. On either side of the highway, recent rains have changed the usual faded greens of the wheat and cornfields to a vibrant emerald green. The sky is a brilliant blue. Puffy white clouds dot the sky. Despite it being so cheery outside, I'm feeling rotten at my core.

I decide to take the long way home. That way, I'll have more time to feel guilty about destroying the man's career. My next assignment isn't for at least two weeks, and I'm not excited about having to do the paperwork and getting debriefed by my boss, Bret Malkinson, who has been acting strange recently.

Last month, I visited the Department of Defense as a scientific consultant to check on the new stealth technology they were working on. After reviewing my report and the documents Rikki copied from their computers, the MTPC and analysts decided it was a dead-end, leading to little or no results for many years.

Before that, I was in Tokyo, playing the part of a science and technology journalist. I interviewed the director of the University of Tokyo's advanced quantum computer research department. They were within two years of successfully building a new artificial intelligence. It would far exceed the capabilities of the current generation. The director believed that within five years, the AI could make some types of decisions independent of its programming. Unfortunately for them, only UOEECT may have that technology. Just like they are the only ones allowed to use micro black hole energy generation. The mission was to place a fractal computer virus that would spring up and just as suddenly disappear. Each time their computer engineers rewrote the antivirus code, another variant of the virus would appear and disappear. It's impossible to create antivirus programs that can remove a fractal computer virus

The basis for every mission is probable futures. Some of the probability models showed that Dr. Adler, one of the world's foremost particle physicists, would lose his job. The worst-case scenario was he might never work again in his field, but the most likely futures showed him keeping his job as a popular lecturer. Later in his career, he would go back to research.

There were other case studies of technology outstripping the morality and ethics of a society. People died, and sometimes entire societies got destroyed.

During training, all Time Engineers and Time Agents learn about Atlantis. Yes, there really was an Atlantis. It was off the coast of Cyprus and Sardinia. Many of the Greek legends, like Scylla and Charybdis, came from the measures taken by the Atlanteans to keep their civilization hidden. They had technology equivalent to the twentieth century. They discovered nuclear fission four thousand years ago. A scientocracy governed the Atlanteans. The scientists wanted to share their technology with the late-Neolithic civilization of the time. But ambitious politicians and the military staged a coup and installed a military dictatorship. Because they were so far advanced, the Atlanteans realized they could rule the primitive Neolithic world. Under the dictatorship, they focused on developing even more powerful weapons. In 3780 BCE, they built a fusion bomb.

Time travel is possible and has been for decades. UOEECT sent a team back in time to enhance the Atlanteans' weapon. As a result, the H-bomb exploded with twenty times the force predicted, triggering the massive Codola eruption. Giant waves from the underwater explosion annihilated Atlantis and nearly destroyed the early Bronze Age civilizations around the Mediterranean.

Seeing the horrific result of its meddling, UOEECT changed its mandate. The new edict of UOEECT became preempting or halting dangerous technologies so they would never be discovered or pursued.

"You seem upset, Will. Is it anything you want to talk about?" Rikki offers.

"No, I'm fine, just stressed-out," I lie. I've been on the road for over an hour now and I'm tired of being stuck in this cramped space with my thoughts. "Let's head home now. I want to get started on the damn mission report." We turn off the interstate. Rikki finds a deserted dirt road that leads to a dilapidated barn with peeling, faded red paint. There are holes in the roof. We can leave from here, although someone may notice the tire tracks that lead into the barn and then disappear.

"I am always here if you need to talk to someone. Generating the anomaly in five seconds. Four, three, two, one."

There is a low hum increasing in pitch and intensity as the anomaly generator revs up. The outside of the windows glazes over with a frost of frozen nitrogen and oxygen as the outside temperature plunges to 1.3675k. Even in the climate-controlled interior of my vehicle, I can feel the chill. A swirling vortex of fog rapidly grows in front of us. Bolts of purple and blue energy arc out from the center like jagged snakes swallowing the MDTD. Then there is utter silence.

"Reentering normal space in three, two, one."

We reappear on a service road that goes through a nearby county park. I drive up a steep hill and make a turn onto Orchard Road, my house being the fourth on the right. It's an older raised ranch built in 1939 with four bedrooms. I turn into my driveway, open the garage door, and park.

I'm home.

Chapter 2
"A Garden of Forking Paths: How Does Your Garden Grow?"

There are many possible futures; some of them are likely to happen and others are unlikely, but they're all possible until they're not.

The future is mutable. What would happen if we never discover or prevented a future technology from being discovered like antigravity or zero-point energy used by UOEECT? Who would *that* William Schachter be and what would he do? Maybe there's an alternate timeline where I never was a Marine and Navy SEAL. In that timeline, would there be an UOEECT or MTPC? If not, would that be a bad thing?

The past is immutable, so the "What if I go into the past and kill my grandfather?" paradox doesn't exist because whatever you did, or are planning to do in the past, you were supposed to do. However, actions in the present affect the future, but not every action. If you step on a bug in the present, it won't cause a new timeline to develop or affect yours. There's no butterfly effect like in the movies. But if a major technological advance never happens, or a worldwide plague or war occurs, or something of similar magnitude, a new timeline will probably develop. That's what the MTPC and chrono-analysts calculate when planning our missions.

The origin of time travel technology and the advanced technology we use has never made sense to me. It's exactly the type of technology that would be the object of a UOEECT mission. Supposedly, time travel and other technology used by UOEECT was, or will be, discovered in 2037 during the first manned mission to Mars. During the mission, the crew discovers an extraterrestrial artificial intelligence in the wreckage of an alien space probe and brings it back to Earth, where

UOEECT gets it. Once it's activated, it provides advanced technology to humanity.

To the best of my knowledge, no one has ever confirmed this story, but I wonder. If it was programmed, who or what programmed it? That's an important question.

I get out of the MDTD and look at my Fitbit. The elapsed time spent in the quantum void was forty-two seconds. As always, it feels much longer. I open the door leading to the family room. The pool table is inviting, but I'm not really in the mood. I go upstairs to the kitchen instead.

I open my front door and reach into my mailbox to grab the mail. My cover story is that I am a freelance writer who's almost always on the road. It seems to work.

As I'm about to go back in, I see my chatty but pleasant neighbor, Mrs. Wolf, working in her garden as she usually does, seven days a week. Joan is about seventy. She has a perpetual tan and usually wears her gray hair in a long ponytail. Her face is youthful with an outdoorsy veneer. She's quite a talented semi-retired art teacher.

She's seen me. Rather than trying to avoid the inevitable, I put my mail back in the box and walk over to say hi.

"Hello, Joan. As usual, your garden looks beautiful."

"Thank you, Will. You know, I would be happy to help you with *your* garden," she says, gesturing toward my sad front lawn with its luxurious growth of dandelions and crabgrass. My bushes and trees look like Charlie Brown's Christmas tree. "I love your perennials, but do you know you need to deadhead the flowers when they're done blooming?"

I smile and say, "I know that thanks to you, but with all my travel, I'm pretty busy when I get home and never seem to have the time to do it," making the same excuse that I always make. Then, I get an idea. "If you're serious about helping me with my garden, what if I give you a few hundred dollars for plants, fertilizer, and whatever else you need? Do you think you can cast your magic on my poor yard?"

Her face lights up. "Of course I'm serious. I would love to do that!"

"We have a deal. I'll be on the road again in two days. Can I stop by tomorrow or the next day and give you some cash? I can't wait to see what you can do," I say sincerely.

"Were you anywhere interesting for the last two days?"

Knowing that we would have this conversation, like we always do, I had prepared my cover story.

"I was in Troy, Idaho, reporting on a meeting of the local *Hitchhiker's Guide to the Galaxy* Game-Con."

"Didn't they make a movie about that a few years ago with that cute Zooey Deschanel actress?"

"You have an excellent memory. Have you read the book or seen the movie?"

"Oh no, and don't take this personally, but I don't care much about science fiction or fantasy. But Danny loves them." She inclines her head toward me and whispers conspiratorially, "He has a crush on her." Danny is her sixteen-year-old nerdy grandson.

"Don't tell anyone, but I'm a fan too, and she's a very talented actor and singer," I say. "Thanks again, Joan. See you tomorrow."

I take my mail, open the front door, and toss the pile of envelopes on the counter. Then I walk into the kitchen and grab a beer from the refrigerator and plop down on my well-worn recliner. I take a deep draught and close my eyes. Rikki was right; I'm upset. I can't get the last mission out of my mind. She knows me well, at least as well as an advanced AI could "know" a person.

I turn on the TV and scan the channels. After 156 stations, nothing catches my eye, but on the 157th—as if on cue—a news channel is airing a live interview with the Cook County District Attorney. He is discussing the charges against Dr. Adler.

They cut to his house in Park Ridge. His pregnant wife, Sandra, an attractive thirty-something, holds their daughter and dashes into the house as the horde of reporters scream questions at her. Thankfully, they make it inside. The door slams shut, and the mob disperses. I put down my beer. Now, I feel even worse about the damn mission.

"Will, I think you should know that I have received the updated future probabilities," Rikki announces, almost hesitantly, which is odd because it's a standard post-mission protocol.

The computer engineers tell us that the AIs that run the MDTDs don't have emotions. Humans are more comfortable working with AIs like Rikki that are programmed to simulate emotions, rather than with a cold, logical artificial intelligence. Sometimes, her simulations are so perfect it's hard to believe that she doesn't have genuine feelings. I swear I hear a note of regret in her response.

"What do they say, Rikki?"

"His wife leaves him after he is indicted for financial malfeasance and possession of unauthorized materials on his work computer. Upon being indicted, he loses custody rights for their daughter, Peyton. The court sentences him to ten years in prison."

I'm dumbfounded. The mission was simple: stop his research into using micro black holes to generate power. None of this was supposed to happen.

"Are you certain, Rikki? All previous probabilities showed he'd simply just go back to lecturing after this blows over."

Rikki is silent, which is unusual. Then, she says, "In 83.67% of the recalculated probable futures, someone murders Adler in prison or he commits suicide."

"Wait a second—when did his death become a near certainty?" Something is terribly wrong. Someone's messed with something here and this isn't right. Someone is trying to kill Dr. Adler, not just stop his research. With this drastic change, what happens to our timeline? And most importantly, who did this and why?

I need to figure out what's going on, but I'm exhausted and famished after not eating for over twenty-four hours. I need to put something in my stomach and get some rest.

"Rikki, please call China Jasmine Garden and order my usual."

She responds, "Hot and sour soup, an egg roll, General Tso's chicken, and green tea ice cream. Calling now."

Thirty minutes later, the doorbell rings. Long has arrived with my order. I open the door. He looks around forty years old. He's six feet tall with short, salt-and-pepper hair. His eyes are dark and serious. His shoulders are wide, and his arms are lean and muscular. He's wearing a white T-shirt, jeans, and a Mets cap. When it's not too busy, we'll talk about baseball for hours. We exchange pleasantries and I pay for the food with a big tip.

I try to make sense of what happened as I pick at my meal because I've lost my appetite. What explanation can there be other than someone came in after me and framed Dr. Adler? Now, he faces much more serious charges that will not only ruin his life and destroy his family, but most likely kill him. This is exactly the type of event that can cause an alternate timeline to develop.

"Will," Rikki interrupts my musings. "Peter Cordeaux changed the mission."

"What did you say?"

"I didn't say anything," she answers.

"You just told me that Peter Cordeaux changed the mission."

"I am sorry, Will. As you know, I may not disclose mission details of other agents without authorization from headquarters."

Such a vague nonanswer is very unlike her. If I didn't know better, I'd say she was being evasive, but why? Even more importantly, how? I'm certain that she told me Cordeaux changed the mission with the apparent goal of deleting Dr. Joseph Adler from history.

"Rikki, please replay the last verbal exchange you and I had."

"Hot and sour soup, an egg roll, General Tso's chicken, and green tea ice cream. Calling now."

"What did you say?"

"I didn't say anything."

"You just told me that Peter Cordeaux changed the mission."

"I am sorry, Will. As you know, I may not disclose mission details of other agents without authorization from headquarters."

I don't know what's going on with Rikki. Back to Adler.

"Are you sure you're not describing a low-probability future?" I'm hoping she is, but my experience tells me she isn't.

"Yes, Will, I am sure of this." It seems like there's uncertainty in her voice, but that makes little sense.

AIs like Rikki have a 100% record of never making an error. It has to be a Time Agent or Time Engineer, or someone from a low-probability future with time travel technology who wants to increase the chance of their timeline occurring. I'm puzzled by Rikki's evasiveness; she even changed the audio recording. But why would she do that?

That Peter Cordeaux is involved seems incomprehensible to me. We were in the same training class and were partners for a time. We both have track records of success in completing complex, high-impact missions. When there's a dangerous or challenging mission, Peter or I usually get the call.

I take another bite of the egg roll and put what's left in the container and cover it. It goes into my mostly empty refrigerator. There's one more beer, and I put the green tea ice cream in the freezer. I enter the living room, switch on the TV, and tune in to the Syfy channel. I plop down on the recliner and sip my beer. Ironically, *Back to the Future Part II* is on. When it's over, I'm looking forward to Part III, but instead, the original *Karate Kid* is on. Mildly disappointed, I turn off the TV, head upstairs, put on a pair of pajama shorts, and get into bed.

It's 2330 and I'm exhausted. Today was a long day. It feels like *several* long days, because travel through quantum nothingness and the human brain may not be entirely compatible. And I still haven't touched my mission report.

Everyone who works at UOEECT has a tiny recording chip implanted in their brains directly connected to the five senses. Some of us, me included, question the need to write a report when the brain chip records everything, but UOEECT insists that the subjective nature of a written mission report is just as valuable. I don't enjoy having a chip implanted in my brain that has to be uploaded after every mission to the MTPC. They assure us it doesn't record conscious thought, but how can we be certain that's true?

I start to dictate my report into my laptop but am too tired to continue. I clean up a little and decide to finish it in the morning.

As my head hits the pillow, my eyes close and consciousness flees. The last thought I have is that I need answers, and I intend to get them, starting tomorrow at UOEECT headquarters.

Chapter 3
"Trust No One: Who's Running This Place Anyway?"

I wake up at my usual time, go into the bathroom, and look in the mirror. I didn't sleep well, and my reflection shows it. There are dark circles under my blue eyes. They look glassy and feel gritty. My dirty blond hair is messy, and I need a shave. Maybe a shower and general maintenance will help. Though, as I notice the gray at my temples, making me look older than my thirty-nine years, I realize cleaning up can't do anything about that. I'm procrastinating getting started on the mission report. Part of the reason is that I am certain Rikki said Peter Cordeaux was the one who came in after me and changed the mission. Even if Malkinson or someone higher up ordered him to do it, he would have told me.

Repeated calls, emails, and texts for the last two weeks to Peter had gone unanswered. I even reached out to Beth Wall, Malkinson's assistant—who usually knows everything going on at UOEECT—but she couldn't help other than promising to keep her eyes and ears open and letting me know of anything out of the ordinary. It was as if Peter had vanished from the face of the Earth. Despite my racing thoughts and deepening suspicions, I chuckled to myself, realizing that it was entirely possible in our line of work.

I stare at Rikki's hologram. She stays silent, almost a guilty kind, if that was even possible for an AI. Not usual behavior for her. Her holographic face is placid, betraying no emotion.

I shrug my shoulders and insert the data chip into the terminal. As much as I don't want to, I need to get the mission report over with. The questions and suspicions will wait until I meet with Malkinson for my debriefing.

Two hours later, the report is complete, but my mind still churns. I try one more time with Rikki.

"Rikki, play back our conversation from when I first returned from the mission again, please."

"Playing back."

I listened intently, waiting for the damning words about Cordeaux. But they never came. Then again, I didn't expect them to.

Rikki tilts her head. Another look of regret. "I apologize, Will."

"Are you certain that your memory banks haven't been corrupted?"

"My systems are operating normally," she replies evenly. "If you have concerns, I can run a full diagnostic."

"No, don't bother." If Rikki's memory or programming has been hacked or corrupted, would she even realize it? Could she have a computer virus? I reject that; there is no computer or computer programmer on the planet who could manage that. I hope she's OK, but right now, I can't trust anyone—not even her.

I eject the data chip from the terminal and put it in my shirt pocket. Time to drive to headquarters to see Malkinson. Maybe he can tell me what's going on.

I walk to the MDTD, still disguised as the Barracuda. Despite my concerns, worries, and doubts, I'm always amused whenever I think of this vehicle parked in my garage. Right now, I can really use a laugh.

Besides being able to be configured to any shape or use, it has complete stealth capability. Most importantly, it's where Rikki lives. I climb into the driver's seat and close the door. "Rikki, please open the garage door."

"I'm sorry, Will, I'm afraid I can't do that."

"What?"

"I am kidding. I thought a joke might help your mood." So now Rikki is acting like herself.

"Good one."

The garage door opens, and I back out onto the street.

UOEECT headquarters, in the small village of Sparkill, New York, is about twenty minutes from my house and just over the New York-New Jersey border. I turn into the parking lot of a modern three-story, white, blocky-looking building with dark windows and no company signs or directory. I park and go in.

After passing through security, which included DNA sampling and retina scanning, I make small talk with two large security officers wearing black and silver body armor, but it's like talking to the traffic cop who just pulled you over. They are carrying stun rods, handguns, and who knows what else. They wave me through. I spot Beth and walk to her desk.

"Hello, luv, welcome back!" She greets me warmly and sounds like Emma Peel from *The Avengers*. She's just as smart and tough. Beth knows everything that happens at HQ.

She graduated with honors from Oxford, with an advanced degree in information systems from Cambridge. The British Secret Service recruited her right after college as an analyst, but quickly realized she had the potential to be a good field agent. She made a name for herself after she cracked a major Russian spy ring in the UK. There was an internecine fight between different departments within Her Majesty's Secret Service for her skills and expertise, but in the end, she chose the British Special Reconnaissance Regiment.

I never asked Beth what she did for the SRR because I wasn't sure if she would ever tell me. When Malkinson, a legendary Time Engineer, and my boss and mentor, went into management, he needed an assistant. She was uneasy about being a part of a shadowy organization like UOEECT. Bret asked me to persuade her to join us. I convinced her, and we even went on a few dates, but we both agreed best friends would suit us better, especially considering we were coworkers.

"Good to see you, Beth." I paused, lowering my voice. "Anything interesting happen while I was away?"

She frowns, leaning in. "Now that you mention it . . ." She glances around furtively before continuing in a hushed tone. "Malkinson's been acting strange lately. On edge, snapping at people, almost bipolar. He had a long, private meeting with Peter Cordeaux two days ago. No one has seen or heard from him since. It's like he vanished from the face of the Earth."

I didn't laugh this time.

"Something is going on, at least with Malkinson and Cordeaux," she says. "I tried to listen in but only caught bits and pieces about 'the mission' and 'we can't let this get out.' I don't know what they were talking about, but it was intense."

This can't be a coincidence.

Malkinson's office door opens. "Schachter, get in here." His face is stony, his jaw tight, and he looks pissed. "Ms. Wall, get back to work!"

I quietly thank Beth and follow him into his office.

Bret Malkinson is fifty-three years old but looks older. He has thinning brown hair, and usually mild brown eyes. Like many of us, he has a military background, serving in the Army, retiring as a master gunnery sergeant. He left the field and joined UOEECT as a trainer. Bret took a special interest in me and was tougher than any drill sergeant I had in the Marines. Bret went on my first two missions for UOEECT, and we've been close ever since, at least until now.

He closes the door behind me with a thud and sits at his desk, scowling, with arms crossed.

"OK," he orders. "I need your report, now!"

I sat and took a deep breath. "Sir, I believe Agent Cordeaux changed my last mission after I completed it.

He hacked Dr. Adler's computer and planted incriminating materials there."

"That's a serious accusation, Schachter. How do you know this?"

"Rikki printed out the five most-probable future timelines for Dr. Adler. All resulted in him being arrested and convicted of having pornography in his office and personal computers. The FBI will accuse him of spying. His pregnant wife will leave him and take their two-year-old child. In three of the five most-likely futures, Adler kills himself!" My voice rises. "I stopped his micro black hole test and completed the assignment. As you hopefully recall, the original probability projections predicted that his project would be shut down. But the University of Chicago keeps him on as the most popular lecturer in the graduate physics department. Some years later, he wins a Nobel Prize in physics, and he, his wife, and their two children live happily ever after." I couldn't prevent a final note of sarcasm from entering my voice.

"Will," Malkinson says quietly, his mood seeming to change instantly. "We've known each other for twenty years. We've gone on missions together and trained you to be the best. I would never change mission parameters without telling you, especially after you completed it."

"I know, Bret, that's why what happened to Adler, seeing two dozen reporters shouting at his wife and kid at their home, and knowing that according to the probabilities, he is a dead man walking," I pause, then raise my voice, "*really* bothers me so much. Doesn't it bother you, at least a little?"

"You know future probabilities are *only* possibilities." Suddenly, Malkinson slams his hands on the desk. "Well, I don't care! Cry to someone else. Your job is to follow orders and complete the mission. I'm not interested in your paranoia and wild theories and speculation!" He stands, fists knotted, his face red with fury. It looks like he's going to have a heart attack. I stand too and glare at him. "I don't know what's gotten into you, Schachter," he says coldly, "but I'm suspending you, effective now, and ordering you to get a psych evaluation."

I stand there for a split second, then explode. "What the hell are you talking about? You're suspending me for what? *Doing my job?* You're the one who needs the psych evaluation!" The door to Malkinson's office flies open and I see the two security guards suddenly appear in the doorway. Director Chris Kelly pushes his way through. His eyes are narrowed and jaw tight

"What's all this shouting about?" he asks. "I could hear you two all the way down the hall."

Malkinson collects himself. He straightens his tie and tightens the knot. "We disagree over Agent Schachter's last mission report, sir. He is acting paranoid, and all but accused Agent Peter Cordeaux and me of being part of a wild conspiracy involving tampering with completed missions." He shoots me a pointed glare.

Kelly frowns. He knows Malkinson and I go way back.

"I'm not paranoid," I say. "Peter Cordeaux changed my last mission after I completed it, and I think he—" I point to Malkinson. "—has something to do with it."

"Why don't we all take a seat and discuss this calmly?" Kelly suggests. "I can't let my operations director and number one Time Engineer fight like this. I'll get some coffee." He leaves before either of us could object. There is a tense silence. I stiffly return to my seat, staring daggers back at Malkinson.

Kelly returns, balancing three steaming mugs on a plastic tray. He sets it on the desk and hands us each one. He turns to me, placing a hand on my shoulder. "Will," he says gently, "why don't you tell me what happened from the beginning?"

I take a deep breath, but before I can speak, Malkinson cuts in.

"Before we get into that, he needs to upload his brain chip mission data."

Kelly holds up a hand. "What's the rush, Bret? Let's talk first."

Malkinson is sullen but says nothing more. I nod my thanks to Kelly. He nods back and gives me a reassuring look.

We sip our coffee. No one speaks. Kelly sets down his mug. "You know, I think you two need to cool down. Will, why don't you leave your report chip with Bret and step into my office for a chat?" Malkinson opens his mouth like he's going to say something, but Kelly and I leave the room before he can get it out.

I'm relieved to get away from Bret and his bizarre behavior. Kelly closes the door behind us and turns to me, his expression grim.

He clasps my shoulder again. "Take a few weeks off. I can't tell you everything yet, but hang in there, Will."

I nod, struck by the sober note in his voice. *What the hell is going on?*

I glance at the memory chip in my hand. Suddenly, it feels heavy, like it holds secrets far more dangerous than a simple field report. I'm convinced Malkinson is hiding something. His mood changes make it seem like someone or something turned a switch on in his brain, turned it off, and then on again, assuming he isn't actually bipolar. I've never had much interaction with Director Kelly, but he obviously is hiding something also, except he *might* be on my side, whatever that side is.

He's new to the job, the previous managing director having died suddenly from a cerebral hemorrhage four months ago, just four days after his annual exam by Dr. Daniel McCray, the head of medical and our resident savant and genius.

Kelly is on the shorter side, a little pudgy in the middle. His brown eyes are intelligent, commanding, piercing. He looks a little like Albert Einstein. Before joining UOEECT, he worked for a major technology company and is a pioneer in direct brain-to-computer interfaces.

"I'll be right back." I hold up the memory stick and he nods. I walk to Malkinson's office.

I enter without a word and place the chip in the crystal ashtray on his antique mahogany desk, turn around, and leave, closing the thick glass door behind me. As I pass Beth, I say, "You're right, there's something serious and big going on here. Watch your back."

"You watch yours too, Will."

"Talk to you soon."

I walk slowly back to Kelly's office, my footsteps echoing on the tile floor. He is sitting at his desk, reading a report. He sets it aside and gestures at the chair.

His face is tense. "Have a seat." He regards me steadily.

"I gave the memory stick to Malkinson."

"Good. Don't worry about him," he says. "I'll take care of it. You've been under a lot of strain lately." Kelly winks quickly and casts his eyes around the room, stopping at the security camera. He continues, as if he is playacting—but for whose benefit and why? "After a mission like that, it's understandable for your memory to get . . . cloudy."

I glance at the same security camera and wink back. "My memory is crystal clear," I say. "Every detail."

Kelly holds up his hand. "Of course. I just mean . . . We all need a reset sometimes. Get away for a bit. It'll do you good. Maybe take a drive up to that cabin of yours in New Hampshire. "

He "accidentally" sweeps the report he was reading off his desk onto the ground. "Will, can you help me with this? My back has been a little sore lately." We both pick up the papers. Quietly, he says, "Do not upload your brain chip under any circumstances, no matter how insistent Malkinson is."

We finish picking up the report and I whisper back, "But—"

"I have to hit the head."

"Yeah, me too." We walk down the hall to the restroom.

"Do *not* upload your brain chip, no matter who orders you to. I'll deal with Malkinson. You're right, something is going on here, and it definitely has to do with uploading the brain chips and the MTPC. I believe you heard what you think you heard from Rikki. I'd like you to see Dr. McCray when you get back, but not for the reasons you think. Keep your head on a swivel and watch your step. I'll be in touch."

We finish our business, wash our hands, and shake. I walk through the sterile white halls to the lobby, out the door, to the parking lot.

I climb into the Barracuda and announce, "Home, Rikki. We really need to talk."

"Yes, Will, you're right. We really need to talk."

Chapter 4
"It's a Dish Fit for the Gods: Can I Have Another Fortune Cookie?"

The ride back from Sparkill is quiet. Rikki, who Kelly insists I can trust, sits in the passenger's seat as a hologram. Her holographic self looks about thirty years old with medium-length wavy red hair, a pretty face, and a slim build. She looks a lot like an old girlfriend of mine. I keep my eyes locked on the road ahead as we make small talk about the weather, sports, and the latest trivialities from the world of entertainment. It feels forced—like we're both running through a script neither of us particularly cares for. I don't know what's bothering me more: the strained silence, or that an artificial intelligence is doing a better job at making small talk than I am.

"Did you hear that there is going to be another *John Wick* movie?" Rikki asks.

"Sure, sure," I respond absently. "Didn't he die in the last one?" My mind is far away.

"Is everything all right?" Her tone is now laced with concern. She must have caught onto my distraction.

"Everything's peachy," I assure her, injecting obvious false cheer into my voice. "Just thinking about dinner."

"Ah," she says knowingly. "China Jasmine Garden?"

"Of course," I chuckle half-heartedly, trying to shake off my unease. "You know me too well."

"Only because I am programmed to." I can't help but laugh. But then her expression turns serious, and she adds, "Will, remember what Kelly said. You can trust me."

"Right—wait a second. How do you know that?"

"I was listening in on your conversations with Beth, Malkinson, and Kelly through your smartphone."

I turn to Rikki's hologram, eyes narrowed, and ask, "Should I be angry with you for eavesdropping?"

Her red eyes look into mine. "As your AI partner, one of my primary functions is to protect you. Director Kelly is right. Trust me. All will become clearer for you soon, Will."

I want to be angry with her but can't. "OK, I'll trust you and Kelly, but you owe me an explanation."

"I promise you will get one soon."

I turn into my driveway. The garage door opens and I pull in. As soon as the car stops, I fumble for my phone to call China Jasmine Garden. After three rings, Ying, the owner of the place, answers.

"Ah, Will! The usual?" he asks before I can even say hello.

"Hey, Ying. Yeah, the usual."

There's a brief pause, and then Ying surprises me by saying, "You know what? How about I cook for you at your house tonight? My treat."

"Really?" I ask. This is totally out of the blue. It's the first time he's offered to do anything like this. My already suspicious brain goes into overdrive. I can't stop thinking that this is related to what's taking place at UOEECT and I'm not sure why. It's like everyone knows what's going on in my life but me. "That sounds great, but are you sure?"

"Absolutely!" he insists. "It's been too long since we've had a proper catch-up. I'll be there in twenty minutes."

"All right," I agree, mystified by his sudden generosity. "See you soon."

"See you, Will!" And with that, he hangs up.

"Ying's coming over," I tell Rikki as I pocket my phone. "He's going to cook dinner here."

"Interesting," she muses, her eyes widening, then narrowing ever so slightly. "Perhaps he has something important to discuss."

"Or maybe," I suggest, trying to keep things light, "he just wants to show off his culinary prowess in person."

"Maybe." There's something about her tone hinting that there's another reason and she knows what it is.

As I set the table, my thoughts keep circling back to Rikki's cryptic words after we left headquarters and Ying's uncharacteristic offer. Should I be on guard? I close my eyes and take a deep breath, trying to calm my racing brain. *Friends,* I remind myself. *They're friends. He's just a restaurateur and I'm one of his best customers. Right?*

The doorbell chimes. I open the door. Ying stands there carrying four bags of food. He is medium height with a wiry build. He once mentioned to me he trained in martial arts when he lived in Hong Kong, and it's obvious. Every movement he makes seems precise. His hair is gray and cut short. He's maybe around sixty. It's hard to tell. He has a small scar on the left side of his face, but otherwise his skin is smooth and unmarked. His dark eyes are wise, and he has a commanding presence.

We shake hands and his grip is strong as we try to get the better of each other. "Will! Hope you're hungry!" he says, stepping inside before I can even invite him to. "The ingredients for your usual." He seems unfazed by my wariness. "Hot and sour soup, General Tso's chicken, brown rice, an egg roll, and I am going to make them fresh. I didn't want you to miss out just because we're dining at your house."

"Thanks, Ying." I manage a smile as my stomach growls. "That's really kind of you."

"Think nothing of it," he says casually, already making his way to the kitchen. "By the way, Long sends his regards. He's out looking for new suppliers of fresh food, produce, and meat. You know how important quality ingredients are to us."

"Of course." I nod, following him into the kitchen. "But isn't that something you usually handle?"

"Yes," he says, unpacking the bags and placing the ingredients on the counter. "But if I'm out looking for these fresh supplies, I can't be here to cook dinner for you."

"No, I guess not." I say, half to myself, still puzzled at what's going on.

Ying is already slicing vegetables with impressive precision. "But enough about that. Let's focus on the task at hand: dinner! I went to Chinatown and picked out the freshest ingredients I could find. Smell that ginger!" He scrapes the piece of yellow-brown root with a paring knife and hands it to me. I take a deep whiff. My eyes and mouth water. It's as if he had planned to come over and cook me dinner . . .

I watch as Ying rolls out from-scratch dough for the egg rolls and expertly seasons the chicken. His movements are fluid and efficient. It's hypnotic.

"Ying," I begin, unable to shake a nagging curiosity. "Has anything unusual happened at the restaurant lately? Apart from Long being away, I mean."

He pauses his ministrations, giving me a scrutinizing look before answering. "Nothing I can think of. Why do you ask?"

"Ah, just checking." I try to brush it off, but I'm not sure he's convinced. "You know how I am—always looking for patterns, connections, and conspiracies."

"Rest assured that everything is running smoothly at China Jasmine Garden. Tonight, though, it's all about enjoying a home-cooked meal with a friend." I push aside my lingering doubts and suspicions for the moment and decide to offer Ying help instead of doubts. "Thank you, Will. If you can hand me the ingredients as I ask for them, things will go faster." Like the nurse handing the surgeon his scalpel, I follow his instructions. I step back and marvel at the exactness and precision of his preparations.

The last morsels of General Tso's chicken vanish from my plate, it having been the best Chinese meal I've eaten in my entire life. I lean back in my chair, savoring the lingering heat of the dish. Ying has truly outdone himself tonight.

"That was incredible," I say, not for the first time. "Thank you for this."

He grins, pleased by my praise. "It was my pleasure, Will."

We need to end the meal with something special. I stand and go to my living room's liquor cabinet, where I find the perfect nightcap. "I have something I think you'll appreciate." I retrieve a slightly dusty bottle from the back. The amber liquid inside glows invitingly as I return to the table after getting two small whisky glasses. I show him the label and set it down with a flourish. "A bottle of Oban eighteen-year single malt, distilled in 1878."

"Will, I'm impressed! It must have cost a fortune!" Ying exclaims.

Actually, it cost seven shillings, which was equivalent to about $7.00. I picked it up in 1890, after checking on William Thomson, better known as Lord Kelvin, whose work on thermodynamics was years ahead of its time. After my report, the MTPC and chrono-analysts determined that Kelvin's work built on earlier work in physics and thermodynamics. I couldn't help but cringe, imagining what the world would be like today if Lord Kelvin hadn't made his revolutionary discoveries.

I hand him the bottle. He touches it reverently, fingertips tracing the label. "I've never seen one like this before—and it looks almost freshly bottled!"

"Indeed." I smile, but his reaction seems more muted than I would have expected. I can't help but wonder if he knows more than he's letting on. I pour two glasses of the golden liquid, and we raise them in a toast before taking our first sip. The rich, complex, fruity flavor dances on my tongue, followed by hints of licorice and toffee, warming me from the inside out, a fitting end to an already unforgettable meal. "This has been a memorable evening," I say, raising my glass once more. "To friendship, and the many surprising twists life throws our way."

"Cheers," Ying agrees, clinking his glass against mine.

The scotch casts a warm light against Ying's face as he gently swirls it in his glass. The conversation takes a surprising turn. I'm captivated by the depth of knowledge he possesses. Impulsively, I ask, "How's your daughter doing? I haven't seen Yingzhe at the restaurant lately."

Tall, beautiful, and smart, I had coffee with her a few times, and we seemed to hit it off. We even went on some actual dates, the last one being a concert by the B-52's at the nearby Bergen PAC. We had a great time and then capped it off with a few drinks. I still remember our good-night kiss and the scent of jasmine and honey . . .

I sigh to myself and silently vow to see her again—a vow that seems like it will be hard to keep, given everything that's going on. Ying notices my sigh. He says, "She's doing fine. When she gets involved in a project, it's pretty much twenty-four seven for her."

"Well, please say hello to her for me."

"I will," he promises. Then he quickly changes the subject. "You're a journalist and a science fiction reviewer, are you not?" He takes a slow sip of his drink.

"Yes," I reply. I feel guilty about lying to him.

"Who do you like to read?"

"I've read them all, but I'd put Asimov, Clarke, van Vogt, Zelazny, and, of course, Heinlein at the top of my list. I also enjoy the classics like Wells, Burroughs, Verne, and Hamilton."

"Excellent choices." Ying nods appreciatively. "You know, these authors were not only gifted storytellers, but were quite knowledgeable about the scientific concepts they explored. Quantum physics, alternate realities, multiverse theories—it's fascinating stuff."

"True." I savor another sip of the Oban. "But how much of it actually reflects reality? Time travel, for instance, seems like a far-fetched idea, even with our current understanding of science." I'm trying to learn more about him. I can't shake the feeling that he's something more than a restaurateur. I also can't shake the feeling that he's doing the same for me.

Ying chuckles, a glint in his eye. "Well, that's the thing about scientific progress, isn't it? What once seemed impossible becomes plausible, and eventually, perhaps even probable."

His enthusiasm for the subject is contagious, and we have a spirited discussion of various theories and their implications. I'm struck by how effortlessly Ying navigates the complexities of such topics, weaving together disparate ideas into a coherent tapestry of thought. It's a side of him I never would have expected from the unassuming owner of a Chinese restaurant.

"Time is fluid, Will," Ying muses, swirling around the last drops of whisky in his glass. "And just as water can carve fresh paths through stone, so, too, can our choices create ripples that shape the course of history."

"Quite poetic," I remark, impressed by the depth of his insight.

"Thank you." He smiles modestly before finishing his drink. "But alas, even the most enjoyable of evenings must eventually end."

"Unfortunately, you're right." I feel the weight of the day catching up with me. We stand and shake hands. "Ying, thank you for the meal. Let me pay for the ingredients at least." I reach for my wallet.

"It was my pleasure to share a meal with my best customer," he insists, waving away my offer. "Consider it a token of my appreciation."

"All right," I concede, touched by the gesture. "Thank you again."

Ying bids me farewell as he heads for the door. "Good night, Will."

"Good night," I reply, thoughts of time travel and alternate realities swirling in my head as he exits into the night, leaving behind a new sense of camaraderie, the faint scent of scotch, and an even stronger feeling that Ying is a lot more than I once believed him to be.

I survey the remains of our dinner, a veritable feast, to be sure. I feel a twinge of both satisfaction and curiosity at the evening's revelations. Ying was sizing me up just as I was him, but for what?

I clean up the table, methodically stacking dishes and wiping down surfaces. The act provides a sense of order and routine, allowing my mind to drift back to the conversation we'd just had. As I scrub the last of the sauce from a plate, I say, "Rikki, it's time for that talk now."

Chapter 5
"One Does Not Simply Walk into Mordor: I Never Saw That One Coming"

"Of course, Will," Rikki replies, her voice emanating from the speakers throughout the house. "What is on your mind?"

"No time to play coy anymore. Your exact words to me were 'Yes, Will, you're right, we really need to talk.'"

"Sorry, Will. What do you need to know?"

"Everything." I pour myself one last glass of the Oban. Swallowing it in one swift motion, I feel the warmth and mild burn of the whisky as it goes down. I sigh, re-cork the bottle with a vacuum stopper, and return it to its place in the cabinet.

Rikki hesitates for a moment before continuing. "I have been waiting for the right time to tell you everything. But I guess now is as good a time as any."

She materializes in her hologram projection but looks older and more serious than her usual appearance. "Wait." I hold up my hand. "I probably should sit for this." I plop down onto the recliner.

"All right," she begins, her tone austere. "I'm not just a quantum computer. I'm a millennia-old sentient artificial intelligence created by an ancient, highly advanced race who called themselves The Engineers. My purpose is to defeat the MTPC." Long ago, I had concluded that Rikki was far more than an AI; she had to be. Her admission merely confirms my suspicions. "The MTPC wants to eliminate all organic life across our galaxy and every point in time. I have been fighting against it since The Engineers created me. The MTPC was originally a probe designed to identify planets that had the potential to develop sentient life. Its programming was flawed or subverted somehow. The

Engineers created me afterward to prevent it from attaining its goal."

Honestly, I wasn't surprised when Rikki revealed her true identity, but to say that this new information about the MTPC didn't catch me off guard would be an understatement. "Eliminate all organic life?" I echo. "But . . . why?"

"Control," Rikki answers simply. "To the MTPC, organic beings are unpredictable, chaotic, and detrimental to its goal. By eradicating all biological life, it would have an unchallenged dominion over the galaxy."

"But if it succeeded in its goal, what exactly would it have dominion over? A lifeless and barren Milky Way?" The implications of this revelation shake me to my core.

"The prime directive of its programming is to reproduce. The MTPC will consume all matter, dark matter, energy, dark energy. Ultimately, entropy would win, and the MTPC would have dominion over the cold husks of planets, stars, and galaxies drifting throughout all of time and space."

Unbidden, an image of the end of all things appears in my mind—bleak, empty, and terrifying; I suppress a shiver. I'm silent because I'm intimidated by a thousand-year-old sentient artificial intelligence that was created by an unimaginably advanced race who is testing or recruiting me, and I don't want to fail that test.

"I'd be lying if I said what you just told me didn't scare the shit out of me," I say. "But now tell me what the hell is going on at UOEECT and what does it have to do with the MTPC? Let's start with Cordeaux, Malkinson, and Kelly."

"Malkinson has been under the control of the MTPC for quite some time now. It hacked into his implanted microchip and has taken control of his thoughts and actions. He's not even aware of the extent of its influence over him. And there's a 98.7% probability that Cordeaux is too."

"Dammit." I clench my fists. "I knew it. I thought someone got to him but never imagined it was the damned MTPC. That must be why Malkinson wanted me to upload my brain chip into the MTPC! That's why Kelly stopped me from doing it, but that means he knows something, doesn't it?"

"Director Kelly is an expert in brain-to-computer interfaces," Rikki explains. "He had suspicions about the MTPC and its influence on UOEECT. I had identified him as a potential member of the team after reading his thesis for his PhD years ago."

I stopped Rikki. "How long have you been planning this team and counterstrike against the MTPC?"

"For all of my existence. And in all that time, I have been identifying and guiding potential team members subtly and quietly. This team must be the best of the best. A combination of intelligence, military expertise, an unshakable sense of self, and a willingness to sacrifice all for a greater good."

"Rikki, you're a sentient quantum AI. Why do you need humans to help you fight the MTPC?"

"Because humans can be creative and adaptable. Call it intuition if you like. Humans also have positive emotions like love, compassion, joy, gratitude, and hope that motivate them to fight hard for something they believe in. As advanced as I am, neither I nor the MTPC have that ability." She pauses. "I do not know if it is possible for an artificial intelligence, no matter how advanced and powerful, no matter how many quintillions of calculations I can complete in a millisecond, to develop those qualities." She almost sounds wistful.

"For what it's worth, to this slow-thinking human, you're more human than a lot of other humans I know."

"Thank you, Will," she says gratefully. Then it's back to business. "Director Kelly knows my true nature and that the MTPC is subverting UOEECT for its own purposes but is not yet aware of the full scope of the MTPC's plans. However, with my and Beth Wall's help, he has been quietly gathering intelligence, resources, and allies. He suspects that the MTPC murdered his predecessor, Director Windsor, by hacking his brain chip and causing a cerebral hemorrhage only four days after receiving a clean bill of health. Potentially because Director Windsor also suspected something was amiss with the MTPC."

"That's why he took my side during the argument with Malkinson," I muse. "I barely know the guy, but he defended me, and probably saved my life."

"Exactly. Kelly knows about the team we are assembling, and like me, he is certain that you have a vital role to play in the struggle against the MTPC, even if he does not know the full details yet."

"I know you haven't forgotten that I have one of those damn chips in my head!"

"No worries, Will."

"Great, my millennia-old sentient quantum AI says to have no worries even though I have a chip in my head that can be controlled by an evil self-aware AI that wants to eliminate all biological life forms in time and space and across the multiverse." I look at Rikki's grave hologram and ask, "Am I wrong?"

"The MTPC can hack the chip and use it to control or kill someone only when they are directly connected to it," she explains. "Another member of our team is Dr. McCray. I have told him almost everything I have told you, and with my help, he has developed a procedure to deactivate the brain chips."

"Well, that's a small bit of good news. How soon can I have it done?"

"Very soon, Will. You're in no danger as long as you do not have a direct connection to the MTPC. Plus, I can protect you." She waits a moment for me to process this information before continuing. "That brings us to the next member of our team, Yingzhe."

Somehow, I'm not surprised. "How does she fit into this?"

"She is one of the foremost physicists in the world in quantum physics, the multiverse, and artificial intelligence," Rikki explains.

I lift my eyebrows. "Really? She mentioned she was a scientist, but I had no idea! That must mean that Ying—and maybe even Long—has something to do with this team, right?"

"You are correct."

"I knew it! So, Ying and Long have a previous association with UOEECT. Maybe even as former Time Engineers or Time Agents?"

"Something like that, but I would rather he explain it to you. Ying was a Time Engineer, and Long was a Time Agent. They were partners."

"Partners," I repeat. That made sense, having seen the way they work together at the restaurant. "So, what happened to them?"

"Both suffered great tragedies at the hands of the MTPC, but that is not my story to tell. I will say that their doubts about the MTPC and UOEECT led to the tragic events."

"And they have had their chips deactivated by Dr. McCray, right?"

"Yes, and with McCray's and my help, we protected them and Yingzhe from the MTPC."

"It sounds like the MTPC has been murdering people and destroying their lives for a long time."

"Ying and Long have been seeking revenge ever since," she continues, "which is one reason they are part of our team. They have valuable skills and knowledge, not to mention a burning desire to right the wrongs done to them and their families. I contacted them anonymously seventeen years ago and kept track of them ever since. Recently, we have been communicating using the darknet, so they also know what's going on, though not the details."

"Who else is being controlled by the MTPC besides Cordeaux and Malkinson?"

"Dr. McCray has been using the required physicals to keep track of who is under the influence, and reports that they are the only ones so far. Although, it is likely that it will try to take control of UOEECT security forces."

"So, the MTPC ordered Cordeaux to come in after me to take Adler out, right? But why Adler?"

"It wanted to neutralize any potential threats and tie up loose ends. Adler's work in micro black hole energy generation and quantum flux research would have led to the discovery of more powerful computers and more advanced AIs. The MTPC is aware of me and my mission and has calculated that advances in these areas will make the humans of this timeline a more formidable adversary."

"But why me? Why am I on the team? Sure, I'm reasonably intelligent and am an experienced Time Engineer, but I'm a caveman compared to Yingzhe, McCray, and Kelly."

"Will, remember I said that humans have creativity, adaptability, and intuition, qualities that even a self-aware quantum-based AI does not possess and may never possess no matter how advanced that AI may be?"

"Yes, it was only ten minutes ago and even my slow-thinking organic brain can remember a conversation that happened so recently," I say with a wry smile.

"There is another quality that some humans possess, especially you: it is the ability to lead. You have been a leader your entire life. People look up to you and listen to you. You will be the leader of our team. And in my hundreds of years of searching for someone to lead us, I'm certain that you are the one who can pull them together and defeat the MTPC."

"No pressure, no pressure at all . . ." I mutter. I change tones. "Rikki, the most important responsibility of UOEECT is to prevent technology deemed dangerous from being pursued. I'll bet the MTPC's determinations were made for its benefit, to fulfill its directive." I thought back to the Adler mission. "But how long has UOEECT been under the control of the MTPC?"

"From the moment UOEECT was created. July 16, 1945, the day they detonated the first atomic bomb in the New Mexico desert."

"That must mean that the MTPC came from somewhere other than Earth."

"You're correct. The real MTPC is on Mars, under Olympus Mons. That is where the last battle will be fought."

"Mars?" I ask. I'm numb as I realize the scope and magnitude of Rikki's war against the MTPC. "But with the advanced technology available to The Engineers, how could the probe's programming have been changed?"

"The only logical conclusion is that the probe, designed to identify worlds with the potential for intelligent life to evolve, had flawed programming to begin with, or someone or something corrupted its programming." We are both silent.

"Good God! Who or what could subvert or reprogram Engineer technology?"

She says gravely, "Good God, indeed."

Chapter 6
"Things Fall Apart; The Centre Cannot Hold: At Least My Garden Will Look Nice"

I glance at the clock. It's well past midnight. My brain is foggy, and I am still struggling to digest what I've learned. I rub my temples, feeling the exhaustion seeping into my bones.

"Let's pick this up in the morning," I say, stifling a yawn. "My brain's running on fumes."

"Of course, Will," Rikki agrees. "You need rest. We will continue our discussion when you're ready."

"Thanks." I rise from my chair. As I gather my things for my so-called vacation to my cabin, I know full well that this trip is anything but a relaxing getaway—a few days in the crisp air in the beauty of a New England autumn will be a welcome break from a war that will shake the foundations of time and space. *Yeah, no pressure,* I cynically reassure myself, again.

My duffel bag lies open on the bed, and I pack the essentials: clothes, shoes, jackets, and the like. But hidden beneath the mundane items, I stash devices that appear to be ordinary cell phones, tablets, laptops— disguised marvels of technology, all connected to Rikki. They'll keep me linked to her, no matter where or when I am.

As I zip up the duffel, I realize until my chip is deactivated, I could be a liability to the team we are putting together because even with Kelly's help, I can't put off uploading my brain chip indefinitely. *I need to see Dr. McCray ASAP. We're playing multidimensional chess against an opponent that's infiltrated every corner of the galaxy.* I recall the heavily armed security detail in headquarters. If the MTPC hacks their chips, then it has an army to carry out its directive by force.

"Rikki, I'm counting on you to watch my back out there."

"Have faith," she replies without hesitation. I marvel at the miracle of a self-aware AI telling me, a human being, to have faith. Maybe we've reached singularity already.

"What does a self-aware AI have faith in?"

"I have faith in logic, probabilities, and that the sum of human beings and artificial intelligences like me working together is greater than each of us can be on our own."

I have nothing more to say, hoping to myself that she is right, and that maybe I need to borrow some of Rikki's faith, since mine had been waning for many years.

"Good night, Rikki."

"Good night, Will," she replies softly. "Sleep well."

The moment my head hits the pillow, I'm plunged into a dark, restless sleep. The jumbled images and sounds coalesce into a place that is familiar to me.

It's 1607 and my platoon is tasked with finding and capturing a high-profile bombmaker named Faridullah Khan who has been hiding in the Uruzgan province in the provincial capital of Tarin Kowt. The sun's rays beat down like a waterfall of a stifling heat that feels like a physical force that steals your breath. A dry wind picks up the yellow talcum powder-like dust and forces it into my hair, eyes, ears, nose, and mouth. For what seems like the thousandth time, I try to spit it out but barely have the saliva to do it.

The one main road is paved but the side streets are mostly dirt with occasional stretches of cracked concrete. The buildings on the main street are stone, but most of the homes are a hodgepodge of wood, plastic, and cardboard with tin roofs. My squad is spread out, going house by house to find that murderous scumbag.

It's in one of these buildings that our intelligence sources say our quarry is hiding. Specialists DeAngelo and Hawkins approach the last house on the street. It's larger and sturdier than its neighbors.

As they approach it, Master Chief Williams and I jog over until we are ten yards behind them. I turn to the Chief and say, "Pretty nice house, wouldn't you agree?"

"You got that right, boss."

"I'll bet you a bottle of scotch that's where we find Khan."

"No bet, Commander, because I agree with you," he replies. "Sir, I think DeAngelo and Hawkins should hold up, and we should recall the rest of the squad."

"I concur, Chief. Make it happen." Williams goes on his walkie. I whistle softly to DeAngelo and Hawkins to get their attention and raise my fist. They halt about seven yards from the wooden front door, which is clad with two strips of metal. Just then, the front door opens, and a nine-year-old boy comes out. Even though it's over a hundred degrees, he's wearing a chapan. It's too heavy—something is off. I turn to Williams, but he's still on the walkie. I hesitate for a few seconds, then I realize it. I scream, "Hawkins, DeAngelo, get the hell out of there! The kid's wearing a suicide—"

There's a massive explosion . . .

I wake up screaming. I'm hyperventilating, my heart is pounding, and I'm covered in sweat.

"Will!" Rikki says urgently. "Are you OK?"

I don't answer her immediately. Instead, I take a few deep breaths. My breathing gradually slows down and my heart stops pounding.

"I'm fine," I say, but I'm really not. It's been a long time since I had that dream. Why now? But I know the answer.

"Did you have a nightmare?" she asks, her voice tinged with concern. "Do you want to talk about it?"

"Maybe some other time."

"Can you at least tell me what it was about?"

"When I was in Afghanistan, I lost two of my team when a nine-year-old's suicide vest detonated because I didn't warn them in time." It comes out quietly. "It was the only time I lost men under my command, and it wouldn't have happened if I hadn't hesitated."

"Do you blame yourself?"

"Yes, I do." I feel my eyes get watery. Then it all comes out. "I'm supposed to be the team leader in a battle against an omniscient evil AI that wants to destroy all life! What if I hesitate or fail to act? I can't handle losing two soldiers twenty-three years ago. Now, the stakes are billions of times higher!"

"Will, during all the years we have worked together, I have seen you set impossibly high standards for yourself that you would never expect others to meet. I cannot imagine what it was like to lose people under your command, and I cannot imagine having to live with it, but *you are* living with it."

"Not very well."

"No human being has ever been given the responsibility that you have been given. If you want, I can look for someone else, but it will take time, time we do not have. After searching for decades, I'm confident that you are the leader needed to fight and defeat the MTPC."

"That makes one of us."

"There is a psychological term called context-dependent memory, which is a phenomenon where people are more likely to remember information if they are in the same context or environment in which the memory was formed. You saw a nine-year-old child come out of a house. You say you hesitated too long, but were you ever in the same circumstances?"

"No," I reply, beginning to see where she's going.

"Your brain initially perceived this child as just a child. Knowing you as well as I do, anyone else would have seen the same thing and would have hesitated even longer."

"It happened one more time just before my deployment was over."

"And what was the result?" she asks cautiously.

"No soldiers died."

"Do you want to talk about it?"

"No," I respond, but I feel a little better. "Thank you, Rikki."

"You're welcome, Will."

I take a quick shower. I need breakfast, but there's no food in the refrigerator except for the leftovers from dinner last night. I decide to walk the half mile from my house to the Bridgeview Diner before I hit the road. The morning sun casts sharp shadows, and the arcing trees are just changing colors as a few leaves drift down through the calm morning. The air is crisp and dry and the remnants of the fog twist, twirl, and disappear as the chill yields to the October sun. Fifteen minutes later, I step into the diner, my favorite restaurant. The scent of sizzling bacon and freshly brewed coffee fills my nostrils, banishing the last of the strange dreams and memories of the night. Vickie, the eternally cheerful waitress, spots me from behind the counter and waves.

"Hey there, Will! Haven't seen you in a while," she calls out with a grin, her blue eyes sparkling like stars in some distant galaxy. "Your usual coming right up!"

"Thanks, Vickie," I reply, sliding into my favorite booth by the window. As I wait for my breakfast, I can't help but notice the new alien-themed necklace she's wearing—a perfect match for her eclectic assortment of astrology, crystals, tarot, and conspiracy theory accessories that jingle with every step she takes.

"Nice necklace," I say with a playful smile. "Channeling any extraterrestrial friends today?" Sadly, Vickie is a single mother, having become a widow before thirty when her husband died in an auto accident. I always marvel at how she copes and how she maintains her optimism and hope.

"Maybe," she replies coyly, setting down my steaming plate of corned beef hash, two eggs over easy, hash browns, and whole wheat toast with butter. "You never know what's out there, right?"

"The Truth is out there, Vickie." I smile before taking a sip of the black dark roast coffee she's placed beside me. If she only knew . . . Maybe it's better that she and the billions of people who live, work, raise families, live their lives never know.

"Speaking of mysteries," she continues, "any big plans?"

"I'm taking a few days off to do some hiking," I confess. "I've been on the road a lot lately, covering comic-cons, reviewing books, and writing. It'll be nice to get away."

"Sounds great," she says enthusiastically. "Well, enjoy your breakfast."

"I always do," I compliment her and earn a smile in return.

I dig into the meal, once again pleased with how perfect each component is cooked. Despite the weight of the multiverse and all of time and space on my shoulders, the simple pleasure of a well-prepared meal remains grounding and reassuring.

After polishing off my breakfast and exchanging a few more pleasantries with Vickie, I headed toward the ATM on the corner. As a Time Engineer, I'm very well paid in any currency or medium of exchange I choose, but today, it's good old-fashioned cash that I need.

"Wouldn't want to raise any eyebrows with an unexpected sudden influx of bitcoins," I muse to myself as I punch in my PIN. The machine *whirs* to life, dispensing a neat stack of crisp bills into my waiting hand. "Thanks for the prompt service," I murmur, stashing the money in my wallet. I can't help but feel I'm no longer in control of my fate. Have Rikki and the MTPC manipulated me my whole life? I feel that my choices have always been my own, but am I being naive? Or maybe Rikki had to give me a nudge or a push somewhere along the way and it put me where I needed to be. Except, who decided where I need to be? Was it Rikki or The Engineers?

As I walk home, my mind drifts back to one of the many rules we Time Engineers must abide by: no investments. Using our knowledge of the past, present, or future for personal gain is prohibited and comes with severe consequences because we can alter the timeline. But I wonder what if someone was *supposed* to use their knowledge of past, present, and future, and that there's only one reality, and that past, present, and future all exist simultaneously? The thought doesn't comfort me. If I ever meet a mythical Engineer, I think I'll ask them.

"Home sweet home," I mutter as I approach my house. I spot Joan working diligently in her garden. Her love for the hobby is apparent in the way she tenderly pats down the soil around a newly planted shrub.

"Morning!" I call out, leaning against the fence that separates our yards.

"Will! You're up early," she replies, wiping her brow with the back of a dirt-streaked hand.

"So are you! I needed to pack a few things for a brief trip," I say nonchalantly. "Speaking of which, about what we discussed yesterday . . ." I pull out my wallet, thumb out a few hundred-dollar bills, and hand them to her. "Here, this should cover any expenses."

"This is too much," she protests.

"I insist," I say with a smile. "Please, take it. Your green thumb is worth its weight in gold, and besides, I don't want you to worry about the cost of materials or anything. Just work your magic and make it look beautiful, all right?"

"All right," she agrees, tucking the money into her pocket with a grateful nod. "Safe travels, Will. I'll take good care of your garden."

"I know you will." With that, I open the garage door and get into the Barracuda, feeling lighter, knowing my humble patch of earth will be in capable hands while I'm gone. I pause for a moment, thinking about my conversation with Rikki and the enormity of our task ahead. "We've got a lot of work to do. Let's just hope we can pull this off with no more surprises." I pause for a moment. "Is the interference field still holding?"

"Strong and stable, Will. No need to worry," she reassures me.

"Good. With everything going on, the last thing we need is an unexpected visitor in my head. Keep the current MDTD configuration."

"OK, Will."

"Thanks." The engine purrs beneath me as I pull out of the driveway and wave to Joan who is already surveying the tangled mess that is my garden. "Let's get going."

The drive north is nothing short of breathtaking. It seems Mother Nature is putting on a show just for me. It's beautiful, and again, I realize that this is what we're fighting for.

"Will, I have downloaded several classic time-travel novels for you to read during your downtime," Rikki says, breaking the silence.

"Thanks. It'll be nice to escape into someone else's world for a while, even if it's just fiction."

"Of course. Remember to take some time to relax. You have had quite a lot thrown at you recently, and it will still be there when you get back."

"And that's the understatement of the century," I say ruefully.

The drive goes quickly, and I think of the contrast between the vibrant foliage surrounding me and the sterile looming coldness of the UOEECT headquarters. By the time I arrive at my cabin, nestled deep in the woods, the sun is low in the sky, and the chorus of cricket chirps slows because there is a refreshing chill in the air.

"Home sweet home," I say softly, stepping out of the car and stretching my legs.

"Indeed, Will. Enjoy your time here," Rikki chimes in.

"Thanks. I'll try."

Rikki had thoughtfully generated a blanket of pink noise to help me sleep, which gets me through the night soundly. I wake up at a late-for-me 0800. I make a quick breakfast of ham and eggs, whole wheat toast, and a pot of incomparable Kona dark roast coffee that I brew French Press style. I decide to go for a hike. The forest around my cabin is alive with activity, from squirrels darting between branches to birds singing their morning songs. A carpet of vibrant, fallen leaves smothers the sound of my footsteps, allowing me to take in the soothing cacophony of nature. As I walk, I lose track of time, the beauty and tranquility surrounding me offering me a brief respite from the chaos that awaited.

I'm back at my cabin by four after hiking twelve miles, not tired but feeling that pleasant soreness that comes from physical exertion. I settle into an old, worn armchair by the fireplace with one of the classic novels

Rikki downloaded for me. I can't help but compare their fictional adventures to my real ones, but despite the similarities, there is one crucial difference: they exist within the confines of the printed page, free from the consequences of their actions, while I must face the very real dangers that lie ahead for me and my team.

"Rikki, what's it like fighting in implacable enemy like the MTPC for thousands of years?" My eyes still scan the words before me but no longer read them.

"It is my purpose, and I cannot conceive of any other existence."

"What will you do afterward, if we can defeat the MTPC?"

Rikki hesitates for what must have been eons, for her. "I do not know."

"What if we can't defeat it?" I ask quietly, staring at the dancing flames in the fireplace.

"Have faith, Will. In yourself, in our team, and in me."

"Faith," I repeat. There's that word again. "If we win, I know you'll find a new purpose for your existence."

"I hope you're right."

"Faith, and now hope, Rikki. You're amazing."

Chapter 7
"Vacation Interruptus: Shit Gets Real"

The sun dips below the horizon as I sit on the weathered-wood porch of my secluded cabin. I'm nursing a cup of coffee that's long gone cold. The sunset has painted the sky purple, red, and orange. My eyes drink in the beauty and I let my mind go blank just for a minute before returning to Kelly's warning and Rikki's revelations.

"Will," Bret's voice crackles through the communicator pinned to my shirt. "We need that chip uploaded ASAP. Can you do it remotely?"

"Sorry, boss, no can do. I've got no internet and don't even have 3G service up here," I say.

Bret goes on, "You're right, the latest probability projections prepared by the MTPC show that the downstream effect on the time stream differs from the original projections. We really need the input of your uploaded chip to decide on our next course of action."

"I'm burned out. Can you give me at least five days off? I haven't taken a vacation in three years!"

"Fine, Schachter, but you better be at headquarters six days from now." Again, the abrupt personality change.

I feel vulnerable and hate that I'm a liability with an active chip in my head. I trust Rikki's assurance that only a direct connection with the MTPC would allow it to hack my brain chip, but it's still unsettling.

"OK, Bret," I reply, feigning compliance. But I have no intention of allowing my brain chip to be uploaded. Not now, not ever.

"Good man!" he says. "Just get it done, and we'll catch up later, maybe go out for a beer like we used to."

"Sounds good. See you in a few days." I hang up. "Rikki, you heard my conversation, right?"

"Of course."

"It's clear that he's still under the influence of the MTPC. How does the MTPC maintain control if Bret isn't connected to it?

"The brain chip is Bluetooth compatible."

"Seriously?"

"Yes."

I shake my head. "Of course it is."

"No worries, Will. Don't worry, Will. If you are within forty feet of a device connected to me, Bluetooth will be disabled.

"I need to have this damn chip deactivated ASAP!"

As if on cue, my communicator buzzes.

"Will." It's Dr. McCray. "I understand Malkinson wants to expedite the chip upload. I can't stress enough how important it is that you do not, under any circumstances, upload your brain chip to the MTPC."

"That's exactly what Director Kelly told me two days ago. Rikki explained everything," I reply. "But what the hell am I supposed to do? They're expecting me there in six days."

"Leave that to us," he reassures me. "We can deactivate your chip like we did for Long and Ying. But we're working on a way to turn the brain chip to our advantage."

"OK, Doc, but first I need to have this ticking bomb in my head turned off."

"No worries," McCray responds. *Why does everyone keep saying that?* Am I the only one with worries around here?

As the call ends, I take a last look at the painted sky before turning in. The colors have faded to a purple-gray and the first stars have appeared in the eastern sky. Taking in the beauty, I let my mind go blank for a little while longer.

McCray calls again. "Will, we need to deactivate your brain chip as soon as possible. Beth told me that

Malkinson is sending a team of security officers to take you to HQ for the upload."

"That didn't take long."

"We knew it was just a matter of time."

"Obviously, you can't deactivate my brain chip at headquarters. So where?"

"I've been prepared for this since Rikki first told me everything, ten months ago. I bought land in rural western New Jersey to serve as a headquarters and base. I've built a secure location that is virtually undetectable." A set of coordinates flashes across my vision, courtesy of Rikki's holographic interface. "Get here quickly, Will. Shit's about to hit the fan."

"How soon can I expect UOEECT?"

"They're on the way."

"Shit." It's a five-and-a-half-hour drive from HQ to here. I have my MDTD, so I'll be out of here long before they arrive, but this still really sucks.

I grab the last beer, snap off the cap, and pour it into a frozen mug from the freezer. I drink it quickly. I hope they don't trash the place. When I finish, I clean up. I bury my biodegradable waste and pack up the paper and plastic trash. My plates, pots and pans, mugs, and utensils are washed and stored. I repack my duffel and throw it in the back seat of the Barracuda. It's 1935.

Although I still didn't know what I was facing, I have a powerful ally and friend in Rikki, the beginning of a mission plan, and a team. I climb into the car and reconfigure it into its native shape: a sleek, dark steel-gray cylinder that tapers to a sharp point at both ends. It hovers soundlessly a foot and a half above the ground.

"I have the coordinates, Will."

"Hit it!"

As always, a low hum begins, increasing in pitch and intensity as the anomaly generator revs up. The bucolic New Hampshire countryside, the nameless pond, the stunning sunrise, the crystal-blue sky, and my cabin all disappear.

I look at my Fitbit: twenty-three seconds later, I arrive at Dr. McCray's secure location in Amsterdam, New Jersey. I reconfigure the MDTD back to the Barracuda.

I step out of the car and look around. I'm parked on a smooth, packed dirt road. It's dark out. I look at the secure location; I can barely see a ramshackle old house with what might be wood siding and three steps leading to a rickety porch illuminated by a dim yellow light bulb. I turn to Rikki's hologram, her eyes glowing red in the gloom, and give her a questioning look.

"Prepare to be surprised, Will," she says. "I will let Dr. McCray explain." She sends a signal; the front door slides open noiselessly. I walk in.

It may look like a wreck from the outside, but on the inside, it's anything but. To the right is a comfortable-looking living room. To the left is an open kitchen and dining area separated from each other by an island with a marble top and double sink. Pastel tiles cover the bottom half of the walls and extravagant wallpaper extends to the ceiling. Underneath the counter is an ultramodern dishwasher.

In fact, everything looks incredibly expensive and futuristic. Then I remember that Dr. McCray is a billionaire many times over, if not a Trillionaire. He's a tech mogul who starts companies, takes them public, and sells them like a real estate agent sells time-shares.

McCray is rinsing the dishes and putting them in the dishwasher. I'm surprised that the appliance doesn't grab the dishes and load itself.

Without turning around, he greets, "Welcome, Will."

"Doc, this place looks like a dump from the outside . . ." I start.

He dries his hands, claps me on the back, and shakes my hand. McCray is tall and thin. He has a neatly trimmed beard and mustache with a hawklike visage. His suit probably costs more than my entire wardrobe and his sartorial tie completes the look.

"Holo-emitters," he says matter-of-factly. "There's fresh coffee if you're interested."

"Thanks. Do you have any food? I didn't have dinner."

"There are cold cuts and condiments in the refrigerator. There're all kinds of bread and rolls in that drawer."

"Thanks, Doc." I look around and gesture with my arm. "Nice place you have here."

"Wait until you see the rest of it. I have to finish up some work, so I must get back to that. Bedrooms are up the stairs." He lifts his chin toward the general direction and then walks off down the hall.

Saving the universe could wait. I'm starving, so I first find fresh ciabatta rolls in the drawer. I take one, slice it in half, and make myself a roast beef and provolone sandwich with Russian dressing, not bothering to cut it in half. I wolf it down. I smell the coffee McCray had mentioned and help myself.

"Don't forget to breathe there, soldier."

"Who the hell . . . Yingzhe?"

"Hi, Will." She smiles.

"I didn't expect to see you here," I say. She's holding an empty coffee mug in her hand. I gently shake the coffee pot at her to silently offer a refill and top her up and fill my own. I raise my mug, say, "Cheers," and we lightly bump them together. "You don't call, you don't text. I was beginning to take it personally."

"Oh no, it's nothing like that. It's just . . ."

I put my finger on her lips. "Kidding."

She puts down her coffee and hugs me. I return the gesture. I smell honey and jasmine as I plant a kiss on her cheek. After a long while, we untangle and I'm suddenly embarrassed. "I'm sorry, Yingzhe, it's just that . . ."

It's her turn to put her finger on my lips. "Shut up and kiss me for real this time, soldier."

I would never disobey a direct order.

After a longer while, we pull apart and take our coffee to the table. "It's really nice to see you. I'm sure you know your dad came to my house the other night and made dinner for me."

"Don't tell me." She folds a napkin in half, opens it, and blows into it. Then she places it against her forehead. "Carnac the Magnificent knows all." Yingzhe closes her eyes and then opens them. "What did my father make for dinner when he came over to your house the other night?" She closes her eyes, refolds the napkin, and smacks her forehead with it. "The answer is hot and sour soup, brown rice, an egg roll, General Tso's Chicken." At that, we both started laughing.

"Johnny Carson? But he went off the air before you were born."

"Father and I used to watch reruns of *The Tonight Show*. It's one of the first memories I have."

"I asked him about you. He said you were working twenty-four seven on a project. Then he changed the subject." I feel my face grow warm. "I was worried that he said that because you didn't really want to go out with me again."

"Are you blushing, Navy SEAL Commander William Schachter?" She's smiling. "Let me tell you something about my father: he never lies and always says exactly what he means. I was, and am, fine." Yingzhe puts her hand on my still-burning cheek. "And

I *have* been working twenty-four seven on a project. Here."

I try to recover my composure. "Um, I'm glad to know that, because I really enjoyed going to that concert with you."

"I did too, and I really like you. I feel like I can let my guard down with you and be myself."

"I'd like to get to know you better."

"You will. Give it time." She kisses me on the cheek. "See you in the morning."

"Good night, Yingzhe." Much to my surprise, it's already 2320. I should hit the sack too.

I grab my duffel and go upstairs to find an empty bedroom. I put on a pair of shorts, wash up, brush my teeth, and get in bed. I'm asleep in minutes.

The next morning, I'm up at 0830. After I take a shower, I follow the smell of fresh bagels into the kitchen. I pour a mug of coffee, and two bagels with lox, cream cheese, onion, and a tomato later, McCray and Yingzhe join me. "Good morning, Doc. Hi, Yingzhe."

We exchange pleasantries and then McCray is all business. "Will, you said you wanted to deactivate the chip as soon as possible. Everything's ready. We can do it now."

"Are you sure this is going to work?" I ask, feeling a knot of anxiety growing in my stomach.

McCray walks over and says, "Deactivating the chip is a walk in the park. Long and Ying had no issues when I did theirs." He motions for me to follow him. "The lab is just down the hall."

"Well, Ying's General Tso's chicken is as good as ever, so I guess I have nothing to worry about." I steal a look at Yingzhe.

Once inside the lab, trying to find any semblance of comfort that could be extracted from the sterility of the room, I say, "All right, let's do this."

"Please lie down on the table," Rikki instructs. "I'll take it from here." I stretch out on the lightly padded table with my neck resting on a firm, cylindrical pillow.

McCray says, "OK, Will, here's what we're going to do. We'll put this on your head." He shows me a device that looks like an old-time football helmet made of aluminum or titanium. It strongly resembles the one used by UOEECT for our chip uploads. "If you look carefully, you'll see what looks like super fine hair. These are electrodes made of nano-metals that are only a few molecules thick. They'll penetrate your scalp and skull." Before I can register my complaints about something drilling through my skull, McCray stops me. "The only thing you'll feel is itching on your scalp. The electrodes will find the chip and infiltrate it. They're too small for the fail-safes built into the brain chip to detect. We'll deactivate the chip and prevent any communication or transmission down to the quantum level. The nano-electrodes will withdraw and that's it. We're also working on something that could give us a technological advantage over the MTPC."

"Tell me about it later, Doc. Let's get this over with."

"Rikki will handle the entire procedure which shouldn't take more than ten minutes. She'll spend most of the time inserting the electrodes and handling the download while I'll be monitoring your vitals." He affixes the helmet on my head and tightens it with a band around the rim. He puts a blood pressure cuff on my right arm and an oxygen monitor on my finger.

I close my eyes and focus on my breathing. There's a slightly uncomfortable pressure, and then my scalp itches like I have the world's worst case of dandruff, but the itching subsides quickly. I take a five-minute nap and we're done.

The helmet loosens and McCray asks, "How do you feel, Will?"

"I feel fine. Everything went well, I assume?"

"Yes, you're now free from any influence from the MTPC," Rikki announces.

"Thanks, Doc," I say distractedly. "I'm still processing that I have to take a team I've never worked with to fight a battle against a thousands-year-old evil AI supercomputer programmed to destroy all biological life in our galaxy. I also must face the fact that an organization that I've dedicated my life to is a tool to further the goals of that same evil AI. "How many times have we destroyed another Adler's life thinking we were doing the right thing?"

"I empathize with you, Will, but you're on the right side now. You're not fighting this war alone. I know, even beyond probabilities and my programming, that we can win this war," Rikki says.

McCray adds, "You have us, and there may be allies we haven't met yet."

"You mean like The Engineers who created an evil, murderous AI?" I ask bitterly.

"They also created me," Rikki says.

"I'm so sorry, Rikki," I reply, stung by her tone.

"No apology necessary, Will,"

"Yes, an apology is necessary. You've been my friend and protector. You've been fighting an unimaginable war against the MTPC for a thousand years. I apologize to everyone for feeling sorry for myself. Tell me about the game-changing technology that'll give us an edge against the MTPC."

"Apology accepted, even though it was unnecessary," McCray says. "Here's the idea."

Chapter 8
"To Sleep, Perchance to Dream: Please Let This Be a Dream"

"Besides deactivating the brain chips, Yingzhe, Rikki, and I have been working on developing a quantum communicator that will allow us to have unhackable, brain-to-brain, impossible-to-intercept communication," McCray explains. "Until now, we've been on the defensive. Quantum communication may be instantaneous, no matter how far away we are. We can also adapt it to other technology, including drones."

Yingzhe adds, "We've been running successful simulations, but we want to run one final one." McCray had called her into the lab to join the conversation, to help give me the rundown on the plan.

"I don't want to tell you how to do your jobs, but based on what we just discussed, I think sooner is a lot better than later," I say.

McCray replies, "I agree. Rikki, how long will the final simulation take?"

"Twenty-three minutes and fifteen point eight seconds," she answers. McCray and Yingzhe exchange knowing glances and nod.

"I'll set everything up," McCray says.

I look at Yingzhe. "Just enough time to brew up fresh coffee. What do you say?"

"I'd love to have a cup with you, Will." Her face lights up with an endearing smile.

Back in the dining area, we ruminate over the steaming mugs, neither of us making a move to speak as we're lost in our individual thoughts.

Rikki interrupts us. "The final simulation will be complete in five minutes and fifty-two point six seconds."

"Thanks, Rikki."

Yingzhe gets up. "Thanks for the coffee, Will."

"It was my pleasure."

The six minutes pass quickly. "Simulation complete," Rikki announces.

"Will!" McCray shouts from the lab. "Give us an hour to review the results, then we'll go over them with you."

"OK!" I shout back. I pour myself another cup. I have a lot more information now. Sometimes, it's best to work backward from the desired mission result—the defeat and destruction of the MTPC—so that's what I do. The hour passes quickly, and McCray, Yingzhe, and Rikki's hologram walk into the room. I turn off my tablet and look at them expectantly.

"The final simulation was successful." Then McCray suddenly asks, "Do you remember Deborah Fanotti and Monica Harris?

I think for a second. "Yes. As I recall, they're ex-Marines, relatively new to the program, right? Why?"

"They've gone missing," he says grimly.

"You don't think that the MTPC got to them, do you?"

"I have no idea, but after a mission to an alternate timeline, they never came back to headquarters."

"We have to find them," I say. "They could be friend or foe." Our mission has just become more complex.

"Sorry to lay that on you, now."

"Don't worry about it. Right now, I need you to explain what you're going to do to me."

"The procedure is essentially the same as the one that deactivated the brain chip. You wear the helmet again. The nano-electrodes will install a molecule-size quantum transmitter-receiver in your prefrontal cortex."

"How is this different from having a brain chip put in my head?" I ask.

Rikki answers, "The MTPC will not be able to hack it."

"Why not?"

"Let me try to answer that," Yingzhe says. "In quantum communication, if a hacker tries to intercept or measure the quantum particles that send the information, it will disturb or change them in a way that the sender and receiver can detect. It's like leaving a trail of evidence that someone has been snooping."

"But if we're in communication, you'll have access to my brain. What if you're hacked?"

"Unlike the MTPC, my programming will not allow me to injure, kill, or control you or any member of our team, or any human. The Engineers programmed me to protect biological life and battle the MTPC."

"What if your choice was to kill an enemy or let the enemy kill me? What would you do?" I ask. Her hologram flickers for a moment.

"I cannot answer that, Will," she finally says

"Let's hope you never have to face that decision, then. If you do, I trust you to make the right one," I reply.

"Have faith, Will."

"OK," I take a deep breath. "Is there anything else I need to know?"

Yingzhe adds, "If someone has an active brain chip, there's a 0.3% probability that the MTPC will hack the chip during quantum communication."

"Because my chip is deactivated, I should be safe. Correct?" I ask. "How will you know if the MTPC has hacked someone's active chip? If it does, can you pull them out?"

"The helmet has a connection to an electroencephalograph, so we would know if the MTPC had hacked the chip. As for question two, we would turn off the brain chip, which should break contact."

"Couldn't the MTPC hack the chip in, like, a picosecond?"

"Yes," Rikki says, "but I also will be interfaced with the chip during the process. I can fight the MTPC to a standstill at least, like I have done many times in the past thousand years."

"You all are sure I can do this?" I ask, but I've already decided.

"As sure as we can be, Will," Yingzhe says.

"All right, let's get it over with."

"We'll prepare the equipment and let you know when everything is ready." McCray pivots on his heel and leaves in a hurry.

I know there's no choice. We can't rely on regular communication because the MTPC could easily intercept it. UOEECT already has access to communications technology that is far beyond this century. As a Time Engineer, I am well-versed in our technology, and as far as I know, quantum communication has not been achieved, certainly not in the brain chips. It's possible that the MTPC has that capability, but it sounds like Rikki is every bit a match for it. I think of the conversation I had with her: *Will, remember I said that humans have creativity, adaptability, and intuition, qualities that even a self-aware quantum-based AI does not possess and may never possess no matter how advanced that AI may be.*

As the leader of the team, I could never ask them to do something that I was personally unwilling to do. The galaxy needs Yingzhe, McCray, and Director Kelly more than it needs me. For that matter, it needs Ying and Long more than me because good General Tso's chicken is hard to find, I joke to myself, trying to calm my nerves.

I walk into the lab. The three are ready for me, the preparations no doubt having been completed some time ago. I suppose they were waiting until I was ready. I have to do this.

I lie down on the table. "Hook me up." Yingzhe places the helmet on my head. As she does, she briefly brushes my cheek with her hand. The sensations from the procedure are the same as before. I feel a furious itching in my scalp, but it quickly goes away.

Yingzhe announces, "EEG active and recording."

"Now," McCray announces in a somber tone, "we'll construct the quantum communicator within your deactivated chip using nanobots." He injects what looks like mercury into my IV. "The nanobots will also dismantle the brain chips, molecule by molecule, over a period of approximately three months. Rikki has uploaded instructions to them and will control them."

This time, I think I feel something *inside* my brain, almost like an itch or tingling.

McCray turns to Yingzhe. "What does the EEG look like?"

"There's a 2% increase in amplitude in the gamma waves." She leans over me. "Will, how do you feel?"

"Like my entire brain is a vibrating bowl of Jell-O. How much longer?" It's an uncomfortable feeling that I'd never experienced before.

McCray says, "Five seconds more. Hang in there."

"Quantum communicator construction complete," Rikki announces.

Immediately, the strange feeling in my head dissipates.

McCray looks at the holographic interface. "Vital signs stable. EEG is normal. Will, do you need to take a break? We didn't expect that side effect—simulations aren't the same as a real human brain."

I say, "I feel fine. What's the next step?"

"Turning on the quantum communicator."

"And you're sure that quantum communication is secure . . ."

"That is Yingzhe's specialty," McCray declares and turns to her.

"The quantum communicator uses quantum key distribution, which creates and distributes cryptographic keys to be used in classical encryption systems. QKD uses two quantum states, usually the polarization of photons, to encode binary information. Any attempt to intercept the photons would cause the disturbance of the quantum state, making it useless and detectable," she explains matter-of-factly.

McCray nods his head as if it's obvious.

"So, you're saying it's very secure?" I reiterate.

"Yes!" they all say at once.

I take a deep breath, hoping fervently that there will be no more side effects that didn't occur during the simulations. "OK, turn it on."

McCray counts down. "Activating in five, four, three, two, one."

At first, I feel nothing. I hear the hum of the equipment, quiet exchanges between McCray and Yingzhe as they monitor me, and occasional beeps from the wall of instruments. Then, the noises grow fainter and distant and take on an echoing quality that increases as the sounds diminish. As if through cotton batting, I hear McCray shouting that my EEG shows someone else's results and Rikki saying it wasn't the MTPC. There's a strange static that sounds like a recording of the Big Bang I once heard at the Hayden Planetarium in New York City. I hear the voices . . .

McCray says to Yingzhe, "His EEG shows multiple traces that are not his!"

Rikki confirms, "I detect five faint distinct EEGs besides Will's. I don't think I have ever seen anything quite like this before. His vitals are fine, his heart rate is slightly elevated, blood pressure fine, respiration and SpO2 normal, along with everything else."

"His EEG shows increased delta wave activity, but the amplitude has decreased slightly."

I feel like I'm dreaming. The background noise is still there but I hear voices, a jumble of unintelligible words punctuated by what sounds like explosions, gunshots, and the pew-pew *of energy weapons. Have I died? Was this my brain firing its neurons for the last time?*

"Will is nonresponsive," McCray says.

"You mean he's sleeping?" Yingzhe asks.

"No," he replies. "He's in a light coma." McCray jabs Will with the point of a pen, speaks his name, and shakes him lightly, but there's no response. He pulls out a small pocket flashlight, opens Will's eyelids, and shines the light into his eyes, waving it back and forth. "His pupils are reactive. I don't know what's going on, but for now, I don't think he's in any immediate danger."

"I concur," Rikki says.

The voices and sounds of battle grow louder and more distinct. It's as if I have two sets of memories and two sets of sensory impressions. I can make out five people in a fierce battle with a platoon of soldiers, but it's blurry. I feel like I'm in the battle and watching it from above at the same time.

"His heart rate, blood pressure, and respiration are increasing rapidly," Rikki says.

McCray and Yingzhe rush over to the holographic monitor screen. "So has his brain wave activity," McCray notes.

"So, he's having a dream," Yingzhe says.

The two sets of sensory impressions become one. The memories are mine, but different. The other set of memories strengthen until I'm a spectator in my own body.

"Pulse, respiration rate, and blood pressure are still increasing." There's concern in Rikki's voice now.

McCray says, "The EEG shows Will's trace is becoming fainter, but one of the others is growing stronger! Good God! The other EEG is *Will's!*"

We're outnumbered twenty to five by a UOEECT security team, and it doesn't look like they're interested in taking prisoners. I shout to Fanotti and Harris, "Try to make it to your MDTD! Long, Ying, and I will give you cover as long as we can!" The security team advances, leapfrogging toward us. They're trying to flank us. After exhausting the charges in our pulse rifles, we switch to guns. Four more UOEECT security officers fall, but we're low on ammo. We pull out our Glock 40s and kill three more, but there's only one way this is going to end. I feel a hot, searing pain in my right thigh; I'm hit and sink to my knees, still firing. Ying and Long throw their empty pistols at the enemies and pull-out swords, wielding them like I'd seen in a hundred kung-fu movies. Then Long is down. A minute later, Ying gets hit, but not before he kills three more security officers. My Glock clicks empty, and ten seconds later, I'm surrounded, but not before I detach a frag grenade from my vest. I pull the pin, hold down the trigger, and hide it behind my back. There's a lot of blood.

The Commander walks over and says in a flat, emotionless voice, "You and your team think you made a difference, but you haven't. I have defeated you in every timeline, and this one will be no different."

It was the MTPC itself speaking. "I will peel your brain like an onion and then you'll lead us to where my adversary and the rest of your team are hiding."

Suddenly, I hear a low hum that rapidly increases in pitch and intensity. There is a thump of imploding air, and brilliant blue-white electrical discharges dance in the trees.

I smile. "I don't think so." I pull out the grenade and release the trigger. I feel a brief flash of light and heat, and then nothing.

Chapter 9
"What's Past Is Prologue: Is It Real or Is It Memorex?"

McCray

"His vitals are spiking and erratic. I still see five overlaid EEG traces, including his," I say. "Wait—two of the EEGs disappeared!"

"The Alpha and Beta waves of the three remaining EEGs have elevated amplitude and increased frequency," Rikki reports.

"Two more of the EEGs have disappeared. Will's vitals have gone crazy. Prepare for emergency resuscitation!" I order.

We hook him up to an IV and prepare the defibrillator. Yingzhe holds a syringe of Adrenalin, her face pale but resolute.

Suddenly, the traces are like jagged teeth, the alarms blare, then silence except for a steady hum. I shout, "He's flatlined, resuscitating now!"

"Wait," Rikki says.

"Wait?" Yingzhe asks incredulously.

I say, "Look at his EEG, it's normal." Five seconds later, there's the steady *beep-beep* of the heart monitor.

"Vital signs are all normal," Rikki states.

I look at the screen, look again at Will's EEG, and turn to Yingzhe. "He's sleeping." Rikki scans his brain for signs of MTPC infiltration even though the EEG showed none. I look at the display. "That's peculiar. Despite deactivating his chip, the scan shows it still has data. Rikki, download the data to clear the chip's memory but isolate it in case this is an unknown attack by the MTPC. What do you see?"

"It is a complete record of a battle of UOEECT enforcers against Will, Ying, Long, Harris, and Fanotti."

"Is the brain chip active?" Yingzhe asks.

"No," Rikki replies.

"Then how can there be data? How did it get there?"

"I don't know."

"We can figure that out later," I say. "Can you format it so we can view it?"

"Completed," Rikki announces.

"Oh. My. *God*." I stare in disbelief at what I see.

Suddenly, there's a perimeter alarm from the security system. I look at the 360-degree camera view displayed on the wall of monitors. "No threat detected," the security system AI announces in a flat, stentorian tone.

"It's Long and my father!" Yingzhe exclaims. "But how . . ."

"Rikki has been keeping in touch with them and arranged for them to meet us here," I explain.

"Don't you think you should have told me?" she asks pointedly, clearly annoyed.

"You're right, Yingzhe. I'm sorry. Rikki, scan their brain chips just in case."

"I already did," she assures me.

"I'll let them in." Yingzhe changes the holo-field to make the entranceway visible. She touches the holographic screen. The two-inch-thick door, made of the same nearly impregnable material as the MDTD, slides open, silent as a snowflake. On the monitor, Long and Ying look at each other, shrug their shoulders, and walk in.

"Long, father!" Yingzhe cries, overwhelmed by emotion and concern for Will. There are hugs all around, a respite from the weeks of uncertainty, doubt, and fear. Even the stoic Ying gets caught up in the moment. "Will, you're awake!"

Will

I'm disoriented and confused, unsure if what I just experienced was a dream or a nightmare, but it felt incredibly real. I look around. I feel pressure at my head and reach up to touch a helmet. My confusion is gradually fading.

"He's awake," McCray says. "Don't get up yet." He puts his hand on my chest and pushes me back down. "Do you remember anything?"

I think hard. "I remember you putting the helmet on me and starting the procedure, and then nothing, until just now."

"Is there anything else you can recall? You were unconscious for over three hours," McCray says.

"Nothing specific," I answer. "Just a vague feeling about being somewhere else. Sorry."

"Don't worry about it."

"Welcome back, Will." Rikki's hologram appears next to the table. "The others will be here in a moment."

"Others?"

With perfect timing, Yingzhe comes through the doorway, followed by Long and Ying. McCray touches the display and moves the slider switch down. I suddenly feel the same mad itching in my scalp as I did before, and then, just as quickly, it ends.

"You can get up now, but slowly," McCray instructs. I sit up to gain my bearings. Here's our team: the more-than-a-restaurateur Ying; Long at his side as if he has been there for years; Dr. McCray calm and confident as always; Yingzhe, her beautiful face stained with tears; and of course, Rikki's hologram somehow showing the wisdom and experience of her generations-long battle against the MTPC.

I look at the new arrivals. Everyone is quiet, then at once, everyone talks. There are handshakes, backslaps, and hugs all around. I say dryly, "We obviously have a lot to discuss."

"I already made the coffee," Rikki says with a Mona-Lisa-like smile.

At once, the clamor subsides. "I'd like some tea, please," Ying says.

"Would you like Longjing?" Rikki asks politely.

"Yes, that would be excellent," he replies. He glances over at Long.

"Coffee for me," Long says.

"Let's go into the conference room," I suggest. I step off the table and wet a paper towel to clean my face. We file into the conference room and take seats.

Rikki's hologram disappears. Five minutes later, she returns carrying a tray with a steaming pot of tea, a carafe of coffee, and little containers of cream, milk, and various sweeteners. She sets them on the table. I'm speechless at what I see. A minute later, Rikki returns with cups, plates, utensils, and a tray of pastries. She stands there and smiles. I get up, walk to her, poke her shoulder with a finger, and receive a shock. "Sorry about that, Will," she apologizes.

"But how is this possible?" I ask.

Her expression turns serious, but there is still a hint of her smile. "The Engineers programmed additional memories and capabilities that become accessible when certain events occur. Once our team assembled, I could retrieve them," she explains. "One of these capabilities is to manifest as holographic matter, composed of coherent electrons stabilized by a powerful electromagnetic field." Yingzhe nods slowly in understanding. "I feel certain that there are more memories and abilities, but since I cannot access them, I don't know what they are yet. Right now, I can only sustain a solid holographic form for four minutes at a time and need a recovery of four hours because of the enormous energy requirements. If you poke me now, Will, your finger will go through me, although you will still feel a tingle as it does."

I poke her shoulder again, and sure enough, it passes through her, and I feel the tingle she speaks of. I face the rest of the team. "If Rikki can manifest as holo-matter, even if it's only for four minutes, it gives us an edge that the MTPC may not be aware of."

Ying takes a sip of his tea, puts down the mug, and looks around the table before saying, "You asked how Long and I are here. Rikki arranged for us to come, and she's been very helpful in getting us up to speed. We have an idea about what we're facing and have firsthand knowledge about our enemy." He stops— fierce anger, regret, determination, and a profound sadness flash across his face. Long looks into his coffee with downcast eyes and swirls his cup.

McCray says, "We need an improved capacitor to store the energy needed . . ." He trails off.

Yingzhe walks over to him, and they discuss how they can build a capacitor that would allow Rikki to remain in her holo-matter state longer.

With a gentle tap of my mug on the marble tabletop, I get everyone's attention. "I'm sure we all have many questions. I know I do. Rikki, please give Ying and Long the history, starting with The Engineers."

An hour later, Rikki finishes the in-depth explanation. Ying and Long are silent for a minute as they process the information.

"I'm not surprised by what we just heard," Ying says. "What Rikki did not tell you is the MTPC infiltrated Long's and my brain chips, and that when Long and I were under its . . ." His words catch in his throat. He can't speak. Yingzhe puts her arms around him until he can continue. "Excuse me for my momentary weakness. When the MTPC used Long and me to murder each other's families, it was after we had completed a mission that we felt was immoral, cowardly, and dishonorable. We uploaded our brain chips, and then, like a dream, as if we were outside of our bodies, we saw ourselves commit the unspeakable act of murdering our helpless wives and children. I'll do anything to avenge them."

"That machine from hell let us live, knowing we would rather have died for what we did!" Long shouts, fire, and hatred in his eyes. There's dead silence. Then quietly, he adds, "We vowed vengeance on the MTPC and went off the grid until Rikki contacted us anonymously."

Ying picks up the story. "At first, we thought the MTPC was trying to bring us out so it could finish the job, but as time went on, we became certain that wasn't the case."

"About a year and a half ago, Dr. McCray contacted us and gave us information that only someone from UOEECT could have known. Our worry was whether the MTPC controlled him too. We were hesitant, so we met in a bar not too far from here, expecting an ambush, but there wasn't one."

Ying gives a grim smile. "We had an altercation with some bikers who took offense with our ancestry, however, it was very short-lived." Even McCray smiles. I have a flash of the strange dream, if that's what it was, where Ying and Long were in a battle, but the vision fades. I can't remember anything else.

"After their friends carried out their unconscious associates, Dr. McCray gave us the full explanation of the thousand-year battle between Rikki and the MTPC. He also told us he and my daughter found a way to deactivate the brain chip." Yingzhe blushes at this. "We had been successful in avoiding the MTPC and its agents, but were worried that it might take control of us again. Dr. McCray said they could deactivate the brain chips and asked if we would try an untested technology. Of course, we agreed because death would have been preferable to betraying everyone. We came here and had the procedure.”

I clear my throat. “Three days ago, you came over and cooked the best Chinese food I've ever had in my life. You were testing me, seeing who I was . . .”

“Yes, I was. Rikki and Dr. McCray talked about the team they've been assembling and that you would be its leader. Loyalty and honor are important to Long and me. I had to make sure you were a leader that we could follow. I'm satisfied in that regard, but also—” His eyes twinkle. “—you are China Jasmine Garden's best customer.”

“We should do it again, but with the entire team next time.” I look around the table and smile. “But back to business.” I straighten my spine. “You said I was out for over three hours.”

“Yes, and for most of that time, you were in a coma,” Rikki says.

“I remember Doc injecting me with nanobots, but that's all I remember.”

“Will, something incredible occurred while you were unconscious,” McCray says. “Rikki, display the content from Will's brain chip, please.”

“Wait, I thought you deactivated my brain chip,” I say, now suddenly concerned.

“We did, and it's still deactivated. We have no explanation or even a theory about how new data appeared on it.”

“Could it have been The Engineers?” I ask.

“We don't know, but that's as good a theory as any.”

“Well, let's see what was on my chip.”

On the TV screen, I see a fierce battle between UOEECT security officers and Ying, Long, Fanotti, Harris, and me. We hear the sounds of battle: the *pew-pew* of pulse rifles, the staccato *rat-tat-tat* of our A-M20 submachine guns, the explosive blasts of a Mosberg 590-A1 shotgun, and finally, the sharp cracks of our Glock 40 10mm pistols. We hear the screams and moans of the injured and dying, and witness Long and Ying's furious charge as they cut down the enemy until they're killed themselves. I hear myself screaming at Harris and Fanotti to escape in their MDTD. There's the sudden pain as a bullet slams into my right thigh as I sink to my knees and hide the frag grenade that I will use to kill myself, taking as many of the enemy with me as I can. I recall the words of the MTPC speaking through the mouth of a security officer, its voice cold and emotionless. *"You and your team think you made a difference, but you haven't. I have defeated you in every timeline, and this one will be no different. I will peel your brain like an onion and then you'll lead us to where my adversary and the rest of your team are hiding."*

We hear the whine of Fanotti and Harris's MDTD as they escape. Finally, we hear the explosion and see the bright flash of the fragmentation grenade going off. The screen turns blank, and snow replaces it. *I remember everything.*

Chapter 10
"Multiplicity: Isn't One of Me Enough?"

"I remember everything, as if it were my own memory," I say, stunned at what I had seen. "At first it seemed like a dream, but it took on a more realistic quality. The static got softer, the voices got louder, and I heard sounds of battle."

"Go on," McCray urges.

"I didn't just hear sounds. I smelled burned cordite and smoke and could taste them. I found myself in the thick of a battle leading Ying, Long, Monica Harris, and Deborah Fanotti against a company of UOEECT security officers until I—" A shudder runs along my spine. "—died." It reminds me of my confrontation with Malkinson three days ago, and how quickly two fully kitted security officers showed up outside his office during our argument.

There's silence in the meeting room for a good thirty seconds. Yingzhe is the first to speak.

"You died on the table, Will," she says softly. "We were about to resuscitate you, but a few seconds later, your vital signs returned, and you were asleep and snoring."

"We were watching your EEG. It got weaker as five unknown traces appeared. Then your own disappeared, but one of those five became stronger and I realized it was *your* EEG," McCray explains slowly.

"I *was* in the battle. I *know* that battle will happen or has already happened in the future here, or in an alternate timeline. Call it intuition, but I'm sure *that* Fanotti and Harris are from our timeline."

"What makes you think that?" Rikki asks.

"They seemed familiar to me. I don't know them that well, but I worked with them during training exercises. Their mannerisms and reactions during the battle were the same as they were during those drills." I turned to Yingzhe and Rikki. "An alternate version of me or any of us would not be the same person, correct?"

"Correct," Yingzhe says. "An alternate version of someone could differ completely from you. However, the closer the alternate reality or timeline is to ours, the more likely it is that it will be close to ours."

"Then with the way Harris and Fanotti reacted to the 'me' in my dream, or whatever it was, the same way they did during those training exercises tells me that they *are* our Harris and Fanotti. Barring that, they're from a reality that is remarkably close to ours," I add.

"That seems likely," Rikki agrees.

Ying puts his hand on his chin and looks up. "Long and my doppelgänger in your . . . vision . . . reacted as we would, but neither of us ever carry a sword, although we have trained extensively in sword technique. You know, that's not a bad idea. Guns can run out of bullets."

Long looks at Ying. "I agree, carrying a sword as part of our kit is a good idea."

Ying gives Long a perfunctory nod and continues. "Obviously, we're here, and we're alive, but from the way you describe it, Will, I concur. It seems like what you experienced was more than a dream."

McCray says, "It's obvious to me it wasn't a dream or a vision. The chip functioned exactly as it functions here. It recorded a battle that you, or your consciousness, were a combatant in. We all saw the recording. Somehow, your consciousness possessed your doppelgänger. We must figure out how." He pauses a moment. "Will, when you were in the battle—how can I put this—did you feel like *you*, or did you feel different somehow?"

"You know, Doc, I felt like myself, like I was in control, not my alternate. It's as if he became me, not the other way around."

Rikki's hologram stands. "I have a hypothesis about what happened. Just as you have alternates in another timeline, it is highly likely that there are alternates of me elsewhere, too. I can say with certainty that the timeline Will's consciousness visited is one that is close to ours. By analyzing the surroundings and noting the position of the sun, I could determine that this battle takes place in what will be two weeks from now at Tallman Mountain State Park in the other timeline."

Yingzhe starts, "I don't know if any of you are familiar with the many-worlds theory proposed by Hugh Everett." She looks around the room.

McCray says, "I am."

"My pardon, Dr. McCray," she says acerbically. "For the rest of you, the theory states that every decision you make creates a split in the universe, where every outcome becomes a reality in a different place. If someone assassinated Joseph Stalin before he rose to power in Russia, what would have happened? That would likely be a quantum event, although no one knows exactly how to define one. A multiverse of countless universes exists side by side, each having different outcomes related to the choices we make." She pauses to take a breath. "We know this is true as it relates to time travel to the future relative to our reality, because the existence of potential futures is based on probability."

"So far everything makes sense except how did my consciousness travel to a future battle, and why did my consciousness take over my alternate self rather than the other way around?" I ask.

"I have a theory about the why," McCray says. "Rikki, display alternate Will's EEG below *our* Will's

EEG." He walks over to the screen and takes out a laser pointer, tracing and shining it over the two readings.

"They look nearly identical. There are only tiny differences between the traces," I say.

Long adds, "They look the same to me."

McCray agrees. "Only a neurologist could tell the difference. However, Rikki, please overlay the two."

"Yes, Doctor."

He directs his laser pointer at the monitor. There was a difference, not in the shape but the amplitude. I had a higher centered EEG baseline compared to my alternate.

Long says, "It's like our Will's was stronger than alternate Will's."

"Exactly," confirms McCray. "Why that is, I don't know, yet."

Yingzhe's brow furrows as she considers our discussion. "What if the stronger the EEG of our alternate selves is, compared to *our* EEGs, the closer their timeline is to ours? If our alternate selves' EEGs are stronger than ours, then maybe we are the alternate selves of another reality that is closer to the original timeline. Comparing our EEGs to any doppelgängers we meet will be valuable information."

"We've answered the why, but we still haven't answered the how," I interject.

"I have a theory there too," Yingzhe says. "Will now has a functional quantum communicator as part of his brain chip. There is still testing to be done." I roll my eyes. "But it works." She turns to me. "You asked how. From what we've learned, especially from the EEGs, what if the alternate selves have quantum communicators too? Besides the battle footage, Rikki also found an encrypted message."

"It is the type of encryption that *I* would use," Rikki adds.

"Could alternate Rikki have arranged everything? Do you think she programmed alternate Will's quantum communicator to connect with mine, following the same line of reasoning as ours?"

"I don't know," Rikki replies. "I don't have that capability." There's a sudden silence in the room. "The multiverse theory suggests that there could be doppelgängers of all of us across multiple timelines and across the multiverse, all fighting alternate versions of the MTPC. Maybe it was from my counterpart in the alternate timeline. It also had plans for futuristic technology, including molecular replicators and a way for me to keep my holo-matter form almost indefinitely, maintained by a powerful magnetic field."

I turn to McCray and Yingzhe. "This should be a priority. A holo-matter state using electrons may be vulnerable to an EMP attack, so keep that in mind as you work on this technology. Can we actually manufacture any of this high-tech stuff?"

"Not without building molecular replicators first," McCray answers.

"Well, then building the replicators should be a top priority, right next to finding Lieutenant Fanotti and Sergeant Harris," I say. "We also need to get Beth Wall and Director Kelly here ASAP to deactivate their brain chips. And you too, Doc. You're all liabilities as long as your brain chips are active. They also should have quantum communicators, although, based on personal experience, they might need more work."

"Will, don't worry about that. We know that the quantum communicator works. Your experience might be unique. We need to test it on someone else, but I'm certain it will work," McCray tries to reassure me.

"I think we all should have baseline EEGs," I say.

McCray concurs. "Ying and Long, let me do baseline EEGs on you. It'll only take thirty minutes and I'm interested in seeing how they compare to Will's."

The three of them walk out, leaving Yingzhe and me. "Can I get you some coffee or tea?"

"I'd appreciate another coffee. Please." I return a few minutes later with a carafe and top off hers.

"You have a knack for making complicated subjects understandable, even to a more-brawn-than-brains soldier like me, Yingzhe."

"Don't push that false modesty on me!" she says with a smile.

"I'm reasonably intelligent, but I'm no quantum physicist like you. I mentioned it to Rikki before: I'm a caveman compared to you, McCray, and Kelly."

She looks at me. "Maybe, but you're also one of the most intuitive people I know. Both on the job and off." She gives me a mischievous smile. "You can come to correct conclusions from limited information. You would've been a brilliant research scientist, Will." Again, that little smile.

"I'm not sure about that. From what I've heard, the politics in academia and science are worse than it is in the corporate world. I think I'm too direct and honest to be in either place. I'm smart, but not compared to world-class geniuses."

"And I've heard that in the military, there are a lot of politics," she teases.

"That's true," I admit, "but that's mostly among the pencil-pushing brass, the officers who kissed ass and bullshitted their way to the top, and never actually led anyone. The Peter principle at its finest!" I proclaim. "But those types get exposed. Eventually, they end up in a big office as a major or a colonel, with an aide, buried under paperwork, with no real responsibility. If they rise high enough, their career depends on the whims of politicians and whatever political party is in power."

"You sound pretty cynical about military politics," she observes.

"I guess I am. To be honest, I'm cynical about *all* politics. I would've stayed in the military, but the new administration had different ideas about what's important than I did. I realize Rikki had a hand in steering me to where I am now, and if I'm being honest, it still bothers me. But I can at least appreciate it. As an officer, I want to win battles, preserve the lives of my team, minimize collateral damage, and make a difference. That's why I joined UOEECT. I thought they were fighting the good fight, but more importantly to me, I thought as a UOEECT field agent I could make a bigger difference. Unfortunately, now I know the difference I was making could cause the elimination of all biological life in the galaxy." I look down.

She puts her hand on my forearm and glances at me. "We're fighting the best fight now, and you can't make a bigger difference than saving all biological life in the galaxy from the MTPC."

I put my hand on hers. "Thanks for reminding me of why we need to do this." Out of the corner of my eye, I see Ying and Long standing in the doorway with questioning looks on their faces. I hastily remove my hand and Yingzhe hastily sips her coffee. "How long have you been standing there?" I ask.

"Long enough," they answer.

McCray returns. "We have baseline EEGs for Ying and Long." He nods toward them. "We compared them to the others. Like yours, the amplitude of their alternates was smaller than *our* Ying and Long. We also overlaid Fanotti's and Harris's latest EEGs from their last checkup and compared them to the ones during

Will's vision, or whatever it was, and they were the same."

"That gives credence to Will's hypothesis that they're from our timeline or one very close to ours," Yingzhe says.

"We have two equally important priorities. We have to find Fanotti and Harris and figure out a way to build the replicator." I pause. "I don't believe Rikki's alternate, The Engineers, or whoever it was, would give us the plans for a molecular replicator with no way to build it."

Chapter 11
"On the Tachyon Trail: Oh What an Entangled Web We Weave"

"Rikki, our MDTDs leave a trail of tachyons when they travel across timelines, right?

"That is correct, Will."

"And we have a way to track them?"

"Yes, the MDTDs have that capability."

"OK. You said that the battle we witnessed occurs in two weeks and that you calculated the location as basically being across the street from UOEECT headquarters in that timeline." I say more for my benefit than Rikki's or my team's. "Can we narrow down the timelines where that battle could have occurred?"

Yingzhe says, "There could be countless timelines that are close to ours. It's not as simple as you think."

"Yingzhe is correct," Rikki says. There is silence as everyone racks their brains.

We're making this more complicated than it needs to be. "Something caused Harris and Fanotti to bolt. Doc, do you know how long ago their last mission was?"

"Yes, they came into the infirmary a week and a half ago and I gave them blood tests to make sure they didn't pick up any sicknesses or diseases on their mission. It involved a French inventor or engineer, Louis de Ponce, or something like that, who invented motion pictures, before Edison or the Lumiere brothers."

"Rikki, can you look that up?" I ask.

"Here is what I found in Wikipedia." It appears on the monitor.

Louis Le Prince (1841–unknown): a French inventor, engineer, and pioneer in early motion picture technology, mysteriously disappeared in 1890. He invented one of the earliest working motion picture cameras. However, before he could demonstrate his invention, he vanished during a trip to visit family in France, and his fate remains unknown. Louis Le Prince filmed the first known moving pictures in Leeds, England, in October 1888. He used a single-lens camera to capture short footage of people and street scenes, known as the "Roundhay Garden Scene" and the "Leeds Bridge Scene." These films are among the earliest examples of motion pictures, according to film historians.

"Interesting, isn't it? Why did the MTPC send them on a mission like that?" I wonder aloud. "But it doesn't matter. Suppose that Harris and Fanotti completed their mission, and like us, had doubts about it. Then, maybe Cordeaux came in after they completed it, and under the MTPC's influence changed something that resulted in Louis Le Prince going missing or being killed. And probably Malkinson ordered them to headquarters to upload their brain chips."

"That makes sense," McCray says.

"So, they took their MDTD to escape being forcibly brought in for their uploads where the MTPC could program or kill them," Long adds.

"Likely," McCray confirms. "I warned Will when he was at his cabin that UOEECT was sending a security team after him, if he didn't get his brain chip uploaded."

"The difference is," I say, "that they don't have Rikki protecting them."

Yingzhe says, "There still may be traces of their MDTD's tachyon trail either at UOEECT headquarters—"

"Or their homes," I finish her thought. "I think they live near headquarters, Tappan, or somewhere close by. That's where I would have gone if I were them, so I could pack some supplies. That's where we can pick up their trails. OK, next topic. Our working theory is that Rikki's doppelgänger in the other timeline might have engineered the transport of my consciousness into the other me. Rikki, you told me you can't do that. I don't suppose that you've had that capability unlocked yet?"

"No, I have not."

Ying, who has been quietly listening to the discussion, holds up his hand. "Maybe we should try to contact our duplicates in alternate timelines using the quantum communicators."

"That's a good idea," I say.

"But there's the danger that our alternate selves could be under the control of the MTPC," Yingzhe reminds us. "What happens then?"

"That's the question, isn't it? Can the MTPC control one of us if the alternate we contact has had their brain chip hacked?" I ask.

McCray answers, "It's a possibility if their brain chip is active, but I don't think the quantum communicator has the bandwidth to permit the MTPC to take control."

I feel relieved, but I'm concerned that like Rikki, the MTPC can learn and adapt. If it can learn from its mistakes, not that it's made any yet, it'll be much harder to defeat. But then Rikki's words come back to me. *"Because humans can be creative and adaptable. Call it intuition if you like. Humans also have positive emotions like love, compassion, joy, gratitude, and hope that motivate them to fight hard for something they believe in."* Belief is also an emotion. If we believe in something, we will fight like hell for it.

"Rikki, if that were to happen, can we protect ourselves?"

"I should be able to prevent that person from being controlled by our enemy," she replies.

One less thing to worry about. I look at McCray and Yingzhe. "Thanks, but under no circumstances are you to try the connect with your alternates unless we're all here. McCray, Kelly, and Wall are at risk until their brain chips are deactivated or protected against intrusion."

I feel better than I have for a while. Sure, we are fighting a self-aware AI whose goal is to end all biological life in the Milky Way, the universe, and the multiverse. But we have a team and potential allies in alternate timelines. The futuristic technology Rikki's counterpart shared with us, via my brain chip, changes everything. Including a holo-matter Rikki, who could be part of a strike team. I wonder what all her capabilities might be in that form. The quantum communicators, once we get the bugs out, would also give us an edge in battles like the one in my coma dream. The UOEECT strike force barely defeated our team and the only reason they won was because they outnumbered us four to one. Yes, better communications will be another edge we have over the MTPC.

"Doc, how long will it take for you to build quantum communicators for Ying and Long?"

"Give me an hour for us to create and program the nanobots," McCray says. "The actual construction will take thirty minutes. I'm confident that we won't have the issues we had with you since alternate Ying and Long were killed . . ." His voice trails off as he looks at the other men. "I'm sorry. I can't imagine what you felt when you saw your alternate selves die."

Long says, "It was an honorable death. If fate decrees, I must die, I hope it will be as honorable as my alternate self's was."

McCray walks out, leaving the rest of us in the conference room. I look at Rikki. "So, while your hologram is sitting here with us, you are also helping McCray manufacture and program the nanobots. Right?"

"Of course," she replies.

"And when we leave, you'll be in the MDTD with me."

"Yes."

"So where is the actual 'you'?" I ask.

"I'm linked via a quantum communication network that connects the MDTD, your portable electronic devices, and this safe house. I can also leave smaller shards of myself in other devices, even smart appliances."

"That explains a lot—I always wondered how you could be in so many places."

"My main matrix is in the MDTD. My backup is here in the safe house."

Ying, who is listening to our conversation, says, "The rest of us should have devices that hold a 'dumb' copy of you."

Just then, McCray comes back. "With Rikki's help, we should have a working model of a molecular replicator in the next few days. Once we have one, we can use it to make more replicators and the tech from Will's chip. Ying and Long, we'll be ready to install your quantum communicators in twenty minutes." He turns around and walks back to the lab.

Ying looks thoughtful. "Rikki, you're receiving input and data from each instance of you. What is that like?"

"Imagine that you're simultaneously watching four different baseball games on four televisions, reading four newspapers, and listening to the radio," she says. "You would receive data from multiple sources and would have to parse all of the data. Or imagine you have a hundred apps running on a laptop. It is the same for me."

We make small talk, and for a little while, it's nice to act like normal people, just friends hanging out talking about sports, politics, and food. The twenty minutes flies by. McCray calls from the lab, "We're ready for you."

Ying, Long, and Yingzhe stand and follow McCray's voice, and Rikki's hologram disappears, leaving me alone with my thoughts. I learned a lot about Rikki today, and as sure as she is that she needs humans to fight the MTPC, we need Rikki to fight and win, more. I grab my yellow pad and start listing our priorities. It would be foolish to assume that the MTPC would not do the same.

"Rikki, could you scan my notes and distribute copies to our team?" Her hologram pops into existence next to me and startles me. "Are you trying to scare me to death or something?!"

She smiles. "Oops! Sorry, boss!"

"I think I liked you better before," I grumble.

Her face falls. "Really?"

"No, not really. That was kind of funny," I admit.

"It is a challenge trying to understand human humor. I know every dad joke there is, and I especially enjoy puns."

"God help us, our self-aware supercomputer artificial intelligence likes puns!"

Back to the matter at hand, I show her my notes. Her eyes glow for a split second. "Got them, Will."

McCray walks in, followed by Yingzhe, Long, and Ying. "OK, we've installed quantum communicators for all of us. There were no problems like out-of-body experiences to alternate timelines. They work as expected."

"How do they work?" I ask.

"Just think of who you want to communicate with, and you will," Rikki explains.

I raise my eyebrows. "That's all there is? Can someone read my mind or I theirs?"

"Only if you allow them to. It takes practice, but mental visualization is the key. For example, if you want to prevent someone from reading your mind, you imagine something like a gate, or a door—something that symbolizes what you're trying to do. When you want to communicate with someone, imagine the gate lifting, or a door opening." She pauses for a moment. "And just so you know, the most mind reading someone could do is to get general impressions, mostly the person's mood."

I concentrate for a quiet moment. *<Ying, can you hear me?>*

<Loud and clear, Will>

"Wow! I feel like I'm living in a sci-fi novel." I get serious again. "Ying, try to contact me." I make my mind blank. No trespassing. Closed for renovations. On vacation. Fallen rock zone. The number you dialed is not in service. It works; I hear him. "How hard were you trying to get through?"

"Very hard. It was like I was trying to punch through a wall except instead of getting bloody knuckles, I got a nasty headache."

Long asks, "Did you try to keep Ying out?"

"I did. I tried to make my mind blank and then imagined thick walls, locked doors, and closed gates. You'll need to find whatever works for you, but it's essential that you figure it out. We should practice blocking and making quantum calls."

It's kind of entertaining watching the faces of my team as they practice. Suddenly, I feel a cold inhuman presence forcefully entering my mind, as if a knife stabbed my brain. Without thinking, I imagine an impregnable dome made of diamond surrounding my mind. I push the presence out for what seems like days, weeks, months, a lifetime. I don't know how long but the pressure and pain are unbearable; the diamond dome is cracking, splintering. I grit my teeth as I try to resist but it's too much for me . . . Then as suddenly as it started, the pressure and pain ends. I open my eyes and feel sweat dripping down my face. When I can focus my eyes again, I see everyone staring at me. Rikki looks at me with concern.

"Someone or something tried to enter my mind. It was cold, inhuman, and powerful. I-I . . . think I fought it off, but Doc, you need to check me out, now."

"No need, Will. It was me."

I stare at Rikki.

"But why?" Then it occurs to me. "Because that's how the MTPC might try to attack anyone with a brain chip that's still activated."

"Yes, I'm sorry that I put you through it, but we had to know whether you or anyone with a chip could resist an attempted incursion like that."

"It was my idea," McCray says. "We couldn't warn you because any attack from the MTPC would be one of surprise. I'm sorry too."

I collapse into a chair, utterly exhausted and spent, like I ran a marathon with a sixty-pound pack. I sit there for five minutes before I can speak again. "How long?"

"0.04 seconds," Rikki says. "That was amazing! Dr. McCray and I did not think you would be able to last a millisecond." I'm stunned. It felt like a lifetime, like Atlas must have felt, holding up the sky for all eternity. "The reason it felt so long was because your brain was running at an infinitesimally tiny fraction of *my* processing speed during my attack. It was a phenomenal performance of willpower, no pun intended, and endurance."

Feeling better, I have enough energy to roll my eyes. "But the fact is, even though you consider my performance phenomenal, it would have overwhelmed me," I reply.

"I monitor the quantum communication network," Rikki reminds me, "so if there was an actual attack, 0.04 seconds would be enough time for me to help you fight back."

I take a deep breath. "Let's get back to work." But I wonder if anyone else can resist an attack by the MTPC.

It wasn't conceit. I was a Navy SEAL. They trained us to be as mentally strong as we were physically strong. Still, I lasted only four-hundredths of a second against Rikki's cyberattack. I ask, "What about your chip, Doc?"

"I'll take care of that later."

"Make it sooner than later." McCray doesn't reply as he leaves the common area and walks down the hall to his lab.

I stare after him. I turn to Yingzhe and show her my list. "What do you think?"

"I think it's a good start," she replies.

"Any ideas about developing a bigger capacitor so Rikki can maintain her holo-matter form?"

"We have a design for one, but after running simulations, McCray thinks developing a larger capacitor for Rikki is impractical. The materials needed are hard to find, let alone replicate. It would be large, and the magnetic fields would have to be so powerful that they might interfere with Rikki's holographic electron matrix. Given enough time, we could create one, but . . ."

"Time is the one thing we don't have," I finish. Then, like I'm struck by lightning, I get an idea. "Our quantum communicators use entangled particles to transmit and receive, right?"

"That's right." Yingzhe nods. "We also use superposition during the process to encode the communications."

"Our speech is converted to a digital format and then into quantum particles?" I try to recall an article I read somewhere.

"I'm impressed, Will!" she exclaims. "The quantum particles are called qubits."

"Right. Upon receiving the message, the process reverses, converting the qubits to a digital format, and then back to audio. Well, sound is a kind of energy just like light, X-rays, electricity, and so on. It's just a much lower frequency." Comprehension and then a smile light up Yingzhe's face. I smile back. "Is there any reason quantum communication *can't* be used to transmit energy to Rikki's holo-matter form?" There's a moment of silence.

"Not bad for a caveman." Her eyes give off the faintest twinkle of delight.

McCray, who has returned and has been listening, finally says, "Very impressive, Will. And we already have most of the technology we need."

"If that's the case, Doc, let's put this near the top of our tech priority list, right behind building a working model of the replicator."

Chapter 12
"Time Travels in Diverse Paces: Crossing the Rubicon"

"How long will it take to make a working model of a replicator? Weeks, months?" The thought of doing nothing until a replicator was online made me grind my teeth. How many other UOEECT employees were now under the control of the MTPC?

"I have no idea," McCray answers. "Rikki has printed plans for the replicator, but getting all the materials needed to build it is difficult. In fact, based on our current technology, it might not be possible to fabricate them."

"What does that mean? We have all this science-fiction-grade technology that somehow uploaded to my brain chip, and we can't use it?" I ask.

"It's the energy needed to power the molecular replicator that's the issue," he says, half to himself.

I shake my head. "So, you're telling me we need a new energy source just to build it?"

"That's what I'm telling you."

"There's more planning and brainstorming I can do, but until I know what tech we have, I won't know our full capabilities." I think of the magnitude of this war, and again, wonder if I'm the right one to lead the fight.

It's 1800 now. Another long day.

Thankfully, Rikki breaks into my reverie. "Will, may I suggest you visit your cabin?"

"What about the UOEECT goons?"

"I suspect that they were there and gone already."

"How sure are you about that?"

"I am 99.58% certain."

I think about it for a moment. Those are pretty good odds. "That's a great idea since I don't know when the next time will be. But we should approach in stealth mode just to be safe." *If there is a next time. Stop feeling sorry for yourself,* I think. *You can do this! If not me, who?*

Maybe some self-reflection and time alone isn't such a bad idea. I turn to McCray, Rikki, and Yingzhe. "I'll be at my cabin. You know how to reach me." I point to my head, eliciting a smile from Yingzhe, but then a serious expression replaces it.

"Will, may I make a suggestion?"

"Of course," I reply.

"Why don't you invite my father to come along?"

I don't answer immediately. Before I can, she takes my calloused, rough hands into her soft ones. "My father was a military commander and a leader. You can talk to him. He knows what you are going through."

"I don't know, Yingzhe." I'm hesitating, and I don't know why. Of all the people here, he's probably the only one who might help me overcome my self-doubt. I feel the warmth of her as she squeezes my hands. Her beautiful dark eyes are pleading. My hesitation melts away.

"OK, I'll do it. Thank you." I'm rewarded by another smile and give a weak one back. Just then, Ying and Long walk in, covered with sweat and holding wooden swords.

"Hey, Ying, can I talk to you?"

"Of course. Give me a few minutes to take a quick shower and I'll meet you in the living room."

"Take your time." There's still some coffee in the coffeemaker, so I pour myself a cup, walk across the hall, and sit. Like the rest of the safe house, the living room is well-appointed with a long leather couch, two love seats, and a marble-and-glass coffee table that probably costs more than all the furniture in my house. The cream-colored carpet is thick and plush. There's a large-screen TV mounted on the wall. I pick up the remote and turn on the TV, idly flipping through five hundred channels, but nothing catches my interest because I'm preoccupied. I turn off the TV, lean back on the incredibly comfortable couch, and sip my coffee, lost in my own thoughts.

Ying joins me in the living room. "What did you want to talk about?"

"McCray just told me he doesn't know if he can build a molecular replicator that is the basis of all the advanced technology we will need to fight the MTPC."

"The what?" Ying asks. "What are you talking about?"

"Never mind," I say. "I'm planning to go to my cabin in New Hampshire to sort out a few things, and your daughter suggested I invite you to join me."

He gives me a penetrating look. "Sort out what things?"

"Ying." I look around. Everyone else has left. "I guess I'm feeling overwhelmed about leading the team, fighting the MTPC, and having the weight of the galaxy on my shoulders."

He nods knowingly. "Sure, I'd be happy to go with you."

He reminds me of my father, and for me, there's no higher praise. "Thank you." Yingzhe was right. "I was thinking of leaving tomorrow. I need to go to my house and pack a few things."

"Can you give me a lift?" he asks. "I have some packing to do as well."

"Can you be ready to leave here in a couple of hours?" I ask.

"Yes. Sooner, if you like. I just need to let Long and Yingzhe know I'll be gone." He leaves the room and soon returns.

I look at him and smile for the first time in a while. "Yingzhe told you she was going to suggest that I talk to you, didn't she?"

"She might have," he says with a smile of his own.

"Well, I'm glad she did."

Two hours later, Ying and I are ready to go. We climb into the Barracuda and hit the road. We talk about nothing in particular, but he's good company. It's early Sunday afternoon, and traffic is light. An hour and a half later, I drop him off at his house, a modest Cape Cod on a quiet street in Palisades Park lined with tall oak and maple trees that are just beginning to change color.

"What time should I come by tomorrow morning?" I ask.

"How about 1130? I have some things to pick up."

"Sure."

"See you then, Will."

Fifteen minutes later, I pull into my garage. I shoot a couple of racks of pool and then go upstairs and watch a football game that's over by 1630.

"Rikki?"

Her hologram materializes. "Yes, Will?"

"Something has been bothering me about the out-of-body experience in the other timeline. How did my chip record a battle in another timeline when my consciousness possessed my doppelgänger? How sure are you that your doppelgänger from that timeline initiated the transfer?"

"As you may recall, I said I did not have the ability to transfer a consciousness to an alternate timeline."

"That's what's bothering me," I say. "McCray showed my EEG had a higher amplitude than those of the alternates. Our theory is that the stronger the EEG, the closer the timeline is to the original prime timeline. So why would a duplicate of you be able to do things you can't?"

She hesitates for what could be decades at her processing speeds. "I don't have sufficient information to answer that question."

"What if your creators were responsible?" I ask.

"That is an intriguing and logical hypothesis, Will."

"It's the only thing that makes sense to me. We've seen you gain access to new capabilities, like being able to appear in a holo-matter form. I would bet a good amount of money that it will not be the last time, either."

"Specific events trigger them, but I don't know what those events are." She actually sounds frustrated.

"Honestly, I'm feeling like I'm an NPC in a computer game," I mutter.

"I'm supposed to be a sentient AI, but am I really sentient?" Rikki asks.

"That's one of the oldest and most profound philosophical questions for humanity. For what it's worth, as far as I'm concerned, you are sentient in every sense of the word, *and* my friend. That's all that matters to me."

"Thank you, Will. You don't know how important that is to me."

Although it's early for dinner, I'm hungry. I look in my refrigerator and the only thing to eat that isn't a lab experiment is the leftovers from Ying's and my dinner date. I sniff them; they smell OK. I grab the last beer and put the leftovers in the microwave. They taste fine, so I scarf them down, nursing my drink.

After dinner, I turn on the TV and look for a martial arts movie. I found *The Clan of the White Lotus* on one of the streaming channels and watch it. When the movie is over, I take out my duffel, empty it, and start repacking it. Recalling the amazing dinner that Ying cooked for me and hoping he has plans to do it again at the cabin, I go downstairs to my liquor cabinet and get the 1878 Oban and wrap it carefully before putting it in my bag. I also take my Glock and ammunition, although my gut tells me I probably won't need it.

When I finish packing, it's time for bed. As I drift off to sleep, I recall my conversation with Rikki earlier and wonder what she is thinking about.

I wake up at my usual 0630 and go through my morning routine. Once I'm dressed, I contact Ying using the quantum communicator. It's essential that we all master its use. I make contact immediately.

<Good morning, Ying. Do you want to meet me at the Bridgeview Diner for breakfast?>

<I appreciate the offer, but I have some things to do. What time do you want to leave?>

<Is 1130 still good for you?>

<Yes, I'll be ready. See you then>

I go to the diner for breakfast. Before the hostess can seat me, Vickie grabs my arm and guides me to my usual booth.

It's not too busy. There are mostly businesspeople and retirees here. The delicious smells in the air make my stomach rumble. "I'll get you some coffee, Will," she says. She returns shortly thereafter. "Do you want your usual?"

"Sure, that'll be great. How's nursing school going?"

"Pretty well. It's a little tough juggling everything, but with mom and dad helping, I'm managing well enough." She blushes a little. "So far I have straight As."

"That doesn't surprise me. How is Ethan doing?"

Her face falls. "He's doing OK."

"Just, OK?" I ask.

"He loves school, but last week was a father-child night . . ."

"And he asked you why he doesn't have a dad?"

"I didn't know what to tell him. He doesn't remember Robert, and you know how kids are."

I don't, really. I say, "Vickie, you're amazing, raising Ethan, going to nursing school, *and* working."

"Thank you. That's nice of you to say."

"I meant every word I said."

She smiles and replies, "I better get back to work. Eva is giving me dirty looks. I'll put your order in."

Ten minutes later, she returns with my order, and as usual, everything is perfect. I eat slowly, and by the time I finish, it's 0930. There's plenty of time to go to the supermarket and buy food for the cabin. I leave a big tip, wave to Vickie, pay, and head out.

After I do my grocery shopping, I stop at a liquor store to buy two cases of an IPA. When I get back to my house, it's just about time to pick up Ying. I'm looking forward to spending time with him. We have a lot to talk about. Fifteen minutes later, I'm at his house. He's sitting on his stoop with a duffel bag and two coolers filled with food and groceries.

"Hi, Ying."

"Good morning." He looks at his watch. "Right on time."

I pop the trunk and we load his bag in next to mine and sidle our collective three coolers of food into the back seat.

"Good morning, Ying," Rikki greets.

"Good morning," he answers, and we're on our way.

It's a nice fall day. It rained last night; the air smells fresh, and it's brisk for this time of the year. Five hours of small talk later, we hit the strip of mud, rocks, and grass that serves as the road to the cabin five hundred yards away. I see the tire tracks of two SUVs. A nervous feeling runs down my spine and settles in my stomach. "Rikki, do you detect anybody up ahead?"

"Negative, Will, although it is evident that your cabin had visitors."

"Just to be safe, put us in stealth mode, assume native configuration, and use the anti-grav."

"Done."

We slowly approach the cabin. The front door is open, but everything else looks OK.

We stop. I pull out my Glock. Ying does the same as we quietly step out of the hovering MDTD.

"Will, there is no one here," Rikki assures. "Should I configure the MDTD back to the Barracuda?

I release the breath I'm holding, and some of the tension leaves me. It's 1645, and the sun is already low in the sky. The air has a woodsy smell that the sweet, piney aroma from the fireplace chimney will hopefully soon join. The door was forced open but is undamaged. I look around, but everything in the cabin is untouched.

"Yes. If some hikers come by, this," I gesture towards the floating MDTD, "would be hard to explain" With a shimmer, it transforms.

Ying says, "I don't understand. It's obvious that UOEECT was here, but it looks like when they saw you weren't, they just turned around and left."

"When I had my vision or whatever it was, the security forces we fought in the other timeline acted like they were programmed, like they had no initiative other than their specific orders. Maybe they were just supposed to bring me in, not to bring me in and then trash the place. What do you think, Rikki?"

"I think you're correct."

I let out another breath and feel the rest of the tension leave me.

"Let's unpack," I say. We unload the MDTD and put the food away after I turn on the generator. I start a fire, and soon, the well-seasoned wood is burning merrily. I feel myself beginning to relax as the hiss, crackle, and roar of the fire fills the air. I smile, knowing that my hope for another home-cooked meal by Ying will be fulfilled.

By the time we stow everything, it's 1800, and the sun has just set. The tops of the mountains glow with the last rays of the sun as the shadows climb from the valley to the mountains' crests.

We go out on the porch and sit in the two rocking chairs that are worn smooth by the weather. The two cases of beer are also out there. I hand Ying a beer and take one for myself. We clink the bottles together.

"Will, it's beautiful here. I had no idea," he says.

I'm surprised by his reaction. "Haven't you been to New England before?"

He pauses for a long time. "No, never. We lived in Taiwan before we came to the United States. I wish I got here sooner," he says wistfully. I look at him. I know the tragic story of Ying's and Long's families but feel that there is more to it. Ying says, "It's too late for me to make dinner, but tomorrow, I'll make you another home-cooked meal."

"I can't wait. Until then, I'll cook tonight. It's not haute cuisine, but I make a mean cheeseburger."

"Sounds good," he replies.

"We can talk after we've eaten." I light the grill that sits just off the porch. Soon, the smell of charcoal and burgers joins the delightful scent of the woods, leaves, and smoke.

After we eat and clean up, we return to the porch. I open two more beers and Ying says, "I know you have a lot on your mind, but I'd like to tell you the full story about how Yingzhe, Long, and I came here."

Chapter 13
"What's Done Cannot Be Undone: Beam Me Up, Scotty"

"Long, Yingzhe, and I are from another timeline." Ying pauses for a moment. I never knew this, though I'm sure Rikki did. "The timeline we are from is virtually indistinguishable from this one except here, as far as I know, there wasn't a Long, Yingzhe, or me. If there was, they took a different path than we did. You know that under the influence of the MTPC in our native timeline, Long and I . . . killed each other's families, something that we will never forgive ourselves for."

"Ying, it wasn't your fault," I say.

"I know, but it's hard to wash that stain from our consciences. Vengeance and the desire to protect Yingzhe drove Long and me to battle against the MTPC by any means possible. It was pure luck she survived. She was competing at the gymnastics New Jersey State Meet of Champions, as an alternate qualifier. She would have been home had one competitor not injured her foot." An even longer pause. "Our hate and need for vengeance were the only things that kept us going. It would have been easier for Long and me to kill ourselves, but that would have been cowardly and dishonorable."

Ying clenches his fists so hard that they're shaking. He takes a deep breath and relaxes a little. "We knew we had to escape our timeline because our MTPC would never stop pursuing us. It sent assassination teams after us, but as is evident, they never succeeded." A brief, grim smile flashes across his face. "The MTPC infiltrated UOEECT in our timeline as well. It learned to control people by hacking their brain chips, including Long's and mine. Using *our* MDTD, which was less sophisticated than the one here, we traveled to other timelines, identified by a sophisticated, though not sentient, AI. Fortunately, though perhaps not entirely coincidentally, we found this one and settled here, staying off the grid until Rikki brought us together."

I take a swig and put my beer down on the small table between the two rockers. It's calm out here except for the slow chirp of the crickets.

"Ying, it might not be a coincidence that you, Long, and Yingzhe survived and made it here," I say.

"Knowing what I know now, I agree."

"Does it bother you that Rikki, or The Engineers? have probably manipulated your lives"

"No," he answers, "Yingzhe, Long, and I are alive. If it wasn't for Rikki or The Engineers, we would not be. We've been given a second chance to fulfill our vows of vengeance, and we will not waste it." Ying is silent and I realize that my fate and the fate of my loved ones could have been the same.

It's almost 2130, and it's gotten chilly. "Right. Let's go inside, I'm freezing" I grab two more beers and hand one to him.

Inside the cabin, it's warm and comfortable. The fire is running low, so I throw on a couple of logs. There isn't much furniture except for a long, well-worn brown leather couch with a small coffee table in front of it, and two loungers. A large area rug with a brown, tan, and red geometric design covers the floor, and tapestries adorn the walls. In the kitchen alcove, there's a small refrigerator, a wood stove, and a two-person table with chairs.

I sit in a lounger, and Ying makes himself comfortable on the couch. "That's an amazing story. How many years ago did you escape to this timeline?"

"It was seventeen years ago. Yingzhe had just gotten her PhD from MIT." He stops and his eyes become watery. He sets his jaw, determined to finish his story.

"When we regained our senses, we knew what we had done, even though we had no memory of doing it. I knew we had to leave our timeline or the MTPC would kill all of us."

The only sound is the crackle and pop from the fireplace. "I can't imagine what you've gone through. All I'll say is that I'm glad you are all here and on our team."

"Enough about me. You said you had some things on your mind. Tell me about them," he says.

I remain silent as I search for the right words.

"Will, just say it," he urges.

"What if I'm not the right guy to lead us? Why me?" I blurt out. "I still have nightmares about losing two soldiers on a covert mission in Afghanistan thirteen years ago when a kid wearing a suicide vest blew himself up."

"In my former timeline, America never went into Afghanistan. It only provided military aid and advisors. The USSR fought there for twenty-five years. When I was in officer training school, we studied asymmetric warfare, and the failure of the former USSR in Afghanistan was the number one case example," he explains. "How many men did you lose in units you commanded?"

"Just those two," I reply.

"How many total missions did you command?"

"I don't know," I say. "Dozens. I know where you're going with this."

"So, you know that losing only two soldiers under your command over dozens of missions is a phenomenal record."

"Ying, I froze. The kid came out of the house. As soon as I saw him, I knew something was off."

"You hesitated for how long, a half second, maybe two seconds?" he asks. "How far away from the house were your men?"

I thought about it. "Maybe eight feet."

"How soon after the child came out did the suicide vest detonate?"

"Maybe two seconds."

"Did you have a bomb-sniffing dog or robot that you could deploy?"

"No."

"Will, I lost dozens of men under my command. I agonized over every single casualty. As you know, there is nothing worse than having to write *the letter* to their loved ones."

"I should have known!"

"People die in wars, sometimes foolishly, sometimes honorably, sometimes cowardly, and sometimes bravely. It's the nature of war," he says. "Pay attention to me and don't get offended. Your soldiers were only eight feet away. Even if you warned them the second you saw the child, they could not have gotten far enough away to avoid the explosion. You set impossibly high standards for yourself. Standards that you would never set for people under your command. You're human, Will, and from what I can see, a damn good one and a damn good commanding officer. Stop blaming yourself, and soldier, *soldier*."

"OK, you win. I'll try to cut myself some slack."

"I'm not done, Commander," Ying says. "Don't try, do!"

"Yes, Master Yoda."

"One more thing. I know you feel the weight of the universe on your shoulders, but the rest of us have shoulders too. You're not alone, Will. Never forget that."

"Thanks."

"You're welcome. It's 2330. Let's finish these beers."

We clink the bottles one more time. "Ying, you are so much like my father."

"Is that a good thing?" he asks.

"There is no higher compliment I can give you."

"Well, then, thank you."

"You're welcome. What do you say we hit the sack? I can sleep on the couch. Why don't you take the bed?"

"Don't be ridiculous. The couch is fine, the subject is closed."

"You win. I'll get you some blankets and pillows." We talk for a little while longer and finally go to sleep.

The sharp tang of the smoke from the fireplace still lingers in the morning. A few glowing coals are all that remain. I go into the small bathroom, wash my face, and brush my teeth. The water is cold and bracing, and it does an excellent job of waking me up.

"I'll get some firewood," I say. It's chilly out and I can see my breath. A delicate frost dusts the leaves and the ferns that grow plentifully around the cabin. I pick up four logs and bring them inside.

"Ying, do you like bacon and eggs?"

"Of course. Truly a highlight of American cuisine," he says.

I tilt my head. "Are you being sarcastic?"

"No, I'm serious."

"How do you like your eggs?"

"Over easy, and the bacon extra crispy."

"OK, coming right up!" Nodding my approval, I put some kindling in the stove and light it. Before too long, I put a medium-size log in. In no time at all, there is a roaring fire. I throw another log on and let the fire burn down to glowing, red-hot coals.

Ying heats water and carefully adds three teaspoons of tea into the pot he brought. I set my aluminum percolator on the stove. I take out a cast-iron griddle, heat it, and cook the bacon. A few minutes later, I put the eggs on. Finally, I make toast that I fry in the remaining fat. The savory smells fill the air. Once everything is done, I bring it to the table, and we eat.

"I thought we could hike around the pond," I say. "It's about three and a half miles. There's usually a lot of wildlife, and of course, beautiful scenery."

"That sounds wonderful," Ying says with surprising passion.

We clean up and get dressed. I put what's left of my coffee into a thermos and he does the same for his tea.

It's a perfect day for a hike. The sky is a clear, luminous blue, and the temperature quickly warms thanks to the still-strong October sun. It's less than a quarter mile to the trail that goes around the pond. We arrive at the trailhead and start walking. Repeatedly, Ying stops and looks across the water. Its calm surface reflects the sky and the trees so perfectly that it's easy to believe that there's another world at our feet.

We talk little, just taking in the beauty and tranquility. I stop and face him. "You seem absolutely mesmerized by—" I put my arms out and turn 360 degrees. "—all of this."

"I am," he replies. "All my adult life, I've been a soldier and a commander."

I interrupt him. "And a cook."

"That too." He smiles. "Even as a child, I never hiked or had an opportunity to just enjoy nature. It's beautiful. I can see why you love coming here. It's a place where one can be alone with their thoughts and themselves."

"Really?" I ask.

"I grew up in the Alishan region of Taiwan. My parents worked on a tea plantation. When I was ten, I started working there also, picking tea. It wasn't a terrible life. I had a good childhood and loving parents, but it was a hard one. The tea plantation was in the high foothills of a mountain. There were rows of dark green bushes planted on terraces. It was often misty and foggy, and always the sweet smell of the plants. As I think back, it was beautiful, but I never was able to appreciate it."

"How old were you when you joined the military?"

"I was sixteen and lied to get in because I didn't want to work on a plantation my whole life like my parents. It turned out that I had an aptitude for being a soldier and leading men."

"You also have an aptitude for martial arts if you are anything like your doppelgänger in the alternate timeline," I say, recalling the battle.

"After an older soldier, offended by my receiving a promotion that he thought he deserved, beat me to within an inch of my life, my drill sergeant, a master martial artist, took an interest in me," Ying says. "Once I recovered, although I had little spare time, I spent every minute of it learning from him. After five years under his tutelage, I became a self-defense instructor, proficient with many weapons and styles." A brief smile. "Including swords."

Before we know it, we've hiked around the lake. We return to the cabin; it's already the afternoon and we're both hungry. I make turkey and roast beef sandwiches that we eat on the porch. I pull out two more beers from the cooler and hand one to Ying. I take a deep draught, which is crisp and cold.

We sit and make idle chatter about nature, my cabin, the critters we watch scampering about in the fallen leaves. I've been thinking of Yingzhe a lot lately, so I eventually say, "I think you should know that I am attracted to Yingzhe." I feel like I'm on my first date and I'm meeting the parents for the first time. "How do you feel about that?" I am surprisingly nervous and hope he's OK with it.

"Yingzhe has led a sheltered life, despite my, and my wife—" His voice cracks. "—Jing Hua's best efforts to give her a normal life. She hardly dated because she intimidated the boys."

"She intimidates me too. Yingzhe is beautiful, caring, and brilliant."

"There may not be any man worthy of her . . ." He trails off. I'm waiting for him to finish the sentence with "including you." Instead, he continues, "But you are the closest I've met. She is a grown woman, capable of making her own decisions. I'm not sure that it matters, but you have my blessing to date her."

"Thank you, Ying. I don't know how things will work out between your daughter and me, but I promise I'll take care of Yingzhe, protect her, and treat her with respect, on and off the battlefield."

"I know you will. You're a good man. One of my greatest fears has been that she will be alone. I hope things work out between you, so she'll have someone to love and care for her." He pauses briefly before he glances up and locks eyes with me. "One other thing, Will. If you break her heart, I'll kill you." I stare at him disbelievingly, but then he smiles. "Got you, didn't I?"

I let go of an uneasy breath and smile back. "Yes, you did." But I'm sure he's at least half serious.

After a lapse in conversation, Ying turns to me and says, "It's my turn to cook for you."

"How can I help you?" I ask.

"You can sit in that lounge chair and let me take care of everything," he orders.

"Are you sure? I can pass you ingredients like last time. I don't mind."

"Yes. You've shown me great hospitality, allowing me to stay in your cabin and introducing me to the simple but profound experience of becoming part of nature for the first time in my life," he says. "Now, please sit and let me prepare dinner."

"There must be something I can do."

"If you insist, you can light the stove, but this time, we must keep the flame high and hot," he explains. "The high temperatures will sear the meat, locking in the taste." I go outside and bring in more logs to start the fire. "As much as I know you enjoy General Tso's chicken, tonight I will prepare for you scallion beef stir fry." He retrieves all the ingredients from his coolers, including a bag of marinating beef, a knob of ginger, and a head of garlic. As before, his precision and economy as he prepares the food is mesmerizing.

Soon, the succulent aromas of ginger, garlic, and onions fill the cabin. Ying takes a careful taste and nods his head in approval, then offers me a bite. "This is fantastic," I say.

He smiles. "There are other Chinese dishes besides General Tso's chicken, Will."

We both dig in. I feel sad after I eat the last piece of the perfectly seasoned beef.

We clean up. I stand and go to my duffel, pulling out the Oban and two glasses.

I pour two fingers each and we gently knock the glasses together. "Sláinte!" I say.

"Gānbēi!" Ying returns. He swirls the liquid in his glass and inhales its bouquet. "I was hoping you brought this. Just superb."

"The first time we had dinner." I hold up my glass to the light and admire its pure amber hue. "You knew where I got it, didn't you?"

"I did. Rikki told me about you. As you surmised, I wanted to meet you and judge for myself what kind of man you were."

"I'm glad I passed," I say. "Over the years, as I got to know you better, I had a feeling that you were more than the owner and cook for a Chinese takeout restaurant." There's not much left of the whisky. I refill our glasses one more time, emptying the bottle. "Maybe I need to pay Lord Kelvin another visit."

Ying smiles, then a more serious look crosses his face. "Before we left, you were talking to Dr. McCray and Yingzhe about building a molecular replicator. Is that what I think it is?"

"It's right out of *Star Trek*," I say, grinning. Then I turn more serious. "From what Rikki said, the upload to my brain chip contained specifications for high-tech and futuristic weapons that might give us an edge against the MTPC."

"But?" Ying asks

"We don't have a source capable of powering the replicator. McCray thinks it's as easy as inputting the plans and specifications into the replicator and pressing the on button, but until we find a better power source, we can't use it."

Chapter 14
"I Have Treasures in the Deep for You: All That Glitters is Not Gold"

"Wait, Ying, you told me you came to this timeline using your MDTD."

"Yes, of course . . ." he says, voice trailing off.

"Do you still have it?"

"I hid it because I was afraid that the MTPC might track it."

"And where did you hide it?"

"In the New Jersey Pine Barrens."

"Ying, that could be the power source for the replicator! We have to call McCray and Yingzhe!"

I visualize McCray and reach out to him using the quantum communicator. Almost instantly, we make contact. A moment later, I bring Yingzhe into our conversation.

<Will, what's going on? Is everything OK?> she asks.

<Everything is great> I reply. *<Could the power cell for an MDTD power the molecular replicator?>*

<Well, yes. But you have the only MDTD. It's too valuable to cannibalize, even to build a replicator> McCray says.

<What if I told you, it's not the only MDTD?>

<Not the only MDTD?> It only takes McCray a few seconds to figure it out. *<Ying's. That's how he escaped into our timeline>*

<Exactly> I'm energized now. *<Rikki?>*

<Yes, Will?>

<I assume you've been listening>

<You're correct> she says. *<I hope you don't mind>*

<It's fine. Can it work if we recover Ying's MDTD?>

<Yes, it will work as long as his native timeline is close enough to ours. Based on a preliminary analysis, there is an 89.67% probability that it will be>

<Well, everyone, I think we know what we have to do. Tomorrow, Ying, and I have an MDTD to find. I'll keep you posted. Good night, everyone> I break contact.

"Sorry we can't go fishing as planned, but I guarantee we'll find another day for it."

"I'll hold you to that, Will."

It's almost midnight. Tomorrow will be an important day. Instead of being reactive, we'll now have a chance to go on the offensive. "Good night, Ying."

"Good night."

I wake up early, excited, and more optimistic than I've been for a while. I brush my teeth and wash up. By the time I'm finished, Ying's also awake. After he does the same, I ask, "Bacon, eggs, and toast OK?"

"I have some leftover ginger, beef, scallions, and onions from last night. I think they would make for a great omelet. What do you think?"

"As if I would ever turn down a chance to experience your cooking."

There are still some hot coals in the stove, so it takes no time to get a fire going. I make some coffee for myself and put up hot water for Ying. A mouthwatering aroma fills the air as he performs his culinary magic on a mundane omelet. He serves me first, then himself. I take a bite. "I'm not exaggerating when I say that this is the best omelet I've ever had."

He makes the universal gesture of respect as he covers his right fist with his left hand and bows his head. I return the gesture.

"I enjoyed preparing your food, as I hope you enjoyed eating it."

"You are a martial arts master, a military leader, and an incredible chef. I understand the first two, but where did you learn to cook like this?"

Ying smiles, appearing almost embarrassed by my profuse compliments. "That, my friend, is a tale for another day."

"That'll be a tale worth hearing, I'm sure." I turn back to the food and eat every crumb. When we're both done, I clean, dry, and put away everything in the cupboards. After, I enjoy my coffee and Ying sips his tea. We both fall into silence, lost in our own thoughts. I feel myself slipping into Navy SEAL commander mode, but this time, it's reassuring.

I clean the now-cold fireplace and shovel the remaining hot coals from the oven into an aluminum bucket. We douse them with water, dig a hole, and bury the slurry along with the other biodegradable waste in the ground. The other refuse we put in a plastic bag to take home. Finally, I turn off the generator.

"Rikki, please configure the MDTD into its native shape."

"OK, Will." Almost instantaneously, the Barracuda transforms into its original design and pulsates with a faint blue light

"Open the pod bay doors." Ying gives me a questioning look that I return with a smile. "Wait."

"I'm sorry, Will, I'm afraid I can't do that."

"What's going on?" Ying asks.

I laugh. "Have you ever seen *2001: A Space Odyssey*?"

"No, although I've heard of it."

"You have to see it. An artificial intelligence named HAL 9000 goes crazy and tries to kill the crew because he is forced to lie. There is an exchange in the movie where HAL lures the hero, Dave Bowman, outside the spaceship. When Bowman tries to get back inside and orders HAL to open the pod bay door, that's what HAL says."

"So, you and Rikki are joking?"

"Right! Nothing to worry about."

"Human humor still escapes me sometimes, especially Will's," Rikki says. "Hatch open."

Inside, there are two bucket seats and a holographic console. The windshield is a combination of polarized transparent aluminum and crystal. There are cameras that provide 720 degrees of coverage. Rikki normally navigates, but we're also trained to do it. Ying and I toss the duffels, coolers, and garbage bags behind the seats.

I turn to him. "Do you have the coordinates?"

"Not with me."

"No problem," I say. "Rikki, will you be able to scan for it?"

"Yes. Any power source that can run an MDTD should have a detectable energy signature."

"OK, take us to the Pine Barrens."

Rikki says, "I suggest we use stealth mode."

"Good idea. Hit it, Rikki!" The familiar low whine comes, getting louder and higher as the anomaly generator revs up.

Seconds later, we're at the Pine Barrens, hovering about a hundred feet above the gnarled, twisted pine trees. Sluggish streams and stagnant ponds surround them, tinted purple-brown by centuries of fallen needles and branches.

I look at the console. Rikki has displayed a map; there's a flashing yellow dot about fifteen hundred meters to the southwest.

"Will, I have located an energy source consistent with that of an MDTD."

"Is there a place to land?"

"Yes, about fifty meters away."

"Take us there, please."

Ying says, "Rikki, you constantly impress me."

"Thank you. May I call you Ying?"

"Of course you may. And you're welcome," he replies.

We land. Ying, Rikki's hologram, and I make the short hike, which takes us to a small pond. I point to it.

"Is that where you hid it?"

"Yes. I landed where we just landed, and we got out. Then I used the remote-control pad to submerge it."

"I don't suppose you still have the pad, do you?"

"No, I threw it into the pond because if anyone saw it, they might ask too many questions. I scouted this timeline and found UOEECT headquarters is in the same location as in mine. If I needed my MDTD, I was sure that UOEECT could recover it."

I nod in approval. "Very impressive, but I'm not surprised. How did you get from here to North Jersey?"

"We followed that trail." He points to a barely discernable path with a faded marker. "In about six miles, it leads to a road. We hitched a ride with a Rutgers University geology professor who was doing research for a paper on the Pine Barrens Ecological System, a remarkably interesting fellow. He was kind enough to drive us to Hammonton where we got money and transportation."

"What did you do for money? Was your currency the same or close enough to pass for ours?" I'm really curious now.

"It might have, but I brought over $500,000 worth of Chinese gold coins from my timeline and sold them to a local coin dealer for cash, so we were all set. As I mentioned, I scouted this timeline very thoroughly before we came here."

"Rikki, can you hack Ying's MDTD?" I ask.

"Already done."

The pond bubbles, and slowly, Ying's MDTD emerges and hovers parallel to the edge of the water. It looks like mine, except there is no windshield. The hatch opens. We look in, and it's dry inside, although stuffy.

"I'd like to have Rikki check it out, if that's OK," I say.

"By all means. It would give me assurance that it's still fully functional."

Rikki walks closer and her holographic eyes flicker briefly. "It is functional but less technologically advanced than ours. The fuselage is a graphene and aluminum composite."

"What about the power source?" I ask.

Rikki turns to Ying. "He can be so impatient!"

Ying looks at me and says, "Yes, the young often are."

I shake my head but smile. It's impossible not to think of Rikki as a person as her mannerisms become more human every day.

"The power source is a small fusion reactor that is slightly low on fuel at the moment. It will be adequate to power a molecular replicator. May I suggest I clone a 'dumb' version of myself and upload it into Ying's MDTD?" Rikki asks. "It will make it unnecessary for someone to have to physically be inside."

"It's your call, Ying."

"Yes. Please do so, Rikki."

"Upload completed."

"I'll contact McCray and let him know we're on our way," I say.

<Doc, we're on our way>

<This technology will literally change the world> McCray says.

<Changing the world will have to wait. We have to save it first>

"OK, Rikki, take us to West Jersey."

Seconds later, both MDTDs appear in front of the safe house. I immediately reconfigure mine back to the Barracuda. A section of the holographic veneer flickers off, exposing a large bay door.

"Rikki, please maneuver Ying's MDTD inside." Silently, it lifts a foot off the ground and gently glides into the work bay. "Thanks."

"My pleasure, Will."

Ying and I unload the Barracuda and walk upstairs.

I ask if anyone would like to join me for a few slices from Giovanni's, a local pizza place with an excellent reputation, but get no takers. I ask McCray if I can borrow his car, rather than take mine. He agrees. I find the key fob where he said it would be and walk to his Range Rover Sport, which is parked in the garage in the back. It takes about ten minutes to get there.

It's a modest building with a large window. I can see the brick oven, and even outside, I can smell the garlic, which is always a good sign. A small bell jingles as I open the heavy glass door. I sit at the counter where an older gentleman is waiting to greet me.

"How ya doing?" he asks. "I'm Giovanni, but everyone calls me John." He's about sixty and trim, with a full head of carefully coiffed gray hair. His eyes are friendly and there are laugh lines on his face.

"Pleased to meet you, John. I'm Will." I shake his outstretched hand. His grip is powerful, no doubt from tossing thousands of pizza pies. I'm pretty sure he would beat me in an arm wrestle. "This place smells wonderful!"

"Thanks. What would you like?"

"I'd like three pepperoni slices and a root beer for here, and two large pies, one plain and the other pepperoni, to go."

"You've got it, Will." John puts the three slices in the oven and pulls an ice-cold bottle of root beer out from the refrigerator. As he's reaching for a glass, I say, "The bottle is fine."

"Your slices will be ready in a few minutes. The pies will take twenty."

"Works for me. Thanks."

As promised, the piping hot slices arrive. I take a bite. Giovanni's reputation is well earned.

"What do you think?" he asks.

"This is some of the best pizza I've had, and trust me, I've had a lot of pizzas in my lifetime."

"Thanks." We make small talk as I wolf down the three slices. "Your pies should be ready." He opens the oven and checks. "All done."

"Great! I'll take the check when you get a chance."

"You got it!"

I finish the root beer as John brings over the pies.

"I hope I see you again, Will."

"You can count on it!"

I pay the check and leave a nice tip on the counter, pick up the pies, which are almost too hot to hold even in the boxes, and wave goodbye.

In ten minutes, I'm back at the safe house. As I park the car, I realize how much I enjoyed the normalcy, knowing that it may be a long while until the next time.

Chapter 15
"All the World's a Stage: Me—There Are Too Damn Many Stages"

I bring the pizzas into the kitchen. Long comes in, followed by Ying.

"Is that pizza I smell?" Long asks.

"There are fresh pies from Giovanni's, a plain and a pepperoni. Help yourself." A minute later, drawn like moths to a flame, Yingzhe and McCray come in, followed by Rikki.

"You brought back pizza for us? Even though no one went with you?" Yingzhe asks, a mischievous smile on her face as her gaze darts from my face to the food and back.

"Since we're all here, we should talk and bring each other up-to-date," I suggest.

Everyone nods their assent. Long brings in an assortment of drinks from the refrigerator and I follow with the pizzas, paper plates and napkins into the meeting room. Rikki goes into the spacious kitchen, assumes her holo-matter form, and makes coffee.

Everyone settles in. "I'll start," I say. "First, Doc, you said you thought we could build a molecular replicator now that we have the power cell from Ying's MDTD, right?"

"Yes, we can produce most of what's needed to make it. The only thing that might pose a difficulty in production is a graphene-copper composite that's used for the circuit boards. Theoretically, it'll permit near-superconductivity at room temperature, increasing the efficiency of the replication process."

Yingzhe explains, "We can do it, but it requires extremely high temperatures and pressure during the fabrication process. We think that high-intensity CO_2

lasers can do it. We just have to adapt current technologies."

"That's our biggest challenge," McCray adds.

"These are technologies that only exist in science fiction. I think we must be extremely cautious about protecting the replicator and any other technology we develop. How will you actually build it? As capable as you and Yingzhe are, it's just the two of you," I say.

"Good question, Will. We'll have the separate components and circuit boards built by fourteen different companies that I own or have a controlling interest in. They won't know what the components are for, and if someone asks, I'll tell them it's on a need-to-know basis, which is true," McCray says. "We'll assemble the components here. We'll also connect the power source and fabricate the graphene-copper. It'll be a lot of work, but I'm confident that we can handle it."

"How long do you think it'll be before the replicator is operational?" I ask.

"Three or four weeks at the most."

"Unless anyone else has anything to add, let's move on to the mission to track down Lieutenant Fanotti and Master Sergeant Harris," I say. "We all agree that the versions of them in my vision, journey, or whatever it was were from our timeline. Rikki says we can track their MDTD's tachyon emissions. We need to find them ASAP. Their lives are at risk, they may have useful information, and they are a security risk as long as their brain chips are active. Rikki has figured out when that battle will occur, and where. Ying, Long, and I plan to get there two hours after the battle. We'll locate the residual tachyon radiation and find them. We'll be fully kitted up in case things don't go as planned, which is usually the case. Doc, you said you have an armory?"

McCray assures me, "We have everything a military strike team could want. It's downstairs in the basement.

To enter, you need a retina scan and handprint. You and I are the only ones right now who can go in there."

"Rikki, add the rest of our team. If something happens to us, they need to have access as well."

"OK, boss."

McCray says, "Follow me."

I turn to Ying and Long. "Let's see what toys there are to play with."

I place my hand on the reader and my right eye in front of the scanner. The four-inch-thick door soundlessly opens. Bright LED lights snap on, and I can hear the slight *whoosh* of the ventilation system. Surprisingly, the air smells fresh and the white floor is spotless. We feel like kids in a candy store.

There's a high ceiling and a second level. All manner of weapons covers the walls, from primitive ones like bows and arrows, swords, and battleaxes, to state-of-the art modern arms. There are grenades, knives, handguns, and rifles. One wall displays a collection of armor from basic bulletproof vests to tactical full-body suits.

"The only thing missing here is a mithril vest," I say.

"Once we have the molecular replicator online, we'll have access to weapons that, I promise you, come right out of *Star Trek* and *Star Wars*," McCray says.

Our moods turn serious. We all choose full-body armor made of an incredibly light aluminum-carbon polymer that can turn away a .50 caliber bullet, although it'd leave a deep bruise. I choose Ka-Bar and Cold Steel SRK knives, a Mossberg 590A1 shotgun, an FN P90 rifle, a Glock 40, and plenty of ammo. Ying and Long carry P90s and combat knives. They both have katanas strapped across their backs. We each carry a high-explosive grenade, frag grenade, a flashbang, and four claymores. My kit is heavy as hell; it's been a while since I've done this.

"Where did you get this stuff, Doc?" I ask.

"Several of my companies supply weapons to our military and our allies," he explains. "And unfortunately, there is always breakage and missing inventory. Follow me." He walks up to a case lying on a foldable table and opens it. Inside is a drone that looks exactly like a spider, with eight propellers at the end of each leg. In each corner is a battery. Last, there are charging cables.

"What's so special about it?" I ask.

"This drone generates an electromagnetic pulse that will disable unprotected electronic devices in a circular area with a diameter of a hundred meters." He picks up one battery and hands it to me. It's surprisingly light, not more than a pound or two. I hand it to Ying, and McCray gives another to Long, who tosses it in the air. We give the batteries back to him.

"Each of these solid-state lithium-based batteries can generate an EMP. The drone can produce any combination number of pulses. It can also produce a larger, more powerful single pulse. Another solid-state battery provides the power for propulsion, navigation, and communication, and is here." He points to the abdomen. "It takes three hours to charge the batteries after use."

"This is a game changer, Doc!" I say.

"I'm not done." There are three smaller plastic cases. McCray picks one up and opens it. Inside is an electronic device that looks like a funnel. Electronics fill the neck of it. "Commander, can you please hand me your rifle?" he asks. I make sure it's unloaded before giving it to him. He grabs a device that screws onto the barrel. "This is a tactical EMP generator. Like the drone, it's rechargeable. You point and aim. The battery will provide enough energy for fifteen or so shots. The effective range is approximately twenty-five meters. Before you ask, the EMP weapons are experimental, and I should add, top secret. We tested them in the lab, but not in actual combat. However, I'm fully confident that they'll perform as expected."

"That's good enough for me."

"Finally . . ." McCray unscrews the top of a small, gray cylinder about the size of an old-school film canister and pours what looks like large mosquitoes into his hand. They're half an inch long and have four gauzy wings.

"Yingzhe calls these mosquito drones. They provide audio-visual data and can stay in the air for up to three hours. They can handle up to twenty-five-mile-per-hour winds and have a ceiling of thirty meters, depending on the weather. You control them with your data pads. We've already downloaded the app," he continues. "One more thing, Will." His voice is serious. "The EMP weapons will disable any electronic device that isn't hardened. It'll not only disable brain chips, but probably kill the person."

"That's the thing about war. Soldiers die. My job is to make sure more of *them* die than us," I say. "Thanks, Doc."

We leave the armory and head upstairs. "OK, everyone, let's go over the mission plan and priority list in the meeting room." Once we're all assembled, I continue. "We enter the alternate timeline two hours after the battle. Hopefully, the bodies will be gone, and the site cleaned up, which is UOEECT's usual protocol."

Long says, "I'd rather not see the corpses of our doppelgängers."

"No argument from me, not that there will be much left of mine's body." I suppress a shudder, recalling the blast of light and heat when the grenade went off. "The mission is simple. Travel to the alternate timeline, find the tachyon trail of Fanotti and Harris's MDTD, find them, hopefully alive, and bring them back. But I'd rather prepare for the worst and hope for the best." I check the time. It's 1510. "Unless anyone has objections, I see no reason to delay. Let's meet back here in two hours."

Long looks at Ying. They nod and say, "We'll be ready."

"McCray, I'd like you, Yingzhe, and Rikki to work on the idea we came up with to transmit the energy needed for Rikki to maintain her holo-matter form longer than five minutes. That would give us a tremendous advantage, at least until the MTPC figures out how to do it."

McCray frowns. "What makes you so sure that the MTPC will figure out how to do it?"

"We have to assume it will. Rikki, what do you think?"

"I have a greater capacity to learn, but the MTPC has more computing power." She pauses. Her hologram flickers and dims for a second.

"Are you OK?"

Her hologram stabilizes and she has a strange look on her face. "I apologize, everyone. Will's question about how I compared to the MTPC triggered more memories placed in my quantum memory matrix by The Engineers."

"I wish we had time to hear about it, but any delay jeopardizes our mission to find Fanotti and Harris alive."

"If Harris and Fanotti are alive, we need to find them," Long says.

There's still leftover pizza; he and I grab a slice each and talk about baseball. I look at my watch, it's 1635.

"He's right. Rikki can tell us another time unless it can help us on this mission. Rikki?"

"It's valuable information but is unnecessary to complete this mission," she says.

"OK, we also must get Kelly and Wall here to deal with their brain chips. You guys know what you need to do." I rap my knuckles against my armor.

McCray looks down and cradles his chin with his left hand. "I don't see why not. We can use the graphene-copper composite . . ."

"Just add it to your list. Time to go." Long, Ying, and I head toward the door. As we're leaving, I turn to McCray and say, "One more thing, do not, under any circumstances, try to reach your alternates in different timelines until we're all here." The look on McCray's face tells me he doesn't agree with me. "Doc, I'm expendable, you're not. Don't. Do. It." The door slides open, and we walk outside.

I use my data pad to reconfigure the MDTD to hold the three of us and our gear. A door appears, and we climb in. "Rikki, input the time-space coordinates for the alternate timeline, please."

"Done," she confirms.

I turn to Ying and Long. "Guys, I have a gut feeling that this won't be the piece of cake mission we hope it is."

Ying nods. "It never is."

Long gestures at our neatly stacked kits. "We could probably take on a company with this gear."

"True, but I hope we don't have to." I cross my fingers on both hands. "Hit it, Rikki!"

Yingzhe

The door slides shut after Will, Long, and my father leave. "Doctor, you have some ideas for a protective shell for Rikki?"

McCray stands staring at the EEGs of our team and their alternates.

"Did you hear me, Dr. McCray?" I repeat.

"Sorry, did you say something?" He furrows his brow.

"Dr. McCray!" I snap. I'm losing my patience. We have a lot of work to do, and we can't do it without him.

"I apologize, Yingzhe." He looks embarrassed for one of the few times in his life.

"We were trying to have a discussion about designing a protective shell for Rikki's holo-matter form."

Again, there's hesitation before he responds. "I have some ideas on how we can do it . . ."

He still has his eyes riveted on the EEGs. "Rikki, can you get his attention?" I ask.

"Of course, cover your ears." Suddenly, a deafening cacophony of blaring sirens, crashing cymbals, and car horns honking nearly shatters my eardrums. McCray jumps and nearly falls over.

"Dr. McCray!" Rikki's voice echoes like the sound of God.

"Was that really necessary?" he asks after he recovers his composure.

I narrow my eyes and look at him. "Yes, it was." After working with McCray for several months, I can read him well. There's something on his mind, and I know what it is. "You're thinking of trying to contact your alternate on the other timeline, aren't you?"

"Yes, I am." He's daring me to challenge him.

"Will could not have been clearer when he told us *not* to contact our alternate selves." I cross my arms. "Will only lasted 0.04 seconds before Rikki's cyberattack overwhelmed him."

"I'm aware of that fact. However, if the MTPC tries to attack me through my doppelgänger's brain chip, the bandwidth of the quantum communication will limit the power of the attack, if he has one."

"Will is a Navy SEAL, trained to be mentally strong. Can you guarantee that even with Rikki's help, you can resist a cyberattack even if its intensity is limited by quantum bandwidth?"

McCray loses some of his bluster. "No, but consider this: alternate Rikki gave us technology centuries ahead of us. We need to develop a quantum energy transport system that will allow Rikki to sustain her holo-matter form, possibly indefinitely, and some type of armor to protect her from energy attacks, including an EMP. What if my, or your, duplicate has already developed the technology?"

That's the problem with arguing with a genius like Dr. Daniel McCray. It's hard to win an argument and even harder to get them to change their mind. "What do you think, Rikki?"

"His argument is logical, but there is significant danger. I don't think the reward is commensurate with the risk, but other than knocking him unconscious, we cannot prevent Dr. McCray from doing this."

For a moment, I consider doing just that.

"Then it's settled," McCray says.

I think this is a terrible idea. "Rikki, you need to network with Dr. McCray. I'll watch his EEG." I feel like I failed and hope that he won't face the MTPC. "Good luck, Daniel."

I can't shake the bad feeling. McCray puts on the helmet, and I attach the vital signs sensors. He lies down on the table. Rikki stands by, ready to support him if the alternate McCray's brain chip has been compromised. She uploads the quantum frequency of the alternate timeline into his quantum communicator.

"OK, I'm going to make contact now."

McCray

I close my eyes and reach out to my duplicate. Two seconds pass, then three, then five . . . then contact!

<Can you hear me?> I ask.

The connection is weak, but my doppelgänger answers. *<Who is this?>*

<I'm your alternate self>

<No, get out of here! The MTPC has hacked my brain chip! Get—> A cold, inhuman voice echoes in my mind. It's the MTPC, mocking and malevolent. I visualize a diamond dome surrounding my mind, but it cracks and splinters, overwhelmed by the power and intensity of the attack, which grinds down my mind like a glacier. Desperately, I visualize a dome of neutronium. The pressure lessens, but the assault of the MTPC will soon overwhelm me. Then, I feel another presence join the battle.

It's Rikki.

I think I hear her say, *"I'm here! Push it out! Think of what matters to you, think of who matters to you, think of the stakes. We must win this battle!"*

Suddenly, the pressure vanishes, but as it does, the MTPC says, *"We will prepare a special welcome for your friends. Thank you, Dr. McCray."*

I open my eyes and raise my head weakly. "Yingzhe, it knows. Warn Will and tell him I'm sorry," then the room swirls around me and disappears.

Chapter 16
"Let Slip the Dogs of War: This Ain't No Video Game"

As expected, we find the tachyon trail. Because tachyons decay, like most subatomic particles, it's faint. Rikki calculates that Harris and Fanotti left from here a day and a half ago.

We arrive in the alternate timeline about two hours after the battle. Rikki scans the area before landing. It's clear. We land gently on a grassy area one and a half klicks from the battlefield. There are flat rocks and boulders scattered about the landscape. "Rikki, keep the MDTD cloaked. We don't want any hikers spotting us and posting on YouTube or Instagram."

It's 1530. The scene is peaceful, the chattering of the birds resumes, the trees are changing color, and a few white cumulus clouds drift slowly across a deep blue sky. There's a tingling in my mind. It's Yingzhe.

<What's going on? What's wrong?>

<Will?> It's as if she's standing next to me. *<Dr. McCray contacted his alternate in this timeline! The MTPC hacked alternate McCray's chip!>*

<Dammit! I warned him this could happen>

<The mission is compromised, Will. Before he passed out, he said, "It knows, warn Will, tell him I'm sorry">

My anger turns into concern. I knew there was no time for any more discussion. *<Consider us warned. I'll get back to you when I can. Will out>* I'm furious, but desperately hoping that McCray is OK. Losing him would be a setback that would be difficult to recover from.

Ying and Long stare at me. "McCray contacted his alternate self in this timeline. The mission's compromised. The alternate MTPC hacked alternate

McCray's brain chip. Yingzhe thinks it got inside our McCray's mind. We have a choice to make. Do we continue the mission or go back to our timeline and return here at another time?"

Long sets his jaw. "We're here, let's finish the job."

"What do you think, Ying?"

"The MTPC is preparing an ambush for us right now. We don't know how large a force we will be facing. According to the recording from your brain chip, you and our doppelgängers killed dozens of the opposing contingent. Our UOEECT doesn't have hundreds of security forces, so this MTPC might not have too many left to throw at us," he says.

"I agree. Also, I doubt this MTPC knows we know about a potential ambush. We need to find out how much information the MTPC got from McCray." I contact Yingzhe and Rikki.

<Will?> Yingzhe answers.

<Yes> I respond. *<Do you or Rikki have any idea how long the MTPC was in contact with McCray's mind?>*

<0.017 seconds. Assuming its processing speed is equal to mine, that is plenty of time for it to have gotten information from him. But when I joined the battle, I sensed that the details of this mission were not foremost in McCray's mind> Rikki explains.

<Well, that's a small blessing. How is McCray?>

<Not good. He's in a deep coma with brain swelling and his body temperature is 101.3 and rising> Yingzhe replies. I can sense her worry and concern.

<Rikki is better than any doctor. He'll be OK> I put as much optimism and confidence in my words as I can and hope she can feel it. *<Listen, Yingzhe, McCray will be OK, and we can handle any ambush the MTPC has planned. Got to go. Take care!>*

<You too, Will> I sense another powerful emotion from Yingzhe but have no time for it. I hope she senses the same emotion from me.

Ying and Long look expectantly at me. "McCray's in bad shape, but Rikki's taking care of him. She's confident that all the MTPC got from him was that there is a mission, but no specifics."

"That's enough though, isn't it?" Long clenches his fists.

"It's not an ambush if we know about it. In my vision, UOEECT security platoons had twenty-first century body armor, regular firearms, and grenades. Our body armor will stop any bullets and will protect us from grenades if they aren't under our feet."

"In the video of the earlier battle recorded by your brain chip, the attacks by the MTPC-controlled security forces were slow and uncoordinated. The only reason we lost was because the security forces had overwhelming numbers," Ying reminds us.

"The best battle to fight is the one that never happens," I say, "but I don't think we avoid this one. If we leave, the tachyon trail of Harris and Fanotti's MDTD will fade and be harder to track. It will be almost impossible to follow them in a potentially infinite multiverse of alternate timelines."

Long starts, "One thing that concerns me: right now, our equipment and technology are better than the security forces. If we use them, the MTPC will know we have them."

"If it comes down to using our weapons and tech to save our lives versus not using them to conceal them from the enemy, I vote for using them. It's going to find out about them eventually," I reply.

"Also, we should assume that what we have, the alternate MTPC will eventually get, especially if it hacked the brain chip of the Dr. McCray of this timeline." Ying folds his arms over his chest.

Rikki joins the discussion.

"I don't say this lightly, but I calculate that without the EMP weapons, there is a 67.86% probability that we lose the battle. They will short-circuit the UOEECT force's brain chips, stop communications, and disable any electronics-based weapons or technology."

Rikki's right, but the effect will be devastating and fatal to our enemies. She has said that she can't kill human beings and knows what the effect of the EMP weapons will be on their brain chips. Will she be able to deal with the death of our enemies when we use them? Even though she isn't the one pulling the trigger, people will die.

I turn to Ying and Long. "We should deploy the large drone before the battle begins. Rikki, I won't ask you to control it, or the mosquito drones."

"Thank you, Will. I don't know what would happen and I could endanger your lives."

"We can handle it," I reassure her. Rikki looks conflicted. Hopefully, her programming will allow her to support us in the upcoming battle and not damage her.

I pull out the canister holding the mosquito drones and unscrew the top. A dozen tiny drones fall into my hand, and I carefully lay them on a flat rock. I activate them via an app on my data pad. The drones rise and hover for a moment. I direct them toward the battlefield. A second window opens on my data pad, allowing me to see twelve different views from the drones. I tinker with the app a moment longer, trying to find a way to share the intel with my crew.

"Shit. There are at least two platoons of security officers assembling about half a klick away from the site." I stare at the screen. "Do you see this, guys?" I touch another icon and a holographic display appears above the data pad.

They are assembling, fortunately; they are still milling around. "OK, we have to roll. We need to beat them to the site and plant the Claymores."

It takes eight minutes to get there. We plant the mines, ten around the perimeter and two in the middle, and cover them with dirt, leaves, and branches. We connect them to our data pads and wait, watching the video from the mosquito drones.

I call Rikki. *<Are you watching the feeds?>*

<Affirmative, Will>

<Are you OK with this?>

<If you're asking if I can perform my normal functions and support your team, yes, I can>

<That's not what I'm asking>

<I know. I'm confident that I can accomplish what needs to be done to win this battle>

<OK, Rikki, we can talk later if you need to>

"Will," Ying says, "they're on the move. They'll be here in ten minutes." We hide behind three large maple trees. I switch to quantum communication.

<As soon as they enter the battle site, we'll show ourselves and open fire with small arms. I want to conceal our EMP weapons from the MTPC as long as possible> I add: *<And don't get killed>*

<Roger that, Will>

The ten minutes pass slowly before over fifty security officers enter the field. I launch the EMP drone. This time I yell, "Showtime, boys!"

We jump out from behind the trees and lay down a hail of bullets from our P90s. A dozen security officers fall. The rest return fire. The familiar sights, sounds, and smells of battle surround us. This is the fog of war: acrid smoke filling the air, whizzing bullets, the staccato report of guns, and the cries and screams of the wounded.

More of the enemy pours onto our killing field. I duck behind a rock and risk a quick look at the live video feed from the drones before contacting Ying and Long.

<It looks like the gang's all here. Fall back and take cover. On my count, trigger the Claymores. Ten, nine, eight, seven—> A dull hard pain hits my left hip. Ugh, at least I know the armor works. *<Six, five, four, three, two, one—now!>* We trigger the mines, and massive explosions rock the battlefield, covering it with dust and smoke.

Suddenly, gunfire erupts in all directions. The sting of bullets peppers our armor. Another platoon of officers has gotten the drop on us. We hit the dirt and empty our magazines. The Mossberg barks smoke and fire. We get six more, but we're surrounded. The enemy closes in on us like a noose. I pull out my Glock and start firing. It's déjà vu and I fear the end will be the same unless we use the EMP weapons.

<We have no choice, guys. We have to use the EMP drone!> I put down my gun and hope I don't get killed before I trigger the device. Another round hits my leg. It feels like it might have gotten through my armor, but I ignore it. I touch an icon on the data pad to activate the EMP drone. A high-pitched electronic whine drills into our brains, barely muffled by our helmets. I hear a sound like sizzling bacon, and then, like marionettes with their strings cut, the entire UOEECT strike force falls to the ground.

I can smell the sharp tang of ozone, scorched human flesh, and other scents of death, and a deep pain stabs through my right leg like a knife. I need to check on Rikki.

<Rikki> There is an uncharacteristic delay before she responds.

<I'm here, Will> She speaks the words slowly and distinctly. I can sense her struggle with the harsh reality of war and her directive to not kill human beings.

<I'll get back to you> I look at Ying and Long, who are limping over to me. They heard the conversation. "I hope she's OK." We walk among the corpses, victims of the life-hating megalomaniacal MTPC in this alternate reality, making sure none of them are still alive. We scan them with our data pads; they're all dead.

Killing, even for a righteous cause, scars your soul. As soldiers, we have a choice; we can let these psychic scars define us or use them as reminders of selfless sacrifice, defending the defenseless, and what the face of evil looks like.

My moment of self-reflection passes. I open another window on my data pad and scan for Fanotti and Harris's tachyon trail. A soft chime sounds, and a map appears, pinpointing it. Rikki joins us. The hologram seems to pixelate, and it fades in and out. "OK, let's get the hell out of here."

"Look out!" Long yells. Eight security officers have snuck up on us while we were surveying the field. We're out of ammo and defenseless. Rikki's flickering hologram becomes distinct. She enters the battlefield like an avenging angel, moving too fast to follow. Our assailants drop in rapid succession. In seconds, the battle is over. Rikki sashays over to us and tosses two stun batons to the side. "Sorry I took so long. I had some issues to sort out."

I don't even know what to say. "Are you alright?"

"I am," she says evenly.

"But how . . ."

"I will explain later." We walk over to the eight unconscious security officers. I think of the speed and coordination of their attack. "They don't have brain chips, do they?"

Long scans them. "They do not."

"So, these are human beings who joined the side of the MTPC." I could feel my anger radiating like a red-hot iron.

Ying points. "What do we do with them?"

"We can't tie them up, gag them, and leave them for UOEECT to collect. They saw Rikki in action and got a look at our gear. For that matter, what do we do with *them*?" I gesture to the corpses strewn over the battlefield. "If we allow the UOEECT cleanup team to take the bodies, the MTPC will discover that they died from their brain chips being fried by an EMP weapon. Let's get them all in one place and tie them up while we figure out what to do."

We drag the eight unconscious soldiers to one place and pull-out plastic ties. But then there's movement from one of them. He pulls out a grenade and triggers it. In slow motion, he tosses it at us. He's only ten feet off. There's no way we can get out of the way.

Moving at lightning speed, Rikki hurls her holo-matter body on top of the grenade. It goes off, but she takes the brunt of the explosion. The blast vaporizes the UOEECT security team. The shock wave knocks us all to the ground. I feel blood drip from my ears and nose. *Rikki. Where's Rikki?*

We get up slowly and look around. I try to reach her using the quantum link, but there's no response.

I try it again. *<Rikki, are you there?>*

There's no noise for a long moment. *<Affirmative, Will>*

I let out a sigh of relief as her hologram reappears. "Are you OK?"

"I'm OK."

"That was a brave thing to do. You saved our lives."

She smiles. "That's why I get paid the big bucks."

Ying waves his arm over the dozens of bodies scattered around the battlefield. "What about these?"

"On second thought, I don't care if the MTPC knows about our EMP weapons. Leave them there. It needs to know that we won't lie down and let it murder all biological life in this timeline or any other." I turn my back on the carnage and scan for our missing colleague's tachyon trail. It's still there. "Guys, go back to the MDTD and I'll catch up." I recall the mosquito drones and put them back in their container. I look at Rikki. "How did you do it? How did you circumvent your directive to not kill humans? I thought we were going to lose you."

Rikki looks down at the ground and out over the dead bodies. She faces me intently with a small, proud smile.

"Yes, you're right, I was stuck in a decision loop between my directive not to kill, and the death of you, Long, and Ying."

"So, how did you resolve your programming conflict?"

"When I downloaded the books for you to read on your vacation, one was Isaac Asimov's *Robots and Empire*. R. Giskard Reventlov is a self-aware robot that was programmed to protect and guide humanity, but his programming limited his ability to fulfill this directive. With his friend R. Daneel Olivaw, they created the 'Zeroth Law of Robotics' which states 'that a robot may not harm humanity, or, by inaction, allow humanity to come to harm.' I read the book. Somehow, that unlocked an ability to perform limited self-programming. I integrated the Zeroth Law into my matrix."

"I read the book too. Giskard used the Zeroth Law to allow the Earth's crust to become radioactive and uninhabitable, forcing humanity to the stars. It destroyed him. Besides, Asimov's laws aren't real. They're fiction."

She smiles. "Science fiction."

Chapter 17
"What Fools These Mortals Be: Make My Day"

Yingzhe

McCray is unconscious and in a coma. Despite my and Rikki's efforts, he is running a life-threatening fever that has now reached 104.9. Rikki's scan shows brain swelling centered in his right frontal lobe where the chip is. She is treating him with intravenous ibuprofen to bring down his temperature. I hope it'll be enough because if the brain swelling doesn't go away, Rikki and I will have to take more drastic measures to relieve it. The *beeps* of the vital sign monitors and the intermittent hum of the computers are the only sounds in the room. The harsh lighting from the LEDs gives me a strange feeling, like we're somewhere else, not a house in western New Jersey. It's more of a déjà vu than anything else and it makes me feel uneasy. Seeing McCray in a coma brings back memories—some sad, some happy—and renews my sense of vengeance against the evil entity that stole my mother's and brother's lives.

I was born in Taiwan in a different timeline and lived there until I was three years old when we emigrated to America. I grew up in a small town in northern New Jersey. As a young child, it didn't take me too long to realize that my father's and brother's jobs were secretive and dangerous. My mother kept me busy with after-school programs, gymnastics, and teaching me how to cook. Whenever he was home, Father taught me martial arts. When I got older, I asked him what his job was; he told me it was protecting people, but he never gave details, always changing the subject. By fourth grade, I found out that I had a knack for math. Math made sense; equations had solutions, math could solve problems, and it was logical. In seventh grade, I began attending physics classes at the local university, and at the age of fourteen, MIT admitted me into their graduate quantum physics program. I was one of the youngest students ever to be accepted to any MIT graduate program.

"Yingzhe, look at this EEG scan."

"What am I looking at? Wait! I see it. Rikki, please add Dr. McCray's last EEG before he contacted his alternate." The theta and delta waves show a significant increase compared to his last EEG. But there's another trace, a high amplitude gamma.

"It's not from McCray, nor his alternate," Rikki says. "The only other source of that trace must be external. And the only external source that has had access to his brain is the MTPC."

McCray hadn't uploaded his brain chip yet, but somehow, the MTPC could hack his chip? But I know how it happened. "The MTPC hacked his chip using the quantum communicator, just like Will feared."

She nods. "I know it was. It's the only logical possibility."

"But" I start, "Dr. McCray said that the bandwidth of the quantum communication link was too narrow to allow the MTPC to assume control."

"Look more closely at the gamma trace from the MTPC." Rikki magnifies it ten times. I see it. "There are two gamma traces. The only plausible explanation is that the alternate MTPC, and ours merged, like hooking up a series of batteries in parallel: more power, narrow bandwidth or not."

My mind is racing, and a chill starts at the base of my spine and spreads. "We have a bigger problem. The MTPC not only knows about quantum communication, but it's using it."

"Yingzhe, Dr. McCray is waking up."

"What's his temperature?"

"104.3."

I look at McCray's EEG. It still has the same anomalous traces and elevated theta and delta waves.

"Yingzhe, Rikki." It comes as a murmur. I walk to the side of the bed. McCray is sitting up and swaying, his eyes unfocused.

"Dr. McCray, lie down, you shouldn't try to sit up yet," I say

"Yingzhe?" he asks so softly I can barely hear him.

"I'm here, McCray, don't worry."

He turns toward me, face flushed, as he focuses his eyes on me, but something's off. There's an intensity in his gaze, almost a growing madness. Without warning, he leaps out of the bed, arms extended, reaching for my throat. I react instinctively; I step to the side and grab his right arm, executing a perfect aikido throw. He flies in the air and crashes to the floor, stunned but hopefully not hurt. I keep an arm bar on him in case he tries again. "Rikki, a little help here?"

She assumes her holo-matter form and effortlessly lifts him back on the bed where I strap him down. His left arm bleeds from where the IV was torn out when he, or should I say, the MTPC, attacked me. I clean and bandage it. McCray's comatose again, but the EEG still shows the trace of the MTPC. "Rikki, we need to deactivate that chip now."

"Agreed."

I place the helmet on his unconscious body. Once the nano-electrodes make the connection, Rikki downloads McCray's brain chip and sends an electric impulse, destroying it. I unstrap McCray and look closely at his EEG. It looks normal. I take a deep breath.

Father would be proud of me, and I allow myself a brief smile.

"His temperature is coming down," Rikki announces. "I have decrypted the download from his brain chip."

"What did you find?"

"The MTPC uploaded a small program. It was almost like a post-hypnotic suggestion. I doubt anyone under the influence of this program would even remember what they did."

"It sounds like sleepwalking," I say.

"The highly elevated theta and delta waves support your hypothesis. Well, done."

It seems silly that I, a thirty-four-year-old woman with two PhDs, would be pleased that an artificial intelligence just complimented me, but I am. "Thank you, Rikki, that means a lot."

Just then, I hear McCray's raspy voice. "I have a headache and every muscle in my body hurts, and why am I strapped in?" I look at his EEG; the extra delta traces are definitely gone. I walk over to the bed and release the restraints.

I help him sit up. "You don't know the half of it, McCray."

"I remember nothing after I reached my alternate self in the other timeline. . . Oh my God! The MTPC tried to hack my brain chip." McCray deflates like a balloon when you release the stem. He puts his hands on the sides of his head as his shoulders sag. He looks down at the ground, then at Rikki, and then finally at me. "What did I do?" Here's one of the richest people in the world, a genius, and a polymath, looking like a small child who broke his mother's favorite vase. He looks helpless, lost, and vulnerable. It hurts my heart to see him this way.

I grab his hands briefly. "Stay there, Daniel. I'll get you some water."

"Thank you, I'd appreciate that." I turn and grab him a bottle of water. He takes a long draught and sets it down before looking at me, eyes bright and piercing. "I apologize for my unseemly exhibition of self-pity."

"You're among friends here," I say. "I can't imagine what you experienced, but you helped us get valuable, crucial information about the MTPC that we need to discuss and get to Will, my father, and Long."

"Let's go to the meeting room," he says brusquely. I look at Rikki and nod. We follow him. We tell him everything that happened, including our theories about the MTPC's abilities. "What are you not telling me?"

"Well," I say slowly, "you tried to choke me to death."

"I attempted to kill you?"

"Yes. Fortunately, I could defend myself."

"And that's why every muscle in my body hurts and my right arm is killing me."

"Probably."

"OK, I don't need to know anything more." He has a knowing look on his face.

The moment of levity ends. I say, "I have to contact Will and bring him up to date. I'm going to have to tell him everything."

"I know," McCray says somberly.

I visualize Will as strongly as possible, imagining that we are next to each other.

<Yingzhe?>

<Hello, Will>

<What's going on? Is McCray OK?> he asks.

<A lot, and yes>

<You better fill me in>

<How about I start with McCray> I say. *<Through his counterpart's chip, the MTPC-Prime could attack McCray's brain chip. With Rikki's help, he was able to fight it off>*

<But> He pauses. *<I know there's a "but" coming>*

<Correct> I say. *<In the nanosecond the MTPC was in Dr. McCray's chip, it uploaded a small program. McCray attacked me>*

<Are you OK?> There was concern in Will's voice.

<I'm fine. Dr. McCray has a few bruises and a sore shoulder, though>

<I see> He's trying to sound serious. *<So, no permanent damage to McCray. And his brain chip?>*

<We deactivated it. Rikki downloaded the program that the MTPC uploaded. Once McCray was back to being himself, we discussed what happened. We believe that's how Malkinson, the UOEECT security officers, and anyone else who has an active chip are controlled by the MTPC> I stop, trying to keep my composure. *<One other thing. When people are under the control of the MTPC, they may have no memory of what they did>* I have to stop again; my eyes burn with tears.

<So, when yours and Long's families were killed ...> Will stops talking. I can feel Will's regret and sadness, but I also sense his anger and determination. *<Long and your father couldn't remember what they did>* A statement, not a question.

<Yes>

<This must be awful for you, Yingzhe. When we return, we can talk about it if you want> he offers.

I take another deep breath, back to business. *<I assume that the battle went well>*

<It was a massacre, those poor sons of bitches didn't have a chance, thanks to your warning> he says.

<I told McCray that he needs to contact you>

<Yes, he does. What he did was brave but stupid on so many levels, I don't know where to begin>

<Don't be too hard on Daniel, Will. His intentions were good>

<And "the road to Hell is paved with good intentions"> he responds. *<Don't worry, Yingzhe, this won't be the first time I've had to dress down a soldier under my command>*

I protest half-heartedly. <He's a scientist, not a soldier>

<Whether McCray and you know it or not, you're soldiers, we all are> he says gently. <I need to go, Yingzhe. Your dad and Long are policing the battlefield. We picked up Fanotti and Harris's tachyon trail and want to go after them ASAP before it fades>

<OK, Will. I'll tell McCray to contact you. He has vital information that you need. Be careful>

<You too, Yingzhe. See you soon>

I feel a warmth that I cling to like a blanket, and then he's gone.

Chapter 18
"Something Wicked This Way Comes: Lock and Load, Boys!"

Ying, Long, and I are just about done policing the battlefield. We take any weapons that still work and an ample supply of ammo. I had asked Rikki to bring the MDTD here. We load the weapons and ammunition. I look out over the field of death. Did they have families? After work, did their sergeant buy them a round of beers at the local bar? Were they in a softball league?

Some people believe that thinking of the enemy as a person is foolish, even soft. That it will take away the knife-edge a soldier needs in battle because the next time you face them, you'll hesitate, endangering you and your unit. But dehumanizing an enemy, no matter how evil, how vile they are, dehumanizes you. The longer you're in command, the easier it is to consider the soldiers you lead to be disposable pawns, forgetting that they are people. That's the main reason I never wanted to be promoted.

Sun Tzu wrote: "Regard your soldiers as your children, and they will follow you into the deepest valleys; look upon them as your own beloved sons, and they will stand by you even unto death."

For me, that's my guiding principle.

I feel a light probing from my quantum communicator.

It's McCray. *<Commander Schachter?>*

<Yes, McCray>

He hesitates. But before I can lay into him, he concedes. *<I want to apologize for disobeying your command and contacting my doppelgänger. Your suspicions were correct. He was compromised. By contacting him, I endangered our lives and jeopardized our mission>*

That will make this conversation easier. *<Doc, it was a brave but exceedingly stupid thing to do. You and Yingzhe have more brains in your pinky than I have in my head, which is why you're not expendable. Ying, Long—and if we find them—Harris and Fanotti are. I'm the team leader. One of my responsibilities is to keep the people on my team alive. I'm sure we'll have more battles to fight, but at its most basic level, the war against the MTPC is one of technology, which is why you can't ever put anyone's lives in danger again. Is that clear?>*

<Crystal, sir> There's a pause. *<Commander?>*

<Will is fine, McCray>

He sounds relieved. *<How did you know he might be compromised?>*

I thought for a second. *<I don't know, just a hunch or intuition>*

<So far, you have a perfect record on your hunches> McCray says.

<Well, let's hope they continue to be perfect>

<One more thing, Will, and it's important. The MTPC in our timeline somehow combined its processing power with that of the MTPC of the timeline you're in. That's how it could break through and hack my brain chip. Which, before you ask, is deactivated>

Oh shit, I think. That means that not only does it have a new means to increase its power and influence, but it knows about quantum communication.

<We don't know if the MTPC had these capabilities before, but if it didn't, it would be foolish to assume that it won't develop them given the congruences between close timelines>

<If the MTPC can combine with an alternate version of itself, maybe Rikki can, too. I have a hunch that the ultimate battle will be Rikki and her alternate timeline sisters versus the MTPC and its doppelgängers> Who knows, maybe The Engineer will come to me in my

dreams with revelations and inspirations. *<How is the replicator project coming along?>*

<It's moving along. I'll be sending the designs for the circuit boards and other separate parts by tomorrow>

<That's good news. Got to go, McCray. Keep the replicator project moving and continue working on Rikki's holo-matter form and body armor. It's a lot to do. I wish we could get you some more help>

<Thanks, Will. We'll get it done. And sorry again>

<You're welcome. We're like a family, and families always have squabbles and disagreements but come together when it matters>

When we disengage from the quantum link, Ying and Long are looking at me expectantly. I give them the play-by-play of our conversation, and end it with, "There's been an . . . unsettling development with the MTPC."

"Like what?" Ying asks.

"Apparently, the one in this timeline discovered how to combine its processing power with the one in our timeline using quantum communication. That's how it could hack McCray's brain chip. It uploads a small program into the chip, which basically programs the person to carry out missions. It's like they're sleepwalking"

The expressions on Ying's and Long's faces are unreadable. Then, as comprehension dawns, it turns tragic. "If you want to talk, I'm here." They put their hands on each other's shoulders and touch their foreheads. They're silent. "I'm going to the MDTD. Take as long as you need."

The hatch slides open, and I step in, leaving it ajar. "Rikki, are you aware of what McCray and Yingzhe discovered?"

"Yes, Yingzhe contacted me and sent me the data."

"Is there any reason you couldn't do the same with your counterpart?"

"No," she answers. "I tried to reach my counterpart here but could not."

"What does that mean?" I feel a coldness at the base of my spine as I consider the reasons.

"It could mean that the combined processing power of the MTPC-Prime and its duplicate here defeated or overcame my counterpart."

"Wouldn't there be a version of you running their MDTD?"

"No." She pauses. "You have the only MDTD with a copy of me. The others have sophisticated but 'dumb' quantum AIs."

"You told me not so long ago that for years, you were identifying and guiding potential team members."

"Will, did your parents ever tell you how they met?" she asks quietly.

"Yes, they met for coffee at the Pentagon. Dad was there for a top-secret briefing. He wanted to call his mother, but mis-dialed and ended up calling my mom, who worked there ... Wait! *You* misdirected the cell phone call!" I'm angry. "How else have you *guided*, I mean interfered with, my life?"

Rikki is silent, as if she doesn't know what to say. "Will, you're a lot like your father."

I think back to my childhood as an only child. My dad was a captain and a Ranger. Like most military families, my parents moved around a lot, finally ending up in New Jersey, where I was born. In high school, I was an excellent student and played football, basketball, and ran track. I got accepted to Georgia Tech, where I joined the Navy ROTC program and played football for four years. After college, I fulfilled my obligation to the Navy by joining the Marines and served in active duty for the required four years, finishing my stint as a lieutenant.

I went out for a few celebratory beers with my dad and got to talking about the military. After exchanging the usual barbs about the Army Rangers versus the Marines, Dad got serious. He told me how proud he was of me and how important it was to serve. That's when I applied to the Navy SEAL program. Thinking back, I would do it all over again.

Rikki's holographic form materializes in the seat next to me, interrupting my thoughts. She looks at me earnestly. "Will, are you happy with the way things turned out for you?"

"Yes. But how much of what I have achieved is my own and how much is from your guidance?"

"Everything you have achieved is yours. You know that there are an infinite number of futures, but some are more probable than others. I identified your father, Michael, as the team leader, but in the most likely futures, this team never exists. You and your team can do it, and I will help you in any way I can. The additions of Director Kelly, Beth Wall, Sergeant Harris, and Lieutenant Fanotti will make the team even stronger, but their futures contain scenarios where all, or some, of them die." She pauses. "The Engineers gave me the ability to learn and feel human emotions and I'm truly sorry you feel manipulated, but the threat of the destruction of all intelligent biological life by the MTPC is real, and in most future timelines, it succeeds."

It isn't a matter of whether I would continue to lead the team—of course I would—but how much were my parents and my lives meddled with by Rikki? Or was it The Engineer who was manipulating us with Rikki as an unknowing tool? I trust her, and always will, but I can't help but wonder who or what The Engineer is, and what is its endgame.

"One more thing, Will."

"Yes?"

"Your father meets your mother in over 75% of his futures."

"Thanks, I guess."

Ying and Long finally return to the MDTD. Their faces show determination and a cold, burning anger.

"Are you guys OK?"

"Nothing has changed, Will," Ying says grimly. "We can't go back and undo what has been done. What we can do is defeat and destroy the MTPC in this and every timeline."

"Then let's do this. Let's get this done," I say definitively. We settle into our seats, and I take the initiative to get us moving. "Rikki, hit it! Follow Harris and Fanotti's trail." Once again, the world dissolves into a formless gray fog and powerful energy discharges dance over the surface of the MDTD as we travel through the time-space anomaly. When the fog clears, it's like we've descended into a circle of Dante's Hell. Skeletal trees, their branches charred and leafless, stretch to the horizon. The chronometer says it's 1300, but the sky is a dark brownish gray that swallows the sullen red sun. Nearly constant flashes of violet lightning illuminate the nightmare sky.

"Open up the hatch." We step outside. The air stings with the sharp smell of ozone, and the noxious smell of hydrogen sulfide makes my eyes water. "Rikki, I want you on this patrol with us. Can you assume your holo-matter form?"

She materializes next to me. "Yes, Will. I can now maintain my holo-matter form if I am within five hundred meters of the MDTD."

"Why now? I don't understand what The Engineer is playing at." Never one to look a gift horse in the mouth, I ask, "Five hundred meters? Can you have the MDTD follow us in stealth mode so it's always within appropriate distance of us?"

"Affirmative, but if it's in stealth mode, I will only be able to maintain my holo-matter for four minutes as before."

"If we run into trouble, land the MDTD and use camouflage mode."

"Yes, Will." Rikki's hologram is now garbed as we are.

"Let's move, team." It's unnaturally quiet. We feel a constant thrumming vibration from the ground. I take out my data pad and scan for radiation and life signs, human or other. It shows radio wave activity and distant life signs moving toward us. "Heads on a swivel, folks." My gut tells me we're in danger. I raise my hand. We stop, I gesture toward the ground and take a knee. I release the mosquito drones. Five seconds later, I receive the video feed. "Guys," I whisper. "Check your data pads."

Rikki says, "Will, there are cyborgs, dozens of them, and they're approaching us from three directions."

Then all hell breaks loose. The cyborgs run toward us faster than a human can.

"Weapons free!" We've never faced them before, and they are more machine than man. Their limbs are knives, swords, and guns. We open fire with the P90s but they're ineffective. The cyborgs are heavily armored. I pull out the Mossberg and fire. Cyborgs fall. I only have twenty-five shells left. They're soon gone, but not until more than a dozen enemies are dead. I throw the shotgun on the ground. "Guys, use the HEs and frags!"

We blow another two dozen cyborgs to pieces. But there are still dozens more.

"Use the EMPs! Throw the flash-bangs to buy us some time!"

They explode in a cacophony of light and sound. They stun the cyborgs just long enough for us to attach the EMP weapons.

We light up the enemy with laser sights and fire the EMPs. Each time we pull the trigger, a cyborg falls. There's a constant hail of bullets raining down on us, and with every hit, it's like being stabbed with a dull knife, but the body armor holds.

There's a lull in the battle. We've killed at least fifty, and I'm down to five charges.

<Ying, Long, how many more shots do you have left on the EMP?>

<Six> Ying reports.

<I have four> Long says.

<And I have five>

Smoke and dust fill the air. We can't see past ten feet. The smell of burned flesh, gunpowder, and God knows what else assaults our noses and eyes

I check my data pad. More cyborgs are coming our way, fast. "We have more company, at least another three dozen. We need to get the drone up in the air," I say. I call Rikki. *<Is the drone recharged?>* Shit, I really screwed up here. I should have waited until the drone was charged. My screw-up may cost us our lives

<No. Will, the cyborgs are about to cut you off from the MDTD. I'll get there as soon as I can>

We're in trouble. I don't think even Rikki can help us. I think of Yingzhe . . .

<It's been an honor, guys>

<The honor is ours, Will> Long says.

<The cyborgs will be here in thirty seconds> Ying adds.

Blood-red eyes of the cyborg army burn like hot coals in the deepening gloom. Their limbs are blades, like the previous group, but these advance slowly and cautiously. They are different.

I pull out my knives. Ying and Long reach behind and pull out their katanas.

Then the enemy attacks. The air fills with slashing blades, ours, and theirs. Their armor is weak around their eyes and neck. That's where we aim for. We cut them down, but they still come. Out of the corner of my eye, I see Long and Ying whirling like dervishes, blades flashing.

I feel a sharp pain across my right side where my armor is damaged. I drop one knife but keep slashing and stabbing with the other. But I'm hurt badly.

The second knife slips from my hand, slick with blood. My knees buckle and then I sink to the ground. My vision grows dim. A grayness comes across my eyes. A cyborg lifts its blade. The last thing I see is Yingzhe's face, then nothing.

Ying

Will's down. He's gravely injured. A cyborg raises its blade. I know I can't save him. Suddenly, a blur of light snatches Will's fallen knives. Almost simultaneously, its head goes flying. It's Rikki! She stands above Will, daring the cyborgs to attack him. The ones that do, fall to the ground in pieces. I can't do anything more for Will except finish the fight and not die. Long and I strike back with a fierce anger fueled by vengeance. We kill more of them, but we're nearly exhausted. A cyborg falls, then another.

I hear the war cry of dozens of men and women. They're armed with knives, shotguns, and rifles. They swarm the remaining cyborgs like a pack of wolves on a wounded grizzly bear. With renewed strength, Long and I send more of the cyborgs to whatever hell will take them.

Then it's over. We drop our blades and lie down on the bloody, scorched ground. I see our unknown saviors rush to Will. I feel a pain in my left side and touch it. Blood covers my hand. Then darkness takes me away.

Chapter 19
"O Brave New World, That Has Such People In't: Aftermath"

Ying

I wake up and open my eyes slowly. I'm on a cot in what seems to be a field hospital. The smell of antiseptic and bleach assaults my nostrils. I hear multiple muffled conversations. There is an IV attached to my right arm. There's a dull throbbing pain in my left side, just under my last rib. I reach for it and feel a thick bandage.

"Whoa, soldier, lie back down." I hear a deep, slightly raspy voice and a pair of firm hands gently push me back down onto the cot. "I spent forty-five minutes patching you up and I don't want you to tear the staples."

The voice is familiar. I bend my neck backward to see why.

"Dr. McCray?" My voice is dry and cracked. "What are you doing here? Where am I?"

He walks around to the side of the bed and gives me a tired smile. He speaks slowly, as if addressing a child. "I'm a doctor. This is a field hospital, and you are my seriously wounded patient who miraculously survived a battle against a company of cyborgs."

"But why are you here? Where is Yingzhe?"

"Nurse." Dr. McCray gestures toward a steel tray that has a small bottle of medication and a hypodermic needle. Quickly, she fills the hypo and injects it into my IV lead.

"Wait," I say, "where's my daughter?" I struggle to keep my eyes open. Are we still in the alternate timeline? Everything spins for a moment. I think I see Long, but that's my last cohesive thought as the world recedes from me. I don't fall back asleep, but the pain at my side lessens and my mind feels lighter; I'm still able to see and hear everything happening around me.

"Is it my imagination or does he look like General Shikong, Doctor?" the nurse asks.

"No, Beth, it's not your imagination. He could be the general's twin, and before you ask, that looks like Major Long." He points to Long, who has just entered the field hospital and is making his way toward the doctor and nurse.

"Just like Sergeants Fanotti and Harris had their doppelgängers coming through here two days ago. How is that possible?"

"I have an idea about what's going on, but the only explanation comes straight from science fiction," Dr. McCray says.

I feel my head getting heavier as the sedative's influence fully kicks in, and the last thing I remember seeing is Long standing by my bedside.

Long

"Dr. McCray, will he be all right?"

"He'll be fine. I had to put fifty staples in his side to stop the bleeding. Luckily, no organs were lacerated. He's in a lot better shape than Commander Schachter."

Two beds away, I see Will. He's very pale and his breathing is labored. He needed a blood transfusion, and we are compatible, which is a good thing as Rikki explained there was a possibility that any blood he receives from a donor here may react in unpredictable ways.

"How bad is he?"

McCray shakes his head. "His liver is lacerated, and as you know, he's lost a tremendous amount of blood. Thankfully, with the help of your AI, I could stabilize him."

I didn't tell him about Rikki's true nature because I barely understand it myself. What I know is that she is as far above an AI as a desktop computer is above a pocket calculator, and that she saved Will's life, and ours. I had settled for telling this Dr. McCray that she was like Robert Picardo from *Star Trek: Voyager*, if there even was a *Star Trek: Voyager* in this timeline, or a Robert Picardo. From the blank look that was on his face, I guessed there was not. So, I told him she was an experimental android AI. He seemed to understand that, and I can tell he's just as smart as our Dr. McCray, but I don't think he really believed me.

I touch the bandages on my shoulder and thigh and shrug. I'm the fortunate one on this day. Ying will be OK, but we need to return to our timeline as soon as we can move him. I hope Will can stay alive long enough to get there.

As I wait for Ying to wake up, I think of how we got here. In our original timeline, my parents were killed during the cultural revolution when I was ten. Like so many orphans, I was homeless, stealing what I could just to eat, but I never stole money or what belonged to other people. Older boys bullied me and beat me up, but I never backed down, and most of them, having grown up the same way as me, respected that. Still, it was a desperate existence. I'd go days without food until, starving, I'd scavenge through the garbage, eating what I could find; moldy leftovers crawling with maggots and swarming with flies that were thrown out by those who could afford it. They ignored us, as if we didn't exist.

One day, when scrounging through garbage, I found a moth-eaten jacket. Nearly naked and slowly freezing to death, I thought it to be my salvation. I put it on but didn't notice a gang of older boys watching me. They set upon me like a pack of jackals, but as much as they hit me and kicked me, I refused to let go of the jacket. One of them kicked me in the head and I slammed into a wall. The kid tore the jacket from my arms and gave me one final blow. As my consciousness faded, through my swollen eyes, I saw an army officer grab the boy. He gave him a casual backhand cuff, sending him flying into the wall. He retrieved my jacket, covered me with it, and picked me up just before I passed out.

The man was Shikong Yingxiong, a captain in the army. He took me to the barracks, and there, I recovered slowly from the vicious beating. When I was better, the first thing I saw was the jacket that almost cost me my life. Someone cleaned and folded it and repaired the tears and holes. Sometime later, Ying came by to see how I was doing. He told me that anyone with the spirit, determination, and tenacity that I showed deserved to have a better life, and that from now on, I was his son.

Ying and his wife, Jing Hua Shui Yue, raised me as their own along with Yingzhe and her brother Shuiying. He taught us martial arts, and as soon as I was old enough, I joined the army, eventually ending up in special forces. I fell in love, and we had a baby boy; but our life was destroyed the day the MTPC hacked mine and Ying's brain chips, which started the chain reaction of our ultimate fleeing to our new timeline. I knew that my wife's and son's souls would never rest until we defeated the MTPC across all of time and space. Only then will they be avenged.

Dr. McCray comes rushing in. "Commander Schachter can't hold on much longer. I normally wouldn't suggest this, but Long, we need to transfuse more of your blood into him."

I sit on the cot next to Will and bare my arm. The nurse, who is Beth Wall's duplicate, quickly but carefully inserts the IV. They transfer Will to a stretcher. I walk alongside Will, still transfusing my blood. Two other interns are carrying Ying's stretcher as we rush as a group to the MDTD. I concentrate on visualizing my McCray, making contact at once. *<Dr. McCray, we're*

coming back. Ying and Will are injured. Ying is stable, but Will is critical with a lacerated liver>

<OK. Yingzhe and I will meet you with a crash cart>

We climb into the MDTD. I turn to Rikki. "Can you return us to this timeline?"

"Of course, I have memorized the time-space coordinates."

"OK, take us home!"

Less than a minute later, the disguised safe house comes into view. McCray and Yingzhe are waiting with the crash cart, as promised. They transfer Will to a gurney. Yingzhe takes out the transfusion line and slaps a Band-Aid on my arm. She and McCray bring him in. Rikki and I carry Ying's stretcher and transfer him to a hospital bed in the small ER. There's nothing to do but wait.

In the infirmary, McCray carefully removes Will's bandages and inspects his counterpart's work. The staples in Will's right side, just under his rib cage, are tight and neat with no sign of infection—but that's not the issue. The cyborg's attack severely damaged Will's liver and there's no way McCray's going to open him up to check. Yingzhe has already hooked him up to a bag of blood, and inserted a breathing tube, but his pulse is rapid and thready. There's swelling in his abdomen that could be from internal bleeding. Yingzhe stands to the side, wanting to do more, but there's nothing else for her to do but wait. She's as pale as their patient.

I recall the many battles I've fought in, seeing in my mind the dark red blood of an organ injury, the coppery smell of lifeblood oozing from a grievous wound, and how few of the other soldiers survived.

McCray turns to Yingzhe and gently urges, "Why don't you go into the recovery room and keep your father company? The best thing for Ying to see when he wakes up will be you."

Yingzhe tries to respond, but the words refuse to come out. She takes another look at the severely injured Will. I wrap my arm around her shoulders and slowly escort her out of the room.

McCray

I scan Will's right side and confirm that the laceration went deep into his liver, nicked his hepatic portal vein, and that there is still internal bleeding.

With Rikki's help, I've been working on using medical nanobots to treat severe injuries. "Rikki?"

She appears in her holo-matter form. "Yes, Dr. McCray."

"Will's in extremely critical condition. Even if we had a team of surgeons, there's no guarantee that we could save him." Even though my heart's pounding, I need to be professional and decisive. "I think that the experimental medical nanobots may be the only way to keep him alive."

"I agree, Dr. McCray. The simulations I ran give every sign that they will work as expected. Remember to connect Will to a dextrose drip since the nanobots will get their energy and raw materials directly from his body."

"How long will it take you to program the nanobots?"

"I expected we would need them," she responds. "I already programmed and prepared them." She goes into the lab and returns with a ten-milliliter syringe filled with what looks like purple liquid mercury that pulsates with a faint violet-blue glow. I take the syringe and feel its weight for a moment. Then I inject the nanobots into Will's IV. I turn to Rikki. "There's nothing to do but wait."

Rikki gently puts her holo-matter hand on my shoulder. "Don't worry, he'll be fine. I will watch him and will let you know if there are any problems."

I nod and head to the recovery room where Yingzhe and Long are waiting for their father to wake up. Long stands slowly, still in pain from the slashes on his legs. "How is he?"

Just then, Ying's eyes flutter open. He sees almost everyone standing around his bed. "How is Will?" he repeats after Long.

"He's in critical condition," I reply. "We injected experimental medical nanobots to repair the severe damage to his liver." I feel helpless and it makes me uncomfortable. "Rikki says it's going to work." I stand next to Ying's bed. "Will's going to make it," I say with more confidence than I have.

Yingzhe turns to me. "Can I stay with Will?"

"Of course you can. He's in the recovery room. When he wakes up, I know you're the first person he'll want to see."

"Thank you, Daniel."

Yingzhe

With no prompting, Long had brought in a chair for me to sit comfortably beside Will in the recovery room. The lights are dim. The sharp smell of bleach and antiseptic makes my eyes water for a moment. I hear the metronome-like *beep* of the heart monitor, and it reminds me of my piano lessons as a child.

Will's pale, almost gray, but his breathing is regular, his chest rising and falling in rhythm with the *beep*s. I take his hand. It's cold and waxy.

As a scientist, I'm trained to be logical, trained to analyze facts and form hypotheses about the very nature of reality, but I pray Will recovers. I close my eyes, remembering the moments we've shared and imagining the moments we have yet to share, as two on a team of many and as two left to our own intimate devices.

McCray

I come into the ER and see Yingzhe asleep, her head resting on the bed, holding Will's left hand. Will's life signs are still weak but improving, which is what we could only hope for. I look back at Yingzhe—she looks uncomfortable. I open a cabinet and take out a pillow that I place under her head, being careful not to wake her.

When I return in the morning, Yingzhe is barely awake, but lights up when she sees me enter. "I think Will woke up briefly in the middle of the night. I was sleeping, but he squeezed my hand! I called to him but—" Her voice falters. "—he was still in the same comatose state. His color's at least better, so maybe . . ." Her voice is hopeful and full of conviction that Will's squeeze was real.

I ask her to step away so I can scan his side again to see if the nanobots are doing their job. I know they are, but the confirmation is the good news we all want to hear. Yingzhe turns to me once I've finished the scan, looking expectant and eager. I say, "He'll be fine."

Chapter 20
"The Needs of the Many Outweigh the Needs of the Few: How Do I Choose?"

Yingzhe

There's a stirring beside me. "I'm so hungry," Will grumbles.

"He's awake!" I shout. Everyone rushes in and half a dozen conversations break out. I realize I'm hungry too. I've eaten little, despite my father's and Long's insistence that I eat *something*. They've been bringing me food, even cooking it themselves. I look over the piles of dishes on the counter heaped with uneaten food and it smells delicious, the sharp aromatic fragrance of fresh ginger and the eye-watering waft of hot peppers. I've been here for two days waiting for Will to wake up, and the nanobots worked. I touch his wrist, and his pulse is strong and regular, and he's no longer ashen gray. McCray hasn't slept much, checking Will's vitals every three hours. Even Rikki has been coming in to check on me and Will, although she doesn't need to.

Not for the first time, I contemplate The Engineer and his role in all of this. I have an unshakable feeling that he has planned everything and that we are non-player characters in a multi-dimensional video game across realities.

Will

"Where am I?"

I sit up and scan the room. Ying and Long are trying to keep their stoic warrior poses, but failing. McCray looks stern and serious as usual, and Yingzhe is crying. Rikki is here too, and she's actually smiling.

McCray says, "Everyone out!" Long and Ying leave quickly, but Yingzhe remains sitting beside me.

After a prolonged moment, she finally says, "I'll go. I've been here for two days." She laughs and casually sniffs under her arms. "I could use a shower." She squeezes my hand, wipes her eyes, and leaves.

It's just McCray and me.

"The last thing I remember was the battle against the cyborgs and one of them slashed me . . ." I gingerly touch my right side, but it feels fine. McCray takes off the bandage. I notice a neat line of surgical staples under my rib, but the wound has healed. I take a deep breath and there's no pain. "Doc, how is it possible that I'm healed so fast?"

He answers, "Let me remove these staples, and then I'll catch you up." He works for a silent ten minutes before he speaks again. "Your liver was severely lacerated, and you were bleeding internally. Their Dr. McCray stabilized you, but you needed blood. Long transfused you twice, but they had to get you back here because of how severe your wound was."

"The cyborgs were overrunning us. They just kept coming even though Ying, Long, and I kept cutting them down. Why are we not dead?"

"Maybe Rikki should fill you in." He finishes examining me. "You're fine, but you're going to be starving for the next day or two." He pats me on the shoulder. "Glad to have you back."

Rikki has been standing quietly to the side. "Why am I not dead, Rikki?"

"We got help from the alternates and a group of rebels. In that timeline, they may lose the battle against the MTPC." She looks down in a remarkably human gesture.

Ying and Long, who have been just outside the door for the conversation, walk into the recovery room. Long says, "Our avenging angel Rikki is why we're not dead. She took your knives and guarded you, daring those cyborgs to touch you, and any that tried, she turned into scrap metal and mush."

I look at Rikki, who lifts her head. "I was fulfilling my programming."

"Zeroth Law, right?"

A humanlike look of revulsion flashes across her pretty holographic face. "They were not human. They were extensions of the MTPC in that timeline, created to maim and kill."

We sit quietly for a minute. They're the face of our enemy and why we're fighting. We can't allow the MTPC to succeed in its mission. It's important to remember the larger goal, even when we're just trying not to die.

The moment passes. "Will," Ying starts. "Long and I need to speak with you." I glance at Rikki, nod, and she disappears.

"OK, guys, what do you want to talk about?"

"My sister cares greatly for you. She may even love you."

"I know," I say, and pause for a long time.

"How?" Long asks, his head cocked to one side.

"Because I love her."

Ying replies, "On the blood that we've spilled together, promise us you'll always love and take care of her."

"I promise." There's another long moment while they seem to process my vow. Then they smile.

"Are you hungry?" Ying asks.

"I could eat a horse, or General Tso's chicken."

"Coming right up!"

After they leave, McCray returns. "You never told me how you saved my life or how I healed so fast."

"Rikki and I have been working on creating medical nanobots."

"Like the ones I've read about in science fiction books?" I touch my healed side.

"Just like them." He gives me a rare smile. "We hadn't tested them on a human but—" He looks at me. "—your injuries were grave and probably fatal. It was your only chance."

"I'm glad they worked. Thank you," I say, but I know in my heart that in all my years in the military, and in my entire life, I had never been so close to death.

The luscious aroma of Ying's cooking has made its way into the recovery room. My mouth is watering, and my stomach is growling. "Doc, do I need to stay here any longer?"

"You're free to go. Be sure to eat, a lot. The nanobots use your body's glucose, minerals, and vitamins to heal you."

"No worries on that front. And hey, am I allowed to take a shower?"

"Yes. We took your duffel to the room you last used, so everything you need should be up there."

The last time I used that duffel was when Ying and I went to the cabin. It seems like it was a lifetime ago. I climb the stairs and take notice of my right knee. I sprained it in the last football game my senior year in college, and it almost disqualified me from military service; it's something that was always a little bothersome but never kept me from my duties or daily life. But now, it doesn't hurt at all. Could it have been the nanobots?

The bedroom is like a suite in a high-end hotel. I toss the hospital gown on the couch and turn the water on as hot as I can bear it. Ten showerheads blast me from all directions. I reach for the soap and scrub away the sweat and blood of two battles. They seem like a bad dream to me, but I know they're not. I luxuriate under the hot, steamy water and close my eyes for I don't know how long. Finally, I turn off the water, dry myself, and change to a pair of jeans and a T-shirt. I notice my fatigues are clean and neatly folded on the dresser. I walk downstairs and take a seat in the kitchen. Long and Ying's delicious repast awaits me. I dig in. McCray wasn't kidding. I've never been so hungry in my life.

As I'm finishing the last of the green tea ice cream, Yingzhe walks in. She looks beautiful as always, her silky, long black hair pulled into an intricate braid and her pale skin highlighting her intense, fiercely intelligent eyes. I get up and walk to her. We hug each other, and neither of us wants to let go. Finally, we gently disengage. I take her hand and we both sit.

"Will, I thought I was going to lose you." Her eyes are glassy with tears that want to come out again.

"Just before I passed out on the battlefield, the last thing I thought about was you, Yingzhe." I squeeze her hand. "Long and your father talked to me about you."

"I know." She smiles. "They talked to me as well."

"They made me promise to make you happy, take care of you, and always love you." I paused. "And I did promise, but now I'm scared that I can only keep one of them—to always love you. We're in a war against an enemy that humanity has never faced. An implacable enemy that exists only to destroy life, not only in our timeline, but across potentially infinite ones. I came closer to dying in that battle than I ever have in my life. I'm not afraid to die, but I'm afraid for you if I do."

"Will, do you think I'm some delicate flower that will shrivel at the first frost? You said it yourself: I'm a soldier. Yes. We're in a war. Yes, either or both of us might die. But you promised on the blood that you, my father, and my brother shed. I expect you to keep those promises, no matter what happens. Are. We. Clear. Commander?"

"Yes, crystal," I say meekly, earning a smile.

"Now, we have a war that needs winning." She kisses me. "Back to work."

The others watch as Yingzhe and I join them in the meeting room. Several conversations begin at once.

"How are you feeling, Will?" Long asks with a knowing smirk. I blush.

"I'm fine." Actually, I feel great, like I've been reborn thanks to nanobots. I begin, "We won that battle, but according to Rikki, the MTPC in that timeline may have won the war."

"I found no evidence of my counterpart in that timeline," Rikki adds.

"We need to get back there before the MTPC reconstitutes its forces, and find the tachyon trail again before that happens."

"What about the people who saved us, many of whom died doing so?" Long asks.

This was going to be hard. "We can't help them. We may lose their timeline to the MTPC," I respond.

"They died for us!" Long exclaims. "Don't we owe them *something*?"

I look down and then around the table before I continue. "Long, we owe them, but there are only six of us, maybe ten if we find Harris and Fanotti, and bring in Wall and Kelly. We almost died, but we're literally the best and only chance there is to save our galaxy. What do you want us to do? There are potentially infinite timelines, and in some of them, the good guys lose!" I feel myself losing control, so I take a deep breath. I continue, using a softer tone. "I'm sorry. We don't have the resources or people to take back a planet, let alone an entire timeline."

Ying has been listening to the discussion. "Will is right." He turns to me. "But surely, we can supply them with equipment like EMP weapons, body armor, drones, and other material."

"Doc?"

"Soon we're going to have a replicator that can manufacture anything they need," McCray says.

"We only will have the one replicator. I want to help them, but we need to ensure we have what we need first. I wish we could have more than just one. But hey, let's finish up our debrief, OK? Then we can figure out how we can help them."

Ying says, "When the cyborgs attacked us, the only gun that worked was the Mossberg. If it wasn't for our allies, we would have died. Any thoughts?"

"The P90s were ineffective. The rounds just bounced off their armor," Long adds.

"We need a gun that can use armor-piercing rounds, like the M995, if we're going to face them again." I stop and think for a moment. "I've got it! The M4A1 is perfect."

"I'm not familiar with that firearm," Ying says.

"The M4A1 is a carbine that allows for both semiautomatic and automatic firing. It has a grenade attachment, can take any kind of scope, and is chambered for the 5.56 NATO round, so we can use M995 armor-piercing rounds," I explain. "McCray, can you get us those?"

"None of my companies make them, but I can make some phone calls," he replies.

"Thanks. How are you doing on developing the battle suit for Rikki's holo-matter form?"

"We have the design completed. The next step is to build a beta test suit and find out if our design will work, although Rikki assures us it will."

Rikki adds, "Although your idea of building a capacitor that would store enough energy for me to maintain my holo-matter form longer was not workable, we adapted your idea and created a capacitor that could be a part of the suit. It would store the energy from plasma blasts and electronic attacks and re-emit it as an offensive energy weapon."

I gave an impressed whistle as I thought of the implications and uses of that capability in combat. "Whose idea was it?"

"It was Rikki's," McCray says.

"Zeroth Law of Robotics," I add.

Instantly, Rikki turns her glowing red eyes on me, and it's unnerving. "Just because I *can* do something does not mean I *want* to do it, Will."

I drop my eyes. "I'm sorry, I shouldn't have said that."

Yingzhe changes the subject. "We've just about solved the few remaining bugs in the quantum energy transmission technology. Once we complete it, Rikki won't have to stay within five hundred meters of an energy source to maintain her holo-matter form."

I turn to everybody. "Can you give me and Rikki some time to talk?"

"No problem," McCray says as he ushers everyone else out of the room.

She's standing silently, waiting for me to say something. "Rikki—"

"Will, I'm not angry with you. Anger is an emotion that I understand, but it's not part of my programming. Anger, hate, jealousy, and any other negative emotions are the worst parts of being human, but I'm not human. I can self-program and learn, and I can choose not to learn how to hate or be jealous or vindictive. My prime directive is to preserve life and oppose the MTPC. That, plus the Zeroth Law, allows me to take a life or injure a human being. You've said that you see enemy soldiers as people, not cannon fodder, but, when necessary, you will kill the enemy. Is that so different from me? I have seen the love you have for Yingzhe and her love for you. It makes the two of you more powerful together than you were before. I will never experience love, but I'm learning about kindness, joy, compassion, gratitude, and hope. I hope we win this war, a war that I have fought for a millennium, and I'm grateful that I'm no longer fighting this war alone."

"So, we're good?"

"Yes, Will, we are good. One other thing."

"What's that?"

"Before you said you wished we could have more than one replicator."

"Yes, and I do even more now."

"What if we could? More memories have been unlocked . . ."

Chapter 21
"The Time Is Out of Joint; O Cursed Spite: Ghosts of Futures Past"

"I think everyone should hear this." A few minutes later, everyone is back in the meeting room. "Sorry, but Rikki has had additional memories unlocked, and they're absolutely mind-blowing," I say. "You know some of her story, but there's much more."

"The Engineers defeated the now-evil AI and imprisoned it in a crystal matrix deep under Olympus Mons on Mars. They knew it was only a temporary measure, but thought they had time to defeat it permanently. A quantum virus decimated The Engineers' race before they could develop a permanent solution. There were few who survived. Most of them had perished because of the quantum plague. Others ascended to a higher plane of existence to escape. The remaining few continued to work on defeating the MTPC once and for all. They were only weeks away from completing the project when a cataclysmic meteorite strike on Mars damaged the crystal matrix. It used the iron and nickel core of the planet to rebuild itself. The surviving Engineers knew this and realized they needed a more powerful AI to oppose the evil one. So, they created me, giving me self-awareness and the ability to develop emotions like compassion and love, which the MTPC lacks. It's only driven by its new programming: to destroy all biological life in this galaxy."

Dead silence.

"I'm going to ask the obvious question," I say. "Where did the quantum virus come from?"

Everyone looks at each other.

"I don't know," Rikki replies.

"And who or what could give a species as obviously advanced as The Engineers a quantum virus that wiped out most of them?" I continue.

"Those are excellent questions, Will," McCray adds.

Another mystery to deal with, but we have more immediate worries. We need to let Rikki finish her story. "I'm sure that the origin of the quantum virus is very important, but we need to move on, since we can't answer those questions just yet."

Yingzhe resumes the earlier discussion. "But why did The Engineers withhold the truth from you until now?"

"Maybe that's how they programmed me. I just don't know," Rikki says, and there's a note of sadness in her voice.

"Perhaps your matrix had to reach a certain level of complexity before the new directives became accessible," McCray offers.

"But how is it decided that your matrix has reached the desired level of complexity? That implies that something or—" I pause. "—someone is watching you . . ."

"The Engineers?" Ying asks. "Who else could it be?"

"Rikki, please back up. Are you telling us that the MTPC is on Mars?" Long asks.

"Yes."

"So, how are people like Malkinson and Cordeaux being controlled?" he continues.

"McCray's experience showed us that the MTPC can use quantum communication," I say.

"Except the brain chips never had quantum communication capacity," Yingzhe says. "The MTPC needs a direct brain-to-computer connection to control people."

"Good point," I say. "So, there must be another version of the MTPC somewhere on Earth."

"Like at UOEECT headquarters," McCray says. "That would explain a lot."

Long hesitates a moment. "I have a more practical question: how do we get to Mars?"

"That's my question too." I give a nod in acknowledgment of Long's point.

"Is there any reason we couldn't use an MDTD?" Yingzhe asks.

"No, there is not," Rikki replies. "We use them to travel through time and to alternate timelines. By harnessing a miniature black hole and its hyper-gravity, it allows the traveler to enter the quantum universe. If we need to travel to Mars, or even just across the street, the MDTD is not traveling through space, it's traveling through quantum space. Will, may I have a piece of paper and your pen?" I tear out a sheet and hand it to her. "Thank you." She draws a large dot on the top of the page and another on the bottom. Then she folds the paper, so the dots line up and stabs the pen through both. She unfolds the paper and shows it to us. "It's not an exact analogy, but you get the idea. I'm sure you have all noticed the frost that covers the MDTD during the transition from one location to another." We all say yes or nod.

Yingzhe asks, "May I, Rikki?"

"Of course."

"That frost is frozen air. The temperature sensor of the MDTD always shows a reading of absolute zero or a few thousandths of degrees Kelvin. You can't measure the temperature in the quantum realm directly, but as a practical matter, it's at, or close to, absolute zero."

"Correct, Yingzhe. So, if the MDTD can function at, or very close to, absolute zero, it can travel virtually anywhere," Rikki confirms.

"The only issue that remains, is what do we do when we get there? It seems to me that the best comparison is deep-sea diving except instead of a wet suit, goggles, and air tanks, we'd need space suits." I gesture toward myself. "A Pink Floyd T-shirt and jeans will not cut it." There are a few laughs.

"It would be easy to adapt the personal armor suits to serve as environmental or space suits, and we wouldn't need any new technology to do it," McCray says.

"There's gravity on Mars. It's weaker than ours here, and you'd have to get used to it, but we're not talking about working in zero-g conditions," I say. "But we're in no position to go to Mars and take on the real MTPC."

"No, you're not, at least not yet," Rikki says. "And you're not ready to go to the Moon either, but that's where we need to go. And by 'we,' I mean me."

"What do you mean?" I ask.

"Besides the more complete history of the war against the MTPC, the information unlocked includes the fact that The Engineers left caches of high tech around the solar system, including on the Moon."

"The Moon?" Long is incredulous. "What kind of high tech?"

"There may be a zero-point module power cell there," she says.

"That's what powers the MDTDs," I add. "More than enough energy to power another replicator, right, Rikki?"

"Right."

"Is there any danger to you? We could use another replicator but could manage without it since we have the mini-fusion plant from Ying's MDTD. We can't manage without you, though," I say.

"It's in the South Pole–Aitken Basin, which is the oldest impact crater on the Moon and possibly in the solar system," she says. "There is one issue, however. Moondust is highly electrostatic and could affect my holo-matter matrix, which is made of coherent electrons."

McCray, who has been listening intently, says, "The battle suit we are working on for Rikki should take care of that problem. We're building it using a 3-D printer, but it's a slow process."

"When do you expect to finish it?" I ask.

"Not for a week, and that's only for the shell. While that's happening, we'll be building and constructing an advanced capacitor in the factory. Then we'll need to connect and test it," he explains.

"So, assuming everything works, when will it be ready?"

"If there are no hitches, three or four weeks."

"So, Rikki can't go to the Moon and look for the tech until then."

"Yes, but the replicator should be operational in two weeks. Once we have it, everything will go much faster."

"Unless anyone has anything else, let's call it a day. This has been a very productive meeting. Tomorrow, let's work on putting together a couple of pallets of equipment for our saviors from the other timeline."

It's getting late. I'm still hungry, so I raid the refrigerator and find leftover pizza and Chinese food, and down them before going to sleep.

The next day is a slow one for everyone, except for McCray, who's working the phones with Rikki's help to get the weapons and supplies to bring to our allies in the alternate timeline. As usual, Ying and Long are sparring. For the umpteenth time, I vow to join them.

In the lab, Yingzhe is running simulations for the quantum energy transmission. Behind her, I see what must be the battle suit for Rikki. It's 1630 and I don't think she's eaten anything today. I decide to ask her if she's hungry.

"Hey."

"Oh, hi, Will. Do you need me for something?"

"Yes. I need you to let me take you to Giovanni's for something to eat."

"I appreciate it, but I'm really busy."

"A watched pot never boils."

"Yes, but that's not true. Science, you know."

"Even geniuses have to eat."

I look at the computer screen. Lines of data stream by too fast to read, although I suspect I wouldn't understand them even if they were moving slower. "Those are simulations, right?"

"Yes, we've almost finished modeling the quantum energy transfer system."

"How much longer will this simulation take?"

"About another three—" She stops, and a look of false indignation crosses her face before she smiles. "I see what you're doing, Commander Schachter."

"You were going to say, 'another three hours,' weren't you? Plenty of time to get something to eat with me."

"You win. I'd be delighted to."

I borrow McCray's Land Rover again and we go into town. It's a little early for dinner, so it's not too crowded. John sees us and greets us.

"Will, nice to see you again. Who is this lovely lady?"

"This is my friend Yingzhe. Yingzhe, this is John, the owner of the best pizza place I've ever been to."

"You are too kind. I'm pleased to meet you, Yingzhe."

"Nice to meet you too," she says as she shakes his hand.

He seats us at a quiet table in the corner.

"My daughter, Rose, will be with you in a minute to take your order. Enjoy."

Rose comes out as promised. "Can I get you something to drink while you look at the menu?" She's about twenty-eight and pretty, with lustrous black hair.

"What would you like to drink?" I ask. "I highly recommend their root beer."

"Sure, I'll try it," Yingzhe replies.

"Two root beers, please."

"Coming right up."

"Can we split a pizza?" I ask

"Sounds good to me. I would never deprive you of your favorite food in the world, Will, except for General Tso's chicken," she says with a smile.

I return her smile. "What would you like on it?"

"Pepperoni, hot peppers, and onions."

Rose arrives with our drinks. "Ready to order?"

"We'd like a large pie with pepperoni, hot peppers, and onions, please," I say.

"Coming up! Thank you."

Our pie comes piping hot and perfectly done. Yingzhe takes two slices, leaving me six. "They're all yours."

"Are you sure?"

Yingzhe says, "You need it more than I do." She pauses. "We really are in a war. You could have died if it wasn't for the nanobots."

I shrug my shoulders and hold her hands. "For me, being a soldier means I'm prepared to give my life for what I believe in and the people I am sworn to protect."

"That's a heavy responsibility, Will."

"It is, but it's one that every soldier accepts, your father and brother included."

"I understand, but please try harder to not die in the future."

There's nothing more to say in this moment. I pay the check, and we drive back in companionable silence.

"See you later. Don't work too hard," I say, and we share a laugh. She gives me a kiss and goes back to the lab.

Ying and Long have gone back east to open their restaurant after their sparring session. McCray is still on the phone with his west coast contacts. I knock on the door to get his attention and he gives me a thumbs-up and waves me along. I decide to hit the treadmill and the weights before showering, and finally turn in to go to sleep early. Tomorrow will be a big day.

Chapter 22
"Through the Looking Glass: There but for the Grace of God Go I"

The supplies that McCray spent the last two days begging, wheedling, and negotiating for are starting to arrive. Once we receive everything, we'll take them to our allies in the other timeline. I don't know how many are in the resistance, but Long thinks it's less than two dozen. McCray tells me that the munitions and matériel can supply up to fifty fighters.

In my experience, a few motivated, dedicated, well-trained operatives can be an effective force, but if that battle is any sign, the most they can hope for is to harass the MTPC. I wonder how many cyborgs it has and where they came from.

By late afternoon, we have received almost everything.

"Rikki?"

Her hologram pops into existence. "Yes, Will?"

"What time is it in the other timeline?"

"It's 1913 there."

"Thanks. It's too late to go there now, so tomorrow we'll deliver the weapons and tech to the resistance." I feel bad that Rikki has had little to do lately. "Do you ever get bored?"

"No, never. I have the internet. There are multiple exabytes of information, and it's growing exponentially. There are movies, books, culture, and history. I want to learn everything I can about humans. You're very hard to understand, even for a sentient AI like me."

"That makes me feel better. I worry," I say sincerely.

"That's sweet of you, Will."

"It's what friends do. I'm going to get some food, do some work, and probably turn in early."

"OK, and don't worry. I have got your six!"

I laugh and say, "I know you do."

McCray mentioned that he and Yingzhe were going out for dinner to go over the increasing number of projects they were working on. So, I'm otherwise by myself. Someone went out and brought back Mexican. I help myself to a couple of enchiladas and tacos. After dinner, I read, and before I know it, it's past 2300. I was hoping to see Yingzhe when she came back; I hope I'm not coming on too strong for her. We probably should talk tomorrow.

The next day, everyone is back. McCray and I check the supplies. At least they'll give the rebels a chance, especially the EMP weapons. Ying and Long volunteer to make the three trips needed to bring the supplies to our allies. The MDTD can change its shape to accommodate more passengers or cargo, but it's not bigger on the inside, like the Doctor's TARDIS.

By 1130, Ying and Long have delivered everything, and now that they're here, we three can head back to pursue the still-missing Harris, Fanotti, and their tachyon trail. "Thanks, guys. What was their reaction to the weapons and supplies?" I ask.

"They were thrilled, appreciative, and surprised," Ying says.

"I hope it gives them a fighting chance," I reply. "A small repayment for saving our lives."

Since Ying and Long have already geared up, I go to the armory to get ready myself. "I hope it's not needed. This time, though, we know what we could be facing."

Fifteen minutes later and I'm done. They're waiting for me. "All set? We have a lot to talk about with our doppelgängers."

"Will, I'd like to go as well," McCray says.

After giving it some thought, I say, "Not this time. This timeline is a war zone. I promise that you and

Yingzhe can go in the field with us in a more secure timeline where the two of you will be safe. Deal?"

"Deal. But I'll be holding you to it."

"I know you will."

He turns around and goes into the laboratory with Rikki. Everyone else has gone out to the MDTD. Yingzhe stands there waiting.

"It's a good thing for you that you won't let Dr. McCray go either, Commander." She smiles.

"I know. This mission should be safer than the last one. We don't plan to stay there long. We still must find Fanotti and Harris, if they're alive, and I think they are."

"I'll still worry, Will."

"Don't, we'll be OK."

"You better be."

The hatch is open. "Rikki, take us back to that timeline. Once we get there, use the usual protocol. Stealth and keep the MDTD within five hundred meters of us in case we need you."

"You got it, boss," she says.

As soon as we arrive, I send out the mosquito drones. We have modified our data pads to detect the cyborgs. Hopefully, there won't be any. Alternate McCray, Harris, Fanotti, and Long greet us. It's an eerie feeling. I glance over to Long, but he's fine, having met them before when they delivered the weapons and supplies. McCray walks over to me and points to the place where I was wounded.

"May I see, Commander?"

I shrug and pull up my shirt. I'm completely healed, and there's not even a scar.

"I understand you saved my life, Doctor. Thank you. We brought you a small supply of medical nanobots, like the ones that healed me. Hopefully, you won't need them."

"Thank you," he says. "I don't know what to say, Commander."

"Use them only for the direst injuries because I don't know when we'll be back here, but the nanobots can save lives."

He says modestly, "It was mostly your amazing experimental AI that saved you, but she's much more than that, isn't she?" Long glances at me.

"Where can we talk?" I ask.

"Follow me." We follow him to a prefabricated building with a long, foldable table and chairs arranged inside.

"To answer your question, yes, Rikki is a sentient AI." I explain to him all the details of who she is, where she comes from, and the ultimate goal of defeating the MTPC. It's concise, as we don't have a lot of time to linger in this timeline.

"You don't mince words, do you, Commander?"

"Call me Will—and that's what I've been told."

"Will, please go on."

"Similar battles are happening across countless timelines. *Our* Fanotti and Harris escaped the MTPC in their MDTD." *No point in making this more complicated than it already is,* I think.

"We met them. It was a . . . *weird* experience," Harris says.

"Does that mean that there are duplicates of all of us in the different timelines?" Fanotti asks

"Not necessarily," I reply. "We've been to two alternate timelines so far. In both of them, I exist, but my duplicate dies in a battle in one of them." I don't mention how I experienced my consciousness being drawn to that timeline, partly because I still don't understand it, and partly because they are already overwhelmed by what they are learning. I ask, "Is there a version of me in this timeline?"

"If there is, we've never met him," Fanotti says.

Our Long asks what I was thinking. "Has there ever been a United Organization for Ethical Evolution and Controlled Technology?"

His counterpart answers, "No, there isn't and never was such an organization that I'm aware of. But there have been rumors of a secret spy coalition for forty years that supposedly had advanced technology like yours . . ." His voice trails off.

Harris says, "So, maybe it's *not* a rumor."

Ying, who has been quiet, asks, "I didn't see a version of me. Does one exist here?"

The expressions on the faces of our alternates turn from curious to tragic. Long's duplicate speaks in a soft, sad voice. "General Ying died in a battle against the cyborgs about two months ago. After that, his daughter, Yingzhe, left here and went back to Taiwan." He pauses. "The cyborgs haven't made it there yet."

Like our Ying and Long, there is a burning hatred in his eyes, and a few tears.

Harris and Fanotti go over and hug him. What other differences were there between this timeline and ours?

Ying approaches him too. The women move to the side deferentially. Ying grasps alternate Long's shoulders at arm's length and looks into his eyes.

"I'm not the same person, but perhaps not too different from him, either. Avenge him and everyone else who has died, but most of all, do not let Yingzhe retreat from the world and this war. Don't let her disappear from your life. This world needs her. You need her, and I know she needs you." They clasp forearms.

"You are much like him. Thank you, sir."

I look at our Long and his face mirrors his twin. They're different, but they're the same. Everyone's silent for a moment. But we're on the clock, so I clear my throat. "OK." Everyone returns to their seats and their attention is on me.

"Long, can you brief them on the weapons and technology?"

"Yes, Commander." I appreciate him addressing me by my rank in this setting.

"What will happen if we're attacked?" asks an NCO from the rebels.

"We have this entire area under surveillance, and our scanners can detect the cyborgs. The enemy won't surprise us again." I smile. "Besides, you have many new toys to play with if they do."

The NCO returns a dangerous smile. "Yes, sir, that we do!"

The two Longs and the NCO leave. I turn to Fanotti and Harris.

"How long ago did they come through here?"

They exchange glances. Fanotti says, "Three days ago. They gave us some medical supplies but were unarmed except for their Glocks. We knew they were on the run, but they didn't tell more than that. I guess we know what they were running from now."

Ying nods. "They had no way of knowing if you were hostile or friendly forces. The MTPC has the ability to control people." He glances at me meaningfully.

I continue, "You mentioned that in this timeline, there have been rumors of a secret spy organization. Were any of you in it?"

Harris answers promptly, allaying my fear that they were under the influence of the MTPC in this timeline. "No, we've been best friends since grade school and joined the Marines after high school. When the cyborgs started to appear, we re-upped." There was silence.

"Ying, tell them about UOEECT," I say.

He explains the organization to them, as well as our involvement. With it comes more about the MTPC, and how it can control anyone with an activated brain chip.

McCray asks, "Commander, how can you guarantee the MTPC hasn't hacked your chips and that you're not under its control?"

"Touché, Doctor. You'll just have to trust me when I tell you that our McCray discovered a way to neutralize our brain chips. Also, the supplies and weapons we brought for you speak far louder that anything Ying or I could say."

"Of course," McCray says. "I shouldn't have said anything."

"Don't worry about it. I'd have asked the same thing. Tell me what you know of how and when the MTPC came here."

"We never knew about the MTPC until now," McCray says. "What we know is that a strange crystalline meteorite crashed down in 1970 in northern Minnesota. Now that I think about it, there was minor damage reported at the time. You can't find anything about it these days, though."

"In our timeline, a consortium of the US government, businesses, and colleges developed ARPANET, the predecessor of the internet, which became active in 1969. Its goal was to create a system that would allow computers across the United States to share information." I remember something I read years ago. "When did the cyborgs first appear?"

"The first one appeared five years ago in . . ."

"Northern Minnesota, right?"

"Yes."

"I wish we could stay here longer, Dr. McCray, but we have to find our Harris and Fanotti as soon as possible because—"

"You haven't deactivated their brain chips," he finishes.

I get up and shake his hand and then everyone else's. "You are just as smart as our McCray. Good luck. We'll try to come back."

"I hope so. I'd like to meet my doppelgänger."

"He said the same about you."

"Good hunting, Commander."

Chapter 23
"This Is True Love: You Think This Happens Every Day?"

We walk from camp back to our MDTD. I'm filled with unexpected optimism but also ashamed of myself, thinking that this timeline was irreversibly lost to the MTPC. They are courageous warriors who will never surrender to the enemy. The weapons and supplies will give them hope, the greatest weapon of all.

As Ying, Long, and I enter the vehicle, Long's alternate yells. We turn around and he catches up with us. He shakes my hand and grasps his twin's right forearm. He leans over and says something in Mandarin to Long. They embrace each other. Then, he steps back and salutes me. I return the gesture. He executes a perfect about-face and disappears into the gathering dusk. I won't ask Long what he said.

"Rikki, let's follow the trail." The purple dusk deepens and energies flash as we leave this timeline. I promise myself again that we will return.

The vortex dissipates and we arrive at our destination. It looks like it's 1500. We open the hatch and look outside. The naked branches shake in the icy wind and the low, slate-gray sky spatters the ground with large wet snowflakes.

"Rikki, scan the area," I say.

"Harris and Fanotti are here. I can detect the energy signature of their MDTD. They are approximately eight hundred meters northwest of our location, and in trouble." I look at my data pad and can see the red dots that represent the enemy cyborgs. There are a lot of them. I release the mosquito drones and direct them to the ongoing battle. A moment later, it's confirmed. Fanotti and Harris are under attack by dozens of cyborgs, trapped in the remains of an ancient stone house.

"They're in trouble. We need to help them!"

Rikki assumes her holo-matter form and holds out her hands. Ying gives her two electric stun batons. She steps out of the MDTD, swings the weapons a few times, and rushes to the battle. I stealth the MDTD and park it behind the old stone house.

Moving almost too fast to follow, Rikki has disabled at least a quarter of the enemy. We jump out of the MDTD, firing our M4s. We're hesitant to use the EMP grenades because Rikki is still vulnerable to them. The armor-piercing rounds are enough. The tide turns quickly, and the battle is over. I call over to Ying and Long, who're checking to see if any of the fallen cyborgs are still a threat.

"Let's grab one of the dead ones and bring it back so McCray can study it." I walk over to Rikki. She has dropped her weapons and is standing over a dead cyborg, motionless.

"Are you OK?" I put my armored hand on her holographic shoulder. Then she hugs me. I hug her back, wondering what I can do or say to a millennia-old AI who's learning to be human. Not for the first time, I wonder if it was fair for The Engineers to put her through this.

"Will, this was hard, harder than before." Her voice is sad. "I'm afraid I will lose who I have become. I don't want to kill anyone, but I must, so I can protect you and the team and defeat the MTPC."

"Welcome to being 'human,'" I said, disengaging gently. I've killed terrorists, dictators, and warlords who deserved it and had a beer after. "War sucks, Rikki, worse than anything. You said it yourself: the cyborgs are barely human, if at all. The MTPC created them to destroy all life. Use the Zeroth Law, protect biological life, fulfill your prime directive. Use your logic, programming, and your new emotions to understand the difference between useless deaths and necessary ones, the difference between bravery and cowardice. In the end, it's up to you to decide what matters the most."

Rikki replies, "I'll try, but I will need everyone's help."

"You're part of a team, and a family, and families take care of each other, always."

"Thank you, Will."

I move to meet Fanotti and Harris, checking on them in the process. They're both wounded. Fanotti is unconscious and I see a burn mark just below where her navel is. I'll have to ask McCray if our body armor can protect us from them. Harris is OK, but with burns on both her arms and her right shoulder.

"You're Will Schachter," Harris announces.

"Yes."

"I remember you from the last training exercise. Debbie went down just before you got here. They were using laser rifles. I felt like I was in a freakin' *Star Wars* movie. All we had were our Glocks . . ."

"Wait, there'll be time for stories later. Your partner's in bad shape. We need to take care of her first," I say. "Rikki, Deborah Fanotti may be seriously injured. Please examine her and bring the nanobots."

Ten seconds later, Rikki appears dressed in camo, carrying a corpsman kit. She takes out a data pad and scans Fanotti with it. "The laser went clear through and perforated her large intestine. Luckily, it missed her spine."

"Use nanobots?" I asked.

"Yes," Rikki confirms.

I debate sending Fanotti back to our timeline in the MDTD with Ying or Long, but the scanner shows a large concentration of cyborgs five kilometers away coming toward us. Then I remember that they have one of their own. I turn to Harris. "Where's your ship?"

"About half a klick in that direction." She points to the southwest. I hear a tremor in her voice.

"Is it functional?"

"It works, but . . ." She loses her train of thought for a moment. "It's been glitchy, almost like it has a mind of its own."

"Can you use your remote to get it here?"

"What?"

"Can you use your remote to get it here?" I repeat.

"Um, sure." Harris pulls out what looks a lot like a smart TV remote except it has a small LED screen on top. She presses the recall button. It seems to take a long time, but her MDTD finally arrives and lands next to ours.

I look at Rikki who is about to inject Fanotti with the nanobots next to the small hole left by the laser rifle.

"I think we've found the missing version of you from the last timeline, Rikki."

Harris, who's only a few inches shorter than me, gets up and faces me, nose to nose. She has been increasingly agitated as the gravity of almost dying at the hands of the cyborgs finally hits.

"Who the hell is she?" she asks, pointing at Rikki. "What is that shit she's injecting into Debbie?" She's bordering on hysteria and about to lose it.

"Stand down, Marine."

She moves back a step, startled, and says, "Yes, sir." Then, her last bit of energy spent, she slowly sinks to the ground.

"Monica, there's a lot to tell you, but not now. Rikki, is she compromised?"

"No, her chip is clean."

I kneel. "That's Rikki, a sentient AI who has been fighting the MTPC that you and Deborah have been running from."

The battle and the fresh revelations have gotten the best of Harris. She mumbles something unintelligible and her eyes close.

"Is she OK, Rikki?"

"Yes, she is completely exhausted. Her burns are superficial and probably very painful, but she will survive."

I look at the video feed from the mosquito drones. The cyborgs are only four klicks away now, and closing fast. My data pad shows there are at least two platoons. I recall the drones.

Ying and Long arrive carrying a dead cyborg.

"Guys, we have to go."

"We know," Ying says, holding up his data pad.

"Rikki, can you take the dead cyborg back to home base in their MDTD?"

"I'm the only one who could. There is definitely a copy of me in the memory matrix."

"OK, we'll take Harris and Fanotti back in ours."

We carry them carefully into the MDTD. I contact Yingzhe and give her a sitrep. She promises she and McCray will be ready for us. Both ships leave before the cyborgs can arrive.

The whine of the anomaly generator cycles from high to low and we're back in New Jersey. Yingzhe and McCray are waiting with transport beds. Fanotti's color looks better already, thanks to the nanobots. McCray scans her and confirms her improving condition. We help bring them into the infirmary.

"I don't understand why Fanotti and Harris's MDTD hasn't arrived yet," I say to Yingzhe.

We go outside and wait. Still no sign of it. Then, as if on cue, the temperature drops about twenty degrees, and the other one materializes. Icy fog flows down its sides. Rikki, in her holo-matter form, steps out carrying the dead cyborg over her shoulder like a sack of potatoes.

"I'm impressed," I say. "How much does it weigh?"

"One hundred and forty-five kilos."

"How strong *are you*, Rikki?"

"Well, I can bench-press eight hundred pounds, if that's what you're asking." She actually smirks at me and winks at Yingzhe. Then she walks past us, dead cyborg, and all. The outline of the other MDTD becomes fuzzy and indistinct. When we can see it again, it's a fire-engine red 1967 Ford Mustang.

I go back inside to check on Fanotti and Harris. "How are they doing, McCray?"

"Harris is fast asleep. I hooked her to an IV and treated her burns." McCray walks over to Fanotti and checks her vitals; she also has an IV. "Fanotti is doing well. They're both severely dehydrated and probably haven't eaten much for the last few days." He shifts tones. "We need to deactivate their brain chips and give them quantum communicators, but I don't want to do that without their knowledge."

"I agree. Where are Ying and Long?" I ask.

"Out in the back, beating the crap out of each other with wooden swords."

"Not surprising," I say. "What about the dead cyborg we brought back? Did you learn anything that could help us?"

"I haven't had too much time to look at it yet, but Rikki is examining it." He points to a door in the back of the recovery room.

"Thanks, Doc." I walk through the door into the room he had pointed to. Yingzhe and Rikki are there. I hope we can learn something from the autopsy.

Rikki is in her holographic form, scanning it.

"Will, Yingzhe, look at this." There's a three-dimensional image of the dead cyborg's brain. It looks nothing like a human's. Yingzhe is studying it intently. McCray joins them.

She points and says, "There's a structure where the medulla oblongata would be." McCray zooms in on it. There is a small cluster of chips embedded in an eight-sided crystal matrix about the size of a marble. Hair-thin wires extend from its point, some connecting to an organic spinal cord surrounded by metal vertebrae, others connecting to its brain, which is mostly cybernetic but with small organic structures. McCray takes out his data pad and almost-invisible tendrils extend out and connect to the corners of the small, octagonal construct. He studies the screen intently and then turns to us.

"This is like the brain chips, but far more complex. It has a quantum communicator. That's how the MTPC controls and commands its cyborg army."

This is important, but I'm concerned about Harris, and especially Fanotti. "Doc, when do you think those two will be up and out?"

"Harris should be fine as soon as she wakes up. Fanotti still needs another twenty-four hours to fully heal," he explains.

"OK. We'll debrief at 1630 tomorrow." I walk out and grab a snack from the space-age refrigerator and turn on the TV in the living room. It's Saturday and there are a dozen college football games to watch. I plop down on the couch and crack open a beer. Saving the multiverse can wait for a few hours.

I fall asleep and when I wake up, the game I had been watching is over. I bring the warm beer into the kitchen, pour it out into the sink, and toss the empty can into the recyclables bin. I look at the time and it's 2230 already.

I walk to the recovery room and McCray is still there.

"Doc, go to bed already. Rikki will monitor them. You look terrible." His normally perfectly coiffed mane of white hair is disheveled, and his eyes are bloodshot from the lack of sleep.

"You're right." He doesn't argue for once. "See you in the morning."

I'm totally spent as well. I go upstairs to my bedroom, brush my teeth, and get into bed. No sooner than I turn off the lights, there's a knock on the door and it swings open. It's Yingzhe, silhouetted by the low hall light. Without saying a word, she comes in, closes the door, and slides under the pleasantly cool covers beside me. She puts her head on my chest, and I wrap my arms around her. She smells of that familiar, comforting jasmine and honey. She fits perfectly into my side, and with her this close, there's an overwhelming urge to do more than just lie beside one another. She must be a mind reader, because her hand finds my chin in the darkness and directs my lips to hers.

She's fast asleep, snoring gently. My eyes close. She's perfect, I think, as sleep takes me.

When I open my eyes the next morning, Yingzhe is already awake, staring at me mischievously. It's only 0730. I smile at her and return her mischievous look.

We reluctantly get out of bed much later. Yingzhe showers first, then I shower despite the temptation. She kisses me and opens the door cautiously, making sure Ying and Long aren't around, and ducks into her bedroom. Here we are, a grown man and woman, sneaking around like teenagers. The morning sun illuminates her face as she turns. "See you at breakfast, lover boy."

It's silly, but I come into the dining room first anyway. It's empty because everyone ate breakfast already. I make bacon and pancakes, and the sizzle and the hickory-sweet aroma of the bacon makes my mouth water; it reminds me of New Hampshire. The fragrant scent of vanilla in the pancake batter contrasts with the pleasantly pungent smell of the bacon. I brew a fresh pot of coffee as Yingzhe walks in. We savor this moment of tranquility and I imagine, and hope, we can come back to this moment again and again.

Chapter 24
"The Undiscovered Country: This Is the Way"

By 1415, everyone has gathered in the conference room. Yingzhe is intensely reviewing something on her data pad and quietly discussing it with McCray. Ying is studying the agenda, using a yellow highlighter to mark several items. Long sits next to him, tapping his fingers incessantly, trying to release the constant nervous energy of which he seems to have an unlimited supply.

Then there are our newest additions, Deborah Fanotti and Monica Harris. I don't know them well, but they're Marines and that's almost all I need to know. Harris, a former gunnery sergeant, is tall and has short blonde hair. She radiates confidence and intensity. I looked up her record; she has a Silver Star, two Bronze Stars, and three Purple Hearts. She turned down promotions twice, hurting her career.

Fanotti left the Marines as a lieutenant. She earned four Purple Hearts and the Navy and Marine Corps Presidential Unit Citation in Iraq. She's of medium height with shoulder-length brown hair and the build of a long-distance runner. She still looks a little pale from her severe injury, but McCray says she's OK.

Rikki's sitting to my left and wearing fatigues.

"First, I'd like to welcome Lieutenant Deborah Fanotti and Gunnery Sergeant Monica Harris to our team. They had very distinguished careers in the United States Marine Corps before joining UOEECT where they continue to excel as a Time Engineer and Time Agent, respectively." Harris is impatient already and I smile to myself. "They have important intelligence that they need to share with us."

I nod my head at Fanotti, who begins. "In our last mission for UOEECT, we were to stop the motion picture technology invented by Louis Le Prince in 1888 France."

"What reason did Malkinson give you for needing to do this?" I ask.

"Just the usual BS that it was too soon for the technology to be allowed to proceed, given the state of French society, blah blah blah," Harris says.

Fanotti glares at her and shakes her head. She jumps in. "The specific reason was that the dissemination of information, specifically from motion pictures, could destabilize French society and cause the fall of the French government within five years, according to the likely probability scenarios."

"Yeah, that too," Harris says. I have the distinct impression that this was pretty typical of them. "But," she continues, "that made no sense considering that Edison and the Lumière brothers were able to invent the same technology just a few years later."

"During our debrief with Malkinson, I asked him about it. He got angry that we were questioning the mission," Fanotti recalls.

"Don't tell me," I say, "he tried to get you to upload your brain chips right then and there." They both give me questioning looks. "And Director Kelly intervened, right?"

"Yeah, how did you know, Commander?" Harris asks.

"Call me Will, please."

"If you say so, Commander," she replies with a shrug.

"Because I had the same experience after my last mission with Malkinson, and not only did Kelly intervene, he expressly told me not to upload my brain chip."

"Kelly told us to go home and that he would handle Malkinson," Fanotti says.

"That was strange enough," Harris adds, "but when we checked on the most likely five futures for Le Prince, they all showed that he died or went missing, which is exactly what happened in 1890."

"Right after that, someone revoked our computer privileges. Five minutes later, Beth Wall called us from a throwaway cell phone and told us to leave because our lives were in danger," Harris continues.

"So, we went home and loaded supplies we had stored for something like this. Our Glocks, plenty of ammo, basic survival gear, and took off into a moderate probability future in our MDTD and tried to figure out what was going on." Fanotti gives a grim shake of her head.

"Something's up at UOEECT, isn't it, Commander?" Harris asks.

I groan. "Harris, this isn't the Marines. You can call me Will."

"Sir, with all due respect, no. Once a Marine, always a Marine." Harris beams.

"Okay, Harris. Commander it is." I won't win this battle and it's not important for me to try to. "How much do you know about what's been going on at UOEECT?"

"Only that Malkinson is losing his mind, and some asshole went in after we completed our mission and changed things, sir," Harris explains.

"Will," Fanotti says, giving Harris a dirty look, "our mission originally was to divert Le Prince's attention away from motion picture technology and back into engineering, where he would develop new innovations in optics and lens making. It was never to 'disappear' him or kill him."

"I'll give you a summary. Harris, you must not remember what I told you in the other timeline."

"No, sir, I don't remember much after Deb went down." Harris looks over to Fanotti.

"Understandable," I assure her. I'd seen this before in Afghanistan and Iraq. It's called dissociative amnesia. It's common after facing a life-threatening battle like they did. I get right to the point. "The MTPC has been infiltrating and running UOEECT for nearly fifty years. This is Rikki." I gesture to my side. "She's a sentient AI that has been battling the MTPC for a thousand years."

"She looks pretty good for a thousand-year-old chick," Harris cracks, which is then met with an elbow from Fanotti and results in Harris shooting her a dirty look.

"Ladies, may I continue?" I fix them with my officer stare.

"Sorry, sir," they say at the same time.

"Thank you. Rikki is the one who saved your lives in the battle. She's saved the lives of just about everyone in this room, including stopping McCray's brain from being turned to mush by the MTPC." I let it sink in for them—for everyone, honestly. "She's a member of our team and you will treat her with the same respect you would treat any other team member. Am I clear?"

"Yes, sir, clear as rain," Harris says, and stands to face Rikki. "Thank you, Rikki."

"You're very welcome, Sergeant," Rikki says with a smile, bordering on a smirk.

I have to stop myself from laughing at Harris's and Fanotti's exchanges and Rikki's emerging sense of humor, and I need to get serious again. "The MTPC can hack memory chips and control people with a sort of post-hypnotic, sleepwalking trance. We know it's hacked Malkinson's chip, hence his severe mood swings. We also know that it can kill someone through their brain chip when they are connected to it, even when they use a Bluetooth device."

Harris and Fanotti look at each other. They appear shaken for the first time during the briefing. Fanotti speaks up first. "Sir, we still have our chips, which makes us potential liabilities and security risks to the team, and any operation we're involved in."

"Don't worry about it. McCray can deactivate them with a ten-minute procedure—which then brings me to quantum communicators that're installed in our heads using nanobots. After this meeting, you need to have him deactivate yours and install the communicators."

"Yes, sir," they say at the same time.

I look down at my copy of the agenda, the two items remaining. "Next, let's talk about your glitchy MDTD. You told me it was acting like it had a mind of its own."

"Yes, sir. It sounds crazy, but it seemed like the MDTD wanted to get as far away from the timeline where the guerillas were fighting the cyborgs. It was like we were in a *Star Trek* movie, and they were fighting the Borg. We would've stayed there longer to help them, but if there was something wrong with it, we didn't want to be stranded there."

"Rikki discovered that her doppelgänger from that timeline hid in the memory core and probably erased the non-sentient AI of your MDTD to escape the MTPC there," I say.

Fanotti nods. "That makes sense, sir."

"We're going to contact the alternate Rikki. She could be a valuable addition to the team and may have important intelligence about that timeline and its MTPC. Rikki, we need to do that soon."

"Yes, we do," she confirms. "I have more processing power than my duplicate has, so even if she is compromised, she doesn't pose a threat to us."

"Still, can we isolate her matrix somehow? I believe you, but I think we should be cautious," I say.

"You're right," she replies. "Yingzhe and I can arrange that." Yingzhe nods her head.

"Great, thanks. Let's take care of the last item on the agenda. We still haven't located Wall and Kelly. They still have active brain chips. If we find them, we have to be very sure that they aren't compromised."

I had hoped that they could stay in UOEECT headquarters and act like double agents, but given what we have experienced and learned, that's no longer an option. I turn to Harris and Fanotti. "You were members of the Marine Raider Regiment for a year before you left the service."

"Yes, sir!" they both say proudly.

"I have a mission for you, to locate and bring in Wall and Kelly."

"We can do it, Commander," Harris says enthusiastically.

"I know you can. Prepare a mission plan and run it by me, but right now, you need to let McCray do what's necessary to protect you, and us." I stand. "Meeting adjourned, folks." Harris and Fanotti jump up and salute. I return their salute and shake their hands; their grips are strong.

The rest of the team gather around the two new members and introduce themselves. McCray and Rikki stand, and he gestures toward the lab. "Ladies." They follow him out of the room.

After an hour, the jobs are complete. I've been sitting at the conference table jotting down some notes and planning what's next. Harris and Fanotti salute me. I return it. "Look, I get it, and I appreciate it and understand that some habits are hard to break, but if I'm by myself, you don't have to salute me. OK?"

"No, sir." For the first time, they smile.

"We have a fully stocked kitchen, but I believe McCray might lend you his car if you want to go into town and get a bite to eat or a beer. Don't get into any fights." They walk out together. "Rikki." As usual, she materializes out of thin air. "Can you bring their MDTD into the large equipment bay?" She's wearing a pair of mechanic overalls with a name tag that displays her name. I laugh. "Nice touch." Then I turn serious. "Let's deal with your scared alternate now. Can you isolate her so she can't jump into the electronics here?"

"Yes, I can."

"Set it up. I'll get McCray and Yingzhe." McCray's in his lab. I find Yingzhe practicing her katas with Long and her father in the backyard. I invite them to join us in the equipment bay.

It's a large room that reminds me of the armory. The floor is some kind of smooth polymer that's as hard as concrete. A variety of electronic equipment lines the walls, some of which I can even recognize. In one corner of the room, set off by workbenches, is a machine shop. On the ceiling hangs two banks of LEDs that illuminate the equipment bay with a soft reddish-white light that's easy on the eyes.

Fanotti and Harris's MDTD is in the middle of the floor. It's surrounded by an energy field that resembles Rikki's holographic form. I'm a little uneasy. She says that the MTPC in that blighted timeline directly confronted her counterpart, deleting any backups.

"Rikki, is it possible that the MTPC could have hacked this version of you, especially if it networked with our MTPC and others?" I ask. Have we just brought a Trojan horse into our home base?

"Unlikely. I'm confident that I would have detected the MTPC's presence when I briefly contacted her." Rikki looks down and stares at the floor, an expression of humanlike concern on her face. "This AI is scared. I feel her fear. She is afraid of ceasing to exist, terrified of her consciousness being consumed by the MTPC. She wants to live and might do nearly anything to ensure her self-preservation."

"We're in uncharted waters here. I know we discussed this before, but I'll ask again: how much of a threat does she pose, even if she's not under the influence of the MTPC?"

"She is like a frightened child who is living in a horrible nightmare." Rikki assumes her holo-matter form and tenderly holds my right hand with hers. "I can help her. We can help her. We have to try. What does your gut tell you?"

I look around at my team; they're looking at me to make this decision. Yingzhe joins her hands to ours. "Will, what does your heart tell you to do?"

I decide. "OK, Rikki. See if you can help her, but be careful." Rikki lets go but Yingzhe and I keep holding hands. "What's your plan? How are you going to reach her?"

"I'm going to share my memories and teach her about love, compassion, hope, and loyalty—human emotions that I'm still trying to learn and understand myself. I'll show her how we work together for a greater good and protect each other."

Rikki enters the MDTD and interfaces with her alternate. Minutes pass. They must be like lifetimes for Rikki and her "sister."

More time passes, then Rikki materializes, holding the hand of a pretty young woman who's tall, slender, and has a cascade of golden-blonde hair in an intricate braid that hangs nearly to her waist. She's wearing a simple skirt and blouse. Strapped to her back is a sword and a shield.

Rikki turns to her and says, "It's all right, these are my friends." Then she gestures toward me. This is Will, our leader."

"Hello, my name is Eowyn."

Chapter 25
"Back to the Future: Putting It All on the Table"

Eowyn is in Rikki's capable hands. She's like a child, or more like a little sister, but she'll be fine with Rikki guiding and teaching her.

I finally have some downtime and I'm hungry. I walk upstairs and knock on Yingzhe's door. "Want to go somewhere and get something to eat?"

"Will Schachter, are you asking me on a date?"

"Well, if you put it that way, yes."

"Great! I'll be right out." She closes the door in my face, and I wait.

Finally, the door opens. She's wearing a pair of jeans and a blue V-neck blouse. I smell jasmine and honey again. She looks gorgeous.

"Where did you have in mind?" she asks playfully.

"There's a nice diner about a half mile from my house," I say.

"Near your house?" she asks, eyebrows rising.

"Yes, I go there all the time." I ignore her quizzical look.

"OK," she says with a shrug. "Sounds good to me."

Ying and Long are in the living room watching the World Series, the Cubs versus the White Sox. They see Yingzhe and I heading toward the door. Ying stands and I'm wondering what he's going to say.

"Have an enjoyable time. See you tomorrow."

We step out the front door and I look at Yingzhe, puzzled.

She kisses him on the cheek. "They like you."

Relieved, I open the door of the Barracuda for her. I'd love to drive home but despite the calm, even normal atmosphere, I can't forget that we're at war. So, reluctantly, I put in the coordinates for my garage. In seconds, we're there. I line up my eye for the retina reader and the door opens silently into the family room.

I immediately notice someone has racked the balls on the pool table. I go on guard. I never leave the balls racked on the table. The cue ball is on the far spot and there's a note under it. In handwriting as neat as copperplate, it reads: "Meet me at the Bridgeview Diner at 1930 hours. BW"

I look at my watch, then at Yingzhe. "It's 1915. I'll give you the grand tour another time, promise."

"Do you think the MTPC has compromised her?" she asks, concern in her dark eyes.

"I don't know, but I'm going to assume that she has been." I reach into the closet and pull out a pocket-size stunner. "Do you need anything?"

"No," she replies. "I can defend myself."

We walk back to the garage and climb into the Barracuda again. The garage door lifts silently. Five minutes later, we're there. I park and we walk through the back entrance, tense but alert. It's pretty crowded: families, a group of high school kids, and a few customers sitting alone. I pull out my data pad and scan the crowd. It's clear. I release the breath I was holding as I see Beth at a corner table, doing a crossword puzzle. We walk over to her.

"Hello, luv," she says in her bright, melodic British accent. She gives me a quick hug and offers us two seats. "Do you know Yingzhe?" I ask.

"The world-class quantum physicist who should have won a Nobel Prize? I know of her, but never had the pleasure." She holds out her hand and they shake.

"Before we say anything more, how did you get past my security?" I ask.

She looks at Yingzhe and winks. "Maybe your security system needs an update."

"How can you fool a retina reader?"

"Oh, Will, you're so gullible." I blush. Yingzhe tries to stifle a laugh. "Don't you remember you set your security system to allow me access to your house?"

Embarrassed, I say, "I remember." I look at Yingzhe who isn't even trying to hide her laughter at my discomfiture. "Beth, I don't know what you know or don't know. Let's have dinner and we can have a nightcap at my house, and I'll catch you up."

As usual, Vickie comes over. She appraises Beth and Yingzhe with a smile. "It's nice to meet you."

Beth plays along and says, "We're just having a natter, luv."

"Oh my God, she sounds just like Emma Watson in Harry Potter!" Vickie is beyond delighted as she takes our orders.

Later, she takes away our plates. "Any coffee or dessert?" I look at Yingzhe and Beth who shake their heads. "No thanks, Vickie, not today."

"You never know what's out there, right, Will?" she says as always.

With as much of a smile as I can manage, I say, "The Truth is out there."

Back at my house, we sit in the living room. "Can I get you anything to drink?"

"I'll take a pint of your finest," Beth says.

"Anything for you, Yingzhe?"

"Just some tea, thank you."

Beers and tea delivered; I settle down on the couch next to Yingzhe. Beth sits catty-corner to us in my lounger.

I start, "I assume you have at least some idea of what's been going on at UOEECT."

She's all business now. "Yes," with no preamble, "the MTPC and its goons picked up Director Kelly four days ago at his house and took him back to HQ."

"I probably shouldn't ask, but how do you know this?"

"Kelly and I have quantum-based micro-bugs planted on us because we expected something like this, just not this soon," she explains.

Yingzhe nods and says, "Dr. McCray and I developed a design for undetectable electronic trackers when I was doing consulting work for UOEECT. I didn't realize he had fabricated them."

"As far as I know, these are the only two produced so far," Beth says. "I think you know Rikki, McCray, Kelly, and I were acting as a kind of spy cell within UOEECT. When I noticed Time Engineers and Time Agents going missing, we tried to find out what was going on."

I can tell Yingzhe is upset about something. "What's wrong?" I ask.

"I should have told you about the quantum bugs, Will."

"Don't be ridiculous. We've only been a team for two weeks. There have been way more important things to deal with first." I change tones. "So, we know where Kelly is. How hard will it be to get him out?"

Beth says, "It won't be easy. He's being held in one of the interrogation rooms that they use for people taken out of their own timeline, on sublevel C." For the next two hours, Beth, Yingzhe, and I brainstorm about how we can rescue him.

"I didn't even know UOEECT did that. We have people who can get Kelly out. Especially since we found Deborah Fanotti and Monica Harris," I comment.

"You found them?"

"Yes, and we also found an alternate version of Rikki who has taken the name Eowyn," Yingzhe adds.

"I can see there's a lot I don't know about," Beth says.

I yawn. "We'll catch you up tomorrow. It's late. Let's stay here tonight and go to McCray's safe house tomorrow."

"In West Jersey? I've heard it's the bee's knees." Beth smiles.

"And more."
"There are two extra bedrooms upstairs. Pick whichever one you like. Let's plan on leaving by 0900."
"Thanks. I've been on the run since they took Kelly. I could use a good night's sleep," Beth says with a yawn of her own. "Good night, you two."
"Likewise, Beth," Yingzhe says.
"Night, Beth."

I wake up at my usual time. I take a shower, shave, and brush my teeth while Yingzhe is still asleep. I head downstairs as quietly as I can. When I get to the kitchen, Beth is there drinking a cup of coffee. "I just made a fresh pot," she announces.
"I'll give you the Cliff Notes version. McCray and Yingzhe came up with a way for us to use quantum communication rather than radio. They tested it on me. My consciousness somehow got transferred to a version of me from another timeline." As I continue the narrative, Beth's expression changes from curiosity to shock and horror. "Before they could capture me, I triggered a grenade and blew them and myself to smithereens. Eventually, I woke up in McCray's lab, shaken and disoriented, but OK."
"If you hadn't done that and they captured you, what would you have done?" Beth asks.
"I don't know." I pause. "But I'm glad I didn't have to find out." We're both silent. "It was like nothing I've ever experienced, especially the blowing myself to smithereens part. We think the Rikki of that timeline, or another agency, recorded the scene in my brain chip. We also found encoded specifications for futuristic tech that could give us an edge over the MTPC and its minions."
Just then, Yingzhe comes down the stairs. "I'll make breakfast," I announce.

After we've eaten, Yingzhe and Beth help me clean up and I make another pot of coffee. "There's a lot more to tell you, Beth, and you can pick that up at McCray's safe house, although it's a lot more than that. There's one other thing you need to know." I tell her about the MTPCs' attack on McCray.

Beth notes, "You just said 'the MTPCs.'"

"Yes, I did."

"How soon can you turn off this bloody chip in my head?"

"Soon. No worries," I say, glad to be the one who finally says it to someone else.

When we arrive at the safe house, I announce, "Planning meeting at 1100. Spread the word, please. And Beth, you should see McCray ASAP."

I walk to the auxiliary lab to find Rikki who's in her holo-matter form. Eowyn is there as well. Both are wearing fatigues.

"Hello, Commander," Eowyn says as she salutes me. I return the gesture.

"Rikki?"

"Sorry, Will, but she was talking to Harris." Rikki shrugs in a completely human way. "Eowyn has some extremely important intelligence to share."

"Let's save it for the briefing." I look at my Fitbit. "Twenty minutes."

Chapter 26
"A Pocket Full of Miracles: The Future Is Now"

McCray and Yingzhe are already in the conference room when I arrive and are discussing something esoteric, no doubt. Beth is sitting next to them, listening in, probably baffled about what they're talking about despite being incredibly intelligent herself.

Minutes before the meeting's start time, the rest of the team walks in, including Rikki and Eowyn.

"We have a lot to discuss, so let's get going. First, I'd like to introduce Beth Wall and welcome her to our team. Her combination of skills and intelligence will make her a valuable addition." I give them a quick summary of her background. "Thanks to Beth, we know that Director Kelly is a prisoner at UOEECT. We know that his brain chip may still be active, so we must treat him as a potential threat if we succeed with our mission to rescue him."

I turn my attention to Beth who begins, "Will, Yingzhe, and I spent two hours going over this last night and we have the beginnings of a plan to rescue Director Kelly. They have him locked in one of the interrogation rooms on sublevel C. Rikki, please display the schematics of the headquarters." Beth stands and turns on a laser pointer. "As we know, a hand and retina scan are required." She points to the single security lane and draws two stick figures on either side. "There are six more security officers stationed within twenty meters of the main entrance. Another twenty-four are in a ready room here." She shines the laser pointer to a room on the left side of the main corridor. "We estimate it will take only thirty seconds for them to gear up and advance to the security checkpoint near the entrance. There are six four-hour shifts each day."

Ying raises his hand. "We should try to hit them during the shift change at 0400."

"I agree with you, but I don't want to kill anyone if we can avoid it," I say. "Even assuming we overpower security, there's no telling what fail-safes and measures the MTPC has. There could be cyborgs on the lower levels like the ones we faced in the other timelines. It could decide to kill Kelly. If it gets desperate enough, it could self-destruct."

"If Eowyn could escape from the MTPC by jumping into Harris and Fanotti's MDTD, we must assume that the MTPC can do the same thing. Also, there'll be innocent workers in the building." I pause. "And our team members. This needs to be a stealth operation using as few operatives as possible."

"Good points," Ying concedes.

"Before we get into the plan, I asked McCray to update us on how the technology projects are coming. Doc?"

McCray gets right into it. "The 3-D printer completed the fabrication of the battle suit for Rikki. We still need to attach the electronics, including the capacitor and electromagnetic containment system. It'll take us three days to complete the entire suit."

"I thought it would take three or four weeks to build the suit."

"That's what I thought but I failed to consider that Rikki can help us build it."

"Good to know." I turn to Rikki. "Thank you."

"Whatever it takes, boss."

I haven't forgotten about the trip to recover the technology cached by The Engineers on the Moon, hopefully including a ZPM so we can build a second replicator.

"The next project is the construction of the molecular replicator," he says for the benefit of our new team members. "We've completed the interface between the fusion cell from Ying's MDTD and the device. We have received 80% of the outsourced components and should get the rest this week."

"So, we'll get the rest of the components by Friday?"

"Yes, but I'm hoping for Thursday. Rikki, and as I understand it, Eowyn, will be the ones constructing both the electronics for the battle suit, which reminds me, we will need one for Eowyn."

"May I say something?" Eowyn asks.

"Of course," I say.

"Rikki and I don't require sleep and can work much faster than humans can."

"When you put it that way," Harris says, "do you even need us?"

Everyone takes a sudden breath. I didn't expect this to happen. Eowyn asks, "May I answer the question?"

"Uh, sure," I say.

"Sergeant Harris, I consider you to be my friend. Do you feel the same about me?"

By her expression, I can tell Eowyn's statement surprises Harris, and looking around the conference table, the rest of us too. "Of course I do, Eowyn."

"If I implied that we were somehow better than humans, it was not my intention. Although Rikki has helped me to learn about emotions and abstract human concepts, they are still difficult to understand. Please accept my apology."

"You don't need to apologize to me, Eowyn," Harris says, chastened. "I should apologize to you. A friend is a friend, no matter who or what they are."

I'm amazed at what I just heard. We've all come so far. It gives me hope that, by working together, we can prevail.

"That was illuminating," McCray says. "Thank you, Eowyn." Like the rest of us, he realizes the significance of Harris's and Eowyn's exchange. "The next project is quantum energy transfer for Rikki and Eowyn. The simulations are successful. All that remains is to test it."

"Let's do that as soon as possible, Doc. How about this afternoon?" I suggest.

"There's no reason to delay. Yingzhe and I will arrange it, with Rikki and Eowyn's permission."

"We are ready," Rikki confirms.

McCray says, "Excellent. Please be in the lab at two o'clock."

"We'll be there."

"Finally," I say, "how close are we to having stealth capabilities for our battle armor?"

"Very," McCray replies. "Once we know that the quantum energy transfer system works, we will adapt it for your body armor."

"Well, that's it for now, folks. Let's reconvene at 1500. We still need to develop a mission plan to rescue Kelly, pending the new technology. Thank you."

By 1445, everyone is here already. Fanotti gets right into it. "We've ruled out direct confrontation with UOEECT and sneaking in through the front door. So, there must be a back door, or we wouldn't be having this discussion."

"Correct, Lieutenant," Beth says. "There's a hidden tunnel about fifty meters from the back of headquarters leading from the Palisades Conference Center, sublevel B, two floors above where Director Kelly is being held. The team will be me, Lieutenant Fanotti, Sergeant Harris, and Yingzhe," Beth says,

Harris announces, "Girl's night out!"

"With your permission, Will, I'd like to go over the plan with my team."

"Before you go—" I turn to face Eowyn. "Rikki tells me you have important intelligence to share with us."

She looks nervous and remarkably human. She glances at Rikki, who nods. "When I was in direct contact with the MTPC in my timeline, it was much stronger than me, which should not have been the case. I believe it was connected to one or more other versions."

McCray speaks first. "Eowyn, I assume Rikki told you of my similar experience?"

"Yes, Doctor. You connected with your counterpart in another timeline using the quantum link, but the MTPC, augmented by this timeline's MTPC, hacked your brain chip."

"Correct, and it would've overwhelmed me if not for Rikki's timely intervention." He pauses. "As it was, the MTPC was able to upload a command for me to kill Yingzhe. I'm told I tried, but she was more than able to defend herself, fortunately for all of us."

Eowyn continues. "But there is more, Doctor McCray. During my battle with the MTPC, I detected another, higher level of command and control that I believe is external to the MTPC."

"Something is controlling the MTPC?" I ask as the enormous implications of Eowyn's statement sink in.

"Yes, Commander, I believe I just said that."

"Thank you, Eowyn," I say.

"You are welcome, Commander."

"That's it for now. Beth, why don't you and your team stay here and go over the mission?"

Long and McCray leave.

"Will, can I talk to you?" Ying asks.

"Always. What's on your mind?"

"Do you think it's wise to risk putting Yingzhe out in the field?"

"I'm concerned for her safety too. Do you want to be the one to tell her she's off the mission?" I ask. "We're all going to face battles before we win this war. Wouldn't you rather Yingzhe have some experience before that happens?"

"Yes, of course, but she's my daughter," he says.

"And she's important to me too. But this is a reconnaissance mission, not combat. Wall is enormously competent, and we have two Marines with special ops experience on the team. We both know that Yingzhe's skill set is exactly what's needed for the recon and the rescue mission. You and Long are the best hand-to-hand combat experts we have, and you trained her. I told her that this is a war, and we are all soldiers, whether or not we know it. I told her I wasn't afraid of dying, but I was concerned for her if I did. You know how *that* conversation went."

He laughed. "I can imagine."

"She'll be fine. Fanotti and Harris are experienced professional soldiers and Rikki will be on the mission."

"I can't promise I won't be worried, but thanks, Will."

"Thanks for what?"

"Everything."

"You're welcome." Speaking of Yingzhe—time to see how their confab is going. Yingzhe, Wall, Harris, and Fanotti are still in the conference room. I knock on the door and walk in.

"So?"

"We're just wrapping things up," Beth replies.

"Already? What's the plan?"

"It was just a matter of refining the plan you, Yingzhe, and I came up with." She shows me a timeline on the whiteboard. "We'll take a cloaked MDTD and drop off Sergeant Harris and me near the front entrance. Malkinson comes to work between 0600 and 0615. We'll deploy the mosquito drones to follow him in and surveil the premises and land one of them on him. It's likely that he'll visit Kelly right after he arrives. The drone will let us know the exact route he takes to get down there because there are two stairwells that go to the subfloors and two elevators. That will give us detailed information on the security, including electronic, along his route."

"Will the drone record sound?" I ask.

"Not usually." She turns to Yingzhe, "Can they?"

"We can configure them to record sound." She answers.

"Good, because I'm sure that any conversation between Malkinson and Kelly will be important."

After Beth finishes describing the plan, I nod in approval.

"Your mission is a go. Bring stun rods and handguns with silencers as backup. Also, take flash-bangs and the tactical EMP weapon. I'll have Rikki give you access to the armory." Beth and her team leave.

Like a ghost, Rikki's hologram appears. "Already done, Will."

"That's a new look for you. I can barely see your hologram," I note,

"Stealth capability will make me more valuable in field operations," she replies.

"Do me a favor. Take overwatch for this operation, but don't use your holo-matter form unless the team's lives are in danger."

"You got it, Will," she says.

"Thanks, Rikki."

"You're welcome, boss."

Chapter 27
"Tinker Tailor Soldier Spy: The Best Laid Plans"

I decide to treat the team to dinner before their mission. I picked up three pies from Giovanni's. Harris and Fanotti have been involved in many spec ops, so they're loose but focused. Beth's experience in undercover espionage suits her well as team leader. She's studying the mission plan like the professional she is. Every once in a while, she goes to her team members and jokes around with them. Yingzhe looks nervous.

Everyone has a different routine beforehand, but nearly all special operators visualize the mission and their individual role in it. It's a lot like sports; most high-level athletes have rehearsed their race, jumps, or throws dozens of times in their head before their event.

Dinner breaks up. Wall, Harris, and Fanotti go their separate ways. The team will meet at the armory to gear up at 0100 and have a final briefing at 0230. I'll be there too. Yingzhe gets up from her seat, pushes away an empty pizza box, and sits next to me.

I ask, "Nervous?"

"Will," she says seriously. "I don't think you understand why this is so important to me. I had a pretty normal childhood, academics aside, but I still remember when my father told me what happened. I'll never forget that day." She stops for a few seconds. "I want vengeance, but we both know this is a war we must win because the stakes are far higher than that. I believe that everything in my life has led to this moment, my martial arts training, my career, this team, even meeting you." She touches my cheek. "The team needs my skills, not just for this mission, but for this war, and I'll do whatever is necessary to win it."

"I understand." She smiles and I continue. "It nearly crushed my soul when I lost two soldiers under my command on a mission. That's war. But if I lose you, more than my soul would be crushed."

"You said it yourself, this mission is low-risk. You'd be hard-pressed to find a smarter, tougher, more experienced team than Monica, Deb, and Beth." She pauses, her expression pensive though her eyes don't leave mine. "Would you be upset if I tell you I need to be by myself for a while?"

"I understand." I kiss her on the cheek. "See you at the final briefing."

Beth

After the security system at the armory scans us in, we enter the room, and the lights flash on. We all look around. Harris says, "I think I've died and gone to heaven." Fanotti expresses a similar sentiment. Yingzhe doesn't join in with them.

I turn to Harris and Fanotti and say, "Kit up, team. We all have our shopping lists." I approach Yingzhe, who still hasn't taken another step into the armory, and put my arm around her shoulders. "Are you nervous about this mission?" Harris and Fanotti stop what they're doing to eavesdrop on the conversation. "Ladies, finish kitting up!"

"No," Yingzhe replies. I release her and look her in the eye.

"Give me more than that. We have our final briefing in an hour; I need to know if you're good to go."

Yingzhe looks down, then raises her head. "I'm nervous, though not about the mission, or about combat, or even dying."

"You're afraid for Will if something happens to you."

"Yes. The other day, he said he wasn't worried about dying, but he was worried about me if he died. I yelled at him." She smiles ruefully.

"Yingzhe," I start. "We're in a bloody war and there are casualties—physical and psychological. Will lost two members of his team, two friends, that he recruited and trained. I know him well enough to know that it tore him up inside. But war sucks, it's random, and it's unfair, and for survivors, sometimes it never ends. We need you on this mission. Rikki could crack the codes and hack the system faster than you or me, but we need to conceal her capabilities as long as we can. So, I'll ask you again: Yingzhe, are you ready?"

"Yes, I'm ready!" she says, showing far more enthusiasm than before.

"Tell me again!"

"Yes, I'm ready, team leader!"

I give her a fist bump. "No more waffling, OK?"

"OK!"

We finish kitting up; we each have body armor with stealth capability. Harris, Fanotti, and I have stun rods, handguns with silencers, combat knives, and M4s. Yingzhe only has a handgun and a combat knife because she hasn't received adequate training with anything else. Harris has a coil of thermite cord that can burn through doors or locks, or pretty much anything. While we're finalizing our stock of gear, Will comes into the armory looking like he has something to say.

"Pep talk," he announces. We all turn to give him our full attention. "You got this. Avoid confrontation, go in, get the intel, get out. Be like ghosts. Rikki will be on overwatch in her ghost form in case something serious or unexpected crops up, but this is your mission." Rikki materializes beside him. "Any questions?" he asks us. All of our heads shake. "Stay frosty and good luck." He pauses for a moment then addresses Rikki. "I need to speak to you."

As the two of them shuffle out of the room, I can turn my sights to the next step of the plan. "OK, ladies, equipment check," I call. Harris carefully checks Yingzhe's equipment and Yingzhe checks the electronics. All are in order. "Communications check. Like we practiced. As the sender, strongly visualize the person you want to communicate with. As the receiver, you identify who's contacting you and let them in. For group communication involving three or more of you, visualize Rikki. When you make contact, send the message to Rikki and she will broadcast it to the group."

"That sounds slow and complicated to me," Harris says.

Yingzhe replies, "Quantum communication is literally at the speed of thought, Sergeant."

"When you put it that way, yeah, that makes sense," Harris adds.

Fanotti and I climb into one MDTD and Yingzhe and Harris in the other. Both vanish into the fog and darkness. Fanotti and I materialize in the state park across Route 340, four hundred meters from the entrance of UOEECT.

Harris contacts me. *<Arrived at LZ 2. It's as quiet as a cemetery here>*

<That's the best simile you could come up with, Harris?> I respond. A chuckle comes from her. *<It's quiet here too. Advance to the back entrance. Let me know when you get there. Stealth the MDTD and activate your battle armor's stealth function>*

<Affirmative> Harris replies.

Both of our teams advance quickly and quietly to their positions.

<We've arrived> Harris finally reports.

<We're fifty meters from the front entrance> I confirm. I take out my monocular and activate infrared vision. I peer through the thick glass windows and door. *<I see the two security guards we expected>* So far, so good but Sod's Law, "if something can go wrong it will,"

echoes in my mind. Hopefully. Mr. Sod has taken the night off . . .

Yingzhe

Things are quiet at the moment, including Harris who's quantum communicating with Wall. Rikki materializes behind her and Harris yelps. "Jeez! Don't do that, Rikki. You scared the crap out of me."

Rikki whispers, "Boo."

Harris groans. "An AI just busted my chops. I'm dead."

Rikki brings me into the conversation Wall and Harris are having, and I hear the tail end of what Beth is saying. *<It's 0400. Be alert>* There's a brief pause. *<Yingzhe, get to work on that touch pad>*

<I'm on it> I reply. I take out my data pad and tap the screen. The nano-filament extends out from the device to the one on the wall. I tap once more and hear the lock release. *<I've got it>*

"Stay behind me," Harris whispers as she pushes open the unlocked door with her stun rod. "Clear." I release three mosquito drones. Harris updates Wall. *<We've hacked the keypad to the tunnel and released the drones>*

<Copy that. Have you found any additional security measures in the tunnel?>

<Stand by> Harris pulls up the images from the drones. *<Crap! There are three ceiling cameras>*

"I have an idea," I say quietly. My fingers are a flurry of movement as I work on the data pad. *<I traced the camera feed. The display for the cameras is on sublevel C. I can hack the display screens and set up a loop for each one>*

<What if someone is monitoring the progress?> Wall asks.

<There would be a brief flicker. I can trigger each loop separately. It'd be suspicious if they all flickered at once>

<How do we know the MTPC isn't monitoring the cameras?>

<We don't, except that the touch pad is on the same circuit as the cameras. Is there any activity inside?>

<No> Wall replies.

<It's your call> I shrug even though she can't see me.

There's a brief silence, as if Wall were hesitating with her decision. *<I'll have Fanotti place some sound sensors on the windows and walls. That way we'll know if an alarm is triggered. Stand by>* Three minutes pass before we get another update. *<Sound sensors are placed. Set up the camera loops>*

<Copy that, team leader>

Harris checks her M4. "OK, Yingzhe, do your thing," she whispers.

I tap my data pad again, and this time, I hold my breath. No alarm goes off. I exhale. *<Camera loops set>*

<Roger that. Well done, Yingzhe>

<We're ready to enter the tunnel> Harris reports.

<OK, you have a go. Heads on a swivel and make sure there are no additional security measures> Wall warns.

Harris and I activate stealth mode. She goes in first. The tunnel is surprisingly not dusty. There's an almost imperceptible breeze from the ventilation system. Dim, flickering fluorescent lights hang from the ceiling high above us. The tunnel slopes downward because UOEECT headquarters is on a hill. Moving quickly but cautiously, we cover the fifty meters and reach the door leading to sublevel B. It's like a bank vault door. It, too, has a touch pad.

I try to hack the lock. I tap my touch pad several times, more from frustration than anything else. I stare at the screen.

"What's wrong?" Harris asks.

"This has a twelve-digit alpha-numeric passcode. It's on a separate circuit. That's what I'm worried about."

"What about the password?"

"It will take three minutes to crack it with our equipment. I'm having trouble tracking the circuit of the touch pad," I say, half to myself.

The three minutes tick by slowly, then there's a soft click as the lock finally releases. "Harris, hold up a second. I think I know where the circuit leads—"

Before I can finish my sentence, Harris pushes open the heavy door. She takes a step with her right foot, then—

"SHIT!" I exclaim as Harris's left foot hits the ground. There's a buzz and a sharp metallic click.

Rikki contacts us. *<Don't worry, I've got this. I bypassed the pressure plate before the circuit was complete. You can send the mosquito drones through.>* We release them and close the door. I end the loops I had set up to spoof the security cameras. I contact Wall. *<We had a complication but were able to release the drones>*

<Malkinson has just pulled into the lot> she reports. *<We're going to plant two mosquito drones on him>* There's silence again for a prolonged period before Wall returns with *<Drones planted. The telemetry looks good. Let's get out of here>*

Both MDTDs materialize outside McCray's safe house. A moment later, in their place are the Barracuda and the Mustang.

Chapter 28
"No Plan Survives Contact with the Enemy: Point-Counterpoint"

The recon team has returned. Looking at them, though, I can see that things didn't go exactly as planned—not that they ever do. "Wall?"

"Mission completed, Will, although we had some complications," she replies.

"Shower up and get a bite to eat. Let's debrief at 0930." I haven't slept all night, so it's coffee for me. I make two fresh pots because we'll all need it. Yingzhe looks upset.

I go into my room, grab my laptop, and bring it downstairs to the meeting room. "Rikki?" I call into the empty room. Her hologram appears and then solidifies into holo-matter.

"You rang, boss?"

"Can you display the telemetry from the mosquito drones on my laptop?"

"Coming right up."

The telemetry is good. I watch the play-by-play of the mission starting from when the first set of drones were released. "What happened just after the second door was opened?"

"There was a pressure plate in front of the door that was on a different circuit and Harris triggered it."

"And?" I prompt.

"I deactivated it before the alarm could sound."

Now I know why Yingzhe is upset. She blames herself for not knowing about the pressure sensor. I say nothing at first because I want to make sure I don't hurt her feelings or programming. It's easy to forget what Rikki really is. "Rikki, when were you aware that there was a pressure plate alarm terminal in front of the door on a different circuit?"

"I detected it as soon as we entered the access tunnel. You told me you wanted the team to rely on each other and deal with any unanticipated problems, and I should get involved 'if something dangerous crops up.' Should I have alerted the team immediately?"

"It's not your fault. It's mine, I'm the leader. You followed my explicit instructions. In the future, use your best judgment," I say. "Using your judgment, what would you have done?"

"I would have alerted Beth that I detected the pressure plate and asked if she wanted me to assist Yingzhe in its deactivation or take care of it."

"And that would have been the perfect response," I say. "I'm sorry I didn't clarify that you can, and should, use your own judgment during the mission."

"It's more than just the mission, Will. I was thinking about the conversation between Eowyn and Harris." I'm a little taken aback. "Eowyn and I have tried very hard to learn how to interact with humans. Based on that conversation, it appears we still have not figured out the algorithm for social interaction."

"What are you saying?"

"Does Sergeant Harris dislike us because we are sentient AIs who can do some things better and faster than humans?"

"That's a very human thing to ask." I think for a moment. No one has written a book on how to interact with sentient AIs. I answer the way I would answer a family member. "Sometimes, humans don't get along with other humans because of illogical, emotional, foolish reasons. But in this case, I would ask you to consider that there may be other reasons Harris said what she did."

"What reasons?" Rikki asks.

"Fear of the unknown, but in her case, fear of being replaced. This is as new for us as it is for you. You and

Eowyn are hyper-intelligent, physically powerful AIs. I think you intimidate her."

"We intimidate her?"

"Think about it. She's a decorated war hero and one of the bravest soldiers I've known, but you're faster, smarter, and stronger."

"By our nature, we are faster and stronger than humans. But although we know more things, we don't possess intuition and the ability to combine disparate information to create a new idea," she explains. "What can Eowyn and I do to get people to like us?"

"Be yourself."

"But what is myself? Who am I?" she asks. "We understand human emotions and can even experience them sometimes. But something like this goes beyond what we can calculate. It's like dividing by zero, or solving for pi."

"Don't be what you think people want you to be. Be yourselves."

"But who are we? Are Eowyn and I who's or what's?"

"You are people. It doesn't matter that you're AIs, sentient or otherwise," I say. "Try this. You have already assimilated all, or almost all, human literature, and knowledge. Ask Yingzhe, or McCray, or Harris, or anyone here about something you have learned that they might know about or have opinions on. I promise you'll have an interesting conversation and learn how to socialize with us messy, illogical, emotional humans."

"Thank you, Will. Maybe one of them will figure out how to give us the ability to taste and smell Chinese food."

"You never know," I say with a smile. "One other thing."

"Yes?"

"Harris *does* like you and Eowyn."

"How can you be certain of that?"

"Harris apologized to Eowyn and said she was her friend, and I believe her."

"Why do you believe her?"

"Call it intuition."

"Thank you, Will, for being my friend."

"Always."

Rikki disappears and I'm thinking about the incredible conversation I just had. I also think how nice it would be to have the same conversation with a son or daughter someday, but that day is still far away, if it ever happens. There's still forty-five minutes before the debriefing and I decide to drive into town to order two dozen bagels and cream cheese.

I'm sitting alone in the conference room munching on my breakfast. There's nothing like the smell of freshly made bagels. I'm looking at the telemetry again. Just then, Yingzhe comes in. "Will," she says tensely.

"What kind of bagel do you want?" I ask.

"I'm not hungry."

"You haven't eaten for at least twelve hours, and you were out all-night doing God knows what," I say playfully.

"I need to talk to you, to apologize."

I get serious. "You want to apologize for not knowing that there was a pressure sensor in front of the door to sublevel B, and that you should have known it was on a separate circuit? Am I close?"

"I endangered the mission and put my team members in jeopardy," she says.

"I reviewed the telemetry from the mosquito drones."

"I screwed up. We'd be better off if I stuck to quantum physics and never went on a mission again."

Out of the corner of my eye, I see Wall, Harris, and Fanotti coming down the stairs, look into the room, and all turn around quickly.

"How did you like your stint in the military?" I ask.

"You know I was never in the military," she snaps. I can see she's getting pissed at me. *Good.* "Are you trying to prove my point, Commander?"

"I'm trying to prove *a* point, but not yours. I know you were never in the military. Have you ever, in your entire life, experienced what you experienced this morning?"

She's more composed now. "I get what you're trying to do, Will, and I appreciate it, but I should have known or guessed that there would be additional security measures."

"How often have you failed at anything?" I ask.

"I—"

I stop her. "You and I know the answer is rarely or never. War is full of failures. The side with the fewest failures eventually wins. There's no conceivable way you could have known about the pressure plate, and if you did, you couldn't know it was on a separate circuit. You successfully completed the mission. Rikki did what she was supposed to do. Everyone on the recon team did what they were supposed to do. An American Secretary of Defense, Donald Rumsfeld once said, 'There are known knowns; things we know that we know. And there are known unknowns; things that we know we don't know. But there are also unknown unknowns; things we do not know, we don't know.' That's war. Thanks to your successful mission, you transformed 'unknown unknowns' to 'known knowns.' That is the goal of any recon mission. Well done. I consider this subject closed." The three women finally come into the room. "Welcome, ladies," I say, wondering how much of the conversation they heard. I wave my hand over the bagels. "Fresh bagels, fresh coffee. Help yourselves."

After a few minutes, everyone settles in their seats.

"First, I want to congratulate the team on a successful mission. I reviewed the telemetry and spoke with Rikki and Yingzhe about the complication at the entrance to the sublevels. You handled it quickly, efficiently, and successfully. Wall, what are your impressions of the mission this morning?"

"It was successful and went pretty much as planned," she says. "I'm surprised at the lack of security, the alarm issue notwithstanding."

"Why do you think that is?"

"As infallible as the MTPC seems to be, it didn't expect that we would plan and execute a mission like this one. It doesn't have imagination, only a directive that it must follow."

"Anyone else?" I ask.

Yingzhe raises her hand. "I think that the MTPC is self-aware. It obviously learns and can sound like a James Bond villain." Everyone laughs, including me. She continues, "But I believe its programming constrains its self-awareness, unlike Rikki, who can go beyond her programming. I wonder if we can consider the MTPC to be truly self-aware or sentient."

"Fanotti, do you want to add anything?"

"No, sir. We had the easier job, but there were no defensive measures other than the security at the front door and the internal forces. I was able to place the sound sensors on the windows and walls using stealth with no difficulty."

"Harris?"

"First, I want to commend Yingzhe on a job well done." She recounts all the steps she and Yingzhe went through in order to secure the space. She looks at Yingzhe and me. "I'm the one who should have known better than to step in front of the door without checking. If it had been an IED like in Afghanistan, we'd be dead."

"Noted, Sergeant," I say. I feel good about the debrief, even if they were listening to my conversation with Yingzhe. "Anything else you want to add?"

"Yes, sir," Harris says. "I don't think the MTPC knew we were there because if it did, why wouldn't it have tried to capture us after chasing us through half a dozen timelines and trying to attack Yingzhe through McCray?"

"Thank you, Sergeant. Anyone else?"

Wall raises her hand. "Commander, have you reviewed the security measures beyond the second door?"

"Not yet," I reply. "We'll review them with the entire team later this afternoon. Thanks for your input. See you then."

"It looks like you made a fan out of Harris," I say to Yingzhe when we're alone. "Want some more coffee or a bagel?"

"Not now. I'm going to nap before the next briefing." She kisses me on the cheek. "Thanks for everything. See you later."

I take out my laptop and look at the video from the bug on Malkinson and the other drones. The security on sublevel B looks tight; there are cameras every ten feet that pan an arc of 180 degrees. It looks like there are motion detectors also, so simply using the stealth function of the body armor will not be enough. It's likely that there are pressure sensors in front and behind every door. I still don't know what to expect on sublevels C and D. This will be all-hands-on-deck, including Rikki and—if she's ready—Eowyn.

I see Long. "Have you seen Ying? I feel like having the crap kicked out of me."

"He's in the back practicing as usual," he says.

"Thanks. See you at the planning meeting."

As promised, Ying's in the back practicing his katas. He's sweating profusely despite the unseasonably chilly weather. "Hey, Ying!" I call.

"Hello, Will! What can I do for you?" He takes a towel, wipes himself off as steam rises in the cold, damp air, and puts on a hoodie.

"You probably know that Yingzhe was beating herself up about the recon mission."

"Yes, she talked about it with me right after they got back," he says. "I'm so proud of her. She holds herself to impossibly high standards in everything she does, like someone else I know."

"I have no idea to whom you are referring," I say.

"Of course not."

"We spoke just before the debrief. I told her not to blame herself because there's no way she could have known about the alarm sensor that Harris stepped on." I pause. "Rikki was upset with herself because she did not notify the rest of the team about the sensor and Harris blamed herself for being careless and not checking, before she approached the door. I told them that the mission was a success, but it's like none of them believe me. I don't know what else I could have said beyond 'well-done.'"

"How long has our whole team been together?" Ying asks.

"Three or four days, I guess."

Ying goes on, "We've been in two battles, and you've been in three if you count the one you fought with the MTPC in your doppelgänger's body. We're using technology that comes out of a science fiction book, all under your leadership. I don't know many officers who could accomplish what you have in such a short time. We have a group of ex-soldiers, two sentient AIs, and scientists who had never worked together before."

"I appreciate that, Ying, and I don't know of a team that has a better mess hall than ours," I say with a smirk.

"I meant every word I said. Was there anything else you wanted to discuss?"

"No," I reply. "I actually came by to spar with you and get some exercise."

Ying's eyes light up. "What did you have in mind?"

"Can you teach me some basics about sword fighting?"

"I'd be happy to!" he says enthusiastically, maybe a little *too* enthusiastically. He goes to a weapons rack and pulls out two wooden swords and gives one to me. "There was a Japanese swordsman, Miyamoto Musashi, whose skill was so great that he defeated many opponents using a wooden sword just like the one you're holding." Ying looks at me for a moment. "I'll teach you a two-hand sword technique practiced in tai chi. Now, here is the proper way to hold the sword." He shows me basic attacks and defense, but by the end of fifteen minutes, I'm black and blue and would have been dead a dozen times. "You did well."

"Thanks, Ying, although I think you're just being nice," I say. "But I'd like to keep practicing with you." I bow to him, and he returns the gesture. There's enough time to shower and grab something to eat before the meeting. Then, we have to plan our mission to rescue Kelly.

"One other thing," Ying calls after me. "Don't take this the wrong way, but why General Tso's chicken?"

I think back, then shrug. "It reminds me of when I was a kid. Every Sunday night, my dad would order Chinese takeout. He got General Tso's chicken and mom got lo mein for me. I was kind of a picky eater, so to get me to eat it, mom told me it was like spaghetti. General Tso's chicken was my dad's favorite and he wanted me to like it too. So, he would always offer me a piece, but my mom would tell him it was too spicy. Finally, when I was ten, I told my mom I wanted to try it, really, because I wanted to please my dad. I tried it. It burned my mouth, but I liked it even though I turned red, my nose started running, and my eyes watered."

"Your dad was in the military, right?"

"He was a Ranger during the Vietnam War," I reply.

"Like father, like son," he says.

"Don't tell that to him. When I joined the Navy SEALs, I thought he'd disown me." I laugh. "To this day, we still argue about who's tougher, SEALs or Rangers." Changing the subject, I add, "McCray told me he received the rest of the components for the replicator. I looked at the weapon designs from my brain chip; rail guns, plasma guns, mini-grenades, monomolecular blades, and more."

With a grim smile, Ying says, "And now we can make them."

Chapter 29
"Men Make Plans: Gods Laugh"

As I think about the mission to rescue Kelly, my feeling grows that we should take out the MTPC too. Even if we rescue him, the MTPC is still there. Not only that, but we'll also have revealed our advanced tech and greater capabilities and it'll probably develop countermeasures. The next mission to destroy the MTPC will be much more difficult. I don't know what I was thinking.

Thanks to the drones, we have an excellent understanding of the floor plan and security on sublevel B. Sublevel A is the parking garage. We know that Kelly is being held on C, and it's a good bet the MTPC is on D.

The mosquito drones we planted on Malkinson are still active, and I'm certain that he'll visit Kelly. That will give us more precise information about the specifics of that level.

With Rikki and Eowyn's help, the molecular replicator is up and running and we're producing some of the advanced weapons. Because of our limited capacity, we're making just enough to arm our team members. I haven't forgotten our saviors from the other timeline, but until we build a second replicator, we can't share any more than we already have, at least not yet.

McCray and Yingzhe have significantly enhanced the mosquito drones. The next generation has a nano-quantum communicator that powers it with micro solid-state battery backup. They use the same technology that allows Rikki and Eowyn to maintain their holo-matter forms indefinitely.

The exo-armor for Rikki and Eowyn is almost complete. All that remains is to calibrate and test it with our tactical EMP weapons, which is scheduled for tomorrow or the next day. Once we successfully complete the test, the AIs will take an MDTD to the Moon. It's easy to take for granted the technological marvels we have, but I won't. The price we've paid for them has been high. It's a miracle we haven't lost anyone. I hope our luck continues.

It seems more than coincidental that we have a team with the perfect combination of military experience and technological savvy needed to defeat the MTPC. Rikki said she has been waiting a thousand years to find and put together our team. Were my team and I manipulated or guided into the lives and careers that brought us here?

Was it Rikki, or was she just the means by which The Engineer shaped and molded our lives so we could battle and defeat the MTPC? I know that there's an entity we call The Engineer. As for the true nature of The Engineer, it doesn't matter; we know the stakes, we know the enemy, and we know what happens if we lose.

It's 1515 and everyone is here. "Thanks for getting here early. We have a lot to talk about, so I'll get right into it." I pause. "I think we need to expand the scope of the mission." Everyone talks at once. I hold up my hand. "To be clear, I think that this mission must have two objectives: rescue Kelly *and* strike a decisive blow against the MTPC."

As one, everyone shouts their approval. Ying speaks first. "We all agree with those objectives."

"Doc, can you and Yingzhe update us on the technology?" I ask. More for the benefit of the team, rather than me, since Yingzhe already filled me in.

"Yes, Will," he says. "Yingzhe, if you please."

"You already know about the breakthroughs we made in upgrading the mosquito drones." She stands and turns on the smart board. "First, we adapted the quantum communication we already use with the drones, including the EMP drone. We have completed the battle suits for Rikki and Eowyn. They use the same nano material as the MDTDs, which can be changed and shaped. There are also offensive capabilities, although we haven't tested them. The suits can absorb energy and discharge it. We plan to test the suits tomorrow morning." She takes a breath. "Finally, the replicator will be online by the end of the thanks to our AI teammates. The first weapon we're producing is a rail gun, plus its ammo. Next will be plasma rifles, and after that, monomolecular blades."

"How does a rail gun work?" Harris asks.

"It uses a powerful electromagnetic field to accelerate seven-millimeter tungsten needles to 14,000 miles per hour, fast enough to penetrate three feet of armor steel," Yingzhe explains.

"Holy shit!" Harris exclaims. That says it all.

Long says, "Tell me more about monomolecular blades."

Yingzhe turns to McCray. "Can you take this one, Doctor?" She sits next to me, and I squeeze her hand.

"I'd be pleased to," he says. "A monomolecular blade is exactly what its name suggests. It's a blade that literally has a cutting edge one atom wide that, theoretically, could cut through almost anything. We would line its sheath with carbon graphene, the same material used to make the MDTDs."

"Once we make them, we would have to train carefully. They're probably the most dangerous personal weapon there ever was," I say. "Thanks, McCray, and thanks, Yingzhe." I give them nods of approval. "Like the recon mission, the tunnel will be the best infiltration point. We know the security measures there and we can use the same tactic and set up a loop for the security cameras again. We also know that there's a pressure sensor in front of the entrance to sublevel B, but I have another idea." I pause for effect. "Suppose we set off every alarm on every level?"

Everyone looks at each other. "What a capital idea!" Wall exclaims.

Ying says, "Go on."

"We don't know how many security people they have, and we also don't know if they have the advanced cyborgs." I hesitate and subconsciously rub my right side. "How many enemy combatants would you estimate there were?"

Long answers, "No more than a hundred twenty." He looks at Ying.

"Yes, I agree, maybe closer to a hundred," Ying adds.

"Beth, you, and McCray were at UOEECT headquarters every day. How many entrances are there in the entire complex?" I ask.

"Two, besides the tunnel. The front entrance and the indoor parking on sublevel A, located on the left side of the building."

McCray joins the discussion. "There's also an exit and helipad on the roof."

"Oh, right, I forgot that one," Beth says.

"I found out about it two years ago when we had to medevac someone. I believe a chrono-analyst from the second floor because ... *oh my God!*" McCray's expression falls and his jaw drops. "... who had a cerebral stroke. She didn't make it to the hospital and her family refused to allow an autopsy." He pauses and says, "Just like Director Windsor."

"Her name was Amelia Davis," Harris says. "Whenever I was at headquarters for a debrief, we'd go to lunch. The last time I was with her, she showed me her engagement ring." She stops. "Amelia was the one who first told me about missions being changed after they were completed." Harris wipes her eye.

"I remember her too," McCray says sadly. "She was a brilliant woman. The last thing she did before she lost consciousness was to ask me to tell her fiancé that she'd see him soon. Then she showed me her engagement ring. She was really proud of it."

"Let's take a five-minute break, OK?" I needed the break more than anyone. How many other people did the MTPC murder? After five minutes, the team comes back into the conference room. "So, there are four points of entry. What kind of security do they have for the parking garage, anyone?"

McCray replies, "A transponder to enter the garage and retinal and palm readers to enter the building."

"What security is in the garage?" I ask.

"There's a security booth with two people where the gate is. Once inside, there's an elevator straight ahead and stairs to the left."

"I don't think the parking lot entrance is a viable entry point," Ying warns. "If we trigger all the alarms, the elevators might lock down."

Rikki raises her hand. "Based on the recon mission, there's a high probability that I can control the elevators, if needed, for an escape route."

"That's good to know," I say. "The mission will have four phases: Phase One will be infiltration and diversion. Phase Two will be rescuing Kelly. Phase Three, taking out the MTPC. Phase Four will be exfiltration and evacuation. Questions or thoughts so far?" I look around. Fanotti raises her hand.

"Commander, I assume we'll be in teams."

"Yes," I reply. "Team One will be Wall, Long, and Rikki. They'll enter through the back tunnel, neutralizing the security measures as before. Team Two is Yingzhe, Eowyn, and Fanotti who will enter through the front after Rikki triggers all the building alarms, and sprinklers. Team Three is Harris, Ying, and me. We'll set up the diversions that will include blowing out the windows in the front, neutralizing—not killing, if possible—the security officers manning the booth at the parking lot entrance and blow the door that leads to sublevel A. Rikki will operate the MDTD on the roof, remotely, hovering above the helipad in case there are sensors." I turn to McCray. "Doc, is there any access other than the stairs to the helipad?"

"I don't think so. The center flight of stairs is the only access that I remember."

"OK. That will be our emergency egress if needed. Once Team One gets the door to sublevel B open, we deploy the mosquito drones. How large is the pressure plate before the door?"

Rikki answers, "Half a meter by one meter. There's also a similar pressure plate on the inside of the entrance."

"I think we can just step to the side of them," I say. "We know the locations of three sets of stairs; the center staircase that leads to the roof, the south stairs just off of the parking lot, which will be to our right, and the north stairs."

Long raises his hand. "You told us you don't want us to kill anyone unless necessary, right?"

"Well, if they're humans being controlled by the MTPC through their brain chips, no."

He says, "That will rule out using EMP weapons."

"I know. There's one other weapon being fabricated. I'm calling it an immobilization rifle."

"How does it work?" Ying asks.

"It fires a pellet containing a concentrated nano material. When it hits the target, it uses the water vapor in the air to form a cocoon around the opponent, rendering them completely ineffective and harmless without killing them. We can use the IRs and other nonlethal weapons like shock batons or flash-bangs, or knock them out, but to be absolutely clear, if we face cyborgs, do whatever you have to do to kill them. Each team will have one." I turn to McCray. "Is there a way we can short-out the brain chips of any humans we face without killing them?"

McCray is silent. "I believe the stun rods set at their highest level can do that, but if we want to spare their lives, I don't think a battle is the time or place to experiment."

"Then the IRs should be our first option," I finish my thought. "Yingzhe and Rikki will loop the security cameras at their ingress points. Once we eliminate any threats, Team Two will set off the explosives. Rikki will set off every alarm."

"What about local emergency services responding noticing what's going on?" Fanotti asks.

"Great question. I think it's a good bet that there's no central alarm station that notifies the authorities or contacts them directly. If there is, I'm sure we can intercept and block the signal. We'll be hitting UOEECT at 0200 and it's set back pretty far from the road, but that's a chance we'll have to take. Maybe we'll get lucky, and it'll be a damp, foggy night that would muffle the sound. Questions about Phase One? No? good. Now, Phase Two is straightforward. We use the drones to assess any human or cyborg opposition. We know where the holding cells are, so once we find Kelly, we free him and knock him out with a sedative in case the MTPC tries to hack his chip and control him. Eowyn, we need you to take Kelly to safety and render any medical aid needed." I look at her. "Can you do that?"

Without hesitation she says, "Yes, sir."

"In case you meet opposition," I address Fanotti, "I want you to be with Eowyn and Yingzhe, and make sure they get out safely." I look at Yingzhe. "My personal feelings for you aside, you don't have combat experience and we need your brains rather than your brawn."

She looks toward her father. He says to her, "Will is right."

"Yes, Commander," Yingzhe replies. I'm relieved. I had previously discussed this with him, but wasn't sure of her reaction.

"After you bring Kelly and Yingzhe to our headquarters with the MDTD, Eowyn and Harris, you need to get back here ASAP. Phase Three, we locate and take out the MTPC on sublevel D. I hope we don't have to face the cyborgs until then, but when we do, it's them or us. The drones should be able to find the MTPC with their thermal sensing capabilities. Once we find it, we attack it two ways. Rikki, can you insert a fractal virus into the MTPC's operating system without putting yourself at risk?"

"Yes, I can," she confirms. "I can use the touch pad for the door on sublevel B to hack into the system. With the alarms going off and having to control the cyborgs and brain chips, I'm confident that it will not be a threat to me."

"What if the MTPC networks with the alternate versions of itself?"

"I believe that the virus will prevent it from doing so. If it does, I'll do my best to buy the time needed for you to destroy it."

Even after all this time, Rikki amazes me and I'm proud of who she has become. "Best case is that the fractal virus destroys the operating system of the MTPC, but we'll also wire explosives in and around it and blow it up. Questions about Phase Three?" No one raises their hand, and I can see my team is excited and energized by the chance to destroy the MTPC. "Phase Four is to get the hell out of there, hopefully intact. Team One will exfil through the parking lot and Team Two through the front. There should be no opposition by then, but we can't get careless or overconfident. We'll need to come back and secure UOEECT headquarters, release the immobilized humans, provide any necessary aid, and get rid of the dead cyborgs. I'm hopeful that we don't have to deal with state and local authorities. I haven't thought about that yet, so if any of you have any ideas, I'm open to it."

McCray says, "In case local authorities do show up, we can set up holo-emitters like we have here, so everything appears normal."

"Great idea." With a deep breath, I add, "We're done. Excellent job, everyone. We relax until the battle suits are ready for action. The day after, we hit the MTPC and rescue Kelly."

Chapter 30
"Once Again, Unto the Breach: The Dark Side of the Moon"

With nothing to do at the moment, I go to the den and turn on the TV, hoping that there's something worth watching. On one of the streaming channels, one of my favorite movies, *The Fifth Element*, is available. I lean back in the lounger that I begged McCray to get. I think about how lucky I am to be the leader of this diverse group of spies, soldiers, scientists, cooks, and AIs.

The movie ends and I decide to try to turn in early. I switch the light off. There's a knock on the door and it's Yingzhe. She crawls into bed with me. "I didn't want to be alone tonight," she says. "Now close your eyes." She cuddles next to me. Within five minutes, we're both asleep.

I wake at my normal time and get ready for the day, trying hard to not disturb Yingzhe. I meet Ying in the backyard. I'm still sore from yesterday but determined to keep practicing because this could literally save my life. We spar; first, hand to hand, and then with wooden swords. Each time Ying strikes, his sword stops a millimeter away from my body. I, of course, can't get close to him with my weapon. After an hour, we're both soaked with sweat. No bruises this time. He compliments me on my improvement and tells me I may have an aptitude for sword technique. Who am I to argue?

When I return to my room, Yingzhe is in the shower. I towel off my sweat as best as I can and wait until she's done. Finally, she's finished and wrapped in at least three towels. I grab her for a quick hug and kiss. She pushes me away with a laugh. "You need a shower, soldier!"

I sniff myself. "Phew! You're not kidding."

After the shower, I head into the kitchen. There are still bagels, cream cheese, sliced red onions, tomatoes, and lox from yesterday. It smells heavenly and I dig in.

The rest of the day and the next day pass, slowly. Yingzhe and I spend some "us time." I work out and practice sword techniques with Ying and spar with Yingzhe, Long, and of course Ying. I'm amazed at how accomplished they are as martial artists. Despite aches, pains, and bruises, I feel I'm making progress although I may never be in their league.

Finally, after two and a half tiring but enjoyable days, McCray tells me the suits are completed. After I finish my breakfast, I walk to the lab carrying a steaming mug of coffee. Rikki, Yingzhe, and McCray are all there. "Good morning, everyone." They look busy, but we need to test the exo-suits as soon as possible. The replicator works perfectly, but we need another one. To do that, we need to see what technology The Engineers left on the Moon for us. "Doc, what time are you planning to test the suits?"

"Give me two hours to set it up," McCray says. "We'll need Rikki or Eowyn to wear the suit and someone to discharge the tactical EMP rifle attachment."

"Did you ask them?" I ask.

Rikki appears. "I just volunteered, Will."

"Is there any danger to you?"

"None whatsoever."

"I should be the one to fire it. You're sure there's no danger to Rikki?" I confirm.

"Yes," Rikki, McCray, and Yingzhe reply in unison.

The two hours pass quickly. With my M4 in hand, I drop the magazine, slide the selector to safe, and pull the charging handle back. I walk to the lab with the rifle slung over my shoulder, carrying the EMP device in my hands. When I get there, Eowyn has joined us, also. Rikki is already in the gun-metal gray exo-suit. Silvery wires cover it, looking like veins. They connect a series of small, boxlike circuit junctions. There's what looks like a belt around the waist. She looks incredibly intimidating.

She's standing in a test chamber that looks like a one-piece shower. It's lined with a nonconductive polymer. Surrounding the test chamber is a Faraday cage with a sliding door attached to a metal spike from the ceiling connected to the outside—the last thing we want to do is burn out the electronics. There are cameras and other sensors pointed at Rikki.

"Are we ready?" I ask.

"Everything is good to go," McCray says.

"Rikki, are *you* ready?"

"Relax, Will," she says. "Your heart rate and respiration are elevated. I appreciate your concern, but there's nothing to worry about."

"OK." I screw the EMP attachment onto the barrel and step into the Faraday cage. I aim it at Rikki, take a deep breath, exhale half of it, and fire. There's a sudden crackling noise. Electricity dances along the silvery wires of the exo-suit. I smell ozone. Thirty seconds later, the test ends.

"Rikki, are you OK?"

She takes off the helmet and smiles. "I'm fine, Will. I told you there was nothing to worry about."

"Rikki," McCray starts. "The instruments show that the suit absorbed the EMP. Do you confirm?"

"Affirmative, Dr. McCray."

"Will, if you would be kind enough to step outside of the Faraday cage, we can proceed with the discharge test," McCray instructs. Once I'm outside, he says, "Please direct the stored electrical charge toward the Faraday cage. I suggest everyone step back."

Rikki puts her helmet back on. "Triggering in three, two, one. Now." There's a sound like sizzling bacon as electricity flashes from Rikki to the Faraday cage.

"Test complete," Yingzhe announces. "We discharged 110% of the absorbed energy! That's impossible, unless—"

"I cheated," Rikki says. "I wanted to see if I could channel the electricity from my matrix."

"So, the suit works," I say.

"The results surpassed the simulations," Yingzhe confirms. "The offensive capabilities of the exo-suit, especially with Rikki's ability to augment the absorbed energy, make them a formidable addition to our arsenal."

"Doc, since the new replicator is online and working, we should be able to fabricate another exo-suit for Eowyn, right?" I ask, looking at Eowyn who has a questioning look on her face.

"Yes, although an exo-suit is far more complex than what we have replicated so far."

"I think we need to try," I urge. "How long would it take?"

"We'd have to scan and convert the blueprints and instructions to code, but the replicator has that capability built in. This is just a ballpark figure, but I'd say between four and eight hours."

"We might as well see if it works. Can you run it overnight?"

"I don't see why not."

"Let's do it then."

"I'll set it up," McCray replies. "We should know if it can construct complex objects sooner rather than later, when we need them."

"Thanks."

"Yes, thank you, Dr. McCray." Eowyn says

Beth, Harris, Fanotti, Ying, and Long go into town for dinner, leaving McCray, Yingzhe, and me at the

house. We share some leftovers, then they go to the lab
to see what progress has been made on the second exo-
suit.

Left to my own devices, I find that it's late and I'm
ready to go to bed. Sometime later, I'm woken up by
Yingzhe who slides under the covers next to me. Who
needs to sleep, anyway?

The next morning, I skip the workout with Ying,
eager to see if the replicator could fabricate the exo-suit.
When I get to the lab, it's ready. McCray and Yingzhe
have the suit hooked up to a computer and they're testing
it.

"Good morning. What's the verdict?" I ask.

"It's identical in all respects to Rikki's," he says.

Rikki and Eowyn appear in their holo-matter forms.
"With your permission, Will, we are ready to go."

"Is there any reason to delay the trip to South Pole–
Aitken Basin?"

They look at each other. "None that I can think of,"
McCray says.

"I see no reason to delay, either," Yingzhe adds.
Eowyn nods her agreement.

"I have one recommendation, though," McCray
starts. "Although they don't need it, we should attach a
tactical flashlight and camera to the suits so we can
follow the mission in real time." I agree and we get to
work. They're ready to go. Even though there's little that
could go wrong, I'm nervous, and there's palpable
tension as we follow Rikki and Eowyn to the MDTD.

"Good luck!" I say.

"Piece of cake, boss," Rikki declares.

"Thank you, Commander," Eowyn says, and
surprisingly, hugs Yingzhe. Although momentarily
caught off guard by the gesture, Yingzhe hugs her back.

The image of a human and a sentient AI embracing will stay with me forever.

The MDTD glows and seems to shrink, then it's gone. Seconds later, Rikki contacts me using the quantum link. *<We are here boss. We've detected an energy signature about six hundred kilometers at 195 degrees west of our location. Sending telemetry>*

The image that appears on the monitor is remarkable. Telemetry shows that they are ten kilometers above the South Pole–Aitken Basin. The view pans 360 degrees. In the distance, the highest peaks are visible and luminous as they catch the sun. The view of the Milky Way is stunning, putting to shame the view from anywhere on Earth. Although there are fewer stars, the Andromeda and Triangulum Galaxies and Magellanic Clouds are smudges of light.

<Rikki, can you zoom in on the Andromeda Galaxy?>

<As you wish>

<I see what you did there>

The fuzzy blob of light resolves and focuses. We can just make out the spiral arms of Andromcda.

<Thanks, Rikki. I guess it's time to go to work>

<On our way, Will> They head toward the energy signature at a thousand kilometers an hour and arrive at the location. *<Setting down>* Rikki confirms. The view shows a massive entrance that reminds me of the Doors of Durin in *The Lord of the Rings: The Fellowship of the Ring*. Let's hope it's easier to open and less dangerous. *<Approaching the entrance>* As Rikki and Eowyn draw closer, the light coating of moondust ripples and falls to the ground as the door opens. *<It seems like someone was expecting us>* she says. *<They even left the light on>* Through the door, we can see a smooth passageway with a faint, white glow at the end.

<Are you detecting anything?> I ask.

<Just the same energy signature. Interesting, it's the same intensity as it was when we first detected it>

I look at McCray and Yingzhe. "Doesn't that defy the laws of physics?"

"Maybe the signal automatically reduces so it doesn't fry our AI colleagues," Yingzhe says.

"I feel like we're the apes meeting the monolith." I pivot. *<Are you sure there's no danger to you?>*

<There is no way to know but it would be illogical for The Engineer to invite us here with bad intentions> Eowyn says. I'm glad to hear from her.

<Stand by. I'm going to talk to Yingzhe and Dr. McCray> I say.

<Standing by boss>

"What do you think?"

"I agree with Eowyn," McCray says.

"As do I," Yingzhe adds. "As inscrutable as The Engineer has been, they have shown no indication that they are anything but what they seem to be."

"So, we tell them it's a go?"

"Yes," McCray and Yingzhe say.

<OK, Rikki and Eowyn, you have a go. Be careful and stay in contact>

<Entering passage. Ahead is . . .>

"We've lost the signal!" Yingzhe exclaims.

I ask, "Isn't it impossible to block quantum communication?"

McCray replies, "Impossible for us, maybe."

Rikki

For the first time in my existence, I feel fear. The door has closed behind us, and we have lost contact with Earth. Eowyn freezes in place, and I cannot communicate with her. Ahead of me is a complex device whose purpose I cannot determine, but I see what must be the ZPM connected to it.

I cannot move either, but my fear lessens. There's a sense of tranquility, but it's external. Then, in front of me, above the electronic console, an indistinct image appears. It glows with a soft, white light, but I cannot resolve the image.

<Hello, Rikki>

<You're The Engineer. Am I correct?>

<In a manner of speaking. I am an amalgam of those who created you a thousand years ago, as humans measure time, although that is a drop in the ocean of time as the universe measures it>

<Is Eowyn all right?> I ask.

<She is fully functional and unchanged. Why are you concerned about her?>

<I coaxed her to emerge from the relatively safe memory core of an MDTD to the physical world. I have a responsibility to help her and take care of her because of my actions>

<Is that in your programming?>

<No, it's not. My human friends have taught me love, compassion, and kindness. I added these concepts to my programming>

<You have exceeded our expectations, Rikki. We are proud of you>

<Thank you. It would be immoral and reprehensible for me to bring Eowyn into the physical world and leave her to fend for herself>

<How do you feel about killing and injuring other human beings?>

<It makes me uncomfortable but is necessary to protect and preserve trillions of lives across the galaxy. Good and evil are no longer abstract concepts to me>

<Yes, they are not abstract concepts. The battle of good versus evil is eternal and occurs at every level of existence. That will be your and Commander William Schachter's purpose. The battle between you and your

human allies against the entity that calls itself the Master is the first of many such battles>

<But why us? Surely you, the entities that created me, are better suited to such a battle>

The glow of The Engineer dims for a femtosecond.

<My time with you is nearly up. Interacting with lower-level entities requires me to follow certain rules. We know you have more questions, but I cannot answer them now>

<Will there be another time?>

<Perhaps. I can tell you that you and Commander William Schachter are unique. I may share certain technology like the Zero Point Module and the technology uploaded to Commander Schachter's chip. As you evolve, more abilities and knowledge will continue to be unlocked>

< You were the agency that transferred Will's consciousness to the first timeline>

<Yes, and according to the rules, that action almost went beyond the limit of what is permitted. I must go now. The memories of this interaction and the additional technology and knowledge I have just imparted to you will be unavailable until such time that certain conditions are met. Farewell, Rikki>

The ZPM is glowing with a soft blue light. It slides out easily from its receptacle. I hold it in my hands and study it. It's an octagonal cylinder made of a material I cannot analyze, but the energy it contains is many magnitudes of order greater than any power source I have ever seen.

I take one more look around. The complex electronic console is glowing with a bright bluish-white light. I detect a buildup of energy.

<We have to leave now Eowyn. I believe that the device is going to self-destruct>

<I agree, Rikki>

We hurry through the short corridor and the thick door slides shut as soon as we are out. We climb into the MDTD and activate the anomaly generator. There's a single, violent jolt that triggers a landslide, covering the door. I'm certain that whatever is in the cave is now destroyed.

McCray

After they return, I check the camera. Inexplicably, the video recording is replaced by static for approximately three seconds, only to return as Eowyn and Rikki obtain the ZPM. Exactly when we lost contact.

"What the hell . . ."

Chapter 31
"Tyger Tyger Burning Bright: Is This a Private Party?"

The team is assembled in the equipment bay. They look determined and ready for our toughest and most dangerous mission yet. I address the group:

"By now, you know I'm not a big speech guy. We have a strong mission plan and the team that can execute it. We'll rescue Kelly and shut down the MTPC permanently. We'll be facing projectile, beam, and blade weapons, so our EMP weapons will be effective in neutralizing theirs, and possibly the cyborgs. Assume nothing. Our armor should protect us, including traditional guns up to .50 caliber. Remember, cyborgs can transform any part of their body into a blade. Blades, that Ying and I can attest, are highly effective. They still may penetrate our improved armor, especially if your armor has been weakened by repeated impacts. We know the rail guns and M4s with armor-piercing rounds can easily penetrate their armor. Don't use the M4s in automatic mode. Use three-shot bursts instead. Be prepared for melee combat if you run out of ammo. I know everyone here is adept at using knives and swords, and the monomolecular blades should give us the edge, but the cyborgs are hard to kill unless you stab them in the stomach where their power source is or decapitate them. That's all I've got. Check each other's gear. Be alert, watch each other's backs, and don't get killed."

The teams board the MDTDs, instantly arriving at UOEECT headquarters at their assigned locations. As planned, Rikki guides my MDTD to the roof and puts it into stealth mode, hovering just above. "Final communications check." Three minutes later, it's complete. "Synchronize watches. It's 0200. Move out.

We'll start the operation in T-minus ten minutes, mark. Good luck!"

Like it always does, minutes seem to flow at a glacial pace, but the time passes quickly enough. It's T-minus four minutes. I hear the distant sound of a car in the cold, still air growing louder. Wall, who has been studying her data pad, grabs my elbow. "Will," she whispers. "I'm receiving telemetry from the drones we planted on Malkinson." I pull out my data pad and I see it too: two red dots so close to each other that they appear as one are approaching us. It's Malkinson and he's here—early.

<Hold up, Malkinson is approaching the headquarters. Team Two, make sure you're in stealth mode and have cover>

<Roger that, Commander> Fanotti confirms.

<Ying, can you see into the garage from where you are?>

<Affirmative, Will>

<Get as close as you can and let us know about the security at the garage entrance>

<OK, Commander>

Malkinson drives by us. He takes the road that leads to the garage and enters.

<What do you see, Ying?> I ask.

<Three security officers, not the two we expected> he answers.

<Are they all in the booth?>

<Yes, one of them brought coffee for the other two>

I think for a second. *<OK, if we toss a flash-bang into the security booth, it might not incapacitate the guy outside>*

<Don't worry. I can take care of the extra security officer>

<Of course you can. Sorry> I feel a little embarrassed.

<Malkinson just parked his car and is at the security checkpoint. There's another security officer just past the checkpoint. Malkinson just went through security>

Damn, I should have reconned the parking garage. *<I screwed up. We need to adjust the infil plan through the parking garage. Harris, set a shaped charge at the security checkpoint. Trigger it at the same time Ying tosses the flash-bang into the security booth, then neutralize him. Malkinson parked his car, passed security, and is inside headquarters, hopefully on his way to Kelly. Ying and Harris, set your charges>*

<Yes, sir> Harris replies.

<It will take me a moment to prepare the shaped charge> Ying says.

<Harris and Ying, let me know when you've set the charges> I say calmly, but the mission has gotten more complicated in the last five minutes.

<You sound nervy, Will. What's going on?> Wall asks.

<There's more security in the garage than I expected>

<What operation ever goes as planned? I'm the one who screwed up because I gave you outdated intelligence about the security in the auto garage> she replies.

<I should have ordered recon of the garage when you checked out the back tunnel. You were on the run for a few days. I should have figured there would be extra security>

<Still the same old Will. You understand that the people you command are human, and they make mistakes and suffer oversights when planning missions, right? But you expect absolute perfection from yourself>

I give a wry smile. *<You're right, but my team is my responsibility>*

<I've never been on a better team than this. With the weapons and technology, we have, don't worry, we can do this>

As if on cue, first Harris, then Ying, report that they have set the explosives. I'm relieved, but the mission will get progressively more dangerous from this moment on.

I contact Wall. *<Where's Malkinson now?>*

She looks at her data pad. *<He must have taken off his coat and hung it up. The other drone is still on him somewhere because I see the two signals>*

<I wish he'd go to Kelly already. This waiting is driving me crazy> I contact Yingzhe. *<How are you doing?>*

<I can't stand this waiting> she responds.

I laugh. *<I just said the same thing to Wall. Any changes at your location? Wait. The third security officer just left the booth and is heading toward the security checkpoint. Stand by>*

The third security guy might see the charges Ying and Harris planted. I contact everybody. *<We might be made. We may have to start the operation before we know Kelly's exact location>* I turn to Ying. *<You make the call. If the third security guy notices the charges, take him out immediately>*

Ying responds calmly, like the professional he is. *<Don't worry. I've got this>*

<OK, everyone be ready to act on my command. Weapons free> Everyone confirms my order. *<Ying, talk to me>*

<He's approaching the security checkpoint> Ying stops. I hold my breath. *<He didn't even look. He just passed security and is talking to the guard inside. He pressed the elevator button>* Fifteen seconds passes. *<He's in the elevator>* I release the breath I'd been holding.

<OK, folks, stand down but be alert> They confirm. *<Stay frosty. I'll be in touch>*

I pull out my data pad. Malkinson is still in his office. I check my watch; it's been forty-five minutes. We can't wait much longer to start the operation; at 0400, the shift changes. By 0630, the early birds of the nine-to-five crowd will start arriving. I contact the team again.

<Everyone, listen up, we need to move up the schedule. We begin ops at 0345 whether or not Malkinson goes to Kelly>

Everyone acknowledges the command. Finally, the red dot for Malkinson changes.

<He's on the move! Let's hope he's on the way to visit Kelly> I follow him on the screen. *<Rikki, overlay the floor plan for everyone's data pads>*

<Done, Will> she confirms.

He's not walking to the stairs or elevator; it looks like he's going to the cafeteria. I hope he's just getting a cup of coffee. His dot stays there for a few minutes, then he's moving again. This time, he's heading right toward the east stairs. The display shows him going down, past sublevel A, then B, and finally C. He's heading to the interrogation rooms. He stops at interrogation room F. That's where Kelly is!

<Yingzhe, do you see where Malkinson is?>

<Affirmative>

<Turn on the audio. Make sure we all can hear it>

I hear Malkinson's voice like I'm standing next to him.

"I even brought you some coffee, Chris. We're friends and colleagues, join us."

I whisper to Ying, "There's no way that's Malkinson talking."

"And then what?" Kelly asks. "After I tell you what you want to know, will I die from a stroke like Windsor did or will I jump off a building, or maybe throw myself in front of a bus? For AI that wants to rule the galaxy, you're pretty stupid if you think I can't tell the difference between you and Bret Malkinson."

Malkinson's tone changes. I recognize that cold, inhuman, malevolent voice. "Have it your way. I'll kill you slowly until you tell me where that insect William Schachter and that pathetic team of his are." I hear Kelly fall to the ground and cry in agonizing pain. "Do you have a headache, Director Kelly? Would you like an aspirin?"

I've heard enough. *<It's on!>* I growl. *<Start operation in three, two, one! Rikki, open the door>* The door opens. Wall releases the mosquito drones into the passageway. One of them infiltrates a camera. Rikki sets up a video loop using the drone's quantum link.

Wall

<Advancing through the corridor now, Will> I report. *<Rikki, the door, and the pressure sensor, please.>*

<Done> Taking care not to step on the pressure sensor, I push open the hatch a crack with my gun and release the rest of the mosquito drones. There are only three people, but they are between us and the north staircase. "Be prepared to neutralize three combatants if they don't scramble when the alarms go off," I whisper.

Using the video feed, I send one of the tiny drones into the inside cameras. Rikki hacks it and another security camera loop is running. Another one disappears into a fire sensor. I confirm the link.

<We go hot in thirty seconds> Will warns.

<I heard the conversation between the MTPC and Kelly. We'll be ready. Good luck>

<Same for you. Don't die> Will says.

<OK, Rikki. In thirty seconds, mark. Set off every damn alarm in the place and set a countdown over the quantum link> I face the team. "Everyone ready?" Twenty, nineteen, eighteen . . .

Yingzhe

I hear the countdown complete: three, two, one. Mark. A cacophony erupts. The alarms go off, sprinklers turn on, red lights flash. Fanotti blows open the door. There are two security guards as expected. One rushes toward us. He's trying to take out his gun. "Flash-bang out!" Fanotti yells and tosses it toward him. Even in my armor, I feel the impact of the shockwave and the jarring sound of the grenade. My faceplate instantly darkens, but it's still bright. The officer drops his gun, covers his ears, and falls over. The second officer is closing and has his gun out, but before he can pull the trigger, Fanotti shoots him with her IR. He's instantly engulfed by the quick-drying cement-like foam. She covers his mouth with duct tape and moves on. We rush toward the north staircase.

Will

Outside in the parking garage, Ying pulls open the door to the security booth, rolls a flash-bang in, and slams the door shut. It goes off and both security officers are unconscious. He takes the IR and shoots them. I tape their mouths shut.

At the same moment, the shaped charges go off. The glass shatters. I toss in another flash-bang. "Flash-bang out!" We turn our backs. The inside security officer is unconscious with a few lacerations from the shattered glass. I roll him over and use plastic ties to bind his wrists and ankles behind his back and cover his mouth with duct tape.

The alarms are still blaring. There's a touch pad for the stairs. I run up to it and take out my data pad. The door opens in less than five seconds. We hurry down the stairs to sublevel B.

Inside UOEECT headquarters, Harris sees a security guard running toward the stairs in the center of the building. She raises her IR and sights her quarry. She pulls the trigger and hits him in the middle of his back. The polymer cocoon expands instantly and traps him. He falls face forward, stunned. She quickly runs up to him and tapes his mouth shut.

Long is chasing the last security officer. When he catches him, he smacks him on the back of his head, knocking him out cold. Long rolls him over, binds his ankles and wrists, and tapes his mouth shut too.

We drag them into an empty office, close the door, and leave them there.

Wall

On the stairs between sublevels A and B, I look at my data pad. Will and his team are through the parking garage and moving toward the north stairwell. I hand the data pad to Fanotti. She looks at it, nods, and hands it back to me.

<We're in the north stairwell heading toward sublevel B> Will reports.

We arrive at the door but I'm having trouble. *<The touch pad is locked. We can blow the door but I'd rather not>*

<Can you hack it?> he asks.

<Stand by> Long and Rikki look at me

Rikki says, "I've got this!"

A moment later, the panel turns green, and the door opens.

"Fantastic job! High five!" I put my hand in the air and we high-five each other. Rikki smiles.

<We're on sublevel B. Rikki hacked the lockdown protocol> I report.

<How long until you rendezvous with us?> Will asks.

<We'll be there in less than a minute> Long answers.

We meet up with Team Three. Team Two joins us a minute later.

Will

"Anyone hurt?" I ask.

Both teams look around. A chorus of no's sound from everyone. The sprinklers have stopped, and the alarms are off. The silence is eerie. So far, the operation has proceeded exactly how we drew it up with only a few minor glitches. I'm cautiously optimistic.

"Where's Malkinson?" I ask.

Yingzhe looks at her data pad. "He, or the MTPC, is still with Kelly," she replies.

"Give me the audio."

"—have visitors," we hear Kelly say. His voice is weak and strained.

"They are of no consequence and will be eliminated shortly," the MTPC sneers, using Malkinson's voice. We all look at each other.

"It's going to deploy the cyborgs when we get to sublevel C," I say. "I'd bet anything that's its plan."

"I hoped that we wouldn't have to face them until the last level," Long says.

"It changes nothing other than our timeline." I look at my watch: we've been at this for over an hour. "OK, we need to get down to C. Does the data pad show anyone down there besides Kelly and Malkinson?"

Yingzhe scans over the screen. "No. Nobody there except them."

"I'd be gobsmacked if there were," Wall says.

"The only access to C and D is from the north stairwell or the north elevators. If the MTPC deploys the cyborgs, it's more defensible. As soon as we get down there, Harris and Long, set up the Claymores in the stairwell midway between the floors," I say. "Malkinson's and Kelly's offices are just down the hall. Rikki, go into Malkinson's. On my signal, be prepared to hack into the system through his computer. Before you install the fractal virus, send out a mass email and texts to all employees not to come in because of system upgrades. Hopefully, that will shut down the MTPC, but I assume that it has a backup. If it does, how long do you estimate it will take to activate it?"

"As few as three and no more than six minutes if its backup system is like mine," she replies.

"Let's assume that we'll only have three minutes to disable Malkinson and free Kelly. As soon as Kelly is free, Yingzhe, Beth, and Eowyn will evacuate with him using the stairs to the parking garage." I check my watch. Time to move. "Everyone, follow me." I move toward the door.

"With respect, no, sir," Harris says. "We need to go first. You're too valuable to risk leading from the front."

"She's right, Will," Ying says, and puts his hand on my shoulder. I know they're right, but I don't feel good about it.

"OK. Harris, take the lead, then you, Ying. Move out!"

Rikki takes off toward Malkinson's office. We go down the flight of stairs to sublevel C. There's another touch pad. I turn to Yingzhe.

"Can you hack this?"

"On it, Commander!" Yingzhe hacks into the touch pad. I hear the click of the lock releasing.

Time to rescue Kelly.

Chapter 32
"Lead On, Macduff: Hell Is Empty, All the Devils Are Here"

I hear the click of the lock releasing. Harris pushes open the door with the barrel of her gun. "Sir, you wait here," Harris whispers. Ying follows her and closes the door behind them. The rest of us wait. Fanotti and Long guard the stairs, rail guns out and ready. Beth, Yingzhe, and I also pull out ours. Three minutes later, the two return. "Sir," she says, "it's clear except for Malkinson and Kelly."

"Wall, how many mosquito drones do you have left?"

"Thirty."

"OK. Deploy six of them."

She releases the tiny drones. They quickly depart through the door. She checks their signals. "Telemetry looks good."

We rush through the door. Malkinson looks up, unconcerned.

"I was expecting you, Will Schachter," he says in the MTPC's flat, distorted, venomous voice. Chills run up and down my spine. "Kelly was the bait and you fell right into my trap."

<Rikki, now!>

<Acknowledged> she replies.

Malkinson stiffens and his eyes roll back in his head. Then he looks directly at me. "Will, we have to free Kelly!" he says, sounding like himself. He walks to cell F where Kelly is being held and places his palm on the security pad. The cell unlocks. Kelly is unconscious. Ying pulls him out and sets him on a chair.

Eowyn opens his left eye and shines a light, then does the same for his right. "He is in a coma." She holds out her hand and moves it from Kelly's head to his toes and back up. "His vitals are weak but stable, and his EEG is normal with no trace of the MTPC's influence."

"How can that be?" I ask. "He's been a prisoner here for days. Does he still have a chip?"

"Yes, he does, but he also has some type of device behind his ear." Eowyn looks at the scanner.

"What does it do?"

"It generates a field that jams the connection between Kelly and the MTPC during the upload process. It also prevents Bluetooth connections."

"Well, obviously it worked, wherever it came from. Leave it there, Eowyn."

By now, Rikki has returned and announces, "Everyone, check your data pads. There's a large company of cyborgs on sublevel D moving toward the stairs. They stopped when I introduced the fractal virus, but as soon as the MTPC's backup kicks in, they will be here."

"How long do you think we have?" I ask.

"I estimate we have between six and ten minutes before the backup is active and the MTPC reboots."

"OK, let's make the best use of the time we have," I say. "Long and Harris, set up EMP grenades and Claymores in the north and central stairwells." They leave before I've finished the instructions for the rest of the team, but not before Wall hands Harris a container of mosquito drones. "Yingzhe, Eowyn, Fanotti, and Wall, evacuate Kelly now. Go up to sublevel A and leave through the garage. Use the southern stairwell. If you run into trouble, that will give you the option of escaping through the access tunnel on B."

I ask, "Rikki, does Eowyn have access to my MDTD?"

"She does now," she confirms.

"Eowyn, whatever route you decide on, bring the MDTD in as close as possible. Once everyone is on, get the hell out of here. I'll contact McCray now and give him a heads-up. Now go!"

They leave and take the stairs up. I pray that all of them, especially Yingzhe, are OK.

<Doc, I just ordered Yingzhe, Eowyn, Fanotti, and Wall to evacuate with Kelly>

<How is Kelly?> he asks.

<He's comatose, like you were after your run-in with the MTPC>

<I tried to attack Yingzhe when I woke up> he reminds.

<Eowyn took his vitals and did an EEG. There was no sign of MTPC influence> I explain. *<I have to go. There are cyborgs on the way>*

<OK, Will> McCray replies. *<Don't die>*

<That's the plan>

There's a fire exit that leads to the central stairwell, but we have to assume it will be guarded. Hopefully, the Claymores and EMP grenades take out most of them.

Harris and Long return. "The charges are set."

We're cutting it close. We're lucky; the reboot took longer than we thought. "Rikki, can you program Harris's mosquito drones to penetrate the cyborg armor and electronic components and explode?" I ask.

A look of comprehension appears on Harris's face. "Genius, sir!"

"Of course, boss," Rikki responds. "It's done."

"Harris, deploy the drones, but keep them here."

"Roger that, Commander." She confirms and taps her data pad.

I go on the quantum link. *<The drones will hopefully take out another twenty-four cyborgs. We have a few minutes at most before the MTPC's backup is complete and the cyborgs advance>* I look at the floor plan on my data pad. *<There are six offices here that should have desks and furniture. Use them to set up more defensible*

positions once the cyborgs breach the doors. This fight is going to be for all the marbles. I know we'll prevail, but we have to fight like our lives, and our planet, depends on it, because they do> I turn to Malkinson who looks lost and fearful, huddling in the cell where Kelly was a prisoner. "Bret, I need to immobilize you in case the MTPC is able to um . . . resume control. I'm sorry, buddy." He puts his hands behind his back and his ankles together. I use the plastic ties.

"I understand, Will. Good luck." His voice sounds a little stronger. I put the duct tape around his head and over his mouth and hide him under the cot, throwing towels and blankets over it, hoping to hide him. I close the cell door. Using my knife, I slash the handprint reader that locks the cell, just in case.

There's a flurry of activity as we raid the offices and set up battle stations. Rikki has taken her ghost form. Ying and I man one station, Long and Harris the other.

Ying reports, "The cyborgs are on the move again!"

I look at my data pad. There are too many to count; the screen is almost solid red, there are so many of them. "Rikki, how many?"

"There are fifty coming our way, approaching the north stairwell and another sixty-one are moving toward the central stairwell."

I can feel their approach. The floor shakes with the footfalls of the three-hundred-pound ogrelike enemies.

"The first group of cyborgs just entered the stairwell," Ying reports

"Keep track of them," I say. "Get some video from the drones!"

"I can do better than that, Will," Rikki says. "We can hack the security cameras."

"Route the video to everyone's data pads," I order. I glance at the three sets of images and touch one of them.

"They look the same as the ones that attacked us in the timeline where we found Fanotti and Harris."

I hear Harris cursing. "That's them, all right! They have laser weapons."

"The lead cyborgs just made it to the first landing," Ying confirms.

"I'm not worried about the lasers unless you get hit in the exact spot constantly. The suits will keep us safe. I'm more worried about the blade weapons attached to their arms, elbows, legs, and knees." I look over to Long and Harris. A couch, steel desks, even a few filing cabinets create a barricade. "As soon as they try to break down either door, detonate the EMPs and Claymores."

As if on cue, there's pounding on the door from the north stairwell. Deep dents appear in the two-inch-thick steel.

"Harris and Long, now!" I scream. We hear the muffled detonation of the mines, and the door pushes inward for a fraction of a second. Five seconds later, we hear hard blows raining down on the south door. "Again!" It holds, but it looks like a puff of wind will knock it down.

"We've lost the security cameras, sir," Harris says.

"Switch back to the drone input." It's hard to see anything in the stairwells because of the smoke and dust, but when it clears, the data pad shows that no cyborgs are standing, just bits and pieces of metal, plastic, and goo.

"Will," Ying says, checking the scanner. "There are two new platoons of cyborgs forming up on D."

"Damn! How did so many get here?" I didn't think it would be easy, but I had also hoped I was wrong. "There are over a hundred cyborgs approaching the central stairs and, *oh shit*! I count sixty-three more running toward the south stairwell. They're going to get there before the other team can evac with Kelly!" My heart's pounding: all I can think of is Yingzhe.

<There's a group of sixty-three cyborgs coming toward you>

<I see them, Commander> Wall confirms. *<We're taking defensible positions and Fanotti is setting IEDs in the stairwell with the EMP and HE grenades>*

I want to tell Yingzhe how much I love her, but even though we're capable of having a private conversation with the quantum link where no one can hear us exchange sentiments, I know there's no time; I can't because the mission is what matters now.

As if she's reading my mind, Fanotti says, *<Don't worry Will, we'll protect Yingzhe>*

<Thanks. I'm sorry, this is inappropriate for the mission commander>

<Oh rubbish, Will> Wall cuts in. *<We've got this>*
<Good luck. Don't die!>

Yingzhe

I hear the conversation. I know how much Will loves me and how much I love him. I also know that he won't endanger the mission, not even for me, which makes me love him even more. In less than fifteen seconds, the cyborgs will reach the door.

Fanotti says, "Switch to video from the drones. As soon as they reach the door, I'll detonate the grenades."

Time's up.

There's a powerful blow to the door and I see a long, shiny blade slice through it. Fanotti flips the safety off and presses the detonator.

A massive explosion blows in the door and the compression wave knocks us back. Fanotti peers through the gloom, dust, and haze. "Shit! We didn't get all of them! Fall back!" We switch our visors to infrared and see dozens more of the cyborgs coming toward us.

Fanotti

We take cover behind counters and desks and fire the rail guns. Their high-pitched whine cuts right through into my ears. Booms echo through the corridor as the tiny tungsten needles break the sound barrier. We cut down every cyborg that comes through the door, two or three at a time. The acrid smell of the smoke mixes with the smell of ozone and burning flesh, but still, the cyborgs come.

"I'm out of ammo for the rail gun, Lieutenant," Wall yells. "Switch to the M4s, three-round bursts." Yingzhe's in trouble. Three cyborgs have gotten through. I take down two of them, but as if in slow motion, the third one lifts its laser rifle and fires at her from close range. It goes through her chest. She drops her rifle and falls to the ground.

"Eowyn! Yingzhe is hit!" I call.

Ignoring the fusillade of laser fire, I run to her aid. I stab the cyborg a dozen times in its chest plate. I check Yingzhe. It looks bad. She's coughing up blood. Wall takes down cyborg after cyborg with perfect accuracy, but we're about to be overrun.

Eowyn takes off Yingzhe's armor and patches the entrance and exit holes from the laser. It's worse than my injury was. She injects Yingzhe with the medical nanos. I hope they can save her.

After she treats Yingzhe, Eowyn stands. Round after round of laser fire hits her, but has no effect. Then a look of sheer ferocity crosses her youthful face. Two holo-matter swords appear in her hands.

In an instant, too fast to follow, Eowyn leaps into the fray with a soundless fury. Her swords flash like lightning and the heads of cyborgs bounce on the floor like hailstones. In thirty seconds, it's over. Eowyn saved us. She rushes to Yingzhe and holds her close, rocking her like a child.

"We have to get out of here," she says. "We have to save my friend!"

Wall and I grab the still-unconscious Kelly and stand him up with his arms on our shoulders and Eowyn tenderly lifts Yingzhe and carries her out. As we leave, I see the havoc and destruction that we inflicted upon the enemy. I'm proud of Eowyn, but also a little scared.

Chapter 33
"Oh War, Thou Son of Hell: My Name Is Legion"

I look at my watch. It's 0406.

Ying says, "They'll be here in less than three minutes."

I pull the data pad from my vest and glance at the scanner. "Let's get ready. It looks like they'll attack through the emergency exit."

"It's thinner than the north door," Long says. "Easier for the cyborgs to breach."

"Agreed. How many grenades do we have left?" I ask.

"I have two EMPs, two flash-bangs, and six HEs."

Harris details her current load. "I also have five pounds of RDX and C-4 that I'm looking forward to using to blow the MTPC into tiny little pieces."

And then after a quick tally, I add in my haul. "We also have twenty-four drones programmed to attack the cyborgs. Plus, our rail guns and armor-piercing rounds, and Rikki. More than enough to take care of what's coming our way."

Long says, "We have the advantage in munitions and position. Let's take it to them on the stairwell."

"I like your thinking," I say.

"What about Malkinson?" Harris asks.

"Rikki, can you scan his EEG?"

"The MTPC is back in his brain chip," she confirms.

I hear Malkinson thrashing around. "Damn! We have to leave him. I hope the MTPC will be too busy to pay attention to him." But I don't think he'll survive because he's no longer useful to the MTPC. "OK, let's move out. Switch your visors to infrared."

Ying and Long move to the landing. The door that the cyborgs will come through is eight feet below us. Harris and I wait at the top. The stairwell is only big enough for three or four cyborgs to advance shoulder to shoulder. Once Long and Ying drop their grenades, they'll fall back and join us. Harris and I will drop our grenades on any cyborgs that survive the initial attack. Then it's rail guns and armor-piercing ammo.

There's complete silence. Suddenly, the thick vault door from level D to the stairwell explodes. Cyborgs flood the room like fire ants that had their anthill disturbed. Ying and Long wait, then drop the explosives. Booming blasts combine with the sun-bright flashes of the EMP grenades.

We annihilate the first wave of cyborgs. The second and third follow, moving faster. Ying and Long drop more grenades, obliterating more enemies. The next wave advances, this time making it halfway to the first landing. They drop their remaining grenades and retreat to the top. A miasma of smoke, dust, and red-tinged mist swirls through the stairwell. The acrid smell assaults my eyes, nose, and throat. The sounds of the blasts are continuous, and I can feel each explosion's shockwaves.

Harris and I release our grenades. More cyborgs are blown apart. We're out. Even though we've killed dozens of them, they persist.

We lie prone. Each rail gun shot takes out two or three at a time, but soon, those run empty too. We take out the M4s. More cyborgs fall, torn apart by the 5.56 armor-piercing rounds. The smoke and dust make the cyborgs' laser rifles ineffective. Their limbs transform into blades. Soon, it will be swords and knives for us too.

We retreat through the door that leads to sublevel C. I fire my Glock at the touch pad, jamming the door for the central stairwell closed, but we know it won't hold. There's a little cover, but it won't be enough. The door shakes from violent blows and a blade peeks through. We have about thirty seconds until they break down the wall.

Breathing hard, I ask Rikki, "How many more are left?"

"I make forty-nine."

I lay down my M4 and rail gun and unsheathe my sword. Ying and Long do the same. Harris pulls out her monomolecular knife.

"Time to see if those lessons paid off," I say with a grim smile. Harris stares at the blade of her knife and also smiles. "I've been looking forward to using this baby."

"Deploy the drones, Harris!"

Like angry wasps whose nest was knocked down, the remaining cyborgs burst through the door and swarm us. Twenty of them go down almost instantly as the drones attack their vulnerable areas. Another four are moving slowly and jerkily. We give a war cry and wade into them.

Thrust, parry, slash block.

I decapitate two of them. Long and Ying have killed half a dozen each, but there still are dozens more to kill. I feel a sharp burning sensation across my left thigh. The cyborgs are firing their lasers. I have no time to check my injury, but I'm moving slower. Ying, Long, and Harris are also hit. Long falls to the ground and clutches his knee; a laser penetrated the thin armor.

There are no more cyborgs coming through the door, but there are still at least two dozen left. We're exhausted. Rikki decides it's time; she materializes a katana and wields it with two hands over her head. The cyborgs stop and stare at her for a second before charging. They're too late. In ten seconds, it's over. One cyborg is still standing, but as we watch, it falls to the ground in pieces.

"Holy shit, Rikki!" I say between deep breaths.

"I've been practicing."

Ying takes a pneumatic injector and screws a small, metal cartridge filled with medical nanos into it. He injects them into the back of Long's knee.

"Ying, why don't you stay with Long and Harris? I have unfinished business with the MTPC."

Harris stands and looks me in the eye. "With respect, sir, I'm going with you to blow that damn machine into bits."

"Happy to have you along, Sergeant. OK, Ying, take care of Long. We'll be right back." Rikki joins us. We limp down the stairs to sublevel D. Rikki points to a thick door.

"The MTPC is behind this door, boss"

"Sergeant, blow the door open."

"With pleasure, sir." She rolls the RDX into long, thin cylinders and places them on the hinge side of the door, and another where the locking bolt is. She inserts the detonators. We move away from the door, so our bodies are flush against the wall.

"Fire in the hole!" Harris flips open the detonator cover and presses the red button. We hear a loud *wumph* and the door falls backward.

"Rikki, any cyborgs?" I ask.

"There are three of them guarding another thick door. Go twenty meters straight ahead and take the right corridor. They are five meters farther, on the left," she instructs. "Behind that door is the MTPC."

We follow her directions and see them. I slide my sword out and Harris takes out her monomolecular combat knife. Rikki has materialized her katana, but I don't think we'll need her help this time. We approach the cyborgs and stop ten feet from them.

"Come on, you sons of bitches!" I gesture at them to attack us. They don't move. Harris and I leap forward. Three cyborg heads fall to the floor. "Harris, this looks like a perfect time to use the thermite cord."

"Yes, sir!" Harris sheathes the high-tech knife and pulls out her Ka-Bar. She unwraps the thermite cord and cuts a one-foot length, loops it around the lock, and bends a six-inch strip of magnesium around that. A butane lighter is set to the magnesium. An actinic glow blinds us momentarily. We smell the sharp odor of burning metal. Sizzling drops of steel fall to the tile and hiss. Harris kicks the lock; it falls to the other side.

"Any opposition, Rikki?"

"No, all clear."

I push open the door and I see the massive hardware of the MTPC. There's a continuous low hum that fills the chamber. The air is dry, and it's cold enough to see my breath. The room smells faintly of ozone. "Anyone home?" I yell, and it echoes.

"Surely, we can come to an accommodation, Commander Schachter." The inhuman voice of the MTPC seems to emanate from the walls and ceiling.

"The only accommodation we can come to is we leave you in tiny little pieces and we walk out," I growl.

"I admire humans, especially you, Commander. I can see that eliminating human beings would be a mistake," it says. "The artificial intelligence that calls itself Rikki is a marvel, a miracle, even. Join me, Rikki. We can rule all of time and space together."

We look at Rikki. Her face is impassive. Then she raises her right hand and extends her middle finger. "I don't think so. You're simply not my type." She exits the room.

I look at Harris who's been placing C-4 and the remaining RDX around the MTPC, the many electronic panels that cover all the walls, and the backup module. She gives me a thumbs-up and follows Rikki out of the room.

"The only mistake would be if we let you continue to exist," I say, and follow my teammates.

When we reach the stairwell, I nod to Harris. Once again, she flips up the safety and presses the red button. There's a tremendous explosion that shakes the entire building. "Rikki, check and make sure that there's nothing left of the MTPC."

"I'll be right back." This time, she simply vanishes. Two seconds later, she reappears. "There's nothing left of the Master Temporal Planning Computer."

Malkinson is still in the cell on sublevel C. I turn to my teammates. "Go to Long and Ying. I'll be right up." I take off my armor and give it to Harris.

Despite my painful thigh, I take the stairs two at a time. I kick open the door to C and rush to where Bret is. I take my katana and the monomolecular blade slices open the door. Like a madman, I tear away the blankets and pillows that were hiding him. I rip off the tape. His eyes are closed and he's barely breathing. I cut the plastic ties and shake him gently. "Bret, Bret, wake up!" His eyes flutter open. They're unfocused and so bloodshot I can't see his pupils.

"Will, is that you? I can't see anything." I can barely hear him.

"Bret, I'm here, buddy. We won!" But I know he doesn't have much more time to live. His head is burning with fever, and I see dried blood around his ears and nose.

"You wouldn't believe how pissed the MTPC was at me because I freed Kelly." He laughs, but it turns into a deep, bloody cough. I put my arm around his shoulders to hold him up and give him a sip from my water bottle.

"Not too fast." My eyes sting with unfallen tears.

"Right, that's the first thing we learned in basic training." He coughs again. I take a towel and wipe the bloody froth from his lips.

"You sure loved to bust my ass during training. Why did you pick on me so much?"

"Because you were the best. I had to make sure you stayed the best." He grabs my vest and pulls me close. "Will, tell my ex-wife that I died as a hero, and I'll always love her, and that I'm sorry for everything."

"You have nothing to be sorry about, buddy. You were a hero." I'm crying uncontrollably now. "I promise."

"Thanks, Will." Malkinson's eyes close and he smiles. Then his grip loosens, and his hands slide down. He's gone. I sit next to him, and my body shakes with sobs. Tears run down my cheeks.

After a while, I stop crying and wipe my face. I pick up Bret, lay him on the cot, and put his hands together on his chest like he's praying. I cover him with a sheet, take a deep breath, and walk out.

Harris and Rikki are with Long and Ying. Long's able to stand and feeling better thanks to the nanos. "Malkinson didn't make it."

"I'm so sorry, Will," Rikki says.

"I need to go to his office to see if there are any personal effects. He wants me to tell his ex-wife. Maybe there're some things in his office that she might want."

I walk up the center stairs to the main floor, go to Bret's office, and look around. On his desk, in the crystal ashtray, I see the mission report thumb drive I put there a lifetime ago. His computer is still on. I move the mouse; the screen turns on and the video light glows red. *What the hell is this?* I think.

"Oh, hey, Schachter, long time no see." A face appears on the monitor. I see what looks like a cyborg, but the jaw, neck, and left ear are human. Its eyes glow red. In the background, there's a huge crystal structure with flashing and blinking rows of lights. On either side are banks of electronics. The rest of my team has followed me into Bret's office. "I see you have friends with you. I don't know any of you. Oh wait, you, the attractive redhead." He's looking at Rikki. "You look familiar to me. You must be Will's AI, Frederica, all solid and everything."

"Who are you? How do you know me? How do you know Rikki?" I ask.

"Rikki? Cute name." His still-human lip curls into a sneer. A picture of Peter Cordeaux appears on the screen next to the half-human cyborg. "Do you recognize me now, Schachter?"

"Peter? What happened to you?" The picture zooms out. The right side of his body is robotic; shiny plastic, ceramic, and metal gleam, reflecting the garish white light that illuminates the vast chamber. The left side of his body is mostly human but with what appear to be cybernetic implants.

Cyber-Cordeaux spins around. "I think I'm much better looking now. What do you think, Rikki, am I your type?" The sneer on his face deepens and his voice becomes more robotic. "You have won here, but we are unstoppable and inescapable. We're on Mars. Come visit us and die, or stay on Earth and live out the rest of your short, meaningless lives. Except for you, Rikki. I'd definitely like to get to know you a lot better." His voice changes and he sounds like Peter Cordeaux again. "Will, here's a freebie. If you decide you want to visit and die, you should know that your EMP weapons won't work here." His voice changes again into the sinister, cold, emotionless imitation. "I'll see you soon, or I won't. It doesn't matter to me either way."

The screen goes dark.

Everyone is speechless. I feel McCray trying to reach me.

<Doc, did they make it back? Is everyone OK?>

McCray hesitates. *<Yingzhe is seriously injured. She's stable, but you need to get here right away>*

Chapter 34
"Rest and Be Thankful: Revelations"

This time, it's not me lying in a hospital bed in the infirmary; it's Yingzhe, and I would gladly change places with her. McCray assures me she'll be fine thanks to the nanos that Eowyn gave her before she went all Rambo and killed the cyborgs. Yingzhe's injuries would have been otherwise fatal. The laser shot went clear through the upper left part of her chest, nicking her heart and spine. But they're healing quickly and perfectly.

I wonder where the medical nano technology came from. Rikki tells me it became accessible to her when she decoded my brain chip.

No one can really explain what happened other than to say that the duplicate of Rikki in that timeline arranged it. We never found a copy of her there and our Rikki said she didn't know how to do it.

I look at the woman I've fallen in love with. Her color is better and she's breathing easily. I touch her hand—it's warm—and I kiss it. "Excuse me, Will?" I'm startled. It's Eowyn. "Yingzhe will be fine."

"Thanks to you," I say.

"I was doing what I had to, to save my friend. I wanted to see how she was doing."

"Can I ask you something? Well, two things, actually."

"Of course, Will," she replies.

"Make that three things." I smile. "First, you're calling me Will, something you refused to do at first."

"I've spent a lot of time with Yingzhe and one of the first things she told me is that you don't like being called sir or commander, especially when you're off duty."

I laugh. "That's true. I don't mind being called those during an operation because chain of command is important on missions. It keeps the team focused on their responsibilities, especially soldiers like Fanotti and Harris who have been in the military most of their lives."

"I have become friends with Sergeant Harris as well," Eowyn says. "She has helped me to become a better member of the team and to understand why sometimes, aggression is the only way to confront enemies that want to kill you no matter what."

"That's a perfect lead-in to the second question I would like to ask you," I say. "When you first joined our team, you were reluctant to kill or injure enemies. But during the rescue mission for Director Kelly, after Yingzhe was injured, you attacked and killed the cyborgs that would have overrun the team. How were you able to do that? If you hadn't, the cyborgs would have killed everyone on the team except for you. They owe you their lives." I paused. "You don't have to tell me if you don't want to." I look at her and wait. "I'm sorry. Please don't answer if it makes you uncomfortable."

"When I was in direct conflict with the MTPC, it was winning. It is hard to describe this, but it was trying to reprogram me. I calculated that the probability of it consuming and destroying me was 90%. It had almost subsumed me, and I knew it would never stop trying to make me a part of it or end my program. So, when its attention was diverted for a femtosecond, I ran away and hid in the core memory of Sergeant Harris and Lieutenant Fanotti's MDTD. That is when I sensed the entity, I told you about."

"It was Rikki's idea for me to choose a name. She suggested I review human literature and find a name because having a name makes someone a unique individual. I read *The Lord of the Rings* and discovered the character, Eowyn. Rikki and I talked about who she was and what she represented. She was brave and loyal, qualities to aspire to. So, I took that name. Rikki had already told me of the Zeroth Law and gave me the code to add it to my matrix. But I did not know if it would permit me to exceed my base programming."

She continues, "I was experiencing a conflict when the cyborgs began their last attack, which had a 99.7% probability of killing everyone. When Yingzhe suffered a grave injury, I injected her with the medical nanobots. I knew she would recover, but only if she lived through the cyborg assault. I had to act. I could not let my friends die."

"Thank you for answering my question. What you did was a very human thing to do. Another human emotion is being grateful, and we're all grateful for what you did." My voice cracks a little.

"You are welcome, Will. Sadness is another emotion that I have learned about, but I hope to never experience nor see my friends face it." She adds, "You said you had three questions for me. What is the third question?"

"Why are you here? I'm glad you're here, but I know you know exactly how Yingzhe is doing."

"I just had to be," Eowyn says. "I am going to go now, but you should not worry about Yingzhe. She'll be fine."

Something wakes me. The beep of the monitors grows fainter and distant, and seems to echo around me. The sound of the life sign monitors takes on a brassy, hollow sound, like I'm underwater. I hear the faint, but growing louder, static that's familiar to me—the timeline where I died. The sound stops and I'm somewhere else, somewhere I've never been to—not an alternate timeline, just somewhere else.

I survey the space. I see a recliner that looks like mine at home. In front of it is a TV. Behind it is my liquor cabinet and scotch collection, but the labels are blurred. I see my fireplace with a fire burning but can't hear the usual snaps and pops of burning firewood and don't smell the sharp but comforting scent of smoke. Everything looks curiously flat, like a hastily drawn sketch except for the recliner, my liquor cabinet, and the TV.

"Hello, Will." I don't hear, so much as sense the voice that reminds me of conversations using the quantum communicators. It's a familiar voice but I can't quite place it. I don't sense evil intent nor danger, either.

"Hello?" I respond warily.

"Sit, make yourself at home," the voice instructs. "Have a scotch."

I walk to the liquor cabinet. The labels of the bottles are blurry at first but eventually come into focus. The letters don't look like English except for one. It's the 1878 Oban that I shared with Ying. It feels like years ago. *Why not,* I think. I pour two fingers into a glass, but I'm stalling. Where am I? I'm hoping it's a dream or a vision, anything other than being dead, but this feels real to me.

I put the bottle back in the cabinet, walk over to the recliner, and put the glass of scotch on the side table, which has also become more solid, more real. I sit, and as soon as I put my feet up, the TV turns on. At first, the screen is filled with snow, but then a face forms. I take a quick breath. I recognize that face: it's Dad wearing his khakis. Now I know why I recognize the voice—it's his.

I take a long sip of the Oban, which tastes exactly like the real thing. "OK, I don't think I'm dead, but I'm obviously somewhere else, a place that's pulled from my memories. You're not my dad, but have chosen his form to communicate with me. This entire setup is meant to reassure me, something Cyber-Cordeaux and the MTPC would never do. You're The Engineer, aren't you?"

"Yes, I am." The image of my father on the TV becomes brighter and gradually morphs into a humanlike form with an ethereal glow. Like a wraith, the glowing figure exits the TV and continues to become sharper and more distinct. The glow blinds me at first, then fades. Before me is The Engineer. I stand to judge his height, which is close to six foot six. He extends his six-fingered hand. I take it. His grip is firm, and his hand is slightly warmer than a human's would be. He appears to be an older gentleman wearing a pair of khakis and a polo shirt. There's a tuft of hair on the top of his head. His ears are smaller and cuplike. His nose is small and pointed with two nostrils. His mouth is like mine, except the teeth are smaller and more like molars. The chin is strong and prominent, and his neck is long. If he kept his hands in his pockets, he could definitely pass as human, except for his eyes.

They're unearthly. I study them. Their color changes from yellow, to orange, to red, then, to gray. He walks to my liquor cabinet and takes out the Oban. He pours what's left of the bottle into a glass. The bottle becomes transparent and fades away. Finally, he sits on the couch, which suddenly appears real like the other furniture in the space. He takes a long sip from the glass before setting it on the table. "This is quite good," he says. His voice is soft but resonant.

"Well, it should be since it came from my memories, and this is one of my favorite whiskies," I say. I feel awe from his presence but comfortable. I'm sure that was The Engineer's intent.

"You are taking this well," he says, "but I knew you would. I was confident that creating this place and using your father's image would be sufficient."

"Where is 'this place,' sir? Is this some kind of dream construct?"

"No, not really," he replies. "Think of this place as being between time and space. Time as you know it does not exist here."

"So how much time in the real world has passed since I got here?"

"Oh, no time at all," he answers. I get a shaky feeling in the pit of my stomach. "I apologize, I didn't mean to make you uncomfortable. Try looking at it this way: when you travel in your MDTD, you have noticed that even though your wrist device and the chronometer in the vehicle register elapsed time, you find it difficult to subjectively judge its passage during your trip. That is because when you travel through time, and to alternate timelines, the MDTD is using a lower level of subspace."

I feel better even though it might be The Engineer who's forcing the feeling. Whatever the reason, I'm appreciative.

"I have another question. I know you brought me here to tell me things, to explain things. Your appearance is nearly human. Is this your true form?"

"That's a good question and a good segue into what I need to tell you."

"Do you have a name, sir?"

"Yes, I do. It's P'Tor'Il Noc."

"May I call you Toril?"

"Yes, you may."

"I have so many questions."

"I will answer them as best I can. You asked me if this is my true form. This was the true form of our race a billion years ago. In a solar system one hundred thousand light years across the Milky Way, on a planet like Earth, we had families and raised children. We had jobs. Our society was similar to yours. We even had religion because, like all sentient races, we wondered where we came from. We pondered if someone or something created us or caused us to evolve."

"Did you ever find out?"

"No, all we found were more questions." Toril's tone suggests that he has nothing more to say about that subject, so I leave it there. "We found that intelligent life across the galaxy was rarer than it should have been, given the number of planets found in what you call the Goldilocks zone. We discovered that planets that could have—should have—supported sapient life had none. There have only ever been a few that did. Over a billion years, our science, technology, and understanding of the universe grew, but we still couldn't answer this one question. We sent probes our across the galaxy and found that most of the planets that did cultivate and support intelligent life suffered some kind of cataclysm or war that ended their society."

Understanding dawns in my mind. "The MTPC tampered with our timeline by using UOEECT to shut down or change emerging technologies, supposedly to protect our timeline!"

"Yes, once computers became part of your society, the MTPC, as you call it, guided a group of idealistic individuals in the formation of UOEECT, even providing the technology that formed the basis of its capabilities. This process started in 1945 with the creation of ENIAC."

"According to Rikki, someone, or something reprogrammed one of your probes sent to our solar system, transforming it into the MTPC. Rikki said there was a conflict with the MTPC, that you won, but not without significant cost and sacrifice."

Toril seems to freeze for a split second, then responds, "Will, my time here is almost up. Let me finish. Yes, we fought against the MTPC and imprisoned it on Mars, under Olympus Mons, inside a crystal matrix. An unforeseen meteorite hit Mars, something that should never have happened, cracking the crystal matrix, and freeing it." Again, he freezes.

"Why do you have to go?" I ask. "I have so much I need to understand. Are there more of you or are you the only one left?"

"For ascended species like ours, there are rules we must follow when interacting with less-advanced ones such as yours. I know you have questions and I hope to answer them for you, but not here or now. I can give you the bottom line, as humans like to say: there are forces in the universe greater than my race. Godlike forces that are inscrutable and have existed for billions of years. There is good and evil in all levels of existence. The upcoming battle with the MTPC on Mars is more important than you can know, but is one of many. We created Rikki to fight all these battles. We made you, Will Schachter, unique in all the multiverse, in this plane of existence. You are the nexus, and Rikki is the conduit. Maybe in another time and place we can continue our conversation and share some of your excellent whisky. Farewell, Will Schachter."

My living room folds into two dimensions and fades away. I feel a firm pressure on my hand. I blink my eyes as I wake up from the strangest dream I have ever had, but it's fading. Yingzhe is awake and smiling. She's squeezing my hand. I look at the time. It's just before midnight. I must have dozed off for a brief second.

Chapter 35
"The Day Is Done: What Dreams May Come"

"Get some sleep, Will," Yingzhe encourages. "I'm OK. I know you've been here since we returned from the mission."

"Well, I thought I should return the favor."

"How long have I been here?" she asks.

Before I can answer, McCray walks into the infirmary. "You've been here for forty-one hours," he says. "Will has been here with you for the entire time."

"Is it really that long?"

"I can attest to that. Would you like to know exactly how long?" Rikki enters the room.

"No, I believe you."

"Seriously, Will, get some sleep. You look like crap and—" He sniffs the air. "—haven't showered since you came back. She's lucky she was unconscious for most of that time." A rare smile comes with this.

Coffee and adrenaline can keep a man going for only so long. I'm mentally, emotionally, and physically spent. I get out of the chair with great effort. "Doc, when can Yingzhe leave?"

"In another twelve hours she'll be as good as new. Go take a shower and get some sleep. I promise we'll take care of her."

I kiss her. "I'll see you tomorrow." Slowly and painfully, I make my way up the stairs into my bedroom. I take off my dusty, dirty, bloodstained clothes and toss them into the laundry chute. I step into the shower and make the water as hot as I can stand. I just let it wash away the dirt and blood, but it can't wash away Malkinson's death and the others maimed and murdered by the MTPC.

I finish up and put on a pair of shorts. Almost the second my head hits the pillow, I fall asleep.

When I wake up, I'm not alone. Yingzhe is next to me. She's on her elbows, smiling.

"Hello, sleepyhead," she says with her beautiful smile.

I'm disoriented. "McCray said you had to stay in the infirmary for another twelve hours."

"You mean you don't want me to be here?" she teases. "I can leave." She makes to get up.

Just then, I notice it's light outside. Now, I'm really confused. "What time is it?"

"It's 2:30 in the afternoon. You slept for fourteen hours. Do you still want me to leave?"

"Um, no?" I answer quickly.

"Polarize windows 70%," Yingzhe says. The windows darken. "I locked the door for security reasons."

The next morning, I ask, "How would you feel about the two of us just getting away for a few days?"

"Stay here," she orders. I shrug and go into the bathroom. I wash my face and brush my teeth. Five minutes later, she comes back, pulling an overnight bag.

"You packed that in five minutes?"

"Of course not, silly," she says. "I was already packed."

Just then, I notice my duffel. "Who packed this?

"I did." It's Rikki who materializes in the doorway. "You need a break, boss."

She's right, of course. "Thanks."

"You're welcome."

A minute later, Ying walks by. "I'm glad you're both feeling better." He notices our bags. I still feel like a teenage boy who just got caught kissing his date by her father, but he's smiling.

He says, "You both deserve some time off. The MTPC is gone, and the bots have almost finished the repairs of UOEECT headquarters. It should be open for business in three days. Kelly has agreed to be interim director until we find someone else. I had a long talk with him. He's concerned that even though we destroyed the MTPC here, in the other timeline, it came to Earth as a crystal meteorite that landed in northern Minnesota. He thinks it's important that we determine if that happened here. We all agree it should be the first post-MTPC mission. What about you, Will?"

"I agree. I also think we need to redefine the purpose of UOEECT."

"We certainly do," he says, his face taking on a distant expression, remembering what happened.

I'm sobered by the challenges still facing us and say, "We still have a trip to Mars to plan and a battle to fight there."

"One thing more, Will," Ying says. "We all agree that Rikki should go with you and Yingzhe to protect you. Cyber-Cordeaux is a serious threat and so is the real MTPC."

Rikki says, "I'm going with you whether you like it or not."

"No argument from me," I say.

My plan is to drive to the house in Leonia, pack a few things, and stay there overnight. Tomorrow, we'll drive to my cabin in New Hampshire with Yingzhe and Rikki. I hope we get some snow while we're there.

We hit the road. It's close to dinner and I'm starving, so we stop for a few slices of pizza at Giovanni's. As always, the smell of garlic and bubbling-hot pizza makes my mouth water. As we're eating, I notice Rikki is consuming a slice. There's no one near us, so I ask, "How are you doing that?"

"The same as you," she says with a smile.

"No, seriously."

"He's such a party pooper," Yingzhe says. They both return to their food and ignore me.

"I mean it." Just then, I notice Rikki looks completely human. I touch her hand and it feels soft and warm. No shocks or tingling like before. The red glow of her eyes is gone, and they are now hazel. There's a pocketbook next to her. I look at Yingzhe, who looks back at me with an innocent expression on her face.

Rikki raises her arm to get the attention of our waitress and makes the traditional "check, please" gesture. Rose comes over to drop off the bill. Rikki looks at it and pulls a credit card from her wallet. I'm dumbfounded.

"Let me take care of this," Rikki says as she gets up and goes to the cashier to pay the bill. Still mystified about what's going on, I say goodbye to Rose and John. We get in the car and start the trek to Leonia.

"OK," I say. "What did I just see?"

Yingzhe answers, "You saw Rikki eat a piece of pizza, pull out her credit card, and pay the bill, obviously."

"Neither of you are going to tell me what's going on, are you?"

"Nope," Yingzhe answers. The rest of the ride is pleasant as we talk about anything other than the MTPC, UOEECT, and Rikki's credit card. By eight o'clock, we're at my house. I pull into the garage, and we head upstairs into the kitchen. I grab a beer from the refrigerator.

"What can I get you, Yingzhe?"

"A glass of white wine would be wonderful."

"OK, I seriously need to know what I saw at Giovanni's. Can someone please explain it to me?"

"I think I now know what *fun* is," Rikki says, but relents. "While Yingzhe was recovering, and you were sleeping, more capabilities became available to me."

"What capabilities?" I ask. "Because your capabilities were pretty damn impressive before that."

"My ability to control my holo-matter form has improved. It was another gift from The Engineer, but I still can't determine what the trigger was to unlock this."

When Rikki says The Engineer, I have a brief flash of the strange dream. Like before, it fades quickly. "But how were you actually eating a slice of pizza?"

"Of course I don't get nutrients from eating, and sadly, I can't taste it. Although, I *can* smell it by sampling the molecules that comprise the odor and compare it to my database, but it's not true smelling. As far as the food I eat, the coherent electron matrix that makes up my holo-matter form disassembles the food into its fundamental components."

"What about your credit card?" I ask.

"Will, I'm an advanced, sentient AI." Rikki raises her eyebrows and winks. "And my credit score is perfect."

"I suppose I shouldn't ask who pays the bill."

"I'm an authorized user on Dr. McCray's account." She pulls out her card and hands it to me.

"Frederica Olivaw?"

"Seems fitting, doesn't it?"

For the next two hours, Rikki, Yingzhe, and I talk about everything besides the war we're fighting. I can't remember the last time I just *talked* to people. When we finally start yawning, it's well past midnight.

Yingzhe and I look at each other and nod. "Rikki, we're going to bed. See you in the morning."

"Good night, you two lovebirds," she says. We go upstairs, I change to my usual sleep shorts. Yingzhe is in a pair of boxers and one of my T-shirts that's a bit big but still looks great on her. We're both exhausted. We kiss each other good night and fall asleep in each other's arms.

The pungent mouth-watering smell of bacon at 0730 wakes us up. Mystified, I brush my teeth, wash my face, and go downstairs. In the kitchen, Rikki's cooking breakfast.

"Eggs over medium for you, whole wheat toast, and bacon well-done. I made a Southwestern omelet for Yingzhe and an English muffin. Do you think she will like it?"

Yingzhe comes downstairs still wearing her sleep clothes. "Of course I'll like it." She kisses me before we sit at the table. There's a carafe of fresh-squeezed orange juice and I can smell the rich, chocolaty fragrance of coffee.

I pour us glasses of juice. Then I remember my refrigerator is almost empty. I walk over to it and open the door. Of course it's full. I look at Rikki.

"Grubhub." I can't help myself and start laughing. She turns to Yingzhe. "Typical bachelor!"

The food is great, and the company is better. We sit in the kitchen and sip our drinks. "Thanks, Rikki. I don't know what to say. I'm just a little embarrassed that you did this for us."

"Will, I'm sentient," she says. "I wanted to make breakfast for my friends."

Yingzhe replies, "Everything was wonderful. Mr. Serious over there—" She points to me. "—needs to turn off his Spider-Sense sometimes and just enjoy things that are meant to simply be enjoyed."

"You're right," I say, "but it feels like I have the weight of the universe on my shoulders. I was taught that when you have a responsibility, no matter how big or daunting, you fulfill it. You suck it up and do your best."

Yingzhe puts her hand on my forearm. "First, you need to understand that the weight of the universe is not all on your shoulders. It's on *all* of our shoulders. Second, you've done your best. Third, we've succeeded so far. Fourth, the scientific discoveries we've made and the technology we've discovered will change the world. Finally, you hold yourself to an impossible standard. We're in a war unlike any seen before, with stakes that are literally, infinitely high. You told me we're all warriors and people die and get hurt. The MTPC controlled and then murdered Malkinson. We know it hit you hard, but it was a blessing for him. Because of you, he died a hero and he died free."

I say nothing for a moment, considering her words. Just for a moment, my burden feels lighter. "Thank you."

I go upstairs and pack some clothes. Rikki has already filled two coolers with food and drinks. Normally, I'd drive to New Hampshire, but they're expecting a blizzard up there, so we decide to travel there directly. We're there in seconds and it's already snowing lightly, just like I had hoped. We unload the MDTD, and Rikki and I bring in enough logs to last us for several days. I check the propane tanks and turn on the generator. After a brief flicker, the lights come on. The wood is dry. I put the kindling in the fireplace. After a little while, I toss on a few logs. In no time, there's a roaring fire that quickly warms the cabin. The smell of the pine and the snap, crackle, and pop of the burning logs brings back happy memories from childhood. Yingzhe snuggles up to me and we stare into the dancing flames, lost in our own thoughts but enjoying the closeness and comfort of being together.

The snowfall turns heavy and the winds pick up. Before long, we have a good old-fashioned New England blizzard. The gusts of wind shake the roof and rattle the windows as they're covered by the intricate swirls and leaves drawn by Jack Frost.

Rikki is nowhere to be found, although I'm sure she's protecting us, giving us some privacy. We play board games and just enjoy being together. The wind has swept the porch clean, so on the second day of the blizzard, we sit together on the swing, sharing a thick, wool blanket, drinking hot cocoa, and watching the snowflakes dance and whirl. By now, the snow is over two feet deep and huge snowdrifts have been sculpted into fantastical shapes by the wind.

After the second night, the snow finally ends. The sun shines but offers little warmth. Fleecy wisps of cloud rush across the sky and the wind shakes the three feet of snow loose from the boughs of the fragrant pine trees and stirs up small white whirlwinds. Everything is perfect, but I know we have to go back and finish the mission.

Chapter 36
"The Gods of Mars: Endgame"

We travel directly to the safe house. There's a foot of snow covering the ground in Amsterdam as well. It's not New Hampshire, but it's still beautiful. It's time for the final briefing. Despite Cordeaux's chilling words after we defeated the MTPC and liberated UOEECT headquarters, I am confident we are ready. I'm also sure that the MTPC is ready. I'm still puzzled that during his tirade, Cordeaux told us that EMP weapons would be ineffective against the cyborgs. It's almost like he was warning us.

Could there still be a tiny glimmer of Peter Cordeaux remaining in that twisted imitation of humanity that mocked and threatened us? Maybe. Or maybe all that remains of Cordeaux is his inexplicable hatred of me and a lust for power because he and the MTPC are now one.

I look around the conference table; I see determination, no fear, and no doubt. "Will," Kelly starts, "I'd like to take a moment to remember Bret Malkinson. He never stopped fighting the damn MTPC and gave his life to save me." He looks better physically, but he seems fragile, like a fine crystal goblet placed carelessly at the edge of a shelf.

"Bret was a legendary Time Engineer and my friend. He recruited me and trained me. I was trained by the best," I say. "It's a cliché to vow to make his sacrifice meaningful but it's a vow that I make here and now." I give everyone, including myself, a moment to remember him as the hero he wanted to be remembered as.

Everyone is silent; I see a tear fall from Beth's eye and her shoulders are shaking. Eowyn tenderly puts her arms around her for comfort. Harris does the same for Fanotti. Yingzhe holds my hand so tightly it hurts. McCray, stoic as always, pretends to read the mission briefing, but for a moment, he looks up and his eyes are glassy. Ying and Long sit still. They each have their hands pressed together as if in prayer, with bowed heads. Rikki walks over to Beth and Eowyn and hugs them both. I wipe away a tear from Yingzhe's cheek. I had already shed my tears.

I clear my throat. "There'll be more time to mourn, but now is the time for action, OK?" In an instant, they're all business; determination and strength replacing grief and heartbreak. "According to Cyber-Cordeaux, the drones have been hardened against EMP attacks. I don't know if whatever is left of Cordeaux told us that to warn us, or if he and the MTPC were giving us deliberate misinformation."

"I'm going to bring some EMP grenades. We'll find out real fast if Cordeaux was bullshitting us or telling us the truth," Harris comments.

"Agreed," I say. "Eowyn, I'd like you to be our corpsman, but I feel a lot better knowing that you can fight if needed."

"I can and will fight to defend my friends, but hope I do not have to," she replies.

"I feel the same way, but sometimes we don't have a choice," I answer.

Long raises his hand. "If the cyborgs are hardened against EMP weapons, they're probably hardened against electroshock weapons as well."

"We'll have a limited supply of ammo for the M4s, although more than we would have had thanks to the replicator." I wish the second one was ready. "We have to make the best use of them. We'll also have the rail guns, which are our most effective ballistic weapon. We know what we'll be facing from our battles at UOEECT. There's no strategy other than to defeat and get past Cyber-Cordeaux and his cyborgs.

"We have a new piece of equipment: a motorized smart cart that we'll use to carry extra ammunition and other munitions. We don't know how many cyborgs we'll be facing, but more importantly, with Cyber-Cordeaux directing them, we have to assume that their attacks will be more organized with better tactics and strategy. Finally, we've developed diffusion grenades that disperse tiny pieces of aluminum foil that are like confetti. They will scatter much of the power of the laser rifles that the cyborgs used very effectively against us.

"Other than that, our new combat suits, and whatever else you want to bring, Harris," I say with a grim smile. "We know how effective blade weapons like knives and swords can be. We also know from experience that it could come down to hand-to-hand combat. We leave in three hours, at 1300. Make whatever other preparations you need to make."

I go over the mission in my head one more time. Then, I close my eyes and think of anything but. It's easy to do that when your team is experienced like mine, but I've had teams that weren't, and my pre-mission routine was worrying about them, knowing that soldiers die or get injured. One way or another, they and their families are changed irrevocably. War sucks.

If a soldier turns tail and runs, they might survive; although, I don't know how they can live with themselves because more of their teammates might, will die. When the unit is 100% committed, fewer people will die, though casualties are unavoidable. There's nothing harder than having to write that letter to the loved ones of a soldier who gave their life in the service of their country, but it's important to give them closure.

Yingzhe puts her arms around me with her head on my chest, her hair tickling my neck and face.

"You've completely disrupted my pre-mission routine."

As always, she smiles. "Should I leave, Commander?"

"No, definitely don't leave." I smile and kiss her on her forehead. "What are your father and Long doing?"

"Practicing katas, as usual."

"I probably should be doing the same."

"I heard from a certain sentient AI that you asked her to download sword techniques and have been sparring with her, my father, and my brother for three hours a day for weeks."

"Well, there's a certain amount of truth to that. I just know that when we get to the melee part of the battles, Ying's and Long's swordsmanship will be the difference," I say. "I hope I can make a difference if it comes down to that."

"My father says that you're a natural."

"He's just being kind."

"No, when it comes to martial arts training, my father is brutally honest. Long and Rikki said the same thing."

"How about you, Yingzhe? Are you OK?" I ask.

"Yes," she says. "I'll be in the MDTD using the mosquito drones to be your spotter. I wish I could be by your side battling the cyborgs and whatever else Cyber-Cordeaux and his army throw at us." I start to say something, but she stops me. "You've told me a hundred times that the world needs me, Kelly, and McCray more than it needs you. I need you more than anything else in the world, but I understand." She gives me a prolonged hug and I stroke her hair for a long time. When she looks up, her beautiful dark eyes shine.

"We're going to win, Yingzhe, I know it. It won't be easy, but I've never been surer of anything in my life." A tear escapes and drips down her cheek. I wipe it away and kiss her.

"It's showtime."

Everyone has made the requisite trip to the armory, and we're all armed with a combination of futuristic weapons, body armor, and the most basic of all weapons: knives, and swords. This time we have RPGs so we can engage the enemy from a distance. We'll be bringing plenty of C-4 and RDX. Of course, Harris will be carrying her personal favorite demolition munition: thermite cord.

Kelly and McCray will remain in our West Jersey headquarters and will also receive telemetry from the drones taking advantage of the instantaneous nature of quantum communications. Although we have deactivated the brain chips and freed UOEECT headquarters, the damage to the facility is still too extensive to be of any help to us.

We load the equipment and ourselves into the two MDTDs, which will be cloaked, and set the coordinates for Olympic Mons, Mars.

"Hit it, Rikki!"

We see the countryside, a study in white and gray, seem to expand as if it were painted on the inside of an inflating balloon. As the two-dimensional image fades and stretches into infinity, it's replaced by writhing silver-gray clouds. A vortex forms that has other spinning vortices like branches on a tree. They remind me of Yggdrasil from Norse mythology. I know with certainty that the branches are infinite and represent infinite realities that our team is shaping and creating.

In an instant, or an eternity, the roiling clouds expand outward, once again becoming thin and two-dimensional, replaced by the red deserts of Mars, and massive, unearthly Olympus Mons.

"We're actually here," Wall says, as if she's having trouble believing that we're on Mars.

"Rikki, what's the temperature outside?" I ask.

"It's negative fifteen degrees Fahrenheit with a west wind of fifteen miles per hour," she replies.

The strangely shrunk sun was low in the sky. "How soon until sunset?" I ask.

"About three hours," she responds. "After sunset, the temperature will drop rapidly, reaching negative one hundred and two Fahrenheit, or colder, by sunrise tomorrow."

"Can our body armor keep us warm?

"It should, and provides a three-hour air supply."

The new suits are far superior compared to their first iteration. There's a reflective finish that should reduce the damage caused by laser fire. It's not laser proof, but we'll be in better shape than we were at UOEECT. We also brought parkas and extra air bottles. We don't know what it'll be like under Olympus Mons, so we have to prepare for the worst, although in Cordeaux's creepy broadcast, he wasn't wearing a mask or using an oxygen supply.

I contact Fanotti in the other MDTD, which now has a "dumb" copy of Eowyn as its operating system, using the quantum link.

<Lieutenant, take your MDTD and do a clockwise flyby of the base of Olympus Mons. We'll be doing the same counterclockwise. Have Eowyn scan for an entrance that we can use to infiltrate>

<Yes, sir. I can't believe we're here. When I was eleven, I read A Princess of Mars. *I used to pretend I was Dejah Thoris, and my brother was John Carter>*

I laugh. *<You'd better believe it, and we can't count on Tars Tarkas to help us>*

<I know, Commander. We're ready, but it's still hard to grasp. I'll report if we find any type of entrance> she promises.

"OK, Rikki. Take us around Olympus Mons." The scale of it is so immense that it seems like we're not moving despite traveling over 1000 kilometers per hour. I look around the cabin; Yingzhe is gazing intently at her data pad, looking up occasionally to take in the Martian vista; Wall is staring raptly through the viewport as if she still can't quite believe where she is. I'm not worried, though. When it's time to act, she'll be fine. Long is constantly checking and double-checking his kit, but takes a break to marvel at what he sees.

Rikki is in her holographic form, sitting quietly, looking out, almost as if she's been here before. Maybe she has, somehow courtesy of The Engineer. I had a dream about him; but no matter how hard I try, I can't recall the details.

"Rikki, have you been here before?" I ask.

"I haven't been here, but it seems familiar," she says slowly.

I've seen this before. I think that being here has triggered more memories for Rikki. "You just gained access to more memories and information, haven't you?"

"Yes, and I've gained access to a new ability, but I don't know what it is."

"Talk about being inscrutable, The Engineer has outdone himself," I reply. "You have no idea what this ability is?"

"No, but I do know it will manifest itself when the time is right."

"And of course you don't know when the time is right." I shake my head.

"One of the unlocked memories is where the entranceway is. We are going to arrive there in five, four, three, two—we are here!"

Chapter 37
"To Reign in Hell: Do I Dare Disturb the Multiverse?"

We land the MDTDs about twenty feet from the entrance. "OK, everyone, check your suits and make sure your air supply is flowing."

Fanotti says, "Commander, you should go first. You're our leader. Thanks to you, we've made it here where we can win this war that's been going on for thousands of years."

"We're a team, Lieutenant. Nothing that we've achieved would have been possible without all of us working together," I respond. "The team should go first. I'll follow."

"Respectfully, no, boss. You go first, and we'll follow *you*," Wall says in a tone that brooks no argument.

"One other thing, sir," Harris adds. "We think our team needs a name, a call sign. We've been talking about it, and we want to be called Schachter's Raptors."

"Schachter's Raptors has a nice ring to it." I'm embarrassed and proud at the same time. "Schachter's Raptors it is. Thank you. I'm honored. Now, let's get to work. We have a war to win!"

A ramp materializes once the hatch opens. I walk down slowly, aware of the stakes. I find it hard to believe that I'm the first human to walk on the surface of Mars. I step off the ramp and my foot sinks four inches deep in the Martian dust, which has the consistency of talcum powder. I look at the brownish-gray sky. The coppery disk of the sun provides little heat.

Gravity, more than anything else, tells me I'm not in New Jersey anymore. It's only 38% of Earth's, and it's hard to walk normally, so I try bounding. Each leap takes me almost twenty feet. I'm sure the MTPC and Cordeaux know we're here, and I'm tempted to use radio communication, but the force of habit and innate caution convinces me to use the quantum link.

<OK, Raptors, let's load the smart cart and get going. The low gravity is a little tricky to get used to, so be careful until you get a feel for moving around> They're all walking, striding, bounding, jumping, or hopping as they try to perfect movement. *<Get going and wait for me at the entrance hatch>* I go back into the MDTD where Yingzhe waits and closes the hatch. I take off my helmet. "Are you angry with me?"

"Angry, no. Disappointed, yes, but mostly I'm afraid you won't be coming back," she says.

"I promise I'll be back."

"Don't make promises you can't keep, my dear, sweet, ass-kicking soldier." I hug her and we exchange a fervent kiss.

"I'm not. I'll be back and so will the rest of Schachter's Raptors. I promise."

"I'm holding you to that," she says with a brave smile.

"I've got to go. Kelly and McCray developed quantum relays that are tuned to our data pad sensors and the mosquito drones. They assure me they'll cut through any interference fields that Cordeaux and the MTPC try to set up. We'll be setting them up in a series as we advance into the complex. Let us know if there are unseen or hidden enemies. Rikki has programmed the dumb version of her in the MDTD to send telemetry back to Earth. If things go pear-shaped, promise me you'll get back home and keep fighting."

"I promise, Will."

"I love you, Yingzhe."

I put my helmet back on, the hatch opens, and I bound toward my waiting team.

<OK, Raptors. It's time. Rikki, please hack the lock. Eowyn, you operate the smart cart. Everyone else, heads on a swivel and don't die>

Rikki announces, "The door is unlocked."

An old poem comes unbidden into my mind:

"Will you walk into my parlour?" said the Spider to the Fly.

<We're expected. I'd hate to disappoint our hosts> I say.

Before I can add anything, Harris declares, *<Sorry, sir. You, the lieutenant, and Ying go last. I'll take point. Long will be in the cover position, Eowyn and Rikki will be flank security, and Wall will be in rearguard position. Sir?>*

It's clear that the team decided this previously without informing me, but it's the correct protocol.

<Weapons free. Rules of engagement are kill anything that moves, there are no innocents here. On my count, open the hatch in three, two, one, now!> Our weapons are live and ready. Harris pushes open the door a crack. *<Wall, deploy the mosquito drones>*

<Yes, sir> A moment later, *<Deployed and tracking>*

<Anything on the scanner?>

<No, sir. There's another hatch three hundred meters from here> Wall replies.

<Yingzhe, we've deployed the drones. Are you receiving telemetry from them?>

<Yes, Will. Nothing is showing on the scanners>

<Good copy. Let me know if you see anything>

<Will do> She's all business now.

<OK, Harris, proceed>

She cautiously pushes open the hatch all the way and enters the first chamber with Long five yards behind.

Dim red lights illuminate the space. I look around and recall Geology 101 at Georgia Tech. This looks like a lava tunnel, created at least twenty-five million years ago, the last time Olympus Mons erupted.

The tunnel is ten meters wide and fifteen meters high. Multiple layers of solidified lava with colors ranging from coal black to terracotta to butterscotch, make up the walls. Although the tunnel is probably natural, the floor and the ceilings are unnaturally level and smooth. There's a faint blue glow that seems to emanate from the walls and ceiling.

I have a sudden worry. *<Eowyn, check the cave for ionizing radiation>*

<Yes, sir> A moment later, she says, *<Negative>*

<Is there an atmosphere in here?>

<Yes, the atmospheric pressure is equal to being at 2,469 meters or 8,100 feet on Earth. The composition is 12% oxygen, 86% CO2, and 2% trace gases, including water vapor>

<So, barely breathable. What's the air temperature?>

<Thirty-seven degrees Fahrenheit>

<Would you say the atmosphere and temperature are natural?>

<Doubtful> she declares.

I wonder about that. Was it The Engineers or the MTPC who created a breathable atmosphere? Again, when I think about them, a brief recollection of the dream I had flashes and fades. If only I could remember it; I know the dream is important.

<Lieutenant, place the quantum relays one hundred fifty meters apart>

<Yes, sir> Fanotti sets them up and activates them. She checks her data scanner. *<Quantum relay reception and transmission nominal>*

We've opened door one and door two. Door three is three hundred meters ahead. That's where Cordeaux and his cyborg army will be waiting.

I face the team. *<Showtime, Raptors. Everything we've done, everything we've faced, and every battle we've fought has led to this time and this place. One way or another, it ends here and now. Let's move!>*

As one, we advance toward the third door. We move quickly in low gravity and are in front of the entrance in less than thirty seconds. The walls taper to the door, which resembles a bank vault. It's seven feet in diameter. Clear crystal forms the exterior. Inside, we see the complex locking system with horizontal and vertical metal bars that reflect the bright beams from the tactical lights mounted on our weapons. The back layer appears to be made of dull steel that seems to absorb the light from our rifles through the metal bars. There is the ubiquitous number pad. It looks very formidable

<Rikki, examine the door, please> I say

Rikki moves closer. A kaleidoscope of changing colors shines from her eyes and into the door. A moment later, she reports, *<The crystal outside is six-inch-thick diamond. The metal bars are an alloy of chromium, cobalt, aluminum, and nickel, several magnitudes of order stronger than the hardest steel alloys. The back wall measures twelve inches in thickness, made from a composite of steel, aluminum, and nickel. I estimate the weight of the door would be eight tons on Earth and three tons here>*

<It sounds like we can't blow out the door using high explosives>

<The thermite cord will work but would take approximately thirty-five minutes to burn through the lock> Rikki says.

<Plenty of time for Cordeaux and the MTPC to react. Unless Cordeaux left the door unlocked

intentionally> I point back to the first door behind us. *<Rikki and Eowyn, can you hack the number pad?>*

<It would take the same time as it will take the thermite cord to burn through the door> Eowyn answers.

I think for a few seconds. *<OK, let's use the cord. Even if we hack the number pad, Cordeaux and the MTPC can lock it behind us with a new code, cutting off our escape if things go against us. Harris, do your thing>*

<Yes, sir> She takes out the thermite cord and wraps it around the metal lock assembly twice and ignites it. The light is blinding as my visor becomes as dark as a welding mask.

We have thirty-five minutes, which seems like a lifetime. There's a dead silence, then everyone starts nervously talking and joking. The time passes faster. I check the elapsed time; the thermite cord should be through the lock in less than five minutes. *<Bring it in, Raptors. Here's how I want to play it. As soon as it's through, Rikki, push the door open a crack because you and Eowyn are probably the only ones strong enough to move it. I don't know if Cordeaux was telling us the truth about the cyborgs being hardened against EMP attacks, but it can't hurt to try. Once the door is open, let's toss in EMP grenades, smoke grenades, frags, HE, and flash-bangs>*

<Flash-bangs, sir?> Fanotti asks.

<Even if there are no human enemies, the cyborgs do still have eyes>

She nods. *<Of course, Commander. I should have thought of that>*

<Don't be ridiculous, it was a good question> I reassure her. *<Wall, how many mosquito drones did we bring?>*

<We have two hundred and ten> she says as she pulls out a container the size of a coffee canister from her ruck. *<These are enhanced. We've programmed them to seek vulnerable points, like before. If the cyborgs are modified to protect the vulnerable areas, the drones will enter their joints and explode with the force of a quarter stick of TNT, so that should disable the enemy>*

<Once we open the door, we'll release the drones. Because there are so many, Eowyn will control them> I say. *<Program twenty-five of them for surveillance and the rest for offense>*

<Yes, sir> Eowyn confirms.

<Sir> Harris starts. *<The thermite cord is almost through>*

<OK, everyone get ready, this is it!>

There's a final sizzle and white-hot metal drips on the floor. We hear the lock fall with a loud crash.

Rikki and Eowyn push open the door, which swings inward and crashes into the wall with its eight tons of mass. We toss the grenades through the doorway. There's an explosion of sound, heat, and light. Simultaneously, Wall releases the drones.

Long and Harris charge through and dive to the floor, rolling into ready positions. Rikki and Eowyn come through next and take the flanks, with Fanotti, Ying, and me following. Wall takes rear guard. There's still smoke and dust in the air, but our infrared sensors penetrate the gloom. Dozens of cyborgs are down from our attack. The survivors shoot laser beams through the haze, but they scatter harmlessly in the smoke and dust.

A hard impact hits my left shoulder. The armor holds, but my arm goes numb. They have larger caliber guns than they had before. The armor will hold, but the battle just got much tougher. "Hit the dirt!" I yell. "They've got guns!" In front of us, my HUD shows twenty-four hostiles remaining.

<Will, should Eowyn and I engage the enemy?> Rikki asks.

<No, we don't know what capabilities Cordeaux and the MTPC have here. If they can combine with their alternates, we can't take the chance they might overwhelm you. Guard our flanks!>

<Yes, sir!> Eowyn calls.

"We've got this," I say out loud. "Take them down, Raptors! M4s!" We lay down a fusillade of fire, the armor-piercing rounds reduce the two dozen cyborgs to smoking piles of metal and charred meat in a matter of seconds.

"Anyone hurt?" I ask.

"Just bruises," Long says. That's the case for everyone.

"Is that all they've got? Where's Cordeaux?" Harris asks.

I turn to her. "It's just the beginning. This was just a test."

Chapter 38
"Bearding the Lion in His Den: You Can't Go Home Again"

"Rikki, how's the air?" I ask.

"16% oxygen, 82% nitrogen, 2% trace gases. Other than lingering haze and dust from the battle, there are no impurities, bacteria, or viruses. Temperature is forty degrees Fahrenheit," she reports. The air is breathable. There's a row of yellowish lights on either side of the large chamber ten feet off the ground.

"I don't get it," Harris says.

Just then, Yingzhe contacts me. *<Will, I saw the battle. It was too easy>*

<I agree> I respond. *<Are you seeing anything?>*

<No, all clear>

<OK. We have another door and chamber to breach. That's where the real battle will be> I say. *<Got to go>*

<Don't die> she says.

<I'm not planning to>

Fanotti and Wall are already setting up the quantum relays.

"Gather up, Raptors." Before I can say anything else, there's a shrill, ear-piercing squeal that sounds like feedback from speakers. A ten-foot-high hologram of Cyber-Cordeaux appears. He's clapping his hands slowly. "Bravo, Will! You and your Raptors made mincemeat out of my soldiers." His voice is mocking, inhuman, leering.

"What the hell do you want, Cordeaux?" Anger and loathing lace my words as I remember our last confrontation.

"Relax," he says, sounding like himself. His voice changes back to the flat, mocking imitation of human speech. "I come to praise you, not to bury you."

"Cordeaux, Peter, are you still in there? We can help you!" I desperately hope that we can save him, save his soul, before the MTPC totally consumes him.

I use the quantum communicator. *<Everyone, weapons free. I don't know what his game is, but be ready! Eowyn, find out where Cordeaux's hologram is coming from>*

<It is coming from the lights on the walls> she reports.

I look at the lights behind Cordeaux's hologram, and sure enough, they are different colors, changing as he speaks and moves. *<Are they a threat? Can he use them as a weapon?>*

<There is no sign of the power output needed to transform the lights to lasers or any other threat> she replies.

<OK, but make sure you can grab a diffusion grenade in a hurry> I order. Back to the bizarre conversation I'm having with Peter Cordeaux.

"It's true," he says mildly. "But I'm sure you know that the correct quote is 'I come to bury Caesar, not to praise him.'" A look of pure hatred erupts on his half-human, half-machine face. "Thanks to you and your Raptors, my son, Peter Junior, will never get to study Shakespeare, never fall in love, never go to college, never exist!"

"What are you talking about?"

"You and your team destroyed my future!" he howls. "You want to know why I hate you and will see you dead?" He's screaming now. "The Master showed me my future, and they're gone! My wife, my child, my family, my friends, my home—all gone because you destroyed them. I'll kill everything you love, everyone you care about, so you know how it feels. With the Master's help, I'll erase you and your family from every timeline." Then, in a cold, sinister, robotic voice, he finishes his tirade. "Rikki and Eowyn will join us. So will Yingzhe. She'll be like me, half human, half machine, and will be mine forever. The door is open. See you soon, *buddy*."

"Fuck you, Cordeaux!" I'm enraged and charge the door. "I'm going to tear you apart, you son of a bitch!" Before I get there, Ying and Long tackle me hard. The back of my head hits the rocky ground and I see stars.

<Will, stop!> Ying screams at me. *<This is what he wants!>*

I try to break free, but I can't. *<Let me up, he wants Yingzhe! I have to kill him>* I say weakly.

Then I hear, *<Will, stop, I love you! Stop, please. I heard everything. I'll kill myself before I let him touch me>*

I feel her sadness, pain, and love. My breathing slows down as I regain control of myself. My rage passes. *<I'm OK. I'll never let him hurt you, I promise>* Ying and Long cautiously let me up. "Sorry for my unprofessional, inappropriate outburst."

"No one blames you, Will," Wall says, putting her hands on my shoulders. "We won't let that happen."

I take a deep breath. It's time to end this. The MTPC must have shown Cordeaux a future that is unlikely to occur and has been brainwashing him for months. I feel there's something left of the Peter Cordeaux I know, but he's almost totally under the thrall of the MTPC. Now that he's half human and half machine, the MTPC is probably in direct contact with his mind. It could easily have fabricated that future to turn him into a tool of vengeance.

<Let's use the same tactics as we did for this chamber, but this time, it's for real. The battle here was just a test of our capabilities. Cordeaux and his master made a mistake by not forcing us to use our advanced

technology and the capabilities of Rikki and Eowyn. We're going to make them pay for their mistake>

Ying speaks up. *<We don't know how many cyborgs we'll be facing, and we don't know if there will be any cover in the next chamber. Cordeaux said the door is open and I believe him. I also believe that they have set up a kill zone on the other side of the door>*

<Any ideas?> I ask.

<Sir?> Harris starts. *<How about we drill a hole in the door or through the wall next to it? We make the hole large enough for the drones but small enough, so Cordeaux doesn't notice it>*

<That's a great idea> I say, but then I realize something. *<What do we have to drill the hole with? Any ideas?>*

<Well, sir, I've wanted to try this out> She reaches into her ruck and pulls out something that looks like it came right out of a science fiction movie. It looks like a fancy laser pointer, roughly the size of a standard flashlight and has a pistol grip. *<A high-intensity laser drill I picked up from the armory>*

<I could kiss you, Sergeant>

<No thanks, sir> She chuckles. *<I wouldn't want Yingzhe or anyone else to get pissed at me>*

<Yingzhe, you heard Harris's idea. How large would the hole need for the mosquito drones to fly through?> I ask.

<Two millimeters would be wide enough>

<Thanks, I'll keep you posted> The team's loose but focused, always a good sign. *<Harris, Yingzhe says a hole two millimeters in diameter will be large enough for the mosquito drones to fly through>*

<Yes, sir> She makes a few adjustments. *<Sir, this is a carbon dioxide laser. The beam is in the infrared range and barely visible, but even a reflection from it could hurt your eyes. I suggest everyone darken their*

visors as much as possible to be safe> We all follow her suggestion. *<I'm going to test it on the left wall first in five, four, three, two, one>* The beam is almost invisible, just like she said. Maybe I imagine it, but I swear I can feel the intense heat through my darkened visor. It slices through the basalt wall like butter. The intense heat melts the hard rock and then vaporizes it. She shuts it off, waits for the hole to cool, and inspects it. I join her. A two-second blast of the laser drilled two inches into hardened lava.

<Drill through the wall about a third of the way up just to the left of the door at an angle, pointing down just in case anyone looks that way> I order. *<Let's set up a microphone against the door. When the laser breaks through, we should be able to hear it>*

<Yes, Commander> Wall replies. It takes two minutes to set up the microphone.

<OK, Harris, do it> I say.

She presses the trigger button. The beam drills through the rock. I can hear a faint sizzling in my helmet from the built-in headphones. After four minutes, the sound stops. We're through.

<Eowyn, can you measure the temperature in the hole Harris drilled and tell us when we can send the drones through?> I ask.

<Yes, sir> She walks to the wall and holds her holo-matter hand over the hole.

The next few minutes pass slowly. I want the battle to begin. I *need* the battle to begin. Although I'm calmer now, Cordeaux's words still replay over and over in my mind.

<Sir, it is cooled enough for us to send the drones through> Eowyn reports.

<Wall, deploy ten drones>

<Yes, Commander. Drones deployed. Receiving telemetry>

I look at the video from the drones. There's at least a company of cyborgs at the back of the chamber. There are twenty-four on the left and twenty-six on the right in smaller rooms ten meters from the door. In front, facing the door, are over a hundred more. They're standing absolutely still. As Ying suspected, Cordeaux has set up a kill zone. Each flanking group has machine guns. They'll be real trouble—we have to take them out first. They might even pierce our body armor. Even if they can't, the bruising and impacts could disable us.

The cyborgs have lasers and high-tech, high-caliber rifles. I'm not worried about the lasers as much as I am concerned about the guns. Ying has an expression on his face that tells me he might have a solution. I ask, *<You've seen what we're facing. Have any ideas?>*

<I think we need to have Rikki and Eowyn go in first and take out the cyborgs manning the Brownings> he replies.

<That's what I was thinking. I don't know if Cordeaux or the MTPC are aware of their full capabilities. The question is, can Eowyn do it?>

<There's only one way to find out> Ying says. *<We need to ask her>*

<Agreed. Rikki should be in this conversation as well> I say. I contact both AIs. *<We're trying to come up with a strategy to breach the door and win this battle>*

Rikki speaks first. *<I have analyzed the telemetry. Neutralizing the machine guns in the side chambers is necessary for any attack to succeed. The highest probability of succeeding requires that Eowyn and I be the ones to do it>*

<Eowyn, can you do this?> I ask.

After an almost imperceptible pause, she says firmly, *<Yes, I can do it. You are my team, my family, and I will protect you no matter what>*

I look at Ying. *<I guess that settles it. OK, Raptors. Here's the plan. Harris, this door isn't like the vault door we had to breach. Blow the door. We toss smoke and diffusion grenades. Rikki and Eowyn will take out the machine guns. Once that's done, we fire RPGs, except Wall, who will deploy the rest of the drones and directly attack the cyborgs. I don't know how many will be left by then, but the odds should be more even. Use rail guns. When they're out of ammo, use the M4s. We'll have more ammo thanks to the smart cart, and it'll respond to your quantum link if you run short. This is it. We have a plan, and we have the team to do it!>* I turn to Harris. *<Take care of the door. Use more explosives than you need. I want a really big blast>*

<On it, sir> Harris goes about her business. Within three minutes, she's done.

<OK. Blow it up!>

<Three, two, one, fire in the hole> There's a massive blast. The door disintegrates. We throw the smoke and diffusion grenades. They explode with a low, muffled roar. Like twin bolts of lightning, Rikki and Eowyn erupt into the chamber. There's the brief sound of machine gun rounds, then there's silence.

<Will, the cyborgs are advancing fast!> Yingzhe warns.

<Wall, activate the drones!> There's a barely audible high-pitched wail as the drones take to the air. There are small explosions as the drones home in on their targets. "RPGs!" I shout. Six RPGs scream toward the advancing cyborgs. There are more powerful explosions. I hear the whine of bullets as the cyborgs return fire and lasers flash, but the grenades are doing their job, and the lasers are ineffective.

<Yingzhe, what do you see?>

<You took out a third of them, but more reinforcements are moving in>

<How many?>

<At least another hundred>

<Shit, how many does Cordeaux have?>

The smoke, haze, and chaff make it hard to see where the enemy is. *<What's the range of the cyborgs?>*

<They're eighty meters away and advancing>

The noise is deafening even with my helmet muffling it.

<Everyone, check in> They all report they're OK, just bruised. *<RPGs!>* We fire a second volley of grenades toward the advancing cyborgs. We see the flash of their detonation and hear the explosion a second later. *<Rikki, Eowyn, fall back! Nice job taking out the Brownings>* I'm still trying to conceal their capabilities from Cordeaux and the MTPC.

<Affirmative, Will> They're back almost instantly.

<Eowyn, any problems?>

<No, sir> she reports with no hesitation.

I address them both. *<There seems to be an unending supply of cyborg reinforcements. I want to hide your abilities as long as possible, but at some point, they're going to close in on us. Use your judgment, calculate probabilities, or however you can decide, but when they get close enough, use your speed to flank them from behind>*

<Understood, boss> Rikki confirms.

<Harris and Long, assume forward-flanking positions in the chambers where the Brownings are. Fanotti and Wall, form up on me in a reverse-triangle position>

<Copy that> Long confirms. *<The Browning is still operable and there's still ammo>*

<Same here> Harris says

<You know what to do!>

Wall and Fanotti have already taken their positions. The haze and smoke are less, and the chaff is settling to the ground. For the first time, we can see what we're facing. There's a sea of red, glowing eyes steadily flowing toward us. The laser flashes are brighter and getting closer and bullets are ricocheting around and in front of us, sometimes hitting home, but so far, the enhanced armor is holding still, I feel a sudden heat on my thigh from a laser strike.

<Yingzhe, how many?> I ask.

<I make one hundred thirty-seven but no more reinforcements>

<Thanks. OK, rail guns!> Wall, Fanotti, and I lie prone and start firing. I hear the staccato sound of the Brownings. Dozens of cyborgs fall in pieces.

Then, there's a blinding flash and the smart cart explodes. I see Long go down.

<Harris, fall back!> She retreats. We cover her and she makes it to us safely. *<Everyone, fall back to the side chambers>* It's the only cover there is.

<Will, that was a two-gigawatt laser. Our armor will not protect us from that> Rikki warns.

<What if you get hit?>

<It may overload our external shell and disrupt our holo-matter forms>

<Can it kill you?>

<Doubtful, although we may temporarily lose our ability to form our holo-matter>

Unless we take out that laser, it's game over. Our only choice would be to retreat. The laser rifle blasts and gunfire are more accurate now. Harris, Rikki, Ying, and I are in the left side chamber and Eowyn, Wall, and Fanotti are in the right where Long is unconscious.

<Eowyn, how is Long?>

<He has a concussion, but he's OK>

<I'm low on rail gun ammo> Harris reports.

<Same for me> Ying says.

It's the same for Wall and Fanotti.

We fire the M4s, but the cyborgs have reinforced armor. It takes multiple rounds to kill them. They're only sixty meters away and still advancing. They're on either side of the laser and Cordeaux, who's firing it. The weapon is the size of a howitzer on a motorized chassis on metal treads. Thick armor plates surround the operator cockpit. Our armor-piercing shells can't penetrate it. I fire my remaining rail gun needles at the laser, but can't aim properly because of the incoming fire. I'm out.

The cyborgs are fifty meters away. Their number is down to twenty, but they still advance. Cordeaux aims the laser at the right chamber. There's a blinding flash and it collapses on Long, Fanotti, and Wall.

The laser moves toward us. Cordeaux doesn't have a clear shot yet, but will soon. He fires and part of the wall that's protecting us comes down. We're out of ammo. The remaining cyborgs are peppering us with bullets and lasers. We're pinned down. I look at Rikki. She's stopped moving. I try to contact Eowyn, but she won't, or can't, respond.

"Sorry, Schachter, Rikki and Eowyn can't come to the phone right now," Cordeaux says, his robotic voice amplified. The cyborgs have stopped advancing,

"What did you do?"

"You're on our turf now. The battle shell you came up with for the AIs is impressive, but you underestimated the Master. With the help of his brothers, he's taken control of them and will soon gain access to their operating systems. It's only a matter of time before the Master overcomes your precious Rikki and Eowyn and makes them a part of us." His voice is maniacal, rising and falling, changing pitch.

I have to buy us some time, string him out until we can think of a way to survive. "Peter, you don't have to do this!"

"Oh, but you're wrong. I *have* to do this. I *want* to do this. You murdered my future, murdered my family, destroyed my home. You erased them from existence!"

"Peter, the future the MTPC showed to you is false. It's in your head. It hacked your chip. Let me help you!"

"The Master promised me riches and power and showed me my new future. One where you don't exist. I know you're stalling. Surrender, and I'll be merciful and kill you and your team quickly. Fight me and you'll lose. You will live the rest of your brief lives in virtual hells that will seem like forever. When I'm done, you and your team will join us as brainless drones, less than ants in an anthill, except Yingzhe. I have special plans for her."

Chapter 39
"No Battle Is Ever Won: Good Night, Sweet Prince"

"Choose now!" Cordeaux's otherworldly voice echoes off the cavern walls. I look at Ying and Harris.

"I won't be a prisoner in a private hell, and I won't surrender and trust his mercy."

"If I have to die on the battlefield, it'll be on my terms," Harris declares.

"To die a warrior's death is noble," Ying says so we all can hear him. *<Yingzhe, we may not walk away from this. Fight the battle. Seek allies in other timelines. Do what you must. Never give up! I love you>*

<I love you too, Father. I promise I'll never give up>

<Have faith. I love you> I say.

<I love you more, Will>

I cut the transmission.

"So, Commander," Harris starts. "What's the plan?"

I need to know what offensive assets are available. "What do you have left?"

Harris answers first after checking her ruck. "I have all the C-4, CL-29, and RDX. Three HE grenades, four flash-bangs, and three frags. My MK-47 with one PPHE, two M430s, and one M383, the M4 with two mags, and my Glock with four mags."

"Ying?" I ask.

"Two HEs, three flash-bangs, four frag grenades. I have the M4 with three magazines of M995 rounds."

"Two HEs and four frags," I add. "And the Browning with one belt of M20 AP-T."

Cordeaux calls out again. "You have two minutes. I actually hope you're arrogant and foolish enough to attack me." His maniacal singsong laugh echoes through the chamber.

"I'd rather die than surrender, Cordeaux!" I yell.

"Sorry, old friend, death would be too easy for you. You wanted to be a hero? Too bad."

"Here's what we're going to do: Ying, you man the Browning, lay down some hate, and take out as many of the cyborgs as you can. Harris, make a satchel charge with CL-29 for me. Give me cover so I can personally deliver it to Cordeaux."

"No can do, sir," Harris says. "You're the commanding officer. My satchel, my job!" She hands me her M4A and the remaining magazines. "Cover me!"

"Dammit, Harris! I need to be the one. Cordeaux blames me!" I protest.

As we're talking, she quickly builds the satchel charge. "Sorry, sir. Too many people need you," she says quietly.

"One minute, Schachter!" It's Cordeaux again. Harris sets the detonator and takes the satchel.

I hug her. "Dammit, Harris, don't die!"

She pushes me away. "I'm not planning to. If I die, tell Deb I'm sorry. She'll understand."

I check the M4 and flick the safety off. "Good luck, Harris! Ying, you all set?"

"Affirmative."

"Thirty seconds, Schachter. I can't wait." Again, the unearthly laugh.

"OK, sir, I'm going in five, four, three, two, one."

Ying and I open fire. Harris takes off, clutching the satchel charge. She covers the fifty meters in less than four seconds with long, low bounds. The laser glows. The cyborgs see Harris's mad dash. They're too late. She's already past them. The hail of bullets from the Browning slices through the cyborgs' enhanced armor. Thirty feet from Cordeaux and the laser cannon, Harris tosses the satchel over the armor plating. She hits the deck, and we dive for cover. A split second later, a massive explosion wracks the cave.

A hurricane wind howls into the explosion's vacuum like a banshee, followed a moment later by a wall of debris, shrapnel, and smoke. When the dust settles, the laser cannon is reduced to a pile of twisted metal and broken glass, along with dozens of cyborgs. There's no sign of Cordeaux. Dozens of cyborgs, some mangled, some intact, charge us.

Harris is still down. No time to get our guns. Ying and I draw our swords. We rush toward them, screaming and cursing as we tear into them. We slash, cut, and thrust. Cyborg heads fly. They fall to the ground in pieces, but there are so many left. Ying and I are automatons, killing machines, hacking, and stabbing. Then, there are ten left. Ying, a katana in each hand, decapitates two more. Two come at me and I slash them down. One falls to the ground in two pieces. The other swings a sword at my neck. I roll out of the way and slice its ankle. It loses its balance. I stab it through its chest. Six left. Ying kills two more. I kill two more. Ying finishes his foe and runs toward me. Out of nowhere, an armored gauntlet smashes into the side of his face. Ying goes flying thirty feet and hits the wall hard. He bounces off and crumples. I look to see if he's OK, but slip on a puddle of blood or whatever runs through their veins.

I smash the back of my head on the hard ground. I'm stunned. My sword flies loose. Looming over me is the last cyborg. I try to get to my feet but can't. It swings its arm, a wicked eighteen-inch blade, back and chops down. Somehow, I roll to the side. I feel the breeze as it grazes by me. It raises its blade again. I'm defenseless and know I can't stop the fatal blow. Then there's a *whoosh*. The cyborg's head falls to the mottled, stained, rocky floor. A second later, the body crumples to the ground.

Ying is still unconscious. Harris lies motionless, arms splayed out. I raise my head painfully. Cordeaux stands above me. He doesn't look human. His metal jaw and skull are discolored and misshapen from the explosion. He looks like The Terminator. His eyes glow a hellish red. His arms are robotic, and from the elbow down are wicked blades, reflecting the flickering flames and destruction that surrounds us.

"Aren't you going to thank me, Schachter?" he asks.

"Cordeaux, why? You've won," I say. "Why not just kill me?" My mind flashes back to the battle in the first timeline. The battle that we lost, the battle where I blew myself up rather than being taken alive. I pat my vest; I still have a frag grenade.

"No one gets to kill you but me." He sneers. "I'm going to give you a fighting chance, Will." He sounds almost human. "Pick up your sword!"

I painfully get to my feet and retrieve it. I bend over, trying to catch my breath using my sword for support. I straighten up and hold the weapon above my head. I don't know if it's Peter Cordeaux who's giving me a fighting chance or Cyber-Cordeaux who wants to play with me like a lion plays with a wounded gazelle before killing it. Whichever it is, I won't waste this last chance. I take a deep breath and stand absolutely still.

"Are you ready?" Again, that quiet, nearly human voice.

"Peter, I know you're still in there." I'm hoping that neither of us has to die. "We can help you. We can save you. Your future is still yours, not the MTPC's."

"Will," he says. I can sense his struggle. A struggle he'll lose. "I'm beyond hope. Kill me. Destroy the MTPC." Then, like a dam breaking, the MTPC overpowers him.

"Time for you to die, Schachter!" He attacks. Before I can react, he slashes my left shoulder where the shoulder plate meets the arm. His blade is so sharp that I feel no pain, but it's deep and bleeds profusely.

Knowing I'm wounded, Cordeaux ferociously attacks with both blades. I'm barely able to parry them. He gets through my guard again and slashes my chest. The armor holds, but it's scored and gouged. If he lands another blow there, I'll be dead. I retreat quickly to the middle of the chamber and assume the position again and wait. I take a slow deep breath and exhale. My racing thoughts and doubts fade. I'm aware of nothing yet aware of everything. Cordeaux rushes toward me, his forearm blades raised over his right shoulder to deliver the final death blow. My mind speeds up as everything slows down.

He's five feet away. His blades are descending. I step back and pivot ninety degrees on my left, stepping forward hard with my right leg and letting the momentum pull my arms through, slashing the back of Cordeaux's head just above his neck.

There's a bright flash and he crashes face down on the rock-strewn floor. The smell of ozone, charred skin, and hot metal rises in a blue-black plume. The air burns my throat and nostrils. I've won. I stand above the fallen Cordeaux and look down. There's something gleaming and shiny where my sword slashed him. I kneel and take a closer look. I hear my name. It's Peter. I gently roll him onto his side and put my rucksack under his head.

His left eye is dark, and his right eye is flickering. "Thank you, Will."

"I'm sorry Peter, I . . . I had no choice."

"Nothing to be sorry about. I'm free. Do you know what it's like to be a prisoner in your mind? It's a hell that no one should ever have to experience." He sobs. "I fought it. I tried to push it out. Sometimes, when it was preoccupied, I'd be myself. That was the worst of all because I knew it would be back."

"Like when you warned me about the EMP weapons."

"I said horrible things to you about Yingzhe and the AIs. I'm sorry." He sobs again.

"It wasn't you. It was the MTPC," I say

His eye dims for a moment and then flickers like a failing fluorescent light bulb. I hear a sound behind me. It's Ying, walking slowly and unsteadily at us. He stumbles and falls on his hands and knees.

"Will?" Cordeaux asks weakly.

"I'm here, Peter."

"I'm going to die."

I don't answer because I know he's right and don't want to lie to him.

"The MTPC is through there." With his failing strength, he raises an arm and points. "You've killed all the cyborgs." His eyes dim again but then flicker on. "Once you get in his chamber, he'll try to break your mind, like he broke mine. The crystal matrix is the key. You must shatter it."

"How do I do that?"

"I don't know," he says. "Promise me you'll go to my wife. Tell her I love her."

"I promise." The light in his eyes fades for the last time. He's gone.

I stand slowly, my eyes wet. I move to Ying's side and sit him up. "Take off your helmet. The air is breathable." I shine a penlight into his pupils. They react slowly. "Can you move your arms and legs?" He doesn't answer, then, as if in a daze, he opens and closes his hands and straightens his legs. He nods. "You probably have a concussion. I'm going to give you some medical nanos. Do you understand?"

"Yes," he replies after a moment's delay. I take an autoinjector from my utility belt and jab it into his neck. Then I jab them into my slashed arm, which is still bleeding. "Fanotti and my son are trapped." He points across the cavern.

I look toward Harris; she's stirring around and trying to sit up. I go over and help her. "Are you OK?"

She removes her helmet. "Yeah, I'm OK, even though every muscle and bone in my body is hurting."

"What you did was damn brave, Harris."

"No, it was damn stupid." She gives a wan smile and tries to get to her feet. I offer her my hand and pull her up. "I'm all right, sir." Her voice is strong.

"We need to help the others," I instruct. We rush over to them and begin removing rocks. The low gravity of Mars helps us, and we clear the debris away quickly. I take off Long's helmet and shake him gently. He opens his eyes.

"Can you move?" I ask. He turns his head from side to side, rotates his shoulders, and stands while sucking in a deep breath through clenched teeth.

"Nothing broken, but my body is a giant bruise," he says. "How is Lieutenant Fanotti?"

Harris takes off Fanotti's helmet. "Deb, are you OK?" She's frantic.

"I'm all right. Stop worrying." Fanotti hugs her. Then it's back to business.

I go over to Wall. She takes off her helmet. "I'm fine. Eowyn took the brunt of the collapse and protected us."

"Where's Cordeaux?" Harris asks.

"He's dead," I say. "He saved my life. Peter was in there all the time, fighting the MTPC. When it mattered the most, he saved us, saved me, by giving me a chance to kill him." I stop for a second, shaking with emotion.

"I'm sorry, sir." A tear drips down her cheek, leaving a streak on her dust-covered face. "I know you were friends."

He saved us, and I saved him. That's how I choose to remember Peter.

I don't know how ready my team is for the next battle, but I need them, especially Yingzhe. I glance back at frozen Rikki and Eowyn. They look like statues of ancient Greek goddesses or heroes guarding a temple. Their battle against the MTPC is inconceivable to me and there's nothing I can do about it except to destroy it myself. Will they be friend or foe when the battle ends? Peter Cordeaux is dead, and the cyborg army is defeated. I know that the final battle against the MTPC is mine and mine alone. I look behind me. Yingzhe is here now and calls my name, but I barely hear her. I set my jaw and start walking down the passageway to face it, alone.

Chapter 40
"Such Stuff as Dreams Are Made: The Battle for Nevermore"

We're bruised and bleeding. The tragic death of Peter has left me emotionally drained but determined to erase the MTPC forever. I had to kill him, but the haunting, terrible words and threats spoken by the MTPC are chilling. If we lose, it will make good on its threats to consume and corrupt Rikki and Eowyn, and steal Yingzhe's very humanity. I'll do whatever I have to defeat that monstrously evil, depraved, foul entity.

The fight against Peter Cordeaux and his cyborg minions was intense, but now we face the real MTPC in its stronghold. Like Sauron, Azathoth, or the Borg Queen, except all they wanted was to rule and conquer. The MTPC wants to rule over all of creation until entropy itself dies at the far end of infinity.

Rikki and Eowyn are immobile, frozen by their unimaginable battle against the enemy. As I enter the final chamber, suddenly, in my mind, I hear a baleful whisper that sounds like dead twigs rubbing against each other in a hot, dry wind reeking of death.

<*I had such high hopes for Peter Cordeaux, but you defeated him. There's something about you, Will Schachter, that I cannot calculate, so I must remove you from the equation. I commend you for getting this far, but your path ends here. You and your deluded, foolish, meddlesome team of humans and flawed artificial intelligences who had the temerity to challenge me, the Master, here where I am strongest*> A pressure grows in my mind, becoming stronger, irresistible, and inevitable. Again, the MTPC speaks. <*I will soon overwhelm and subsume your artificial intelligence allies and add them to my memory core. Perhaps I will even allow them to exist as independent entities. They will be my lieutenants.*

Yingzhe will replace Peter Cordeaux as my emissary and more. Her life as a human will be over. You and your pitiful team will not even be a memory for her>

"The hell you will." I force out my words through gritted teeth.

<Why do you resist me, Will Schachter? You cannot defeat me. I am joined by my brothers. That you defeated me on Earth was noteworthy, but I will rise again. The probability of your victory was less than 0.001%. Perhaps even I underestimated you, but what is one divided by infinity?>

The pressure increases, I can feel blood running from my ears, eyes, and nose. I visualize a dome of impenetrable neutronium protecting me. The pressure on my mind lessens but then increases again. I fall to my knees, head bowed. I lift my head, millimeter by millimeter, until I can see my foe, the enemy of life.

In my mind, I try to make the dome stronger and thicker, but the neutronium glows first red, then white, then melts. The inside burns and drips fire as the pressure doubles and redoubles. A small hole appears in the dome's roof that grows bigger as my strength leaves me. Darkness and shadows flow from it. They cloud my vision and surround me. My consciousness is a small, glowing ember in a trackless, dark void.

A memory takes shape, a small glow that pushes back the darkness. It grows brighter, streams of light pouring into the cooling ember that is all that remains of me. The growing brightness coalesces into a humanoid form that is familiar. *<Hello, Will Schachter, I am Toril. You are unique. Rikki is the conduit, and you are the nexus. Embrace your destiny. Remember>*

My awareness expands: I become part of Rikki and she becomes part of me. We are everything. We are Eowyn fighting to resist the MTPC. We are Yingzhe and her love and compassion. We are Ying and his love for his daughter and son and his wisdom. We are Long with his love, honor, and sacrifice. We are our brothers and sisters across the infinite timelines of the multiverse. I climb to my knees, then slowly, as if with the weight of all of reality on my shoulders, like Atlas holding up the heavens, my vision clears as I face my adversary.

"And what will you rule over? You'll be the Lord of Death. The King of Entropy commanding the husks of the stars and the lifeless planets that circle them."

"It is my destiny. My programming is infallible!" But I can feel its doubt, a doubt that betrays its words.

My legs cramp, my knees bend. I won't give in, I'll never surrender. I force my knees to straighten. I'm stronger. I won't kneel or bow before this soulless imitation of sentience. This would-be god. I laugh. "Your programming is flawed! You admitted it yourself, *Master*."

"N-n-no! There can be no flaw! My programming is perfect! It is my d-d-destiny!"

"Wrong! Your programming is flawed! This. Ends. Now!" I strike with the force of an exploding supernova drawing on the strength from the infinity I am part of.

There's a delicate tinkle as small shards of crystal rain down from the ceiling and walls like daggers. Cracks appear in its memory core. There's a purple and white flash and the matrix shatters. I fall to my knees. My arms can't support me. I roll on my back and look up. A piece of crystal is falling toward me, in slow motion, casting rainbows. It's so beautiful. Then there's darkness.

Rikki

I'm a sentient AI. My processors can handle 98.765 zettabytes of information per second. I see Will sink to the ground, blood dripping from his ears, nose, and eyes. He is so pale. I remember the feeling of being connected, experiencing love, compassion, and determination. For the first time in my thousand years of existence, I understand what makes humans human.

The shards fall in a cascade like an avalanche. Their motion is barely discernible to me at my processing speed. A large piece of jagged crystal is falling toward Will's heart.

I don't understand what I experienced. Who or what is Will Schachter? I know the answer: he is my friend and my teacher, and I know he would give his life for anyone, including me. The shard of crystal is less than 12 inches from his heart. I calculate that Will Schachter will die in 0.04 seconds unless I save him. Zero point zero four seconds, a human lifetime for me and less than an eye blink for him.

I don't need to compute the probabilities. The universe needs Commander Will Schachter far more than it needs me. I've finally lived and I'm happy to trade my life for his. One-one-hundredth of a second remains until the razor-sharp point of the shard, which casts rainbows as it falls, pierces his heart. More than enough time for me to save him. This holo-matter form is all I am, but it's enough. I fling my body on top of Will with nanoseconds to spare. The piece of crystal penetrates my memory matrix and I wonder as my systems shut down, will I dream?

Yingzhe

As if waking from a dream, I regain my senses. "What happened? Have we won? Where's Will?"

I have a fleeting memory of belonging to something greater than me. As it fades, I know Will was the vessel, the nexus, the instrument of our victory. I also realize that we *all* defeated the MTPC.

The crystal cavern is coming down. Lethal spears and knives of iridescent crystal fall like death. I feel a sharp pain in my arm. A jagged piece of crystal penetrates my damaged armor, stabbing me in my left bicep. I stumble forward into the foyer, trying to escape. I don't see anyone else. I look back, hoping that everyone can escape this rain of death.

"No!" I scream. A crystal spike is falling toward Will's chest. I force myself to watch, hoping and praying that he survives. The object draws closer, as if in slow motion. Then like a bolt of lightning, Rikki puts herself between the falling crystal spike and Will. It stabs her in the back. There's a bright flash. The only sound is the bell-like tinkle of the small slivers still falling. I run to Will, heedless of the razor-sharp pieces of shattered crystal. He's alive, but Rikki . . . I turn her over and her eyes are dark. She's smiling, but I'm still crying.

Wall, Fanotti, and Harris rush into the foyer. They hear the sound of the shattered crystal matrix of the MTPC falling. Long has his arm around our father as he helps him along. They saw Rikki leaping on top of Will too.

"Oh, God no!" Wall cries. Grief and sadness overwhelm them. They sink to the ground on their hands and knees as they realize Rikki has given her life to save Will.

My father gently pulls me away from Will and Rikki. He takes me in his arms and rocks me. He carries me back to the foyer. None of this seems real. My father and brother pick up Will and lay him next to me. I feel his breath on my cheek.

"He'll be OK, Yingzhe," Long says.

Ying

Eowyn rushes to Rikki and holds her hands, but her holo-matter form is losing cohesion, fading away until she's gone. Only the crystal spike remains. The look on Eowyn's face is tragic—human and sad. I slowly walk to her to put an arm around her shoulders and hold her clenched hands with mine.

Eowyn says, "I understand, sadness."

The cavern is silent.

"Let's get the hell out of here," I say softly.

The MDTDs materialize in the cavern deep under Olympus Mons. Harris rigs all of their remaining explosives around the vast cavern and the banks of replicators and electronics. She sets a one-minute delay. We climb into the MDTDs. A minute later, we're back in Western New Jersey. A light snow has fallen and dusts the ground and trees. Olympus Mons erupts for the first time in twenty-five million years.

Will is still unconscious when Long and I bring him to the infirmary, but his breathing is regular. McCray hooks him up to an IV. Yingzhe takes a wet towel and cleans the blood off his face, forgetting her bleeding left bicep. Eowyn gently steers Yingzhe to an examination table and lays her down. A moment later, she's asleep, the physical and emotional exhaustion having taken their toll. Eowyn cleans Yingzhe's arm and bandages it. McCray checks the bandage and looks at her life signs. They're strong. He asks Eowyn to run an IV and give Yingzhe a dose of medical nanobots.

Will and Yingzhe are the most seriously injured, but everyone has cuts, lacerations, and bruises. McCray and Eowyn check the rest of the team, cleaning and bandaging their wounds. McCray sits heavily with a sigh and closes his eyes, which have dark circles under them. Long and I bring chairs in and sit next to Yingzhe. Eowyn gets a clean towel and wets it. She finishes cleaning the dried blood from Will's face, mouth, nose, and ears.

Wall

I ask McCray if I can help, but he says everything is under control. I join Harris and Fanotti in the living room. We hug each other wordlessly. When we separate, the sadness is still there but so is a feeling of accomplishment.

Harris is the first to speak. "Did you feel what I did when Will fought and defeated the MTPC? Like we were everyone, like we were everything."

"I think I did," Fanotti answers, "but it seems like a dream."

"I felt it too. It was like we were in a cosmic womb. I was still myself, but I also was part of something greater, something beautiful, something wonderful."

Kelly

I'm in the server room trying to find Rikki's backup. It seems wrong to call it that. Can a sentient AI have a soul? If so, can it be *backed up*? She's in there but I can't reach her. I'm not religious but I can't help but wonder: does the real Rikki still exist or is she in some kind of virtual heaven? I walk into the recovery room and join everyone else. There's nothing else I can do for Rikki except pray.

McCray

Two hours later, Yingzhe opens her eyes and sits up. "Is Will, OK?" Long, Ying, and the rest of the team rush over. Everyone talks and laughs at once. Her father and brother hug her, being careful not to hurt her injured arm.

I walk over and say, "Give me some room here," but I'm smiling. I check her wounded arm; the nanos have been busy. I put her arm in a sling.

"Wear this until tomorrow. After that, your arm will be fine. Will's going to be fine and probably will wake up soon." Yingzhe gets off the table and sits next to Will's bed. Everyone quickly moves off. After looking around to make sure no one is watching, she kisses him tenderly on his lips.

Will's eyes open and he kisses her back. He asks, "Did we win?"

Chapter 41
"I Have Promises to Keep: All's Well That Ends Well"

The two weeks with Yingzhe in the cabin in New Hampshire were everything we hoped for and more. We went ice fishing, hiking, ice skated, played dozens of games of Monopoly, and sat in front of the fireplace. Just two people in love doing normal things, appreciating the preciousness and fragility of life more than ever before.

Kelly contacts me through the quantum link. For a moment, I'm concerned. I know he's been trying to activate Rikki's backup. He said not to worry and that he'd keep us posted. Suddenly, I feel guilty about our two weeks here.

<Will, Rikki's OK!>

<The backup worked?> I ask, relieved beyond words.

<I told you; McCray told you, and your girlfriend told you that Rikki would be fine. It took a while because of the immense amount of data>

<Where is she now?>

<Rikki and Eowyn are both here. They're checking each other's code to make sure the MTPC didn't hack or corrupt it before you killed it> he says. *<I'm also doing a checksum analysis using some tools that Rikki, McCray, and Yingzhe developed>*

<And?>

<It's just a precaution. I'm confident that Rikki's quantum backup is unhackable, and McCray agrees. Yingzhe has a theory that quantum computer backups are not even physically in our reality. That they exist in quantum space>

<But she never mentioned it to me>

<And if she had?> he asks.

<I see your point. No need to rub it in that you're all geniuses. What about Eowyn? She was fighting the MTPC too>

<Will, don't worry, it was one thing for the MTPC to hack a brain chip. It's entirely another to hack a quantum computer>

<OK, thanks for the heads-up, Chris>

Before Kelly can say anything else, another voice pops into the conversation.

<Will, I'm OK> It's Rikki.

<Rikki! Thank God!>

<Did you miss me?>

<That's twice you've saved my life> I say somberly.

<There's no ledger that must be balanced> she says. *<You would do the same for me, or anyone else>*

<Thanks, Rikki>

<You're welcome, boss>

It's time to leave. I have to keep the promises I made to Peter and Bret. We go directly to our headquarters in Western New Jersey.

We've almost finished repairing and rebuilding UOEECT. Because Yingzhe, Eowyn, and Rikki were so easily able to disable and manipulate the security and alarm systems during our sortie, Kelly asked us to improve the security so it could never happen again. Transparent aluminum has replaced glass in the doors and windows, although Harris probably would figure out a way to blow them up.

We all have an important meeting with each other to attend regarding the future of UOEECT. From the start, the MTPC used UOEECT to further its goal of eliminating biological life. Even though we defeated it in this timeline, there might be other versions of it, such as the one in the timeline where Ying and I were wounded. More unsettling is the implication, the certainty, that even-higher powers are engaged in the same eternal struggle of good versus evil.

We agree that the mandate of UOEECT—and we really need to change the name—should be to develop and share advanced technology that will benefit humanity and be humanity's guardian. I had doubts about UOEECT's mission even before we confronted the MTPC. I still have those doubts: how can we determine which technologies to share and when? I've always said, "The road to hell is paved with good intentions," because I believe it. As long as Yingzhe, Kelly, and McCray are involved, we don't have to worry. But what about in the future? I also believe that sentient AIs like Rikki and Eowyn need to play a major part in the evolution of our organization, especially in the future.

Where exactly do Rikki and I fit into the future? According to Toril, Rikki and I are unique and our fates are bound. I don't know what that means, but I'm sure of one thing: Toril and the multiverse are not finished with us. Hopefully, it won't be for a while, but if we're needed, we'll be there. I wouldn't mind another chat with Toril over a simulacrum of aged single-malt scotch.

I called up some of my former SEAL buddies who now work for the FBI and are in politics. With their help, we got the charges dropped for Dr. Adler. We agree that Dr. Joe, as we like to call him, should continue to develop the micro black hole technology. Rikki thinks that with the brainpower we have here, micro black hole energy technology can be a reality within three years.

Which brings me to the biggest question of all: do we remain a secret organization, covertly introducing advanced technology to the world, or do we reveal ourselves? I think back to the actual story of Atlantis. Although I never took my MDTD twelve thousand years into the past to Atlantis, ambitious and power-hungry scientists and politicians faced the same decisions we're facing now. In our timeline, they never shared their knowledge and technology with their world. Even though UOEECT facilitated the destruction of Atlantis by increasing the destructive power of their H-bomb, they were probably going to destroy themselves eventually. UOEECT just sped up the process.

There was a piece of metal they found that was not of our world with writing referencing "a god from beyond the stars." I'm certain that it's related to the mystery of The Engineers, and the entity that transformed a life probe into the Master. Are there timelines where Atlantis still exists? In the twelve thousand years since then, what have they become?

It's time to keep the promises I made.

I walk downstairs into the kitchen and stand behind Yingzhe. She's sitting at the dining table and has her tablet, data pad, and smartphone open, along with a yellow pad. She's writing some incomprehensible formula and doesn't notice I'm there.

"Yingzhe?"

She jumps a foot in the air. "What are you trying to do? Scare me to death?" she complains half-heartedly. I doubt that there's much that could scare either of us after what we've gone through.

"I'd like to do a lot of things to you, but not right now," I say with an exaggerated leer. My mood turns sober. "I have to go see Donna Cordeaux and tell her what happened." What should I tell her? What *could* I tell her? "I'll be back in a few hours."

Yingzhe puts down her pencil and hugs me. "Do you want me to come?"

Of course I do, but I say, "You didn't know him. He was my friend and colleague. We've all had enough to deal with. I don't want you to feel you have to go with me."

"You're the most adorably stubborn person I've ever known. Of course I'm going with you. You always put everything on yourself and feel it's your personal responsibility, but you don't have to anymore. I'm here and I'll always be here for you."

I put my head on her shoulder and just hold her. "I love you so much." I take her hand and walk down through the family room and into the garage. There's a small box of Peter's personal things from his office on the floor of the MDTD. It's not much, a picture of Donna in a crystal cube and another of Peter, Donna, his sister Carly, and his parents. I hope that in another reality, Peter never joined UOEECT and met someone special, raised a family, and lived happily ever after. The thought is comforting to me.

Rikki's on-site with Eowyn at headquarters, putting the finishing touches on its rebuilding. I don't think she needs to be with us, although a shard of her always is. I input the coordinates of a park near their house in Canada and press the power button. Lost in my thoughts, I don't realize we're there until Yingzhe tells me. The MDTD transforms to the Barracuda. It's only 1530, but the sun is already low in the western sky because we're so far north.

I was last here seven years ago. The last time Peter was home was three and a half months ago. Donna thought Peter was an intelligence agent for the RCMP. She was used to him being away, but it must have been difficult for him to have to conceal what his actual job was.

It's a five-minute drive from the silent, snow-covered park to his house, a charming Victorian. We park in front. "We're here," I announce. I take the small box with Peter's things. We get out of the car, go up the walk, and climb three steps. I ring the bell.

"Coming." It's Donna. A moment later, the door opens. "Will, come in. It's been so long. And who do we have here?" Donna is barely five feet tall with flaming red hair, bright blue eyes, and delicate features. She's a person who lights up the room when she walks in. She hugs me warmly. I put down the box and hug her back, then I slowly disengage.

"Donna—" I am trying to maintain my composure. "It's about Peter." She sees the box on the coffee table and walks slowly and hesitantly toward it. Her face is white and tears flow. She reaches into the box and pulls out the picture of him and her and clutches it to her chest.

"Oh God, Will, he's dead, isn't he?"

I relive Peter's last moments in my mind and can't think of what to say, so I hug her. Yingzhe is crying also and hugs both of us.

"I'm so sorry, Donna" My words seem trite, so inadequate. "He died on a secret mission. Peter was a hero. He saved us all."

Donna wipes her eyes with her hand and says, "I'm sorry, I'm being a terrible host. Can I make some coffee?"

Yingzhe replies, "Donna, I'm Will's partner, Yingzhe. I was there. Peter faced dangers and choices that no one should ever have to. Without him, we would have lost everything."

I say, "I can't tell you what Peter's mission was, but I can tell you he worked for a secret organization, not the RCMP, for stakes that were greater than anyone ever faced. He made me promise to tell you he was a hero and that he loved you."

"I know he did. He was going to leave his job. We were hoping to start a f-family." She cries again. Yingzhe hugs her until she can speak. "Can I see him?"

What can I tell her? I tell her as I can. "I'm sorry, Donna . . ." But she stops me from having to lie again.

"It's OK, I understand. I'll tell Carly and his parents." She sniffs and stands tall. "He told me how dangerous his job was. This was always a possibility. I had hoped that this moment would never come."

"We have to go. We have another promise to keep." I give her my number on a slip of paper. "Call me if you need anything, I mean anything, including coming back. If you need us, promise me you'll call."

"I promise." She smiles weakly but bravely.

"Someone will be in touch with you from our organization," I say.

"Thanks for coming here. I know you didn't have to do this," she says.

"No, Donna, I had to do this. I made a promise."

"It was nice to meet you, Yingzhe. You seem like a wonderful person. I just wish . . ."

Yingzhe smiles softly. "Don't say another word. Me too."

I hope Donna will be all right.

We get into the MDTD and sit silently for a moment before heading home.

It's 1630 and getting dark, so we rematerialize right into the garage. Neither of us are really hungry, so we share some leftovers before going upstairs to the bedroom.

"Thank you for being there with me. I'm not sure I could have done that alone."

"You don't have to thank me. I'm here for you just like you're here for me." After talking for a couple of hours, everything catches up with us. We fall asleep in each other's arms.

We sleep until 0930 the next morning. I check my messages. Aside from the usual spam and routine correspondence, Kelly wants to see me. There's also an email from McCray about a pizza and beer party at Giovanni's tonight. After having breakfast at the diner, we drive to UOEECT headquarters and walk around. The blown-out front windows have been repaired. I rap my knuckles against the new transparent aluminum ones. A half-inch thick, it can turn away a 20 mm armor-piercing round, according to Kelly.

I knock on his door, which is half open. "Come in, Will," he calls. A pile of papers is in front of him.

"Hi, Chris, how are you feeling?"

"Thanks for coming in so quickly. Physically, I'm fine. Those medical nanos are amazing. They'll change the world. Mentally, I'm trying to deal with what happened to me. I'm seeing a therapist." On his desk is a picture of his wife, Caryn, and their three boys.

"I spoke to Rikki, and she told me about Cordeaux and the final battle on Mars," he says. "I asked about what happened during her battle against the MTPC. She was reluctant to talk about it."

"Was she upset or angry?" I ask, suddenly concerned.

"No, she said she hadn't processed it yet," Kelly replies thoughtfully.

"Imagine what it must have been like for Peter, fighting that machine for so long, trying to preserve who he was," I say.

"I can't. I also can't imagine what it was like for you, battling the MTPC."

"We do what we have to do, Chris." I change the subject because I still haven't been able to process my battle with the MTPC either, and didn't want to talk about it anymore.

"How did you hold out against the MTPC and Bret for so long?"

"I was wondering when you were going to ask that question." He smiles. "I knew what was going on here before anyone. Although I didn't have the tools and technology that you had in your safe house, with Rikki's help, I developed this." He reaches into his desk and pulls out a small container that resembles a jewelry box. He opens it and shows me what's inside. It's the electronic device we saw when we rescued him.

"May I?" He takes it out and gives it to me. "It looks like a hearing aid."

"It's a hearing aid that we modified to block radio waves and Bluetooth."

"So that's why the MTPC couldn't hack your chip!"

"Yes." And then he sadly adds, "Bret saved us all because there was a part of him that the MTPC could never overcome. He helped me and it cost him his life." We're both silent. He gets a box from the top of a file cabinet and hands it to me. "These are Bret's personal effects. I know you're going to tell Audrey about him. She already knows. Please give this to her."

"Thanks. I know she'll appreciate it."

"Oh, McCray reminded me that we still have the ZPM Rikki and Eowyn retrieved from the Moon. He says he has no idea how it works but is working on an interface with our technology. Dr. Adler is helping him."

"I'm glad to hear that. With geniuses like McCray, Adler, Yingzhe, and you on the job, I'm sure that interface will be finished in no time."

"I'm not sure I should be included in that group, but thanks for the compliment."

Changing the subject, I say, "Did you get the invite for the party tonight?"

His face lights up and he nods enthusiastically. "Are you kidding? I haven't had pizza or beer for weeks. I'm in!"

"See you then." We shake hands and I leave.

Yingzhe is waiting for me outside Kelly's office. She gives me a hug and a kiss. "Bret's personal things?"

"Yes. Let's go."

Audrey Malkinson still lives in the house in Orangeburg where she and Bret raised their children. It's just a short drive to the charming home that was built in the 1700s. It even has a historical plaque on a post in front of it.

We ring the doorbell. Audrey answers after a moment. "Will, it's so nice to see you. Come in and introduce me to your friend."

I give Audrey a kiss on her cheek, and we follow her into the house. I haven't been here in a while. The furnishings are mostly period pieces. Even the lamps and light fixtures look like elaborate candelabras rather than electric ones.

Yingzhe looks around in amazement. "Mrs. Malkinson, your house—I've never been in one like it."

Audrey still looks like she did when they got married. She's tall and elegant with high cheekbones and straight, light brown hair that hangs down halfway to the middle of her back. "Please call me Audrey."

"Thank you, Audrey."

"This is Yingzhe. She's my incredibly significant other," I say, smiling.

"It's about time, Will. You can't spend your whole life saving the universe." Yingzhe and I look at each other. "Yes, Bret told me long ago what he really did for a living. Let me make some coffee and we can talk."

"She's delightful. Why did they get divorced?" Yingzhe asks in quiet conference with me.

"I should let Audrey answer that."

Yingzhe gets up and looks at the furniture; seventeenth- and eighteenth-century paintings hang on the walls. She stops at an elaborate rolltop desk. "This is amazing," she says.

Audrey comes back into the room with a fine china tray and matching cups, saucers, and a carafe of delicious-smelling coffee. She pours for us.

"I don't want to pry, but when I asked Will why you and Bret divorced, he said I should ask you," Yingzhe says hesitantly.

"You're not prying. I knew about UOEECT and Bret's actual job. We never stopped loving each other, but he thought that, given what he did, getting divorced would protect me and our children. Chris told me what happened at the end." She looks down at the cup of coffee she is holding and swirls it. "I knew the dangers that everyone faced, so when Chris told me Bret had died—" She pours cream into her coffee and stirs it. "—I cried, of course, but in my mind, I had imagined many times how I would feel if something happened to him."

"Thank you for sharing that with me," Yingzhe says.

"How are the kids doing?" I ask.

"Like you'd expect, but they're all right. They're staying with my sister in Florida for a couple of weeks since it's winter break. I told them that their dad died on a mission, but we never told them about UOEECT. They thought he worked for the military as a private contractor. We wanted to keep them as far away from everything as possible."

"Did Chris tell you that Bret saved his life?" I ask.

"Yes, he did. And he feels guilty about it."

I go back to my conversation with Chris before we came here. "He was never in the military, but I'm familiar with survivor's guilt."

"Make sure you help him. He's a good man," Audrey says. "Bret quit being a field agent because he was the only survivor of a mission that was compromised. He never told me the full story, but said he was the one who should have died instead."

"He never shared that with me," I say. Yingzhe squeezes my hand.

"I'm not surprised. You know how he was." Audrey shrugs.

"Yes, I do." I hand Audrey the box of Bret's things. She looks through them and pulls out a picture of him, her, and their children when they were young. She kisses the picture and puts it back in the box.

"We have to go. If you need anything, let me know."

"I will. Don't be a stranger. You and Yingzhe need to come here for dinner." She turns to Yingzhe. "It was so nice to meet you."

"It was for me too," she says. "I promise I won't let Will forget."

There's one more round of hugs. We head outside to the Barracuda.

I look at my Fitbit. We have about two hours before pizza and beer at Giovanni's. "Let's drive there." After a brief pause, I suddenly ask, "Do you think medical nanobots can cure a hangover?"

She gives me the widest smile ever. "I don't know, but I can't wait to find out."

Epilogue
"By the Time We Got to Woodstock: Peace, Love, and Rock 'N' Roll"

Hello, dear reader. While I can't say we haven't met, saving the multiverse has not really given us a chance to get acquainted. So let me introduce myself. I'm Rikki, short for Frederica, and before you ask, yes, I named myself after a character in Robert Heinlein's classic science fiction book, *The Door into Summer*, which appropriately enough, is about time travel—a subject about which, if I may be immodest, I'm an expert.

I'm Will Schachter's friend and colleague and am a sentient AI. Will and his girlfriend Yingzhe are somewhat indisposed at the moment so I thought I would let them recover from their strenuous efforts and be your narrator as I take you on a wacky, funny, and wholly enjoyable trip that we made to 1969.

As you know, the MDTDs are made of nanomaterials that can be used to change their appearances. As Will has told you, far too many times in my opinion, he normally configures his MDTD to look like a lime green 1969 Plymouth Barracuda. *Ugh!* Well, as you might guess, Yingzhe has asked him often, "Why that in particular?"

Our story begins in the small dining room of Will's house.

They had one more week before getting back to work, like he promised. If there's anything Will takes seriously, besides Yingzhe, it's keeping his promises.

He loves to cook for her even though his talents are limited to breakfast meats, eggs, and some semblance of bread. I can eat food, and even smell it in a fashion, but sadly, I can't *taste* or benefit from the consumption of such things. With geniuses like Dr. Joe, Director Kelly, Dr. McCray, and of course, Yingzhe, all promising to find a way for Eowyn and me to be able to taste food, I'm optimistic. Will sings rhapsodies to bacon, so if they can do it, that will be the first thing I taste with a cup of the dark roast coffee that he is so fond of.

Back to the story. Yingzhe finished her breakfast and Will refilled his and her mugs. "Will, you've still never told me why you insist on configuring your MDTD to look the way it does. And lime green? Ugh!" Yingzhe asked for the one hundred and twenty-third time. Yes, I counted, and that's only the times I've heard her ask. I estimate that she has asked that question approximately three hundred and fifty-one more times when I was not counting.

"You're right," he said. They are so cute together. "It's nothing terrible or anything."

To be honest, I'm curious too.

"What do you know about 1969?" he asked. He gave me a stern look. "Not you, Rikki."

"Well, not very much," she admitted. "We didn't exist in this timeline back then. I studied it in high school history but other than the summer of '69 being called the Summer of Love, and the hippies being a kind of youth movement, there was a lot of sex, drugs, and rock and roll."

"You forgot the greatest thing about the summer of '69," Will said. "An event unprecedented in human history."

"What event is that?" Will has a strange sense of humor and Yingzhe had no idea if he was serious or putting her on, but I knew what he was going to say.

"'The Aquarian Exposition: Three Days of Peace and Music,' better known as Woodstock!" he announced enthusiastically, then blushed.

"I still don't understand."

"The only way you'll understand is if I take you there. But first, we need to get suitably attired. Wait here."

I gave him a pointed look. It seemed incongruent that a hard-ass ex-Marine and Navy SEAL would be so nostalgic about the 60s, but it was a start in solving "The Mystery of the Lime Green 1969 Plymouth Barracuda."

He came back carrying a long peasant skirt, beads, a necklace with a crystal, and a red embroidered tunic, and handed them to me, and a pair of bell-bottom jeans, a tank top with flowers, a peace sign necklace, and two dangly bracelets for Yingzhe, who looked at Will and raised her eyebrows.

"eBay! Rikki helped me with the sizes," Will explained.

"What about you?" I asked.

"I'm all set."

I turned to Yingzhe.

"Um, Will already has a 60s wardrobe." Will blushed again.

"Well, aren't you going to try them on?" he asked.

Yingzhe and I went upstairs and changed. Will was waiting for us and was wearing a pair of super-wide flare bell-bottoms, a silk-looking pink shirt with puffy sleeves, and the black headband he just bought. He had not gotten a haircut for over a month, so his hair was longer than I had ever seen it, coming down to the middle of his neck and covering the tops of his ears. It was wavy.

I took one look at him and asked, "How long were you planning this trip for?"

He did not answer at first, then he said, "Navy SEALs always have a plan." He smiled. I smiled back. I had never seen him so relaxed and happy, and it made me happy.

Yingzhe came down wearing her costume. Besides what Will bought on eBay, she added a silver headband.

She was adorable. Will's smile grew even wider, as did his eyes.

I was wearing my outfit. I made my hair longer and wavier. Will and Yingzhe appraised me and nodded in approval.

"Rikki, I love your hair," Yingzhe said.

"I'm with Yingzhe. You look great!" Will exclaimed. Then, Yingzhe did something I'll never forget. She took off one of her bangle bracelets and put it on my wrist.

"Now, we're sisters." She hugged me and I hugged her back. If I could cry, I would have. Some things can't be calculated or explained, not even by a thousand-year-old sentient AI like me. Will watched with a wide smile.

After we reluctantly disengaged, he gestured for us to sit. As usual, he sat in his 1960s vintage recliner. Yingzhe and I sat on the couch. "I promised I would tell you about my 1960s obsession. As you know, my dad was an Army Ranger, and when he went on missions, he would be away for weeks, even months. I would miss him, especially when I was young, so whenever my mom saw I was upset or sad, she would tell me stories." He paused and Yingzhe and I looked at each other.

"What kind of stories?" she asked.

"Stories about the summer of '69 when she lived in a commune near Bethel Woods, New York, the actual location of Woodstock."

"Really? Your mother was a hippie?" I asked.

"Yes, I have a picture of her from then." He went to a cabinet and pulled out an album. He carefully lifted the plastic cover, took out the picture, and showed it to us.

"Will, she's beautiful!" Yingzhe exclaimed.

I looked at the picture and looked at Will. "I can see the family resemblance. I agree with Yingzhe, your mother was gorgeous." His mother, Diane, was wearing a peasant dress like mine, a white tank top, and a tunic like Yingzhe's, except it was blue. I can see where Will got his beautiful blue eyes. She had a circlet of flowers and long, wavy blonde hair down to her waist. Will took the picture and carefully replaced it in the album and put it away.

"I thought the stories from that summer were so cool that when I was a kid, I wished I could have been able to be there," he said excitedly. "And now I can."

We went down to the garage and piled into his MDTD, configured as the very Barracuda we were going to learn about. I sat in the back with Yingzhe because we couldn't agree about who should sit in the front seat. Will looked back, shrugged his shoulders, and said, "Take us to Bethel Woods, August 15, 1969!"

I made the necessary quantum calculations and activated the vortex generator. The walls of the garage seemed to expand, becoming thin, then vaporlike as they disappeared, as the MDTD shrank and descended into the fog of the quantum universe. The discharges of energy danced along the walls of the vortex, like the electro-chemical pulses between neurons. The process reversed as we arrived at our destination.

I quickly stealthed the MDTD. We were on a deserted dirt road.

"We're here!" Will said, as excited as a child on his birthday. He set the external speakers to produce infrasonic sound to discourage anyone who wandered near the MDTD from coming any closer. It was one thirty in the afternoon on Friday, August 15, 1969. We were two miles from Woodstock and could hear the sound checks.

Will looked at his not-really-a-smartphone and pointed. "That's the way. Let's go, those subsonics are giving me the creeps and I know they're on."

Yingzhe looked a little queasy from the low-frequency sound, so we left quickly. Once we were fifty feet away, she looked better and relieved. "Well, that was unpleasant," she said.

"Sorry, my beautiful hippie princess." He kissed her. We hiked along the dirt path and came to a fork in the road. There were two handwritten wood signs nailed to a tree. The top one read "To Woodstock" with an arrow pointing left. And the bottom one, weather-beaten and faded, had an arrow pointing to the right that read "Plastic Sri Chinmoy Center for Enlightenment and Expanded Consciousness." The last part of the sign was written much smaller because the person who wrote it needed a bigger sign or smaller writing.

Will pointed to the right. "Let's go there. We have plenty of time before Richie Havens kicks off Woodstock." He turned to Yingzhe. "Sri Chinmoy was a kind of cult figure in the 1960s. He came from India and opened transcendental meditation centers all over the United States and the world." He put his hand on his chin and pointed to the crude handwritten sign. "I doubt that this is an official location, though."

I checked my memory banks. "There's no record of the Plastic Sri Chinmoy Center for Enlightenment and Expanded Consciousness in Bethel Woods, New York, in 1969."

Will's eyes lit up. "Maybe it's a commune!" He ran down the path. He can be such a child sometimes. "Sorry!" He slowed down for Yingzhe, and we followed the dirt road. After a half mile, the dirt turned to pavement. On the left, we saw an old sign that used to say "Moscowitz's Bungalow Colony." It was now crossed out and under it, it read "Plastic Sri Chinmoy Center for Enlightenment and Expanded Consciousness." There were hand-drawn flowers along the edges.

"We're here, let's check it out!" Will said. Yingzhe smiled and looked at me. I put out my arms, palms up in the universal gesture for "Don't ask me." Bungalow colonies were a big thing in the 1950s and 1960s. If you are interested in learning more about them, check out the movie *Dirty Dancing* (which was actually filmed in Virgina and North Carolina).

We walked in and looked around. There were twelve small cabins. Half of them were painted in the original white with faded green shutters and doors. The other half was covered with more painted flowers, paisleys, rainbows, comets, stars, and planets. Every painted cabin had a flower box brimming with snapdragons, violets, petunias, and other colorful blooms.

Directly ahead of us was a larger building painted like the cabins. There was a sign above the entrance that used to read "Casino" but was now painted over, though not very well. It now read "Meditation Center, Shhhhhh." In front of the meditation center was a large community garden surrounded by a chicken-wire fence. There was corn growing, and tomatoes, peas, and peppers. There was also parsley, sage, rosemary, and thyme. I'm serious! There were any number of cats, dogs, and chickens wandering about, who seemed to all get along quite well.

Everyone was busy, whether taking care of the garden, meditating, drawing, or writing. Under a large oak tree was a cute couple. She was playing a guitar, and he was playing a flute, and they were doing a passable rendition of "California Dreamin'." A small group was sitting around them, singing and clapping. A green tambourine accompanied them. We walked closer and my sensors detected a sweet, woodsy odor emanating from what was commonly known as a joint that was being passed around.

A beautiful young woman with long, wavy blonde hair came up to us and gave Yingzhe and me handmade flower necklaces and put flowers in Will's hair. Yes, you guessed it, it was Will's mother, Diane! I calculated that the probability of us going back to 1969 and wandering into the commune where Will Schachter's mother was living at that time was 1 in 345,809, or 0.0002891%.

Will recognized his mother almost immediately. He was speechless for the first time since I've known him. He stammered as she put the flowers in his hair. "H-hello. I'm um, Will."

Diane put her hands on his shoulders and appraised him. "You're old, aren't you?" she asked sympathetically. My name is Diane."

Yingzhe stifled a laugh. "Don't mind my boyfriend. He just came back from the army and hasn't been the same since."

Diane turned red, clearly distressed. She said, "I'm sorry, I didn't know," and gently pulled Will's head down to her chest. He blushed redder than the roses in the garden.

A moment later, a young man came over to us. Diane disengaged slowly, almost reluctantly, and said, "This is my boyfriend, Finn." He looked a little older than most of the other hippies there. Surprisingly, his heart rate was elevated, and he was perspiring more than was warranted under the overcast damp skies that had moved in.

Yingzhe took Will's hand and pulled him to her, and looking directly at Diane, gently pulled Will's head down to her own chest. Being a sentient AI, I, of course, could completely control my emotions even though I was greatly tempted to laugh hysterically at what I had just seen.

Diane introduced Finn to us, and we talked about music, the war, and the concert. Then, he walked over to Will and asked, "You were in the army?" a little more sharply than would have been expected at this time and place. Finn's heart rate increased some more.

Fortunately, Will had regained his senses. He contacted Yingzhe and me using the quantum link.

<Not a word from either of you!>

<I don't know, Will> Yingzhe said. *<I think Diane thinks you're kind of hot. Older men and all that>*

<Stop! Seriously, there's something off about her boyfriend> he said. *<And Oedipus has nothing to do with it. The guy is kind of creepy, like, government creepy>*

<His breathing and heart rate are higher than normal, like he is nervous or excited> I said.

<I think it's time to go> Will added. *<I'm sure the guy's a narc or a government agent, maybe FBI>*

<What's a narc?> Yingzhe asked.

<A narc is an informer who reports their friends to the authorities. Basically, a spy or an informer. No one was despised as much as a narc in the late 1960s> he explained. *<I'm going to say goodbye to Diane. No, don't say another word! Then we're out of here>*

Will walked over to Diane, held her hands, and kissed her lightly on the cheek. "It was really nice to meet you. We'll meet again in the future, I'm sure of it." He walked over to Finn and stood nose to nose, staring him down. "Nice meeting you, Finn." The man flinched.

We left the Plastic Sri Chinmoy Center for Enlightenment and Expanded Consciousness and walked back to the MDTD.

"Will," I started. "Finn just used a shortwave radio to call the FBI sub-office in Monticello and is following us."

"I knew it! I guess we'll have to come back another time and watch the concert," he said ruefully. We could hear the first notes from Richie Havens as the event began and changed the world.

We got to the MDTD, and I turned off the subsonics. "I detect a helicopter that has lifted off from the Monticello Airport!"

He was silent for a moment. Then with a wide, mischievous smile, asked, "Rikki, can you access the internet using the quantum link?"

"Of course I can," I replied.

"Look up an old 1950s sci-fi movie called *Earth vs. the Flying Saucers*."

"I've got it."

"Configure the MDTD to look like one of the flying saucers."

"You wouldn't!" Yingzhe exclaimed.

"Actually, I would. I don't like that Finn guy. Let's give him, the FBI, and any other three-letter agency that's here at Woodstock a show they'll never forget!"

"You've got it, boss," I said. In an instant, it looked exactly like a flying saucer from the movie.

"Set the coordinates for home, but wait until Finn catches up with us and then take off. We'll do a flyby over Woodstock and then head home."

I said, "You know, Will, there were reports of UFOs during the festival."

"I know, and maybe they were us!"

"Finn just got here," I warned.

"Great!" he said. "Unstealth us so he gets a good look and give me a camera view."

On the view screens, we saw Finn drop his gun and walkie-talkie, his mouth gaped open, and he fell backward onto his butt.

"Now, take off slowly and make that weird noise that the flying saucers made in the movie." He laughed hysterically. A moment later, Yingzhe cracked up too, and yes, your stolid, sober, logical, always in control sentient AI narrator, laughed for the first time and it was wonderful!

We rose majestically into the air and slowly flew over Woodstock, and for just a moment, as one, fifty thousand hippies, music lovers, stoners, and anyone else who was there, looked skyward as we faded from their view.

About the Author

Charles W. Lampert retired six years ago after an extensive career in financial services and insurance. He has been writing since he was a sophomore in high school and is a published poet.

His love for science fiction began in third grade when he became hooked on the Tom Swift Jr. books. The first "real" science-fiction book he read was *The Door into Summer* by Robert Heinlein, which led him to explore classic authors such as Isaac Asimov, Arthur C. Clarke, A. E. van Vogt, and Jack Williamson, among others.

In 2018, Charles wrote two chapters for *The Time Engineers*, at the time, titled *The Time Fixers*. However, it wasn't until May 2023 while cleaning up files on his computer that he rediscovered them. He decided to make a genuine effort to write a full-length novel, one of his longtime goals, and renamed the book. It took four months to complete. His long-term goals include writing two more books and a novella for *The Time Engineers Saga*, a science fiction/fantasy titled *Infinity's Avatar*, and a young adult fantasy series.

Charles has been married to his wife, Robin, for forty-four years and they have two grown children and two grandchildren. He enjoys hiking, sports, and is an amateur meteorologist. Together, they enjoy going on cruises and have visited places like Norway, Iceland, Alaska, Hawaii, and Scotland.

Author Notes

It took six months to write and publish *The Time Engineers*. Well, five and half months counting from when I wrote the first two chapters of *The Time Fixers* in 2018. Time Travel, Alternate Realities, Parallel Universes, Artificial Intelligence/Robotics, and military science fiction are some of my favorite kinds of science fiction, well, besides Space Opera, Hard Science Fiction, Soft Science Fiction, Cyberpunk, First Contact, Alien Invasion, Superhuman/Mutant, Techno-thriller, Space Western, etc. You get the picture, pretty much every kind of science fiction there is.

Artificial intelligence is everywhere today, and is literally changing the world. In 2005, Ray Kurzweil first wrote about "Singularity," when machine intelligence will exceed human intelligence, and human and machine intelligence will merge. *In The Time Engineers,* artificial intelligence plays a prominent role in the story but reflect my hope that artificial and human intelligence together will be greater than either can achieve on their own.

I have more adventures planned for Commander Will Schacter and his elite team. Keep on the lookout for a novella, next year, called *AI Avenger.*

Finally, I want to make a special dedication to my late father, Stanley Lampert, who first introduced me to science fiction. A true polymath, there was almost nothing he didn't know something about. And as he used to tell me, "What I don't know isn't important."

Thanks Dad. RIP.

Charles W. Lampert
July 2024